T0000137

PRAISE FOR
ᴆRAGONꙅ OF ᴆECEIT

"I love Dragonlance and I love Margaret Weis and Tracy Hickman: plain and simple. Their books are my favorite fantasy series of all time. I love the stories and ideas but most of all, I love the characters. Why do we all feel like we know them? They are what spurred me to start working for D&D and inevitably what inspired me to pursue a career in show-running."

—Joe Manganiello

"A love letter to fans." —*Nerdist*

"It is truly a very nice return to a well-loved world, and it is handled with care and great passion by the two authors who introduced us to Krynn all those years ago. *Dragons of Deceit* is fun, adventurous and heartwarming in all the right spots. Those new to this land, welcome. Sit back, open up and enjoy the journey."

—*Bookreporter*

"If you love all things *Dragonlance*, please read this book."

—*Geeks of Doom*

"Reading *Dragons of Deceit* was like catching up with friends I haven't seen in a while. They've had new adventures, met new people. The world has kept going, but it happily welcomed me back. . . . The story was fast-paced and exciting, the sort of adventure I love reading about. It ended with a bang and left me wishing I had a Device of Time Journeying of my own, so that I could travel forward and read book two. Unsurprisingly, *Dragons of Deceit* was incredible."

—*Grimdark Magazine*

DRAGONLANCE DESTINIES

DRAGONS
OF
FATE

DRAGONS OF FATE

DRAGONLANCE DESTINIES:

VOLUME 2

MARGARET WEIS
& TRACY HICKMAN

RANDOM HOUSE WORLDS

NEW YORK

Dragons of Fate is a work of fiction. Names, places, and incidents either are products of the author's imagination or are used fictitiously. Any resemblance to actual events, locales, or persons, living or dead, is entirely coincidental.

2024 Random House Worlds Trade Paperback Edition

Copyright © 2023 by Wizards of the Coast LLC

All rights reserved.

Published in the United States by Random House World, an imprint of Random House, a division of Penguin Random House LLC, New York.

RANDOM HOUSE is a registered trademark, and RANDOM HOUSE WORLDS and colophon are trademarks of Penguin Random House LLC.

DUNGEONS & DRAGONS, WIZARDS OF THE COAST, DRAGONLANCE, and their respective logos are trademarks of Wizards of the Coast LLC and are used with permission. All Rights Reserved. Licensed by Hasbro.

All DRAGONLANCE characters and the distinctive likenesses thereof are property of Wizards of the Coast LLC.

Originally published in hardcover in the United States by Random House Worlds, an imprint of Random House, a division of Penguin Random House LLC, in 2023.

Song of Huma reproduced with permission from Michael Williams, copyright © 1984

LIBRARY OF CONGRESS CATALOGING-IN-PUBLICATION DATA
Names: Weis, Margaret, author. | Hickman, Tracy, author.
Title: Dragons of fate / Margaret Weis & Tracy Hickman.
Description: First Edition. | New York: Random House Worlds, 2023.
Series: Dragonlance Destinies volume 2
Identifiers: LCCN 2023033477 (print) | LCCN 2023033478 (ebook) | ISBN 9781984819413 (trade paperback) | ISBN 9781984819406 (ebook)
Subjects: LCSH: Dragons—Fiction. | Fantasy games—Fiction. | Dungeons and Dragons (Game)—Fiction. | Prophecies—Fiction. | Imaginary places—Fiction. | Quests (Expeditions)—Fiction. | LCGFT: Novels. | Fantasy fiction.
Classification: LCC PS3573.E3978 D7384 2023 (print) | LCC PS3573.E3978 (ebook) | DDC 808.83/8766—dc23/eng/20230720
LC record available at https://lccn.loc.gov/2023033477
LC ebook record available at https://lccn.loc.gov/2023033478

All illustrations from stock.adobe.com by the following contributors:
Book 1: t_dalton; Chapter 1: Mateusz; Chapters 2, 3, and 6: aksol; Chapter 4: Turaev; Chapters 5, 7, 40 and Book 2: Danussa; Chapter 8: VictoriaBat; Chapters 9 and 23: channarongsds; Chapter 10: Татьяна Гончарук, ilonitta; Chapters 11 and 33: Good Studio; Chapter 12: AkimD; Chapters 13 and 38: vectortatu; Chapter 14: Christos Georghiou; Chapter 15: ilyakalinin; Chapter 16: pandavector; Chapter 17: kuco; Chapter 18: Rustic; Chapters 19 and 39: Rawpixel.com; Chapter 20: acrogame; Chapter 21: silvano audisio; Chapter 22: Dmitriy Vlasov; Chapter 24: ~ Bitter ~; Chapter 25: Nick_D_Zen; Chapter 26: Aleksandr; Chapter 27: MicroOne; Chapter 28: jenesesimre; Chapter 29: Rashevskyi Media; Chapter 30: arkadiwna; Chapter 31: desertsands; Chapter 32: Oleksandr Babich; Chapter 34: PikePicture; Chapter 35: istry; Chapter 36: asiah; Chapter 37: Alexander Pokusay; Chapter 41: warmtail
Maps: Jared Blando, © Wizards of the Coast

Printed in the United States of America on acid-free paper

randomhousebooks.com

2 4 6 8 9 7 5 3 1

Book design by Alexis Flynn

To Ray Puechner and Jean Blashfield Black.
Both were dear friends and without them
there would have been no Dragonlance.
MARGARET WEIS

To my beloved grandchildren:
Angel Jane, Alexandria, William, Alice, Maxwell, Violet,
and Arthur
TRACY HICKMAN

Song of Huma

By Michael Williams

Out of the village, out of the thatched and clutching shires,
Out of the grave and furrow, furrow and grave,
Where his sword first tried
The last cruel dances of childhood, and awoke to the shires
Forever retreating, his greatness a marsh fire,
The banked flight of the Kingfisher always above him,
Now Huma walked upon Roses,
To the Wilderness, where Paladine bade him to turn,
And there in the loud tunnel of knives
He grew in unblemished violence, in yearning,
Stunned into himself by a deafening gauntlet of voices.

It was there and then that the White Stag found him,
At the end of a journey planned from the shores of Creation,
And all time staggered at the forest edge
Where Huma, haunted and starving,
Drew his bow, thanking the gods for their bounty and
     keeping,
Then saw, in the ranged wood,
In the first silence, the dazed heart's symbol,
The rack of antlers resplendent.
He lowered the bow and the world resumed.
Then Huma followed the Stag, its tangle of antlers receding
As a memory of young light, as the talons of birds ascending.
The Mountain crouched before them. Nothing would change
     now,
The three moons stopped in the sky,
And the long night tumbled in shadows.

It was morning when they reached the grove,
The lap of the mountain, where the Stag departed,
Nor did Huma follow, knowing the end of this journey
Was nothing but green and the promise of green that endured
In the eyes of the woman before him.
And holy the days he drew near her, holy the air
That carried his words of endearment, his forgotten songs,
And the rapt moons knelt on the Great Mountain.
Still, she eluded him, bright and retreating as marshfire,
Nameless and lovely, more lovely because she was nameless,
As they learned that the world, the dazzling shelves of the air,
The Wilderness itself
Were plain and diminished things to the heart's thicket.
At the end of the days, she told him her secret.

For she was not of woman, nor was she mortal,
But daughter and heiress from a line of Dragons.
For Huma the sky turned indifferent, cluttered by moons,
The brief life of the grass mocked him, mocked his fathers,
And the thorned light bristled on the gliding Mountain.
But nameless she tendered a hope not in her keeping,
That Paladine only might answer, that through his enduring
    wisdom
She might step from forever, and there in her silver arms
The promise of the grove might rise and flourish.
For that wisdom Huma prayed, and the Stag returned,
And east, through the desolate fields, through ash,
Through cinders and blood, the harvest of dragons,
Traveled Huma, cradled by dreams of the Silver Dragon,
The Stag perpetual, a signal before him.

At last the eventual harbor, a temple so far to the east
That it lay where the east was ending.
There Paladine appeared
In a pool of stars and glory, announcing
That of all choices, one most terrible had fallen to Huma.

For Paladine knew that the heart is a nest of yearnings,
That we can travel forever toward light, becoming
What we can never be.
For the bride of Huma could step into the devouring sun,
Together they would return to the thatched shires
And leave behind the secret of the Lance, the world
Unpeopled in darkness, wed to the dragons.
Or Huma could take on the Dragonlance, cleansing all Krynn
Of death and invasion, of the green paths of his love.

The hardest of choices, and Huma remembered
How the Wilderness cloistered and baptized his first thoughts
Beneath the sheltering sun, and now
As the black moon wheeled and pivoted, drawing the air
And the substance from Krynn, from the things of Krynn,
From the grove, from the Mountain, from the abandoned
    shires,
He would sleep, he would send it all away,
For the choosing was all of the pain, and the choices
Were heat on the hand when the arm has been severed.
But she came to him, weeping and luminous,
In a landscape of dreams, where he saw
The world collapse and renew on the glint of the Lance.
In her farewell lay collapse and renewal.
Through his doomed veins the horizon burst.

He took up the Dragonlance, he took up the story,
The pale heat rushed through his rising arm
And the sun and the three moons, waiting for wonders,
Hung in the sky together,
To the West Huma rode, to the High Clerist's Tower
On the back of the Silver Dragon,
And the path of their flight crossed over a desolate country
Where the dead walked only, mouthing the names of dragons.
And the men in the Tower, surrounded and riddled by
    dragons,
By the cries of the dying, the roar in the ravenous air,

Awaited the unspeakable silence,
Awaited far worse, in fear that the crash of the senses
Would end in a moment of nothing
Where the mind lies down with its losses and darkness.

But the winding of Huma's horn in the distance
Danced on the battlements. All of Solamnia lifted
Its face to the eastern sky, and the dragons
Wheeled to the highest air, believing
Some terrible change had come.
From out of their tumult of wings, out of the chaos of
    dragons,
Out of the heart of nothing, the Mother of Night,
Aswirl in a blankness of colors,

Swooped to the east, into the stare of the sun
And the sky collapsed into silver and blankness.
On the ground Huma lay, at his side a woman,
Her silver skin broken, the promise of green
Released from the gifts of her eyes. She whispered her name
As the Queen of Darkness banked in the sky above Huma.

She descended, the Mother of Night,
And from the loft of the battlements, men saw shadows
Boil on the colorless dive of her wings:
A hovel of thatch and rushes, the heart of a Wilderness,
A lost silver light spattered in terrible crimson,
And then from the center of shadows
Came a depth in which darkness itself was aglimmer,
Denying all air, all light, all shadows.
And thrusting his lance into emptiness,
Huma fell to the sweetness of death, into abiding sunlight.
Through the Lance, through the dear might and brotherhood
Of those who must walk to the end of the breath and the
    senses,
And the long lands blossomed in balance and music.

———————

Stunned in new freedom, stunned by the brightness and colors,
By the harped blessing of the holy winds,
The knights carried Huma, they carried the Dragonlance
To the grove in the lap of the Mountain.
When they returned to the grove in pilgrimage, in homage,
The Lance, the armor, the Dragonbane himself
Had vanished to the day's eye.
But the night of the full moons red and silver
Shines down on the hills, on the forms of a man and a woman
Shimmering steel and silver, silver and steel,
Above the village, over the thatches and nurturing shires.

Karthay

Kalaman

Istar

Taman Busuk

Neraka

...nction

Thoradin

Losarcum

Monastery

Blöten

Silvanesti

Balifor

Balifor

Silvanost

Courrain Ocean

Scale in Miles

Capital   City   Town   Fortress

POST-CATACLYSM
ANSALON

DRAGONLANCE DESTINIES

DRAGONS
OF
FATE

BOOK ONE

CHAPTER
ONE

Dalamar the Dark was centuries distant from those who had been stranded in time by the destruction of the Device of Time Journeying. Yet he had them on his mind as he left the office of Astinus carrying the shattered remains of the Device in a black velvet sack.

He kept seeing over and over the moment when he had entered the Artifact Room in the Great Library of Palanthas at Astinus's bidding to find the monk, Brother Kairn, standing motionless among the wreckage of the Device. The floor was littered with debris: cogs, wheels, jewels, metal shards, a broken chain.

"I ordered him not to move until you arrived," Astinus had told Dalamar, "to see if you could salvage it."

"But what happened to those who traveled with Brother Kairn? Lady Destina and Tasslehoff?" Dalamar had asked, aghast. "Where are they? What of the Graygem of Gargath the lady wears?"

"Brother Kairn returned alone," Astinus had replied, maddeningly dispassionate.

Dalamar had used his magic to gather up the fragments of the Device and place them in this bag. Astinus had given him permission to take the remains of the Device to Justarius, head of the Conclave, to determine if it could be repaired and to tell Justarius about the catastrophe that had left four people and the Graygem of Gargath stranded in time.

Dalamar first returned to his own tower, the Tower of High Sorcery in Palanthas, to make certain all was well. His *Shalafi*, Raistlin Majere, was purportedly stranded in time. Knowing Raistlin as he did, Dalamar would not have been surprised to find his *Shalafi* once more master of the tower, and he was relieved when the Black Robes who guarded it reported nothing amiss had occurred in his absence.

"I am traveling to the tower of Wayreth," Dalamar told them. "Close the magical portals to all except me. No one is to leave or enter."

Having no idea how long he would be gone or what dangers he might face, Dalamar replenished his spell components and selected a variety of magical scrolls with spells that could be cast swiftly and at need.

As he worked, he considered reporting what he had learned about the whereabouts of the Graygem to the gods of magic. They knew Chaos was roaming the world, but nothing more. And the other gods did not know that much. The gods of good and those of evil all believed the Graygem was still in hiding, as it had been for thousands of years.

If Astinus was the god Gilean, as some believed, he alone knew it had gone back in time, yet Dalamar had no fear Astinus would intervene. He never intervened, but merely recorded what he saw as he sat with his hand on the Sphere of Time. When the world ended, the last sound would be the scratching of Astinus's pen.

"Better if I deal with this disaster quickly and quietly without divine interference," Dalamar said to himself.

He did not have time to send word to Justarius that he was coming. Walking the paths of magic, Dalamar arrived at the tower of Wayreth without warning and the sudden appearance of the master of the tower of Palanthas materializing in their entry hall threw the guardian mages into confusion and alarm.

Every master refurnished the tower to suit himself or herself. Since mages came from all over Ansalon to take their Tests at the

Tower of High Sorcery in Wayreth, Justarius had designed the entry hall to be welcoming. Tapestries celebrating magic lined the walls. A rug carpeted the cold marble floor. The guardian mages were playing at khas on a board they had set up, when Dalamar's arrival triggered the warning bell that sounded throughout the tower. The two guardians jumped to their feet, ready to defend their posts. Both immediately recognized Dalamar, who was the only elf archmage to ever take the black robes.

"I must speak to Justarius," said Dalamar.

The guardians sent for the chief apprentice. Once she recovered from her shock, she approached him.

"Master, this is an unexpected—"

Dalamar cut her off. "I must speak to Justarius on a matter of the utmost urgency."

"I fear the master is not here, sir," the apprentice told him. "He has traveled to his home to dine with his wife and their new baby daughter."

"Fetch him," said Dalamar. "Now."

"Yes, Master. Right away, Master."

She escorted Dalamar to one of the antechambers where the students usually waited to take the Test. The small room was furnished with chairs and a table where nervous applicants could study their spells. Dalamar had forgotten until the apprentice mentioned dinner that he had not eaten all day. The apprentices served him bread with clotted cream and honey and brought a flagon of elven wine. By the time he had finished his meal, Justarius had returned.

Justarius was in a good mood following his visit with his family, but when he saw Dalamar's expression, his pleasure evaporated.

"What has happened?"

Dalamar glanced about. The apprentices had disappeared, leaving the two alone. But the walls have ears, especially in magical towers, and he did not want to say more than necessary. "The Graygem."

Justarius was grave. "We will go to my quarters. We can speak in private there."

He escorted Dalamar to his private chamber.

People were always amazed that two men who were so vastly different and should have been sworn enemies were, in fact, extremely good friends. Both were dedicated to the magic and to the gods they served.

Justarius was a human in his early fifties who wore the red robes of those dedicated to Lunitari, the neutral goddess of the red moon. He walked with a crutch, for his Test in the Tower had left him crippled in body, though stronger in spirit and resolve. He was still hale and fit. Only the few strands of gray in his hair and beard gave evidence of his age.

Dalamar was a Silvanesti elf with black hair and almond eyes. He wore the black robes of Nuitari, the god of the dark moon. He was over a hundred years old and in the prime of his life. Acting as a spy for the Conclave, Dalamar had served Raistlin Majere after his *Shalafi* had claimed the Tower of High Sorcery in Palanthas. Raistlin had discovered his betrayal and Dalamar still bore the marks of his *Shalafi*'s wrath on his flesh.

The master's quarters were designed for comfort rather than elegance, with several large, overstuffed chairs that were cozily shabby. The walls were lined with shelves of books. Justarius placed a warding spell on the door and, leaning on his crutch, turned to his companion.

"You spoke of the Graygem. You have news?"

"The worst possible," said Dalamar grimly. "Lady Destina and the Graygem have traveled back in time to the Third Dragon War. Tasslehoff Burrfoot is with her, as are Sturm Brightblade and Raistlin Majere—both men very much alive. That is the bad news. This is what makes bad news worse."

He placed the velvet bag on a table and opened it.

"Look inside."

Justarius peered into the bag and saw a rod, two orbs, a chain, myriad jewels, and bits and pieces of broken metal. Justarius stared at the objects in what appeared to be confusion, then he realized what he was seeing and looked up at Dalamar in horror.

"Is that—" Justarius couldn't finish.

"The Device of Time Journeying," said Dalamar. "Or, rather, it *was* the Device. Right now, it is a collection of junk. It blew apart, leaving those who went back in time stranded."

Justarius gaped at him, bereft of speech.

Dalamar sighed and ran his hand through his long black hair. "I was hoping you and I might be able to repair it. If so, we could send someone back to rescue them."

"We can try to fix it," Justarius said, but he didn't sound hopeful. "Let us take it to my laboratory."

The laboratory was the beating heart of the Tower of High Sorcery. Here mages conducted experiments to create new spells or worked to perfect or enhance old ones. The walls were lined with metal shelves containing jars and bottles and cannisters of spell components, all neatly labeled and placed in alphabetical order. Since the risk of fire was high, given the nature of some of the spells, no spellbooks were kept within the laboratory, although they could be brought inside. Those who worked or studied here sat on metal stools.

The familiar smell of spell components enveloped Dalamar as he entered: pungent spices, acrid chemicals, drying herbs, and the sickening smell of decay. He glanced swiftly about. He did not expect to see any secret experiments—Justarius was far too careful for that. But he might gain some idea of the field of study the archmage was pursuing. He saw nothing of interest, however.

Apprentices working in the laboratory jumped to their feet in respect when the two masters entered. Justarius ordered them away, shut the door, and cast a locking spell on it.

Dalamar carefully emptied the bag onto a marble worktable whose smooth surface contained no runes or any other symbols of magic that might interfere with the magic of the Device.

Justarius gazed in dismay at the pile of glittering jewels, the numerous tiny cogs and small wheels, the chains and orbs. "Did you find all the pieces? Is this everything?"

"I have no way of knowing," said Dalamar with a helpless shrug. "The remnants were scattered everywhere around the Artifact Room in the Great Library. I cast a revealing spell that caused the magical parts to glow, and I gathered up all I could find. But I could have easily missed some. And since the Device blew up during the spellcasting, it is possible some pieces could be in the past."

Justarius sat down on a tall stool and laid aside his crutch. Dalamar drew another stool near him. Together, they gazed in glum silence at the remains of the Device. Justarius picked up the rod and one of the orbs and attempted to fit them together. When that failed, he shook his head despondently and set the pieces back down.

"Tell me how this happened," he said.

"As you know, Astinus asked me to loan him the Device of Time Journeying so that his aesthetics could use it in their research," Dalamar began.

"I always thought that was a mistake," Justarius growled.

"I could not very well say no to a god," Dalamar replied.

Justarius grunted, conceding the argument. "Go on."

"I told you before about the human woman, Destina Rosethorn, and how she traveled to the dwarven kingdom to find the Graygem of Gargath."

"In which accursed gem Reorx imprisoned Chaos," said Justarius. "The fool!"

"Destina or Reorx?" Dalamar asked with a faint smile.

"Both!" Justarius grunted. "Go on with your tale."

"When Destina returned to Palanthas, I laid a trap for her in order to take it from her, employing my most powerful mages to seize it. The Graygem thwarted them, nearly costing one the use of his hand. Destina then took the gem with her to the Great Library with the intention of stealing the Device of Time Journeying so she could travel back in time to the War of the Lance. Her father had died in the fighting and she wanted to restore him to life."

"Which meant she would change history," said Justarius, frowning.

"That is why she needed the Graygem. To give her credit, she believed the change would be minuscule, a mere drop in time's vast river. And she might well have been right."

Justarius gave a violent snort.

Dalamar faintly smiled. "You and I can say she was misguided, but given the choice, Master, both of us might have done the same to bring back someone we love."

Justarius was silent, perhaps thinking of his beloved wife and the baby girl he had so recently cradled in his arms.

"The time for judgment is past. Continue," he said brusquely.

"Destina managed to steal the Device, undoubtedly with the

help of the Graygem. She couldn't make it work, however, and she asked the kender, Tasslehoff Burrfoot, to assist her. As you know, he had mastered its use."

Justarius groaned and put his hand to his head.

"The story is complicated, so bear with me," Dalamar continued. "According to Brother Kairn, Destina transformed herself into a female kender named Mari. She asked Tas to take her to the High Clerist's Tower to save her father, but Tasslehoff had other ideas. He wanted to take her to the Inn of the Last Home to introduce her to his friends. That was the same night Goldmoon arrived in the inn with the holy Staff of Mishakal."

Justarius was grim. "I begin to see where this is going."

"Brother Kairn tried to stop Destina and Tas but ended up traveling with them. Because he had been the last person to use it, the Device of Time Journeying remained with him. Raistlin Majere was there with the Staff of Magius and Destina possessed the Graygem. Acting on impulse, she seized the Device from Kairn and activated the magic with the intention of taking Sturm Brightblade to the High Clerist's Tower to save her father. Raistlin struck her with the staff to try to stop her. Tasslehoff saw Raistlin attacking his friend, so he hit Raistlin with the Staff of Mishakal. Holy and arcane magicks collided, with the Graygem in the center."

"The gods save us," Justarius murmured.

"A little late for that," said Dalamar dryly. "The Device transported Sturm Brightblade, Raistlin Majere, Destina, and Tasslehoff to the right place—the High Clerist's Tower. But to the wrong century—the time of the Third Dragon War. The Device was apparently too fragile to withstand such a confluence of powerful forces, and it shattered, throwing Brother Kairn back here and leaving the others stranded, unable to return. And now the Graygem is with them at one of the most pivotal points in history. Undoubtedly by Chaos's design."

Justarius sat in appalled silence for long moments.

"Are you certain of this information?" he asked at last.

"I have only just returned from the office of Astinus, where I have seen proof," said Dalamar. "Brother Kairn showed me the writings of Astinus from that time, thousands of years in the past. I saw

Sturm Brightblade listed on the roll of knights defending the tower, along with Huma Feigaard. Two war wizards—Magius and Raistlin Majere—were also listed."

"The great Magius," said Justarius, distracted. "To think they might get a chance to meet him! I almost envy them."

"I thought much the same myself," said Dalamar. "But that does not solve our problem."

"Which is?"

"I fear it is possible Chaos could wreak havoc in the past and thus alter time."

"That seems far-fetched."

"I fear the alteration has already begun," said Dalamar. "We looked for Lady Destina and the kender, Burrfoot, in the writings of Astinus, hoping to read what he had written about them, but . . . the pages were blank."

Justarius frowned. "How could the pages be blank? Astinus would have recorded what happened."

"He said it was because the history of that time has yet to be written. That we might yet escape drowning, but the waters are rising."

"What in the Abyss did he mean by that?" Justarius demanded impatiently.

"The waters of the River of Time rise slowly. What happens in the past has yet to reach us in the present, which means we have time to salvage the situation by going back to rescue the four before they can do irreparable harm."

"Given that the Graygem is with them, we may already be too late," said Justarius.

"My *Shalafi* is also with them," said Dalamar. "Raistlin made an extensive study of time travel, as I am certain you know, for that is what eventually led to his doom. He understands the perils of traveling through time. He will do what he can to be certain time remains unchanged."

"Unless he figures out how he can use this disaster to his advantage," Justarius said caustically. "We could wake tomorrow to find Raistlin a god."

Dalamar said nothing. They both knew Raistlin and knew what Justarius said was quite true. They gazed at the pieces of the Device. Justarius gingerly nudged some of the jewels with his index finger.

"I know nothing about creating artifacts, let alone repairing them," Justarius said.

"I was thinking we might find information on the Device in your Silver Book," Dalamar suggested. "Since the previous master, Par-Salian, gave the Device to Caramon and told him how to use it, he may have recorded information on it."

Every Tower of Sorcery possessed a Silver Book that contained powerful magical spells known only to the masters of the towers. The books were as old as the towers themselves. The spells had been handed down through the generations and only the masters held the magical keys to open them. Originally there had been five Silver Books. Now two were left; the others had been destroyed by their masters for fear they would fall into the wrong hands or be lost in the destruction of the towers.

"The book is in my office, guarded by a warding spell only I can remove," said Justarius, reaching for his crutch. "Please do not disturb yourself. I will fetch it."

Dalamar smiled in understanding. All the masters jealously guarded the secrets of their Silver Books. Much as he liked and trusted Justarius, Dalamar would not have allowed him to be present in the same room as he retrieved his own Silver Book.

Justarius soon returned, struggling to carry the immense book in one hand and his crutch in the other. He dropped the book on the marble table with a ringing clang. The Silver Book was, as the name implied, bound in silver.

The Silver Book contained a thousand spells or more, but fortunately they were cross-referenced and indexed. The various masters had also added descriptions of artifacts they had created, notes on ancient artifacts, and other information they felt would be useful to future generations.

Justarius smiled in satisfaction when he located a page written in Par-Salian's hand entitled: *Device of Time Journeying*.

The entry was long and, according to Par-Salian, contained all the information he knew about the Device. Justarius and Dalamar hunched over the book and studied it together. They were initially disappointed to find that much of what they read they already knew.

The Device of Time Journeying had been forged on the Anvil of Time. The Anvil itself was now lost and no one had been able to discover who had forged the Device or when. It had been first mentioned in the Silver Book of Wayreth following the Cataclysm, which had shaken the tower, split the ground, and unearthed a chamber beneath the tower whose existence had been previously unknown. The master of Wayreth at the time had found the Device in the chamber, along with the poem that provided instructions for the Device's use.

The master had recorded its discovery in her Silver Book and locked the Device away for safekeeping.

When Par-Salian became master hundreds of years later, he had read about the Device in the Silver Book and sought it out, then had made a study of it.

The Device is old and fragile. Although it was forged on the Anvil of Time and that is now lost, I hope to either replicate the Device or create a new one to replace it in case it breaks, he wrote.

He had gone so far as to draw a diagram of the Device, and had provided a list of selected materials and suggested spells that could be used to make the Device functional. Apparently, that was as far as he got.

I have come to the conclusion that the magicks used to create the Device cannot be replicated, Par-Salian wrote. *I can well imagine some long-ago crafter adding magic to the molten metal and hammering the pieces with a magical hammer on the magical Anvil. If something were to happen to this Device, an artifact maker might be able to repair it, but I believe it would not be possible to create a new one without the Anvil.*

The proper study of artifact-making is a lost art these days, one that I lament. Young mages only want to learn how to hurl fireballs and cast other such flashy spells. The days of the great artifact makers, such as the revered Ranniker, are no more.

Dalamar and Justarius flipped through the pages, only to find that all mention of the Device ended there.

"It seems Par-Salian was more interested in inventing a new Device than he was in maintaining the old one," Justarius remarked, closing the book in disappointment. "He says nothing about how to reassemble it if it was broken."

"According to legend, the last time the Device broke, a gnome fixed it," Dalamar said thoughtfully. "I suppose we could . . ."

"No!" said Justarius firmly. "I will have nothing to do with gnomish infernal devices. Their enthusiasm outweighs their technical expertise, which means their inventions have an unfortunate tendency to explode."

"True," said Dalamar, smiling. "Perhaps Par-Salian attempted to create a new Device and it did not work. Thus he concludes one would need the Anvil of Time. Which makes sense."

Justarius sat frowning at the book. "Ranniker. Why is that name familiar? I seem to recall I have heard it before in reference to the Device and the Graygem."

"You are thinking of Ungar, the mage who urged Destina to bring him the Graygem. He destroyed Ranniker's Clock, which showed us a vision of doom."

"Ah, yes. Is Ungar still languishing in your dungeon?"

"I will let him go eventually," said Dalamar coolly.

Justarius snorted. "He destroyed a rare and valuable magical artifact crafted by the most gifted artifact maker of all time. You are kinder to him than I would be. But I am thinking of something different. When you first told me about the clock, the name 'Ranniker' jogged my memory. Gather up the pieces of the Device and meet me in my office."

Justarius picked up the Silver Book and carried it off to return it to its hiding place. Dalamar carefully gathered up all the pieces of the Device and went to the office, where he found Justarius giving instructions to a White Robe who served as his secretary.

"I received a letter some time ago from a young mage who asked to be considered for the Test," he told his secretary. "The name is Ranniker. You will find it in the file marked 'Rejected.'"

The secretary left and was gone some time searching the files, for the number of rejected applicants was extensive. He finally returned and handed the letter to Justarius, who noted the name of the applicant and nodded in satisfaction.

"Alice Ranniker. I remember wondering at the time if she was a distant relative of the great Ranniker." He handed the letter to Dalamar. "As you can see, she was not qualified to take the Test. She lists very few of the most rudimentary spells we require to demonstrate proficiency in the art. I doubt she could have magically boiled water."

"But she does say she is knowledgeable in regard to artifacts," Dalamar remarked. "You did not think to ask her about her work in that regard?"

"Given that if a mage fails the Test, the penalty is death, I did not want to give this young woman the slightest encouragement," said Justarius. "I had my secretary send back the standard reply: 'Continue to pursue your studies and contact us again at a later date.' That was over a year ago and we have not heard from her since."

"You are thinking she might be able to repair the Device. She lives in Solanthas, but she doesn't say where," said Dalamar. "As I recall, a member of the Conclave lives in Solanthas."

"You are thinking of Bertold. I have been a guest in his house," said Justarius. "I will contact him and ask him to find her. I fear repairing the Device is a forlorn hope," he added somberly.

"But better than no hope at all," said Dalamar.

CHAPTER
TWO

estina Rosethorn sat alone beneath the sheltering arms of an oak tree and watched the sun of a distant past flicker among the leaves and branches. She sorrowfully recalled the words of her dwarven guide, Wolfstone.

The Graygem has chosen you. It's yours now, for good or ill.

Destina clasped her hand over the gem that hung on a red-gold chain around her neck. The Graygem was cold and, at the same time, uncomfortably warm. Yet she felt compelled to constantly touch it, constantly reassure herself of its presence, though at the same time she longed to snap the chain and throw the Graygem into the deepest part of the sea. The one time she had tried to rid herself of it, the Graygem had grown so hot it had burned her hand, and she had been forced to let go of it.

She would have liked to have blamed Chaos for the bad choices she had made, but she could only blame herself. The Graygem might have chosen her, but she had chosen to set out on the ill-fated quest to the dwarven kingdom to find it.

If only she had not gone!

If only . . . The saddest words in any language.

If only her father had not died at the Battle of the High Clerist's Tower. If only she had not let her grief consume her and made the foolish decision to go back in time to save him. If only she had never walked into Ungar's mageware shop in search of the Device of Time Journeying. If only she had never sought the Graygem!

Destina felt the gem tingle, as though it laughed, mocking her, reminding her that she was wearing Chaos on a chain around her neck. And now she and Sturm Brightblade, Raistlin Majere, and Tasslehoff Burrfoot were trapped back in time.

"And it is all my fault," Destina murmured.

She had tricked Tasslehoff into showing her how to use the Device of Time Journeying by shapeshifting into the body of a kender female named Mari. After Tas had told her she could find the Device in the Great Library of Palanthas, Destina had abandoned Tas and the kender body and traveled to the Great Library, where she had tried to persuade a monk, Brother Kairn, to give her the Device.

But when Tas had arrived in the library, searching for Mari, Destina had changed back into the kender and stolen the Device. She had intended to travel back to the High Clerist's Tower to save her father, but in her panicked desperation, she had forgotten the complex poem needed to use the Device. She had turned for help to Tas, but he had wanted to introduce Mari to his friends, and before Destina could stop him, he had activated the Device to take her back to the Inn of the Last Home. At the last second, Brother Kairn had grabbed hold of the Device, and the River of Time had carried all three to the inn on the night the companions had agreed to reunite after five years of searching for the true gods.

Raistlin Majere and Sturm Brightblade were among those present, and Destina conceived the ill-fated idea of taking Sturm back to the High Clerist's Tower. She had grabbed Sturm and activated the Device of Time Journeying, and after that—disaster. The Device had transported Destina, Sturm, Raistlin, and Tas through time to the right place—the High Clerist's Tower—but the wrong century. They did not arrive at the tower during the War of the Lance. The Graygem had instead thrown them back in time to the Third Dragon War.

They made the discovery when they overheard two men talking—

two men who turned out to be Huma Dragonbane and his friend, the wizard Magius. They could see the High Clerist's Tower in the distance and were astonished to note that it was under construction, as it had been during the time of Huma. The curtain wall was covered in scaffolding, only half completed.

And now they were stranded here in this time, for the confluence of powerful magicks had caused the Device to explode, leaving them with only a few broken pieces and no way to escape.

They had taken refuge in the woods, for Huma and Magius had talked of goblin raiders in the area. Sturm had left the shelter of the trees to reconnoiter. Raistlin and Tas had gone off on their own to talk in private; she could see them through the leaves and could hear Raistlin trying to explain to Tas that his wife, Mari, a kender, was in truth Destina, a human.

"Destina used a magical artifact to shapeshift into a kender," Raistlin said.

Tasslehoff was having none of it. "I know you mean well, Raistlin, and you're almost never wrong, except that time you were wrong about trying to become a god and a couple of other times before that. But I saw that Destina woman suck Mari up in a stardust cyclone and whoosh her away. I even got stardust in my eyes and my hair! Mari *must* be around here somewhere, so I have to find her!"

"If you want to understand what happened to Mari, you will keep quiet and listen to me."

"I'll be quiet, but it's just that—"

Raistlin glared at him.

"Being quiet now," said Tas meekly.

"What you saw, Tas, was not a magical stardust cyclone, but rather the effects of the shapeshifting spell Lady Destina used to transform herself from a human into the kender you knew as Mari and then back again."

"If I wasn't being quiet, I'd tell you I saw a magical stardust cyclone," said Tas.

Raistlin gave an exasperated sigh. "Answer me this: Did you ever see the two of them—Mari and Destina—together?"

"Of course I did! I remember one time . . . No, that was just Mari. It must have been . . . No, that was just Destina. . . . And then . . . No, that wasn't them either." Tas sighed unhappily. "I guess maybe I didn't."

Destina couldn't bear to hear the pain in his voice, and she shrank back into the shadows of the trees and ducked her head. Seeing the horrible brooch of shapeshifting still pinned to her wool jacket, she tore it off, buried it in the underbrush, and covered it with a pile of dirt and wet leaves.

"But if what you say is true, Raistlin, and Destina was really Mari all along, does that mean I'll never see Mari again?" Tas asked.

"I could tell you that you never saw Mari at all, Tas," Raistlin replied. "But I know that she was very real to you, and the loss of your friend hurts very much. I am sorry."

Destina wondered what she could say to Tas, to all of them, to make them understand that she was sorry. So very, very sorry. Wiping the dirt from her hands, she touched the ring her mother had given her when she was young. The ring was on the little finger of her left hand, and she had worn it so long she often forgot about it. A gold band set with a small emerald, the ring had been blessed by the goddess Chislev. According to her mother, the goddess would guide her if she was ever lost in the darkness.

Destina gazed at the ring in sorrow. She felt very lost now, but she doubted if even a goddess could help.

She was startled and alarmed to hear the rattle of armor and the sound of boots crunching through the leaves and brush. Recalling that a party of goblin warriors had only recently passed by their hiding place in the forest, she hurriedly scrambled to her feet. She was relieved to see Sturm enter the forest and walk toward them. He was wearing old-fashioned plate armor that she knew from stories about him had been his inheritance from his father—the armor and the family sword. He kept his hand on the hilt.

Sturm glanced at her and his face hardened. He made a polite bow, but it was stiff and cold. He walked past her toward Raistlin and Tas.

Destina could not blame him for reviling her, for she had attempted to dose him with a potion of cowardice. She wished she could sink into the ground and not have to face him or the others, but that wasn't likely to happen. And she was no coward. She was the daughter of a knight and she had to accept responsibility for her actions. She shook out her skirt, brushed off the dead leaves, and prepared to face them.

"I guess I understand, even though I don't," Tas was telling Raistlin. "So because I married Mari who is really Lady Destina, does that make me Lord Tasslehoff?"

"You are not married, Tas," said Sturm sternly, overhearing. "Lady Destina married you under false pretenses."

"Actually, I married her under a roof, not a false pretense," Tas stated. "But I see what you mean. If I marry a kender she needs to be a kender and not a human or a bugbear. Although I guess if I wanted to marry a bugbear, so long as the bugbear *was* a bugbear and not a three-headed troll in disguise, I could do that. Kender law is very generous on that point."

"Did you see any sign of the goblins—" Raistlin began, but he was interrupted by a fit of coughing. The cough sounded terrible— a deep, hacking cough that seemed to be tearing at his lungs. He drew a handkerchief from the sleeve of his red robes and pressed it over his mouth as he struggled to breathe.

Destina should have probably offered help or sympathy, but she kept her distance. Like most Solamnics, she had an aversion to all magic-users, and he frightened and intimidated her. He was young, perhaps in his twenties, yet his hair was white. His skin glowed with a golden metallic sheen in the sunlight and the pupils of his eyes were in the shape of hourglasses. A faint odor, as of rose petals and spices and decay, clung to him. She guessed she wasn't alone in her dislike. Sturm watched Raistlin cough until he doubled over in pain, yet Sturm made no move to assist him.

Tas regarded Raistlin with interest.

"Still got that cough, huh?" he said. "I was thinking being dead might cure it. Is that bad wizard, Fistandoodle, inside you?"

Raistlin pressed the handkerchief to his mouth and stared at Tas. Slowly he lowered the handkerchief. Destina saw blood on it.

"What did you say?" he asked Tas.

"About Fistandoodle?"

"No. About being dead."

"That I thought dying might have cured your cough," Tas repeated.

Raistlin stared into the shadows of the past. "There is no cure.

The cough, my frailty, are part of the price I paid for my power. And I was powerful. One of the most powerful mages to have ever lived, Master of Past and Present. I died . . . I remember. . . ."

"You *were* dead in the past, but I guess 'past' is still to come in the future," Tas said helpfully. "Sturm is dead, too. But if it's any comfort, you both look pretty lively right now."

Sturm was frowning in perplexity. "I remember the High Clerist's Tower. I remember Laurana and Tas . . . and a dragon orb. . . . I held the dragonlance in my hand. . . ." He rounded angrily on Raistlin. "What manner of foul magic have you worked this time? You have dragged me from eternal rest!"

"*I* cast no magic," said Raistlin. His glittering gaze went to Destina. "This is none of *my* doing. Five years ago, we separated, agreeing to meet again at the Inn of the Last Home on the anniversary of that last day we were together. We were sitting around the table when you and a monk joined us. I saw you pour a potion into Sturm's drink that would have turned him into a coward. I caught you, and when that failed, you seized hold of him and activated the Device of Time Journeying."

Raistlin turned accusingly to Tas. "Did you give the Device to her? You were the last one to have it, at least in my time."

"It wasn't my fault!" said Tas. "Astinus had it after me, and she borrowed it from Astinus."

"Yet I doubt Astinus taught her how to use it," said Raistlin, fixing his strange gaze on the kender.

Tas fidgeted. "It's . . . uh . . . possible I may have taught her how to use it. Or rather I taught Mari. And Mari didn't take it, Destina did. So, you see, it's still not my fault!"

Raistlin sighed and turned back to Destina. "Using the Device, you brought us here to the time of the Third Dragon War. Now the Device is lost and we are stranded here. You owe us an explanation, Lady."

Destina clasped her hands together to hold fast to her courage. "First I want to apologize to you, Tas. Raistlin is right. I used a magical brooch to turn myself into the kender Mari. I am truly sorry for deceiving you. Please believe I never meant to hurt you." Destina looked around at the others. "I never meant to hurt any of you, and

I will do whatever is in my power to fix this terrible situation. I truly never meant for any of this to happen!"

"Yet, you meant for *something* to happen, Lady," said Raistlin. "Where were you planning to take Sturm and why?"

Destina twisted her hands together. "My father fought at the battle of the High Clerist's Tower during the War of the Lance. At one point, he feared the battle was going to be lost. He and the other knights intended to leave the tower and return home to defend their families. My father was going to return to me."

She raised her eyes to look at Sturm. "You were his commander, and you gave him permission to leave. You told him you understood. Then you faced the Dragon Highlord alone and you died on the battlements. Your sacrifice lit a flame in my father's heart. He stayed to fight the dragons and they killed him! I lost my dearly loved father. Then I lost his legacy, our castle, and our lands. I lost everything."

"We know about loss," said Raistlin grimly. "That doesn't explain your actions."

"I'm trying to tell you," said Destina desperately. "One of my father's favorite books was an account of Huma's life written by a scribe who had served with the army during the Third Dragon War. I remembered reading a passage in that book in which Huma's friend, Magius, mentions a Device of Time Journeying. Magius had been in love with Huma's sister, who had been wounded in battle and died. Magius wanted to go back in time to prevent her death. My father had underlined the passage about the Device. I believe he had some idea of trying to go back in time to try to prevent the war. If so, he never acted on it. I was thinking that if I gave Sturm the potion of cowardice and took him back to the High Clerist's Tower . . ." Her voice trailed off.

"Sturm would run from the battle and your father would live," Raistlin finished her sentence for her.

Sturm was clearly shocked to the core of his being.

"If you had succeeded, Lady Destina, I would be forever branded a coward, a disgrace to my name, a disgrace to the knighthood! You should be proud of your father. He fought to save Solamnia from the forces of the Dark Queen. He died with honor, as befits a knight."

"Honor?" Destina repeated bitterly. "Where is the honor in leaving a fifteen-year-old girl without a father? I needed him! Solamnia didn't. He was only one man, a drop in the river. His death meant nothing."

"Sturm Brightblade was one man," Raistlin said sharply. "Yet you said yourself his sacrifice resulted in the knights triumphing over the forces of the Dark Queen. One man can make a difference."

"So can one kender," said Tas. "I made a difference when I found the dragon orb in the High Clerist's Tower. True, I was going to smash it, but—"

"Not now, Tas!" said Raistlin impatiently. "Continue, Lady. Why bring us to this time?"

"As I told you, I never meant to!" Destina said. "Sturm and Brother Kairn were talking about Huma Dragonbane, so perhaps he was in my mind."

"We are not in this predicament because Sturm was thinking of Huma!" said Raistlin. His hourglass eyes glinted. "Only truly powerful magic could have thrown us back in time and left us stranded here. My guess is that it has something to do with the gem you are wearing."

Destina was reluctant to tell them about the Graygem, but the Measure says that "Half a truth is naught but a whole lie."

She put her hand to her throat. The Graygem was hidden beneath her collar hanging on a golden chain. She slowly lifted the chain and drew out the gem. It faintly pulsed with a dull gray light.

"The Graygem of Gargath," said Raistlin. "I suspected as much when I noticed it in the inn. You would need the Device to travel back in time, and the Graygem to alter time—to save your father. I must say I admire you, Lady Destina. You thought of everything."

"But the Graygem is only a myth!" said Sturm. "No one in his right mind believes that tale about how Reorx captured Chaos inside a gemstone and it went flying about the world changing gnomes into kender."

"I was never a gnome," said Tas firmly. "I've always been a kender. Just so we're clear on that."

"Whether or not it flew about the world, the Graygem is very real and very dangerous, and the lady is wearing it around her neck," said Raistlin. "You noticed it in the inn. I know you did because I saw the expression of disgust on your face."

"It gives you a squirmy feeling if you touch it," Tas added. "And not the good kind of squirmy feeling. The bad kind."

"I grant you, the gem is loathsome to look upon, but that does not make it the Graygem," Sturm argued.

Raistlin stirred in annoyance, his red robes rustling. "Do I tell you how to wield your sword, Sturm Brightblade? My knowledge of magic is my sword, and you would do well to pay heed to me!"

"Please don't quarrel," said Destina, her cheeks burning with shame. "Raistlin is right. This is the Graygem."

Sturm still appeared unconvinced, but to continue to argue would be to accuse her of lying and he would never do such a thing. He turned from her to Raistlin.

"The question is, what do we do now that we are stranded in a time that is not our own?" Sturm asked.

"You and I are alive again and I, for one, intend to stay that way," Raistlin replied. "We *must* stay alive until we can find a way to return to where we belong. Otherwise we will change time. And that could be catastrophic."

"Raistlin knows all about time travel," Tas offered helpfully. "He went back in time to try to become a god, and Par-Salian sent Caramon and me back in time to stop him. That is, Par-Salian sent Caramon. He didn't send me, but I couldn't let Caramon go alone, so I changed into a mouse and—"

Raistlin rounded on him. "Do you remember the talk we had about a cricket? My threat still holds."

"I remember," said Tas, sighing. He added in an aside to Destina, "He told me he would change me into a cricket and swallow me whole."

Raistlin pointedly ignored him and turned to Sturm. "Did you see any goblins?"

"None near us, but signs of them are all around. And I recognize our location. We are in the wooded flatland known as the Wings of Habakkuk, south of the High Clerist's Tower. The knights will be gathering their forces to defend the tower and the Dark Queen is summoning her forces to attack it. Those goblin raiders are probably advance troops."

"Thus begins the Third Dragon War, and we are caught in the middle," said Raistlin. "And now I believe I know where to lay the blame."

"I didn't do it," said Tas promptly, then realized Raistlin was looking at Destina and came to her defense. "She didn't, either. Or at least, she didn't mean to!"

"I am aware of that," said Raistlin. "We are all of us here on the whim of Chaos."

CHAPTER
THREE

The wind blew through the branches of the tree beneath which they were standing. The leaves stirred and rustled, almost as if the tree was alive and it, too, was afraid.

"I have tried to rid myself of the Graygem, but I can't take it off! It won't let me!" said Destina. She took hold of the Graygem and gave it a tug, as though to break the chain. Gray light flared and sizzled. She snatched her hand away and held out blistered fingers.

"Interesting," Raistlin murmured. "You have not yet learned how to control it."

"I can't control it," Destina protested. "I can't even touch it! You see what it did to me."

"Because you are afraid of it," said Raistlin. "Only when you overcome your fear will you be able to exert control over it. Yet the Graygem has been lost for centuries. How did you find it?"

"It was hiding in the dwarven kingdom beneath the mountain," Destina replied. "A mage named Ungar claimed to know its location. I went in search of it, and I found it."

"Or rather it found you . . ." Raistlin murmured.

"Stop being so damn mysterious!" Sturm told him, exasperated. "Speak plainly for once in your life."

"Very well," said Raistlin. "To speak plainly, the Third Dragon War happened at a critical moment in time when the fate of the world hung in the balance. We are not here in this place at this time because you and the monk were talking of Huma! We are here because of that."

He pointed a long delicate finger at the Graygem.

"You are saying Chaos is going to change history," Sturm stated, frowning.

"I doubt if even Chaos knows what Chaos is going to do," Raistlin said caustically. "But I do not believe we are here by accident. After all, it was the lady's intention to change history."

Destina gasped in horror. "Oh, no! I never meant—"

"Yes, yes," said Raistlin impatiently. "So you have told us. But your remorse does not help us."

"Don't be mad at Destina!" said Tas, coming to stand protectively at her side. "She was wrong to bring us here and to pretend she was Mari when she wasn't, but she said she was sorry. She didn't know the Device was going to blow up in the future and strand us here in the past."

"The past . . ." Raistlin repeated softly. He stared at her intently, though she had the feeling he wasn't seeing her.

"And you have to admit, Raistlin," Tas continued, "the fact that we're stuck here where we're not supposed to be, and you and Sturm aren't dead anymore, is kind of exciting!"

"I find nothing exciting about it," said Sturm dourly.

"But aren't you glad you're not dead?" Tas asked.

"Be quiet, all of you!" Raistlin ordered. "Let me think!"

They all heard the note of excitement in his voice. Sturm was silent and even hushed Tas when he would have spoken. Destina could only hope he had come up with a plan to save them.

Raistlin turned to her. "You said that a book of your father's gave you the idea of going back in time."

"A book about Huma . . ." Destina faltered, not knowing what he wanted of her.

"Describe the book. Your exact words!" Raistlin insisted.

Destina thought back as best she could through her weariness and fatigue. "I think I said that in that book, Huma's friend, Magius, mentions the Device of Time Journeying—"

"That's the answer—" Raistlin began in triumph, then started to cough.

The others impatiently waited for him to resume. He wiped his lips, drew in a breath, and continued speaking. "We may not be stranded here after all. According to the account in her father's book, Magius intended to use the Device of Time Journeying to go back in time to save Huma's sister. That means he knew where it was located."

Sturm made an impatient gesture. "But the Device was destroyed—"

"In *our* time, yes," said Raistlin. "But in this time, the Device will be whole and intact. And Magius knows where to find it!"

"So we might be able to go back!" Destina said, hardly daring to hope.

"All we have to do is locate Magius in the midst of a war, then persuade him to tell us where to find the Device, all the while refraining from getting ourselves killed, and taking care not to change time while doing any of it," Sturm stated in exasperation.

"Do you have a better suggestion?" Raistlin demanded.

"Unfortunately, I do not," Sturm replied and even faintly smiled.

"Huma and Magius were going to go after the goblin raiders," said Tas. "Couldn't we just go after them going after the goblins?"

"I was hoping we would not have to reveal our presence to anyone in this time, but it seems we have little choice," said Raistlin. "And we must not run blindly into the middle of a war. What do we know of Huma and the Third Dragon War? Sturm, you must have studied him."

"There is not much to study," Sturm said. "The Third Dragon War happened centuries ago, and a great deal of knowledge about it was lost during the Cataclysm. I am most familiar with the story as it is told in the *Song of Huma*."

"I remember the part of the song when Huma followed the stag because you followed the stag, only that was after you'd been hit on the head," said Tas. "Tell us that part!"

Sturm lowered his voice and spoke quietly, reverently.

"'It was morning when they reached the grove, the lap of the mountain, where the Stag departed, nor did Huma follow, knowing the end of this journey was nothing but green and the promise of green that endured in the eyes of the woman before him.'"

"Huma Dragonbane met the silver dragon who had disguised herself as a mortal woman," Sturm continued. "They rode into battle and used the first dragonlance ever forged to drive the Dark Queen and her evil dragons back into the Abyss. But you must know something about the Third Dragon War, Raistlin. You carried what you claimed was the Staff of Magius."

"It was his staff. Magius made it himself," said Raistlin. "And the staff is his now again, for, as you see, I am no longer in possession of it." He stood in silence, brooding, then stirred and shrugged. "Magius was said to be the greatest wizard who ever lived. Beyond that, I know little."

Sturm grunted, clearly not believing him.

Tas raised his hand. "I know all about the Third Dragon War! Uncle Trapspringer and the gnomes forged the first dragonlance and gave it to Huma. It's a very interesting story—"

"And one we do not have time to hear," Raistlin interrupted. "Go keep watch on the road."

"I don't need to watch the road," Tas protested, aggrieved. "I can see the road from where I'm standing and it's not doing anything. But I could go find Magius and the goblins! I'll do that."

"No, Tas!" Raistlin exclaimed. "We need to stay together—"

Tas didn't wait to hear. Sturm made a grab for the kender, but Tas deftly dodged out of his reach and was off among the trees, heading for the road.

"We cannot have him running about loose!" Raistlin said grimly. "The gods know what mischief he will do."

"I will fetch him," said Sturm, sounding resigned. "You and Lady Destina wait here."

"Come right back. And don't get yourself killed doing something noble," Raistlin added.

Sturm set off in pursuit, but kender tended to be fleet of foot, having had to run from various enraged individuals over the years. Thus Tas had a good head start, while Sturm was slower and encumbered by his armor. The kender vanished from sight.

Destina sat down, exhausted, on the fallen log.

The afternoon was warm and sultry with no breeze stirring. They had arrived in Palanthas in early summer, and she was wearing clothes intended for traveling in the winter: a wool jacket, a blouse beneath, and a wool skirt. She was hot and she longed to take off the jacket. Instead, she buttoned the collar up to conceal the Graygem.

Raistlin coughed again, but only briefly. He was pacing back and forth, his arms in his sleeves, absorbed in his own thoughts. Destina didn't like being alone with the mage. She didn't like the way he looked at her, as though he knew all her secrets and all her fears.

Destina recalled the dark stories she had heard about Raistlin Majere when he became master of the Tower of High Sorcery in Palanthas. People whispered of the terrible things he had done there, and she wished Sturm and Tas would return. She didn't want to talk to him, but she was desperate for answers and he was the only one who seemed to have any.

"Raistlin . . ." she said timidly.

He cast a sharp glance at her.

"Tas said you know about traveling through time. Do you believe that if you find the Device, we can go back to our own time and nothing will have changed?" Destina asked.

"The River of Time flows so slowly that if we can leave here without doing anything to drastically alter time, we will be as drops in the water. The river will wash away all traces of us. You should know," he added bitingly. "You hoped the same would happen with your father."

Destina didn't want to talk about her father, and she asked no more questions. She watched the sun glide through the sky, watched the shadows of the trees shift at her feet. She was starting to grow worried about the others and she was relieved to hear Tas calling out to them.

"Destina and Raistlin, where are you?"

"We are here!" Destina answered, waving to him.

Tas peered through the trees, saw them at last, and came running toward them.

"I found a new hoopak," he announced, flourishing a long, forked stick. "And I found Magius and Huma. A bunch of goblins are attacking a village down the road and Huma and Magius are fighting them. But there are only two of them and an awful lot of goblins, so Sturm stayed to help. He sent me back to tell you."

Raistlin sucked in an irate breath. "Sturm finds you and loses himself? One would think we were on a kender picnic! Now I must go after him."

"He didn't find me. I knew where I was," Tas protested, offended. "I know where he is, too. I'll show you."

"I will come with you," said Destina, rising.

"Neither of you are going anywhere!" Raistlin told them. "You will both stay here, so I know where to find you. Do not move until Sturm and I return."

Raistlin shoved up the sleeve of his robes to reveal a knife strapped to his left forearm, held in place by a leather thong. He flicked his wrist, and a silver dagger slid from the thong and into his hand. He offered it to Destina.

"I doubt the Graygem will let anything happen to you, Lady, but take this, just in case," said Raistlin.

The dagger was devoid of decoration and seemed very ordinary, but Destina was reluctant to touch it. "Is it magic?"

Raistlin gave a contemptuous laugh. "You wear around your neck the most powerful and dangerous magical artifact in this world. This dagger is a butter knife compared to the Graygem. Take it or leave it."

Destina noticed he didn't answer the question about the magic, but she accepted the dagger. The knife had weight to it, and the blade was extremely sharp.

"Where is this village?" Raistlin asked Tas.

"A mile or so in that direction," Tas said, pointing with the stick. "You can see the smoke and flames from the road."

Raistlin pulled his hood over his head and walked off swiftly, his robes snapping around his ankles. Destina soon lost sight of him in the forest, though she could hear him coughing.

"Could I hold the dagger?" Tas asked. "I'm sure Raistlin wouldn't mind."

"I don't think he would like that, and I wouldn't want to make him angry," said Destina. She hurriedly tucked the knife into the leather belt she wore around her waist and sat back down on the log. She could now see smoke drifting among the trees and smell the odor of burning and destruction. "You have your own dagger. I know you call it 'Rabbitslayer.' You never told me why."

Tas proudly exhibited his knife. Sitting down beside her, he used it to begin trimming small branches and leaves from the forked stick.

"I found it years ago in the ruins of Xak Tsaroth. Or I guess I find it years ahead in Xak Tsaroth. Anyway, Caramon said the knife would be useful only if we were attacked by ferocious rabbits and so I named it Rabbitslayer. It's magical."

"What does it do?" Destina asked.

"Every other knife I ever owned had a way of losing me when I wasn't looking. Rabbitslayer has never lost me once! Not even the time I traveled to the Abyss to talk to Takhisis. Would you like to hear that story?"

"Very much," said Destina.

"I just went to the Abyss to pay a friendly call on her, to see how she was doing after losing the war. But I guess Takhisis wasn't doing all that well because she sent a demon to kill me. I stabbed the demon with Rabbitslayer and the knife got all slimy with demon blood and was so slippery I dropped it, and I didn't have time to pick it up because I was being chased by an angry demon. I managed to escape the demon and I got out of the Abyss, but I was sad because I had been forced to leave Rabbitslayer behind. But when I looked at my belt, there was Rabbitslayer! So that's how I know it's magic."

Tas had finished trimming the stick. He began to kick his heels against the log. "It's kind of boring without Sturm and Raistlin, isn't it?"

Destina remembered the old saying that the most dangerous thing in the world was a bored kender.

"I'm not bored," she said quickly. "Tell me another story."

"I would, but I'm awfully thirsty," said Tas. "It's hard to tell stories when you're thirsty. I'm hungry, too, but I'm more thirsty than hungry. I guess I'll go look for some water."

"Raistlin said we weren't supposed to leave," Destina reminded him, alarmed.

"I'm not leaving," Tas argued, jumping to his feet. "I'm going to look for water. Besides, I want to try out my new hoopak."

"Tas, I really think you should stay here!" Destina said. "Raistlin said we should stay together."

"But he didn't do what he said. He's not staying together. He went off after Sturm. Don't worry," Tas assured her. "I won't be gone long."

He picked up his forked stick and ran off into the forest, heading in the opposite direction of the road. Destina wondered if she should go after him, then decided against it, for she had no idea where she was and she was afraid of getting lost.

The forest seemed unnaturally quiet. Nothing stirred except faint tendrils of smoke writhing around the trees. The woodland creatures had gone to ground, probably due to the fighting. She didn't like being alone, and she started up in fright when she heard a crash behind her. Putting her hand on her dagger, she stared fearfully into the shadows.

"Tas?" she called.

No answer.

"It was only a branch falling," she said to herself.

And then she heard Tas yelling, "Look out" as he came tearing through the brush, brandishing his forked stick.

"Goblins!" he shouted. "Right behind me!"

CHAPTER
FOUR

Tas skidded to a halt and turned to taunt the goblins, who came crashing through the woods after him.

"You can't catch me, you ugly, flea bitten squeakers!" Tas yelled. "You sawed-off excuses for hobgoblins! Half the brains and twice the ugly!"

The goblins howled and gibbered in rage. Tas whipped about and ran toward Destina, waving his hoopak. "I'll lead them to you. Be ready to smack them when they come by!"

He tossed her the hoopak as he dashed past and continued on with the goblins in mad pursuit, charging after him in blind fury.

Destina didn't have time to think or even be afraid before the goblins were on her. She swung the forked stick as a goblin rushed at her and smashed it in the face, then struck another goblin on the head and knocked it flat.

Tas was dancing about, jabbing Rabbitslayer at a goblin who took a wild swing at him with its sword. Tas ducked and the sword whistled harmlessly over his head, then he again leaped to the attack with Rabbitslayer. The goblin flung itself on him bodily, and they both went down. The goblin got its hands around Tas's throat and tried to wring his neck.

Destina grabbed her knife and was about to go to his rescue when she again heard a rustling in the branches. A woman dropped down out of the tree and landed beside Tas. The woman stabbed the goblin in the ribs with a short sword, then dragged the body off Tas and looked around at Destina.

"Behind you!" The woman pointed.

Destina swung around just as a goblin lunged at her throat. She slashed frantically at it with her knife. The goblin knocked her blade aside and seized hold of the Graygem.

Gray light flared. The goblin gave a fearful shriek and stumbled backward, yelping in pain and wringing its charred hand. Destina scrambled away from the creature as it limped off. The rest of the goblins lingered, their eyes balefully reflecting the eerie gray light. Destina clutched her knife, ready to fight, and the strange woman came to stand beside her, holding her sword. The rest of the goblins turned and ran away.

Destina stood panting for breath, trying to rid herself of the terrifying memory of the goblin's hand at her throat and the stench of its fetid breath.

"Are you all right?" the woman asked her.

She was an elf and the most beautiful woman of any race Destina had ever seen. Tall and slender, the elf was dressed in a summer-green belted tunic with darker green leggings and brown slippers that blended well with the colors of the forest. Her features were delicate. Her hair was silvery white, the color of moonlight shining on snow, worn in a single braid down her back. Her eyes were as green as dew-sparkled leaves.

She carried a short bow slung over her shoulder and a quiver of arrows, as well as her sword, and she regarded Destina with a frown, her gaze fixed on Destina's throat. Destina looked down to see the Graygem still shining brightly. She hurriedly clasped it and tucked it away beneath her collar, hoping without much hope that the elf hadn't noticed. But Tas ended what little hope she had harbored.

"I saw the Graygem burn that goblin, Destina!" Tas cried excitedly, running over to join them. His voice was raspy, and he had bruises on his throat, but he appeared otherwise unharmed. "When I touched it, it only gave me a squirmy feeling. It didn't try to set me on fire! How did you do that?"

Destina pretended she hadn't heard him and turned back to the elven woman. "Thank you for coming to our aid."

"Yes, thank you," Tas added. He wiped the goblin blood from his hand on his tunic, then politely extended his hand. "I am Tasslehoff Burrfoot and this is Lady Destina Rosethorn."

"I am called Gwyneth." The woman shook hands with Tas. "And I believe the ring you are holding is mine."

Tas opened his hand and turned it palm up. He seemed extraordinarily surprised to find a silver ring.

"You mean this ring? I guess you must have dropped it," Tas said.

"I guess I must have," said Gwyneth with a smile. "Thank you for finding it. The ring is dear to me. It was a gift from my sister."

She slid the ring onto her finger, then shifted her gaze to Destina. "So that is the Graystone, the jewel you humans call the Graygem. I heard you and your friends talking about it."

Destina thought she should deny she was wearing the Graygem, tell the elf that the necklace was a family heirloom or something, but she was too tired to lie. Besides, denying it seemed pointless anyway. Gwyneth had overheard them discussing the Graygem. She had seen it in action, and Tas had provided confirmation.

"How did you come by the accursed gem?" Gwyneth was asking. "Why are you wearing it?"

"Would you like me to tell her?" Tas asked, seeing Destina's hesitation.

"No, Tas, just stop talking about it!" Destina said wearily.

Gwyneth shook her head. "The knight and the wizard were wrong to leave you to fend for yourself while you wear such a dangerous gem."

"Destina's not fending for herself," Tas protested indignantly. "She has me, and I have Rabbitslayer, only I'm going to change the name to Goblinslayer."

"You are a valiant bodyguard, Master Burrfoot," said Gwyneth, "but Lady Destina is in great danger. The Dragon Queen has come to Solamnia, where she is gathering her forces for a final assault on the High Clerist's Tower. If she learns the Graystone is here, within her reach, she will stop at nothing to get hold of it."

"What would Takhisis do with it?" Tas asked with interest.

"The Dragon Queen would try to harness the Graystone's awful power and if she succeeded, she would be stronger than all the gods combined," Gwyneth replied. "She would try to corrupt and control all the existing races and ultimately remake the world, creating new beings and races to serve her. It would give her an unending well of power."

Destina clasped her hand around the Graygem with a sick feeling of dread. Gwyneth saw her misery, and the elf's stern demeanor softened.

"I am sorry, Destina. You are in trouble, and I am adding to your burden, not helping to lift it."

"You don't need to worry, Gwyneth," Tas stated. "When the Dark Queen attacks the tower in a few days, a knight named Huma is going to attack her and drive her back into the Abyss and she'll have to stay there until the War of the Lance."

Gwyneth stared at Tas in perplexity. "What do you mean—"

"He likes to make up stories," said Destina and quickly changed the subject. "Did you find any water, Tas?"

"I found a creek, but then the goblins found me and I had to run away. The creek is not far from here. I could go—"

"You should not be wandering off alone," Gwyneth admonished him. "I have water. I will be glad to share."

She removed a small jug from her belt and held it out to Tas. The jug was made from a turtle shell with a cork stopper. He took a long drink, then regarded it admiringly.

"I've never seen a water jug made from a turtle before. It's awfully nice, though I'll bet the turtle didn't much like being made into a jug."

"The turtle's spirit had moved on to the next stage of its life's journey by the time I found its shell," said Gwyneth. "Are you still thirsty?"

Tas nodded. "That was the very best water I ever drank, though it did taste a little of turtle. But the jug is empty."

"Look again," said Gwyneth.

Tas peered into the jug, then tilted it to his lips. "More water! It must be magic! I don't suppose you have any magical sausages to go with it, do you?"

"I am sorry, I don't," said Gwyneth.

"You should try this magical water, Destina," said Tas, handing her the jug.

Destina hesitated, uncertain.

Gwyneth saw her concern. "The water is not magical. Only the jug."

Destina was parched, and she drank from the jug, then handed it back to the elf.

"Would you like to hear the song about Huma and how he's going to attack the Tower, Gwyneth? I know some of it," said Tas.

"We don't have time, Tas. You and I should go find our friends," said Destina, thinking goblins were not nearly as dangerous as the kender's tongue.

"You should come with us, Gwyneth," Tas invited. "In case we meet any more goblins."

"I am certain Gwyneth has better things to do," said Destina. She didn't want to be rude but she didn't like the fact that the elf had been hiding in the trees, eavesdropping on them, and had only decided to help when she learned about the Graygem. "Thank you for coming to our aid, Gwyneth. Tas and I can manage on our own."

"I will accompany you until you find your friends," Gwyneth said. "You should not be alone with the Graystone."

"Why should we trust you?" Destina demanded, rounding on her. "Your homeland is far from Solamnia. You say the Dark Queen is gathering her forces. Perhaps you are a spy!"

"And why should I trust you, human?" Gwyneth countered. "You carry the most dangerous artifact known to both mortals and immortals."

Destina was confounded. She had no idea what to say.

Tas looked from one to the other.

"I think we should all trust each other because we get into trouble when we don't," he stated. "I trust you, Gwyneth, because you could have stayed hidden in your tree, but you didn't. You jumped down to save us from the goblins. And, Gwyneth, you can trust Destina because even though she is wearing an ugly gem that can roast a goblin, she feels really bad about bringing us here by accident. And you can trust me because kender are very trustworthy people."

"I know kender are very wise," said Gwyneth, smiling.

She turned to Destina. "I will tell you why I am here in Solamnia, far from my homeland, if that will reassure you. But we should talk as we walk, for you must find your friends. You are wise to doubt strangers," she added, as they set off through the woods, toward the road that led to the village. "You should doubt them more and not talk openly about the Graystone."

Destina didn't like being scolded, but she felt she deserved it, and didn't respond. She fell into step beside Gwyneth, thinking Tas did make sense. If the elf was a spy, she would not have given herself away. Destina was inclined to trust Gwyneth, if for no other reason than she was blunt and could not be accused of trying to ingratiate herself as a spy might have done.

Gwyneth walked with lithe grace and moved silently through the brush. Destina tried to emulate her, but sticks snapped beneath her feet, and her skirt kept getting caught on bushes. Her clothes were hot and she longed to take off the jacket, but she didn't dare reveal the Graygem after Gwyneth's dire warnings. At least Destina didn't have to worry about Tas talking too much. He had ranged ahead of them, tossing his new hoopak into the air and catching it two times out of three.

Destina glanced curiously at her companion. She had encountered elves in her travels and had occasionally seen them in the city of Palanthas, but she had never spoken with one.

"So why are you in Solamnia?" Destina asked abruptly.

"I am here as an observer for my people, the Qualinesti. If Solamnia falls, we fear Takhisis will strike at our nation next since we share a common border."

"No, you don't," said Destina, thinking she had caught her in a lie. "Qualinesti and Solamnia are separated by an ocean."

Gwyneth gave her a strange look. "An ocean of misunderstanding and mistrust, perhaps, but our two nations border each other."

Destina was about to say that the Cataclysm had ended that, when she suddenly remembered where she was and when.

The Third Dragon War had happened in the year 1018 PC, one thousand eighteen years before the Cataclysm, when the gods hurled down the fiery mountain on Krynn. Her father had kept a map of Krynn before it had been sundered as a curiosity and she now re-

membered that during the Third Dragon War, Qualinesti did border Solamnia to the east.

"Forgive me. I am terrible at geography," said Destina lamely.
"What were you doing in the tree?"

"Napping," said Gwyneth. "Much safer to sleep in a tree than on
the ground. You and your friends woke me. I did not mean to eavesdrop. I tried not to listen, but when you spoke of the Graystone, I
could not help myself. And I could not leave the tree without revealing myself. I am not comfortable around humans, particularly wizards like your friend."

"I am not comfortable around Raistlin myself," Destina admitted.

They were interrupted by a yelp from Tasslehoff, who had accidentally tossed his hoopak into an enormous bramble bush.

"How much does the kender know about the Graystone?"
Gwyneth asked, eyeing him thoughtfully.

Destina watched Tas, who was attempting to extricate his hoopak from the brambles and not having much success.

"He knows too much," she said with a sigh. "And I can't stop him
from talking."

"I doubt if even the gods can stop a kender from talking," said
Gwyneth. "But perhaps I can help him at least keep silent about the
Graystone."

Tas had finally managed to retrieve his hoopak and was now
busy plucking thorns from his hands.

"Whoever created bramble bushes made a very bad mistake," he
was grumbling. "I pointed that out to Fizban once. He said brambles
weren't his fault, that they were an accident of evolution. When I
asked what evolution was, he said it had something to do with monkeys. And when I asked what monkeys were, he hit me with his hat."

Gwyneth helped him remove the last few brambles.

"You have goblin blood on your face," she told him.

"Do I?" said Tas, alarmed. He scrubbed at his cheek. "I'm going to
meet Huma and Magius. They're heroes, and I want to look my best."

"I will clean it off for you," Gwyneth offered.

She licked her fingers and rubbed Tas's forehead, leaving a clean
spot in the middle of the grime.

"The blood is gone," said Gwyneth. "Now you are fit to meet this Huma or anyone else."

"Is elf spit magical?" Tas asked, awed.

"Why do you ask?" said Gwyneth.

"Because my head feels all tingly inside."

Destina did not see how the elf spit was going to help Tas quit talking. She said nothing, however, hoping Gwyneth would drop the subject of the Graygem.

They continued walking, keeping to the shadows, not venturing down onto the road. The smoke was growing thicker, drifting among the trees and spreading a pall over the forest.

"It's not every day I get to meet a hero," Tas was saying. "I'll bet Sturm will be excited to meet Huma, too. Sturm can recite the song by heart. Do you know Huma?"

"I do not know anyone who lives in Solamnia," said Gwyneth.

"You do now," said Tas. "Destina is from Solamnia. She and I met in the Inn of the Last Home, which is in Solace. She had shape-shifted into a kender named Mari and I thought we were married, but Raistlin says we weren't—"

Destina hurriedly interrupted. "Are we close to the village, Tas?"

"It's through those trees. It sounds like they're still fighting goblins."

Destina could hear the clash of arms, shouts and cries and goblins screeching. She peered through the smoke and caught glimpses of men and women battling their foes with pitchforks and axes.

"There is still some fighting but the battle is almost over," Gwyneth reported, pointing. "Most of the goblins are running away. Still, we should wait here under cover until we have found your friends. We are near the High Clerist's Tower. You can see it well from here."

The smoke was slowly dissipating, and from their vantage point atop the hill, Destina could see the spires of the High Clerist's Tower, standing tall and stalwart against the backdrop of the snow-capped mountains, guarding the pass that led to the city of Palanthas. The sky above the tower was the pale blue of early summer with drifting, wispy clouds.

But the peaceful scene was deceptive. Long lines of goblin troops bearing the banners of Queen Takhisis were snaking across the plains. A dragon the color of blood flew toward the tower and Destina gasped in dismay.

"Are the knights under attack?"

"Takhisis is not yet ready. The red dragon is Immolatus, the head of the Dark Queen's advance forces," said Gwyneth. "The rest of Solamnia has fallen. The High Clerist's Tower is all that stands between Takhisis and rulership of Solamnia. She will expend all her might on it. She has sent her favorite, the red dragon, to soften the tower's resistance, demoralize its defenders before her arrival."

Destina watched the red dragon circle the High Clerist's Tower, not even bothering to keep out of arrow range, mocking their attempts to harm him.

"I once saw a blue dragon," said Destina, remembering the blue dragon that had attacked Castle Rosethorn, "but I have never seen a red dragon. I had no idea they were so enormous."

"Immolatus is larger than most. He is arrogant and cruel, and he must chafe at being forced to wait for his queen before he can start killing," said Gwyneth. "As it is, he is using his dragonfear to terrorize the knights and their forces who are trapped inside the tower. He is hoping to undermine their morale and weaken them before the final assault. And he is succeeding. Already some of the soldiers have fled, deserting their posts."

"I saw red dragons during the war," said Tas somberly. "I guess I've seen almost every type of dragon there is. I saw a black dragon at Xak Tsaroth. And then there was Fizban's dragon, Pyrite. I liked him, even though he was about as batty as Fizban. I guess my favorite was Silvara. She was a silver dragon, though none of us knew that at first because she looked like a Wilder Elf."

Gwyneth had stopped walking and was staring at Tas, her eyes wide.

"Do you know Silvara, too?" Tas asked.

"I . . . no," said Gwyneth. She seemed shaken.

"Are you all right?" Destina said, stopping with her.

"An old wound," said Gwyneth. "It pains me sometimes. Do not worry. It will ease."

But she kept her eyes on Tas, who had run on ahead, swatting at the smoke with his hoopak.

I am not the only one with secrets, Destina thought.

"We were speaking of Immolatus," said Gwyneth. "He has been an enemy of my people for many years. I watched city after city in Solamnia fall to the Dark Queen, and I sent swift runners to urge the Speaker of the Suns to come to the aid of the Solamnics. We had a chance to defeat the Dark Queen and slay the red dragon. But Talinthas would not listen. He sent word back to me that this war was the humans' war and to let them fight it."

"I found Sturm!" Tas shouted, running back to join them. "I was going to go help him fight goblins, since I have Goblinslayer, which used to be Rabbitslayer, but which I renamed since we were attacked by vicious goblins not rabbits. Where was I? Oh, yes. But then I thought I should come to tell you that I found him. Sturm, I mean. If you look really hard through those trees—and if that annoying smoke and all those goblins would go away—you can see him. And that other knight with him is Huma! How exciting! He's the one I told you about, Gwyneth. Hey, Huma! It's me! Tasslehoff Burrfoot!"

Huma was still some distance away, in this midst of the battle, but he glanced around on hearing his name and saw Gwyneth, just as a ray of sunlight shining through the leaves gilded her hair with molten silver. The knight stopped where he stood, transfixed.

And Gwyneth saw him. He was not wearing his helm, and she could see his face clearly. Her eyes widened in recognition, and Destina felt her shudder, as though she had been pierced by an arrow.

"What's wrong?" Destina asked, startled, seizing hold of her.

Gwyneth gently pulled away. "You have found your friends," she said in a hollow voice. "I will leave you now."

Destina opened her mouth, but before she could say a word, Gwyneth had run off. Destina watched her slip among the trees and disappear into the shadows. She looked back at the fighting and saw Huma standing, amazed. A goblin wielding an axe was bearing down on him, and only Sturm's urgent warning caused Huma to look around in time to deal with his opponent.

"Gwyneth reminds me of someone," Tas said, wrinkling his brow in thought. "I've been trying to think of who." He suddenly pounced on an object lying on the ground. "Look what I found! The turtle shell water jug. Gwyneth must have dropped it. Hey, Gwyneth!"

He picked up the water jug and ran after her. Destina was going to try to stop him, but she was too tired. She waited for him, and within moments he came bounding back.

"I lost her," Tas said, downhearted. "Maybe she'll come back for her water jug. I'll keep it in case she does. Should we wait for her?"

"I don't think she will be coming back," said Destina. "And we need to go catch up with Sturm and Raistlin."

The sounds of fighting had stopped. The smoke was starting to drift away. The goblins were in full retreat, running down the hill toward the plains, where the enemy's tents were starting to sprout like noxious mushrooms.

Destina looked at the red dragon flying above the tower and the long lines of enemy soldiers marching across the plains, and memories came back of the War of the Lance, the attack on Castle Rosethorn. She could see and smell and hear the terrible sounds of battle and began to tremble.

Tas slipped his hand into hers.

"Don't be frightened, Destina. I won't ever let you fend for yourself."

She squeezed his hand gratefully. "You are a good friend, Tas. Even though I don't deserve it."

"You said you were sorry for changing into Mari, and I forgave you," said Tas. "So that's either water under the bridge or letting the horse out of the barn. I can never remember which."

Tas hung the turtle shell water jug by its leather strap over his shoulder, and they began walking toward the village.

"Wait until I tell Sturm and Raistlin about the goblins attacking us and how I stabbed one with Rabbitslayer now Goblinslayer and one attacked you and tried to grab the—"

Tas was interrupted by a violent sneeze.

"Drat!" he said, wiping his nose with his sleeve. "Where was I? Oh, yes. The goblin and how he tried to take the—"

Tas sneezed again and sniffed. "Maybe a cold is catching me. They do that, you know. Colds catch you when you're not looking. So as I was saying, I'm going to tell Sturm and Raistlin about the goblin that almost had its hand burned off when it tried to take the—"

Tas sneezed again. Destina remembered Gwyneth's words and smiled. *Not even the gods can stop a kender from talking.* But apparently magical elf spit could.

CHAPTER
FIVE

Raistlin walked along the road that led to the village. He was relieved to get away from the others, relieved to be by himself. He had always preferred his own company to that of anyone else—something the outgoing and genial Caramon had never been able to understand. Searching for Sturm had been an excuse to rid himself of Destina and Tasslehoff.

Especially Tasslehoff and his talk of "Fistandoodle." Tas had a disconcerting way of sifting through the chaff to reach the grain most people thought they had safely stored away.

The wizard's name was Fistandantilus and, like speaking the words to a spell, the name conjured up dark and horrifying memories of the lich who had preyed for centuries on vulnerable young mages taking the Test in the Tower of High Sorcery.

The wizards of Ansalon had decreed that all mages who wanted to advance in their art must take a test at the Tower of High Sorcery in Wayreth. The Test evaluated a mage's skills in magic and, more importantly, forced the mage to look into the depths of his or her soul. They emerged wounded in body and soul, humbled and chastened.

But some mages did not leave the tower at all. Those who failed died. And since failure meant death, Fistandantilus had preyed on young mages, offering his help in exchange for a portion of the mage's life force to extend his own.

Raistlin had been one of those young mages. He had not been afraid of death, but he had been afraid of failure, so he had made the dread bargain. He had given Fistandantilus a part of his life. The bargain had left him with the debilitating cough and weakened body. In return, Fistandantilus had given Raistlin the ability to pass the Test. But Raistlin had always been able to hear the evil wizard's voice in his soul, prompting him, guiding him. He had spoken the words to powerful spells with the prompting of that voice.

Until now.

Raistlin slowed his pace. He forgot the danger, forgot everything except those words Tasslehoff had spoken. *Still got that cough. I was thinking being dead might cure it.*

Being dead had not cured him. But death had severed the connection. He could no longer hear the voice. He was on his own, to cast his own magic. The few spells he knew at this stage of his life, five years after passing the Test, were simple spells. He could dimly remember the powerful spells he had cast as the master of the Tower of High Sorcery, but the words were shadows on his mind, for he lacked the ability and experience needed to cast them.

"The voice I hear in my soul is my own."

Raistlin coughed and fumbled for his handkerchief, pressing it to his mouth. The coughing eased. He drew back the handkerchief and saw it spotted with both dried blood and fresh. His blood.

Raistlin looked at the road stretching on before him. He walked alone. He could no longer hear the voice of Fistandantilus.

"I have a chance to live life without him," Raistlin reflected. "At least for a short time."

And hopefully that time *would* be short. He knew better than the others the danger posed by their accidental presence. They had to remain alive, for if Sturm died back in this time, he would not be present at the Battle of the High Clerist's Tower in the future. True, the River of Time might continue to flow without him. Another hero might emerge to battle the dragons assaulting the tower. But they did not dare take that chance.

If Raistlin's theory on traveling through time was right, he had to ensure that he and Sturm returned to the time they had left—the autumn night of their reunion during the War of the Lance. If he was successful, neither of them would have any memory of this time, because it had not happened to them. And without the intervention of Chaos, trapped in the Graygem, it never would. He reasoned out the conundrum.

"Sturm and I are dead when our bodies in the past are whisked back to the Third Dragon War, a time in which we never existed. Chaos snatched our souls from our eternal rest and rejoined them with our bodies. That is why Sturm and I are able to remember our past lives.

"As for Tas and Destina, the Tas of the present replaced the Tas of the past for a brief moment in time, yet when Tas returns to the Inn of the Last Home during the War of the Lance, he won't remember any of this, because that Tas will have never lived it. That Tas will meet Destina in his future.

"If we leave the Third Dragon War without doing any harm, the River of Time will wash away all trace of us. Sturm's soul will go on to the next stage of his life's journey. I will go back to my endless sleep."

He had to consider the possibility that they might not find the Device. They might not even be able to go back. "I wonder what might occur if our future is here in this time." Raistlin gave a sardonic smile. "Who knows? With Sturm Brightblade here to influence me for good, I might even take the White Robes."

He laughed and then chided himself. Speaking of time, he was wasting it.

He quickened his pace down the road and, realizing he could still be in danger, began to pay more attention to his surroundings. The goblin raiders had stolen livestock and produce, then set houses and barns and outbuildings on fire to cover their retreat. The smoke grew thicker as he approached the village, which was still under attack, and he used the handkerchief to muffle his nose and mouth.

During the gaps in the billowing smoke, he could see that the battle was not so much a battle as a pitched brawl. The villagers were fighting the goblin raiders with pitchforks and clubs, rakes and fists, as bellowing cattle, squealing pigs, and frantic chickens charged about with goblins in pursuit.

Raistlin coughed in the smoke and pressed his handkerchief more closely over his mouth. He could not locate Sturm or Huma or Magius. But when he saw a streak of magical blue lightning strike a goblin, he knew Magius was here somewhere.

Clouds were massing in the east. A cool breeze with a whiff of rain sprang up, dispersing the smoke, and Raistlin caught sight of Sturm coming to the aid of a man being attacked by several goblins who had yanked off his helm and stolen his pack and were savagely kicking and beating him.

Sturm shouted to draw the goblins' attention from their victim and swung his sword in a threatening arc. The goblins had come to raid and butcher, not to fight a sword-wielding knight, and they picked up their loot and fled.

The soldier moaned and Raistlin hurried to his aid. He was wearing the padded tunic and breeches that Raistlin recognized from his mercenary days as denoting a foot soldier. The man's head and face were covered with blood, and he clutched at his midriff. Sturm was standing protectively over him, his sword drawn, watching for more goblins.

Seeing Raistlin, Sturm frowned. "What are you doing here? You're supposed to be guarding Lady Destina."

"Given that you are needed in the future to win the Battle of the High Clerist's Tower, I came to make certain you did not get yourself killed," Raistlin snapped. "I will stay with this soldier. Go help the villagers."

Sturm gave him a dark look. "If anything happens to her—"

"It won't," said Raistlin. "The Graygem will see to that. Go. You are needed."

Sturm hesitated a moment, then he heard someone screaming for help. He turned and ran, disappearing back into the smoke.

Raistlin knelt beside the soldier and started to examine him, trying to determine the severity of the injuries. The wounded man felt his touch and his eyes flared open in terror.

"Lie still," said Raistlin. "You are safe for the moment. What is your name?"

He did not speak Solamnic, so he used what was known as camp talk, the language of soldiers, particularly mercenaries, who came from different parts of the world and spoke a variety of languages. Camp talk provided them with a way to communicate. The language was old, as old as war itself.

"Yeoman Mullen Tully," the soldier said weakly. "They just call me Tully."

The soldier groaned again. His face was badly battered, his eyes starting to swell.

"Do you feel pain anywhere else?" Raistlin asked.

"My knee and my ribs," the soldier gasped. "I think they're broken."

As Raistlin started to examine the knee, he smelled the foul stench of goblin and heard the sound of a sword sliding from its sheath and feet shuffling through the undergrowth.

As Raistlin continued to talk to the soldier, he surreptitiously dipped his hand into one of his pouches.

"You may have a mild concussion, Tully, but nothing is broken," said Raistlin. "Your knee is sprained and your ribs are badly bruised."

Tully opened his eyes to look at Raistlin, then caught sight of the goblin. His eyes widened. He struggled to sit up. "Behind you—"

"Don't move!" Raistlin ordered. "I am aware."

He waited one more heartbeat, allowing the goblin to creep closer, then whipped about and flung yellow powder in the goblin's face.

The powder exploded with a dazzling flash. The goblin shrieked, dropped its sword, and began to rub its eyes, howling in pain. Raistlin picked up Tully's sword and clouted the goblin on the head with the hilt. The creature slumped to the ground. Raistlin tossed the sword aside and returned to his patient, who was regarding him with suspicion.

"You're a wizard," said Tully, drawing back from Raistlin's touch. "You're not going to use your magic on me, are you?"

Raistlin did not bother to tell him that what he had used was not magic, but a powdered mixture of the dried spores of the clubmoss plant known as flash powder.

"Lie still," said Raistlin.

"Where'd a wizard learn camp talk?" Tully asked.

"I worked as a mercenary," Raistlin replied.

Tully grunted. "Were you in the battle of Palanthas? Because I heard the city fell to the Dark Queen."

Raistlin was startled and appalled at this unexpected news. He sat back on his heels. "Is that true or just a rumor?"

"It's true," Tully said. "I heard it from the survivors who fled to the High Clerist's Tower. I serve there under Commander Belgrave."

Raistlin cursed the ill luck. He had deemed it likely that the Device of Time Journeying was in the Tower of High Sorcery in Palanthas, for that was the tower with which Magius would be most familiar and where he had probably seen it. If so, it was in Palanthas— a city that was now in the hands of the enemy. Raistlin wondered what had become of the tower. The wizards would have stayed to defend it. Or so he hoped.

Tully's eyelids fluttered. His eyes rolled back in his head.

"Keep talking, Tully!" said Raistlin, rousing him. "You have to stay awake. Tell me more about Palanthas."

Tully blinked and grimaced. "All I know is that ships loaded with minotaurs sailed into the Bay of Branchala and captured the city. Palanthas fell without a fight."

Tully started to heave. Raistlin turned his head so that he would not choke. He had to keep Tully from lapsing into unconsciousness, knowing from experience that those with head wounds who fell asleep often did not wake up.

"If you are with the forces defending the tower, what are you doing here?" Raistlin asked.

Tully nodded and winced in pain. "Commander Belgrave sent me to warn the villagers about the red dragon. I was on my way to tell them when the gobs caught me."

Raistlin considered that an odd story. "Seems to me that if the villagers looked up into the sky, they would notice a red dragon. Why would this commander risk sending one of his soldiers to warn them of something they could see for themselves?"

Tully groaned, his eyes closed, and Raistlin wondered if he was avoiding answering the question. He vaguely remembered hearing something about a red dragon in connection with the Third Dragon War, but he could not bring it to mind.

He roused Tully once more. "When did this dragon arrive?"

"Seems like he's been here forever," Tully muttered. "Flying overhead. Taunting us. Filling our minds with fear. Some of the men couldn't take it and fled."

Raistlin wondered if Tully was one of them. When he vomited again, Raistlin looked around for help. He and his patient were a tempting target, and he could not move Tully by himself. He breathed a sigh of relief when he saw Tasslehoff and Destina emerge from the woods at the top of the hill. Raistlin motioned for them to join him, and Tas came bounding toward him, followed more slowly by Destina.

"We were attacked by goblins!" Tas announced on his arrival. "My knife has a new name. Goblinslayer." He squatted down beside the wounded man. "Hullo! I'm Tasslehoff Burrfoot."

Tully feebly tried to shove him away. "Little thief! Bad as gobs . . ."

"Thief!" Tas repeated indignantly. "I've never stolen anything in my life!"

By this time, Destina had made her way down the hill.

"What can I do to help?"

"This is Yeoman Tully. He is badly injured," said Raistlin. "We're not safe out here in the open. We need to get him into the forest."

"Do you think we can carry him?" Destina asked doubtfully.

Tully wasn't very tall, but he was big-boned and solidly built. He blinked at Destina and struggled to rise.

"You shouldn't be here, Mistress! It's too dangerous. A beautiful lady like you . . ." Tully's voice trailed off in confusion.

Raistlin looked at Destina and supposed she was beautiful. He couldn't tell. In his cursed vision, she was decaying, withering, dying. As were the trees and the grass and everything else around him.

"Thank you for the compliment," said Destina. "But let me help you."

"I can manage on my own, bless you, Mistress," Tully said, flushing in embarrassment.

"Nonsense, Yeoman, you are badly hurt," said Destina. "Put your arm across my shoulder and I will help you stand."

Tully continued to protest. "My clothes are filthy. I'll get blood on your fine dress."

Tas eagerly came over. "You can lean on my hoopak!"

Tully shrank back. "Don't let the little thief touch me!"

"Calling me a thief is very rude," said Tas. "But I'll help you anyway because I'm maniacal."

"He means magnanimous," Destina corrected, exchanging amused glances with Raistlin.

"That, too," said Tas.

The kender got a good grip on Tully, who was now in too much pain to continue to argue. With the help of the hoopak, Destina, and Tas, Raistlin managed to assist Tully to stand.

They started climbing up the ridge toward the woods, but they did not get far before Tully accidentally put weight on his injured knee and collapsed with an agonized cry. They managed to drag him into the shadows of the trees, and he sank back among the leaves. He was sweating and breathing heavily. His head lolled; his eyes closed.

Raistlin called his name, but he did not respond.

"We must find help for him," said Destina.

"Would he like some water?" Tas asked, hovering over Tully. "I have a new water jug. It's made out of a turtle, but Gwyneth said the turtle didn't mind. The jug is magic. When it's empty, it fills back up again."

"Let me see that," said Raistlin. He took the jug and examined it. "This is of elven make. Who is Gwyneth?"

"An elf," said Tas. "I'm keeping the jug for her."

"Where did you meet this elf?"

"In a tree," Tas answered. "I was going to look for water, only I found goblins instead. Destina smashed one in the face with my new hoopak. She's awfully good with a hoopak, probably from her time being a kender. And then one of the goblins tried to strangle me, and Gwyneth jumped down out of the tree and stabbed it. Then a goblin tried to steal Destina's necklace and the—"

Tas sneezed. He blinked his eyes. "I'm sorry. That sneeze snuck up on me. What was I saying? Oh, yes, the goblin tried to take the—"

Tas sneezed again. "The goblin burned his hand on the—"

He sneezed a third time and wiped his nose with his sleeve in annoyance. "I don't know where these stupid sneezes are coming from, but they're starting to bother me!"

"Interesting," said Raistlin. "Skip to the part about the elf."

"I will if I can quit sneezing! Her name is Gwyneth and she was hiding it a tree and helped us fight off the goblins. She heard me say I was thirsty and she gave me some water in this magic turtle jug. I asked her if she had any magical sausages to go with it, but she didn't. She heard you and Destina talking about the—" Tas sneezed again

Raistlin observed the kender closely. "Did this elf touch you?"

"No, I don't think so. Oh, yes! I remember! I had goblin blood on my face and Gwyneth scrubbed it off with elf spit. Did she get all the blood?"

"Most of it. So where is this elf now?"

"I told you. She ran away," Tas said.

"Did you meet this elf?" Raistlin asked Destina.

"She came to our rescue when the goblins attacked us," Destina replied. "She said she was from Qualinesti and was here as an observer for her people. She stayed with us until we saw Sturm and Huma, then she ran off."

"Elves and humans have no love for each other, but they are bound together in their hatred for Takhisis," said Raistlin. "If you see her again, let me know. Meanwhile, we need to get help for the yeoman. The goblins are in retreat. Tas, run to the village and find Sturm. Tell him we have a wounded man and to bring assistance."

Tas jumped to his feet, picked up his hoopak, and dashed off.

"Those sneezing fits are magic, aren't they?" Destina asked.

"The elf cast a spell on him," Raistlin affirmed. "You notice he sneezes whenever he starts to say . . . a certain word."

"You mean the Graygem," Destina said. "Gwyneth said she was going to stop him from talking about it."

Raistlin frowned and cast a warning glance at Tully.

"Come with me," he said abruptly and walked some distance away, out of earshot.

"What's wrong?" she asked, accompanying him. "He's unconscious."

"I do not altogether trust him. He told me that he is part of the force defending the High Clerist's Tower and that his commander sent him to warn the villagers to flee. I think he could be a deserter, but that is neither here nor there. How did the elf come to know about the Graygem?"

"She was sleeping in the tree when we arrived in the forest. She said our voices woke her and she overheard us talking about it."

"Did she say anything else?" Raistlin asked. "We spoke of many things, including the Device of Time Journeying. Did she ask about that?"

Destina thought back. "No, just the Graygem. She warned me I was in danger because of it. Which reminds me." She drew Raistlin's knife from her belt and handed it back to him. "Tas has been admiring it. I think it will be safer with you."

Raistlin took the knife and slid it back into the leather thong. "Why did she leave?"

"She ran off when she saw Huma," said Destina. "I thought that was strange. She started to tremble at the sight of him, as if she knew him and was terrified of him. Then she turned and ran away. And he looked stricken when he saw her."

"I wonder if her sudden departure had something to do with the Graygem," Raistlin mused.

"She saved our lives," Destina pointed out. "You said yourself the elves hate and fear Takhisis."

"The Graygem of Gargath is a powerful artifact," Raistlin said. "This elf might want it for herself, to save her people from the Dark Queen. I have known that to happen."

He recalled the tragedy of Lorac, the elven king, who had stolen a dragon orb to try to save his people and had ended up nearly destroying them.

Destina started to say something more, but Raistlin stopped her. "Quiet! I hear someone coming!"

They kept very still. Raistlin brought the words to a spell to mind—one he had memorized centuries ago—and took out a pinch of bat guano. A simple spell. As a novice mage once again, he lacked the magical skill to cast anything else.

And to think I had the power to challenge the gods, he thought with grim irony.

They heard the sound of feet rustling through the forest undergrowth and a shrill voice, singing.

"'Your one true love's a sailing ship, that anchors at our pier. We lift her sails, we man her decks, we scrub her portholes clear. . . .'"

Raistlin let the words to the spell slide from his mind. "Tasslehoff."

"I found Sturm," Tas announced when he saw them. "He and Huma and some other men are coming to help the soldier. And look who came with me, Raistlin! This is Magius. And see what he has with him? He has your staff!"

CHAPTER
SIX

Magius came into view, walking slightly behind Tas. The mage was a typical Solamnic in appearance, with hair the color of the ripening wheat and blue eyes. He had high cheekbones, a determined jaw, a sardonic smile, and a mocking glint in his eyes. He wore red robes, since war wizards were not permitted to wear the white robes that betokened peace, and a silver ring on his left hand. Eyeing the ring, Raistlin wondered if it was magical.

He knew from history that Magius was now in his thirties, as was his friend, Huma. That meant that Raistlin was the younger of the two, with far less knowledge and experience at this time in his life.

Magius walked slowly, leaning on his staff as though exhausted, which might be true, for he had been casting spells that fatigued the body and drained the mind. But Raistlin was not fooled; he had used the same deception himself, leaning heavily on his staff to lull an enemy into complacency by feigning weakness. With one word of magic, Magius could turn that staff into a deadly weapon.

Raistlin could not fault the mage for taking precautions, for he was now encountering strangers who had been skulking about in the woods during a time of war. But as his gaze swept over the group, Raistlin saw he appeared to be more intrigued than afraid.

"Sturm and Huma are bringing help for that soldier who got hurt," Tas was saying. "Magius wanted to come ahead to meet everyone. This is Lady Destina Rosethorn."

Destina did not look like a noble lady, for her clothes were covered with leaves and stained with blood, and her black hair had come unbound and tumbled down around her shoulders. But she shook out her skirt, brushed off the leaves, and greeted Magius with the poise she would have used to welcome a guest to her manor house.

"Thank you for coming to help us, sir," she said graciously. She gestured to Tully. "This man was attacked by goblins and is wounded."

Magius inclined his head in acknowledgment. "My friend is bringing men from the village with a litter."

His voice was confident, self-assured, taking command of the situation—wary, but not fearful. His blue eyes flicked past Destina to fix on Raistlin.

"And this is my wizard friend, Raistlin Majere," Tas continued excitedly. "I was telling Magius about you, Raistlin. How you cough up blood and you have golden skin and hourglass eyes."

Magius regarded Raistlin with a cool, appraising look. "Golden skin. Pupils the shape of hourglasses. Your hair, prematurely white."

"The Test," said Raistlin by way of explanation.

Magius's expression grew shadowed. He nodded in understanding and said nothing more. He, too, would have taken the Test. And, like Raistlin and all other mages, he would be loath to reveal what had happened to him.

Raistlin observed his fellow mage with interest and some reluctance.

Huma was celebrated as a hero in story and song, but none of the heroic tales mentioned Magius, probably because Solamnics distrusted magic, and they chose to ignore that their hero had been friends with a wizard. But Raistlin had heard stories of Magius all his life, for wizards honored him to this day and kept his memory alive. Yet Raistlin knew the old adage that warned against meeting your heroes, for they can never measure up to your expectations and were certain to disappoint. He wondered if that would be the case with Magius and held himself aloof.

"Greetings, Brother," said Magius. "I have long thought I was the only wizard in Solamnia. I am pleased, albeit astonished, to meet another."

"Raistlin is the friend I was telling you about," said Tas. "The one who owns your staff."

"And to think that all this time I have been laboring under the misconception that I owned my staff," Magius said, his lips twitching in amusement.

"The kender has your staff confused with an old walking staff of mine," Raistlin said.

"I am not confused," Tas said, offended. "I *know* it's the same staff because your staff had a dragon claw holding a crystal ball on top just like this one. I can prove it." He turned to Magius. "Does the crystal ball on your staff light up when you say, 'Shellac'? Because Raistlin's staff used to do that."

Magius had been amused before, but he was not amused now. The magic word used to light the crystal on the staff was *Shirak*, not *shellac*, but the two were close enough to raise questions.

"What else do you know about my staff, Master Burrfoot?" Magius spoke to the kender, but he was watching Raistlin.

"Call me Tas," said Tas. "Everyone does. Raistlin said it was the 'Staff of Magius' and that it had been your staff. He was really proud of it and wouldn't let me touch it even though I promised I wouldn't get it dirty. Although I guess I should say the staff *will* be his, because, of course, it is your staff now."

Magius raised an eyebrow at this puzzling statement. Raistlin was still holding the bat guano, and he seriously considered using it to blast the kender. Fortunately for Tas, Sturm and Huma entered the woods at that moment, and Tas forgot about the staff.

The knights were leading two horses and talking companionably. Huma was dressed for traveling, not for battle. He wore a breastplate and helm, leather boots and chain mail, and carried his sword at his side. His rich brown hair fell in two braids over his shoulders and, like Sturm, he wore the long mustaches that were the hallmark of the Solamnic knights.

But the similarities between the two ended there. Huma had been in his early thirties during the Third Dragon War. Sturm was about the same age, though he appeared the older of the two. Sturm was grave and somber. He viewed life as a struggle, a serious endeavor that was not to be undertaken lightly. He almost never laughed, as though he feared joy might break some strict rule of the Measure. He was withdrawn, even from his close friends. Tanis had once remarked that even when Sturm was not wearing armor, he was wearing armor.

Huma, by contrast, appeared to take life far less seriously. He already had gray in his hair and mustache, and his face was tan and weathered, but the lines around his mouth were from smiling. His blue eyes were warm and welcoming. Raistlin remembered the conversation he and the others had overheard between Huma and Magius.

The two had talked about aiding the village being attacked by the goblins. Although they knew they would be vastly outnumbered, they had jested about the danger, and Huma had even challenged Magius to a bet.

"Let us make this interesting!" Magius had told him. "A cask of dwarf spirits says that I kill my ten goblins before your sword is bloodied."

"A bet you will lose, my friend!" Huma had returned, laughing.

Huma was laughing now, as he and Sturm walked toward them, talking of the fight in the village. "I will never forget seeing you stop in the midst of a pitched battle to salute your opponent! Lucky for you, the goblin was as startled as I was and missed his stroke."

Sturm answered, somewhat stiffly, "According to the Measure, an honorable knight—"

"Doesn't get himself killed saluting a goblin," said Huma, smiling. "Come now, Brightblade, I meant no offense. You are the best hand with a sword I have met in a long time. I would be glad to have you at my side in battle any day."

Sturm almost, but not quite, smiled at the praise, though he resumed his customary grave dignity when he performed the introductions.

"My companions, Lady Destina Rosethorn and Raistlin Majere," said Sturm. "I have the honor of presenting Huma Feigaard, Knight of the Crown."

Sturm had also met his hero, Raistlin realized. Sturm had been brought up to honor and revere—and urged to emulate—Huma, only to find he was not the serious, honor-bound knight he had expected, but one who was friends with a wizard and laughed at the Measure. Sturm was deferential and respectful, but he appeared uncomfortable, perhaps unable to reconcile the myth with the man.

Destina likewise looked awed and made a low curtsy, and Raistlin remembered her saying how her father had revered Huma as well.

The knight did not seem to notice their admiration. He tethered the horses to the tree and walked over to join them. He looked at Raistlin and appeared taken aback by the mage's strange appearance.

"The Test," Magius replied, taking note of his friend's discomfiture and answering his unspoken question.

Huma was grave. "I understand . . . at least as much as I can." He exchanged glances with his friend, then politely changed the subject. "But where is your companion? The elf woman with the silver hair? I would like to meet her. I believe I know her."

"Know her? How?" Magius asked, astonished. "You have never encountered an elf in your life!"

"I did once," said Huma quietly. "As you well know."

Magius looked exasperated. "It was a dream! As *you* well know."

"It was not a dream," said Huma firmly.

"She has gone," said Destina. "We do not know where she went."

"The villagers are following us with a litter," said Sturm. "They should be here soon."

Destina murmured something in reply and an uncomfortable silence fell. Huma continued to cast searching glances around the forest, as though thinking he might yet see the elf with the silver hair.

Sturm cleared his throat. "Huma was telling me about a strange encounter he had moments earlier. He saw a white stag. Please tell the tale again, sir. I think my friends will find it interesting."

"I'm sure your story is very interesting, but shouldn't we be looking for Gwyneth?" Tas asked.

"Gwyneth?" Magius repeated, glancing about. "First Huma claims to have seen an elf with silver hair, and now there is someone called Gwyneth? How many more of you are hiding in the bushes?"

"She wasn't in a bush," said Tas. "She was sleeping in a tree. She's an elf and she has silver hair, so she might have been the elf Huma saw. I think we should look for her."

"Let Huma tell his story, Tas," Raistlin said sharply, realizing Sturm had mentioned this for a reason and remembering another encounter with a white stag. "Don't interrupt. It's rude."

"I'm sorry, Huma," said Tas, remorseful. "The interruption came out of my mouth before I could stop it. You can tell your story now."

"I agree with the kender," said Magius. "Tell us your tale about seeing a deer in a forest filled with deer. Like the kender, I am agog with excitement."

"Not just any deer," Huma said. "I have never seen a stag as magnificent as this one. The stag's fur had a silvery cast to it and there was a look of intelligence in the animal's brown eyes such as I have never seen in the eyes of a dumb beast. I almost thought it would speak to me."

"Sturm saw a white stag once. He said it was leading him somewhere," said Tas, forgetting he wasn't supposed to interrupt. "But he'd been hit on the head. Were you hit on the head?"

Raistlin now understood why Sturm wanted them to hear this tale about the stag. He listened in growing concern.

"No, I wasn't hit on the head," Huma was saying, smiling at Tas. "I was helping the villagers round up some of their cattle when I saw the stag. It had been wounded by a goblin arrow, buried deep in its left shoulder.

"Blood flowed from the wound, and the stag was in obvious pain and growing weak. It tried to run when it saw me, but it staggered and fell to its knees. I could not let it die a long and agonizing death. If nothing else, I could at least put it out of its misery.

"I spoke to the stag gently as I drew near. The beast was frightened and tried to flee, but it was too weak. I knelt beside it and put my hand on its neck and stroked the silver fur, hoping to reassure it.

"The stag trembled at my touch at first, but it soon grew calm, and I swear to Paladine that the creature knew me! I told it I wanted to free it of pain and I asked it to forgive me for what I must do. I was about to draw my sword when my heart misgave me. I could not kill such a wise and noble creature. I decided to try to pull out the arrow, but I feared the wound would bleed even more and the stag would die. Promising the stag I would return, I ran back to the village for bandages to staunch the wound. But when I returned, the stag was gone."

All of them waited, regarding Huma expectantly. He shrugged. "That is the end."

"What do you mean 'that is the end'?" Magius demanded. "The end of this exciting story is that the stag got up and ran off?"

"I am afraid so," said Huma. "I searched, but I could not find any trace of it."

"But that story isn't right," Tas protested. "In the song, the stag leads you on a quest to find the dragonlances."

"There you are, Magius," said Huma, clapping Tas on the shoulder. "The kender has a far more interesting version. Tell us the ending to your story, Master Burrfoot. What are dragonlances?"

Tas gaped at him. "You don't know?"

"Tas, I see men coming with the litter," said Raistlin. "They may not be able to find us. Go show them."

"But Huma doesn't know about the dragonlances!" Tas protested. "The stag didn't lead him anywhere! How is he going to fight the Dark Queen without dragonlances?"

"I will go with Tas," said Sturm.

He placed his hand on Tas's shoulder in a viselike grip and marched him off.

"Do you know what the kender is talking about, Lady Destina?" Huma asked, puzzled.

"We rarely know what he is talking about, sir," said Destina with a strained smile.

"True enough," said Huma. "If you will excuse me, I will go see if the villagers require my help with the litter."

"I proposed levitating the poor chap so that a litter would not be necessary, but you turned down my generous offer," said Magius. "I will remain here and keep watch for silver deer."

Huma laughed and hurried off. Destina cast a worried glance at

Raistlin and nervously clasped her hand around the Graygem. Raistlin knew what she was thinking, for he was thinking the same. History told that Huma and the Knights of Solamnia had fought and defeated the Queen of Darkness using the formidable power of the dragonlances. And it appeared that Huma, at least, had never even heard of such a weapon. Was Chaos already at work?

Raistlin moved to stand near Destina.

"Stop fidgeting with it!" he told her in an undertone. He could see Magius observing her. "You think you are concealing it, but you are only drawing attention to it."

Destina hurriedly released her grasp on the Graygem. Fortunately, about that time, six sturdy men arrived, carrying a door they had removed from the hinges to use as a litter. Two more men walked along behind, armed with bows and arrows.

Destina beckoned to them. "Over here, gentlemen."

The villagers stared at Raistlin in shock and then at Destina in astonishment, undoubtedly wondering what was wrong with him and why she was sheltering in the woods in the middle of a war, and with such strange company. They asked no questions, however, but greeted Destina politely and hastened to do her bidding.

She directed them to place the litter alongside Tully, who was, Raistlin noticed, apparently still unconscious. Huma offered to assist them, and they lifted the yeoman and placed him on the litter. He did not move, did not cry out, although the pain must have been agonizing.

Sturm stood some distance away, keeping a firm grip on Tas. Sturm motioned for Raistlin to join them.

"But we have to do something!" Tas was saying as Raistlin walked over.

"No, we do not," said Raistlin.

"But the song is going wrong!" Tas said worriedly. "The white stag is supposed to lead Huma to the silver dragon and they fall in love and then ..."

Tas suddenly smacked himself in the forehead. "That's it!"

"Keep your voice down," Raistlin admonished.

Tas spoke in a loud whisper. "I said Gwyneth reminded me of someone and I've just remembered who! She reminds me of Silvara!"

"Silvara?" Sturm repeated, troubled.

"You weren't with us, Raistlin, so I'll explain," said Tas. "Silvara was a Wilder Elf, only she wasn't. She was really a silver dragon. She helped us find a dragon orb. We met her when we were in—"

"I know who Silvara is," Raistlin said impatiently. "What made you think of her in relation to Gwyneth? Tell us quickly! The others will be expecting us to join them."

"I should have thought of it when Gwyneth dropped her ring and I found it for her. She said the ring was a gift from her sister. Gwyneth and Silvara both have silvery hair and both are very beautiful and both were disguised as elves. Since dragons live a long time, it seems to me that Silvara could be Gwyneth's sister, and that would mean Gwyneth is the silver dragon in the *Song of Huma* and she is supposed to lead Huma to the dragonlances. She is *not* supposed to run away!" Tas concluded sternly.

"The silver dragons forged the dragonlances with the help of the dwarves and then hid them. Some feared mortals would use the dragonlances against them," Sturm said, troubled. "If Gwyneth is the silver dragon, she knows where the dragonlances are hidden."

Tas shook his head. "I'm sorry to tell you this, Sturm, but the song is wrong about the dragonlances. They were invented by Uncle Trapspringer and the gnomes."

"And may I remind you both that the *Song of Huma* is fiction," said Raistlin, trying to reassure himself as much as he was attempting to reassure his companions. "It is not a true account of historical events, but only some bard's romanticized version."

"And may I remind you, Raistlin, that the Dark Queen and her evil dragons are within a few days' march of the High Clerist's Tower and the knights have no dragonlances," Sturm returned balefully. "Huma has never even heard of them! Lady Destina wears Chaos around her neck. What if our presence here has already changed history so drastically it cannot be repaired?"

"Do you think that has not occurred to me or to Destina?" Raistlin demanded. "What would you have us do?"

"We could tell Huma about the dragonlances ourselves," Tas suggested. "We could tell him to go talk to the gnomes."

"Or we should find the silver dragon," said Sturm.

"We will keep our mouths shut about dragonlances and silver dragons *and* gnomes!" Raistlin said tersely. "We have no way of knowing if history has changed or not. If it hasn't and we go bumbling about trying to fix what is not broken, we could end up breaking it. Do you both understand?"

"I understand that something is wrong with the song," said Tasslehoff somberly. "And someone needs to make it right."

CHAPTER
SEVEN

Raistlin reiterated his warning that Tas should keep quiet about the song, though he doubted it would have much effect.

"Keep the kender with you," he told Sturm. "I have some questions for the villagers about Mullen Tully."

"I can tell you he's not a nice man," Tas said. "He called me a thief."

As Raistlin approached the group of villagers, he found Destina describing Tully's injuries.

"My companion can tell you more," said Destina, looking up as Raistlin drew near. "He found him lying on the road."

"Yeoman Tully told me Commander Belgrave sent him to the village to warn you about the red dragon," Raistlin said. "I was wondering if his account was true."

"He said the commander sent him," said one of men—the eldest among the group. He was apparently their spokesman, for the others deferred to him. "Though it seemed to me that this commander was a bit late with the news. We'd been watching the dragon for at least a day."

The others nodded sagely.

"And where was the yeoman when the goblins attacked?" Raistlin asked.

The elder pondered. "Don't remember seeing him during the fighting. Of course, I might have missed him, what with gobs running amuck and the two knights charging in and that wizard flinging lightning bolts."

The elder gave a grateful nod to Magius. "As a general rule, I don't have much use for wizards, but you, sir, are damn good at killing gobs."

"I am glad I could be of help," said Magius. "I am sorry we could not do more to save your village."

"Not much left of it but blackened rubble, I'm afraid," the man replied. He looked downcast for a moment, then shrugged it off. "But thanks to Paladine and you gentlemen, none of our folk lost their lives, and we managed to save our livestock. That's what counts. We can always rebuild once this war is over."

"Where will you go now?" Destina asked.

"We've been storing provisions in the caves in the mountains ever since the High Clerist sent word that Palanthas had fallen."

"Palanthas has fallen?" Huma gasped, shocked.

"Indeed, Sir Knight," said the elder. "I'm surprised you didn't hear."

"We have ridden from the north in answer to the summons of the High Clerist and only just arrived. We have heard no news since we left our homes," Huma explained. "What happened?"

"The city fell to the forces of Sargonnas. A fleet of minotaur ships sailed into the Bay of Branchala in the dead of night. The city had no defenses for an attack by sea, never believing one would come. Minotaur warriors poured into the streets. The Lord of Palanthas surrendered without a fight. He and a few others managed to escape and fled for safety to the High Clerist's Tower."

"That means all of Solamnia is now in the hands of the Dark Queen," said Magius. "With the exception of the High Clerist's Tower."

"It is now the last bastion of hope," said Huma gravely.

"We sent our families into hiding a week ago and we're headed there ourselves," said the elder. "We can take this wounded man with us. We have a cleric of Mishakal who can heal him and send him back to his duties. I advise the lady to accompany us. You will be safer with us in the caves, mum."

"Thank you, sir, but I will remain with my friends," said Destina.

"As you wish, mum. If you'll excuse us, we should take our leave," the elder added. "The afternoon is wearing on and we have a bit of ground to cover before the sun sets."

"Perhaps you could do us a favor," said Huma. "Would you take our horses with you?"

He indicated the horses tied to the tree. The elder regarded them with admiration and readily agreed, while Magius stared at Huma in shock.

"Why are you giving away our horses?"

"Because if we are going to travel to the High Clerist's Tower in the manner you suggested, we cannot very well take the horses with us," Huma replied.

"You astonish me!" Magius exclaimed. "You are actually going to agree to use my idea?"

"Occasionally you have a good one," said Huma, smiling. "I suggest you unpack what you need."

"I have all I need with me," said Magius, indicating the pouches holding his spell components and his staff.

Huma removed a large canvas bag bound with leather straps in which he carried his armor, then handed the horses' reins to the villagers. The armed escorts mounted the two horses, and the other six men picked up Tully on the litter and they moved out through the forest, heading southwest. The men with the litter went first. Their armed escorts brought up the rear.

The sun was sinking into the west. The afternoon was waning. Time is passing and the River of Time is rising, Raistlin thought. He needed to talk to Magius, find a way to recover the Device of Time Journeying.

"Did Gwyneth come back, Destina?" Tas asked as he and Sturm joined Huma and the others. "I thought she might."

"Is Gwyneth the elf?" Huma asked. "Did she say why she was here in Solamnia?"

"Gwyneth told me she was here as an observer for her people, the Qualinesti," Destina replied. "Their land borders your own, sir. They fear that if Solamnia falls, Takhisis will strike at them next. She was especially concerned about the red dragon. She says his name is Immolatus—"

"Immolatus!" Raistlin repeated, startled into speaking when he had not meant to.

"You talk as if you know this dragon, Brother," Magius said, quickly rounding on him.

Raistlin berated himself. He should have remembered that Immolatus had been involved in the Third Dragon War. The red dragon would be young now, in his prime and eager to impress his Dark Queen with his prowess. But during that war, he had been wounded severely by a dragonlance. He had blamed Takhisis and fled to the Abyss.

Raistlin would meet Immolatus in his guise as a human in the future during the time he served as a mercenary with the army of the Mad Baron. He recalled that centuries after the Third Dragon War, the red dragon had still been bitter, still complaining about the Dark Queen.

He was spared from answering by Tasslehoff, who was, of course, doing his best to land them all in deeper trouble.

"I keep telling you and you're not listening!" Tas was saying loudly. "She ran away and that didn't happen in the song! Sturm can tell you. He knows the song by heart. Sturm, tell them that part of the song about the stag and how its antlers got all tangled up and it led Huma to a bunch of birds and a crouching mountain."

"You have quite an imagination, Burrfoot," said Huma, laughing.

"Doesn't he," said Magius, and he was not laughing.

Raistlin flicked his wrist, and his knife slid into his palm. Using the sleight-of-hand skill he had learned when young, he deftly slit the straps of one of Tas's pouches, causing it to slide off his shoulder and dump his most precious possessions onto the ground. Tas gave a cry of dismay and immediately went down on his hands and knees in a mad scramble to gather everything up—a task that would occupy him for some time.

Huma was talking to Destina, who was still talking about Gwyneth.

"She saved our lives at the risk of her own. I am the daughter of a knight. According to the Measure, I owe her a debt of honor, so I would not betray her if I did know. I hope you understand."

Huma was immediately disarmed and made a courteous bow. "I respect your wishes, Lady Destina, and I admire your loyalty and adherence to the Measure. I will not press you further."

"But I would be interested to know more about you, Lady. What is the daughter of a knight doing wandering about the wilderness in the middle of a war?" Magius asked. "I believe you could tell us that much without going against the Measure."

Destina regarded him in confusion and reached, unconsciously, for the Graygem. Raistlin shot her a warning glance, and she lowered her hand to pluck nervously at her skirt. Sturm was grimly silent. Tasslehoff looked up from his "treasures" and opened his mouth. Raistlin hastened to devise an explanation.

"Lady Destina did not have a choice in the matter, Brother," said Raistlin. "The armies of the Dark Queen were closing in on her castle, and she was forced to flee. Sturm and I are friends of the family, and we offered to serve as her escort. We lost our belongings and provisions crossing a flooded stream. We hoped to find refuge in the High Clerist's Tower."

Destina cast him a grateful glance. Sturm frowned. He disliked being involved in a lie, but at least he had sense enough to keep quiet.

"And what about the kender?" Magius asked, glancing at Tas. "Is he also a friend of the family?"

"Tasslehoff is my bodyguard," Destina replied gravely.

Tas looked up from his sorting to say proudly, "Did you hear that, Sturm? I'm Destina's bodyguard!"

Magius stared at them both in wordless astonishment. Clearly, he had not expected this answer.

Huma chuckled. "Serves you right for subjecting the lady to your interrogation, my friend! Forgive him, Lady Destina. He is suspicious by nature."

Sturm apparently decided he'd heard enough falsehoods. "We do not want to be benighted in the woods with enemy troops roaming about. We must find someplace to safely shelter."

"Somewhere close," Destina added with a wan smile.

She was so weary she was unsteady on her feet. Huma noticed her stagger and courteously assisted her to sit down on a fallen log. She leaned back against a tree trunk and closed her eyes.

The sun had dropped behind the mountains. The forest was starting to fill with the shadows of coming night. The day had indeed been a long one, Raistlin reflected. Spanning centuries.

"We can all use the rest," said Huma. He lowered the pack to the ground—taking care to keep it far from Tasslehoff—then he sat down beside Destina. "We might as well be comfortable as we consider what to do. The nearest location is there." He pointed. "The High Clerist's Tower."

The sun's afterglow filled the sky, but the shadows of the mountains had closed in around the tower, so that it was shrouded in darkness. Between them and the tower were the Dark Queen's forces. They could see the campfires of her troops spread across the plains and dark figures silhouetted against the flames, undoubtedly making preparations for the final assault.

"We cannot very well cross the plains to reach the tower," said Sturm, eyeing the campfires. He remained standing, his hands on the hilt of his sword. "The enemy's forces are between us and the tower, to say nothing of the red dragon. Even if we attempted to cross the plains by night, we would not be safe."

"Magius has a plan," said Huma. "I will let him explain it."

Sturm was already looking disapproving.

"I am thinking of casting a journeying spell," said Magius. "I can take us from this location directly to the tower. Are you familiar with the spell, Brother?"

"I know *of* it. I fear such a spell is beyond my ability to cast," Raistlin replied, unable keep the note of bitterness from his voice.

"It is a handy spell to have," Magius said. "I always commit it to memory when I travel, although I don't know why I bother, since Huma generally refuses to let me use it. We could have walked the safe, dry paths of magic to reach the High Clerist's Tower, but Huma preferred to ride on horseback through wind and rain, soaked to the bone, surrounded by the enemy and in fear of our lives."

"I wanted to see for myself what was happening," said Huma.

Magius shook his head in mock sorrow. "The truth is that he and

I have been friends since childhood, but he still does not trust my magic."

"He is not alone," said Sturm, glowering. "Magic has landed us in trouble enough already. I will have nothing to do with more."

He stalked off, heading for the road, a short distance away. Huma watched him depart in some astonishment.

"We will have difficulty persuading Sturm to come with us if you use magic," Raistlin said. "He would rather face Takhisis and her hordes."

"We will find a way to persuade him," said Huma.

Raistlin grimaced. "I wish you luck. For my part, I think we should simply clout him over the head and haul him off in a sack."

Huma walked over to join Sturm, who was standing with his back to them, his arms folded across his chest, gazing morosely across the darkening plains. Raistlin followed, keeping his distance, but close enough to hear them.

Sturm heard Huma approaching and glanced around at him.

"I mean no disrespect to you, sir, but I will have nothing to do with magic."

"I understand your concern," Huma replied, "but I have traveled the paths of magic with Magius before. Despite what he says, I trust him implicitly, and magic is by far the safest way to reach the tower, especially for Lady Destina."

He glanced back at her. She was sitting slumped on the log, so tired she appeared to have fallen asleep sitting up.

Sturm stubbornly shook his head. "He can take Lady Destina and the rest of you. I will make my own way, take my chances."

"We will need every sword to fight for Solamnia, Brightblade," said Huma earnestly. "You must reconsider."

"We have come this far *together*, Sturm," Raistlin added, moving forward to join the conversation. He laid emphasis on the word. "We need to stay together if we want to return to share a drink in our favorite inn."

Sturm took his meaning. His eyes flickered. "It seems I have no choice. I will accompany you."

"I guess I'll stay here," Tas announced, trying to repair the strap on his pouch. "You can pick me up on your way back."

Everyone looked at him in astonishment.

"Are you afraid of magic?" Huma asked. "I didn't think kender were afraid of anything."

"I love traveling by magic," said Tas, concentrating on his work. "Raistlin magicked me into a duck pond once and it was great fun. But I don't want to go back to the High Clerist's Tower because that was the saddest day of my life."

"What do you mean 'go back to the tower'?" Magius asked. "The High Clerist does not permit kender to enter the tower, so how could you have been inside?"

The kender's shrill voice and Magius's sharp tone must have roused Destina from her nap.

"He is only telling tales—" she began.

Magius raised his hand. "Please let him finish, Lady. I find his stories fascinating. Proceed, Master Burrfoot."

"I haven't been to the tower yet," Tas explained. "I went there in the past which is in the future and it was very sad. I found the dragon orb and the dragons flew into the traps and there was blood on the walls and the floor and ceiling and then Sturm . . ."

Tas blinked his eyes and wiped his nose on his sleeve. "It was very sad. I don't want to go."

"You are my bodyguard, Tas," Destina said gently. "You have to come with me."

"But Magius just said kender weren't allowed in the tower," said Tas. "I don't want to get into trouble going somewhere I'm not allowed."

"Since when?" Raistlin demanded. "You have to come with us, Tas. Much as we might like to, we cannot go home without you."

Tas sighed. He had tied together the straps of his pouch and now he began to gather up his things.

"I must find a place to cast my spell," said Magius. "Come help me search, my friend."

"I don't know what good I will be," said Huma, but he picked up his pack and the two walked off, heading back toward the road, talking quietly together. Raistlin wondered what they were discussing and hoped it was not Tasslehoff.

"We have to do something to keep the kender quiet!" Sturm said, echoing his thoughts.

"Short of murder, I'm not sure what," Raistlin returned. "I will talk to him. Sturm, you and Destina keep Huma and Magius occupied. Tas and I will join you in a moment."

Sturm and Destina walked over to join Huma and Magius. At Destina's gesture, the four of them proceeded to a place on the hill where they could view the tower. As Destina engaged Huma in conversation, Raistlin noticed that while Magius appeared to be listening to Huma's response, his head was slightly turned, keeping watch on them.

Raistlin stood over Tas. "You and I need to talk."

"I didn't do it!" Tas said promptly and proceeded to rattle off a litany of innocence. "It's not my fault. I don't know where that came from. You must have dropped it. I never saw that before. I guess it fell into my pouch."

"Be quiet and listen. You are not in trouble." Raistlin put both hands on Tas's shoulders and looked him in the eye. "You have traveled through time using the Device of Time Journeying. You know that whenever you travel back into the past, you risk changing what happens in the present."

"You mean the future," Tas said. "The past was the past when we were in the present, but now that we're in the past, the past is the present and that means what's going to happen is going to happen in the future. So I shouldn't talk about the future, even though it's the past."

Raistlin was grim. "Past, present, or future, do not talk about any of it! Do not talk about dragon orbs. Do not talk about the High Clerist's Tower or dragonlances or silver dragons. Do not talk about Sturm's death!"

"I think I understand. And I guess I shouldn't talk about the—" Tas sneezed. "Drat!"

"Especially not that," said Raistlin.

Tas sighed. "I'll try to remember."

"You must set a watch upon your tongue and think about what you are saying before you say it," Raistlin admonished. "In the future, you will save Caramon's life. If you do something to change time, you might not be in Caramon's future and he could die."

"Because of you," said Tas accusingly. "You were the one that almost killed him."

"We are not talking about me—" Raistlin stopped. He could feel the familiar painful squeezing sensation in his chest, as though the air was being wrung out of his lungs like water from a sponge. He recognized the sensation, for it had happened to him many times before.

He began to cough, and he fumbled for his handkerchief and pressed it over his mouth. The coughing spell was a bad one. Raistlin knew the sickening terror that came with it, wondering if it would be the last. If this one would kill him.

He was slowly suffocating. He doubled over, coughing, trying desperately to breathe.

"Caramon still talks about you, even after you were dead," Tas told him. "Tika scolds him when he does and says you aren't worth him making himself unhappy. But Caramon only shakes his head and goes really quiet and walks off."

"Caramon was a fool to care!" Raistlin wanted to shout, but the words came out in a bloodstained whisper.

"You could tell him you're sorry," said Tas. "I could give him the message when I go back."

Raistlin drew in a ragged breath.

"Go! Just go!" he wheezed, coughing.

Tas looked at him a moment, then he picked up his hoopak and walked off, going over to stand protectively beside Destina in his role as bodyguard.

Raistlin closed his eyes, sank down on the log, and waited for the coughing fit to pass or death to take him. He was in so much pain he didn't care which.

"Isn't there anything you can do for that?"

Raistlin opened his eyes to find Magius standing in the shadows, leaning on his staff. Raistlin drew in a shuddering breath and another. Each breath grew easier. The coughing spasms would not kill him this time.

"I have herbs," he said faintly, wondering how long Magius had been standing there, what he had overhead. "I can brew a tea. . . ." He coughed again. "I do not have a disease, if that is what you fear. The malady was . . . my sacrifice."

"A sacrifice for your magic. The Test?" Magius asked.

Raistlin nodded, unable to speak. Magius sat down beside him and rested his staff against the log.

"We risk our lives when we take the Test, for we know that if fail, we will die. But the fear of death is not the worst part. The worst is being confronted with the dark recesses of our soul. The Test forces us to see what we are afraid to see, what we work to hide even from ourselves. I do not know for certain, but I have always wondered if those who refuse to look into the darkness are those who fail. The master returns their empty robes, washed and neatly folded, to their loved ones, with a little black-edged card of sympathy."

He paused, thoughtful, then said abruptly, "Have you ever asked yourself why we take the risk?"

"Most believe we do it for the power," said Raistlin.

"I made the same mistake when I was young," said Magius. "Before I had taken the Test I reveled in the thought of the power magic would give me. Afterward, I was wiser. Consider what the magic requires of us. We must spend hours every day studying and memorizing spells. When we cast them, they drain our bodies and our minds to the point of collapse. And the next day, we must do this all again. And what power do we gain? The power to cast a spell over a handful of goblins that does nothing more than provide them a restful night's sleep."

Raistlin could not help but smile. "Then why do you do it?"

"The same reason you do. For the sake of the magic," said Magius. He had dropped the cynical tone, the glib sarcasm, the mockery. He spoke from the heart and Raistlin guessed that this man did not open his heart often. "To feel the magic dance in my blood and sing in my soul."

"Yes," said Raistlin softly. "That is why we do it."

"I have never told that to anyone," said Magius. "Not even Huma. He loves me as a brother, but he would not understand."

"My brother did not understand, either," said Raistlin, more to himself than to his companion.

Magius glanced at him. "My name is not Magius, as you must have surmised. I christened myself. I never speak my true name. And neither does my family. They disowned me."

"I am sorry," said Raistlin.

Magius shrugged. "No great loss." He picked up his staff and rose to his feet. "Do you feel well enough to assist me with the spell-casting?"

"I am quite recovered," said Raistlin, slipping the bloodstained handkerchief back into the pocket of his robes. "But I do not know this spell."

"Then I will teach you," said Magius. "Walk with me. I plan to cast the spell over there."

He indicated an open space, where the trees gave way to a clearing. As they moved toward it, they could hear Huma some distance away, expounding upon the marvels of the High Clerist's Tower to Sturm and Destina. Tasslehoff was shifting from one foot to the other, a sign that he was bored. But at least he hadn't grown so bored he had wandered off.

"The tower is said to be one of the wonders of the world," Huma was saying. "It was designed by Vinas Solamnus to guard Westgate Pass and the city of Palanthas. The main structure consists of a central octagonal tower that stands a thousand feet tall with sixteen different levels. The High Clerist previous to this current one decided that the tower's defenses were not sufficient and ordered that they build a curtain wall around it.

"The central tower is surrounded by eight smaller towers located at each of the eight points of the octagon, connected by a curtain wall. Within the wall, eight additional stair towers rise from the main level, providing access to the interior levels. The tower is guarded by the cliffs of the Vingaard Mountains on three sides, completely blocking access to the pass. It took many years to build. Vinas Solamnus did not live to see it completed."

"He was fortunate he did not," Magius remarked, the sarcasm returning. "Every architect who succeeded him added some flourish so that now the tower is a mishmash, not a wonder. Here we are."

They entered the clearing. Looking up, Raistlin could see the stars and the red moon, Lunitari, goddess of the Red Robes. Magius smiled and saluted her.

"She has always been good to me. And now tell me, Brother, how does the kender know about dragon orbs?"

Raistlin froze, unable to move. For a moment, he was unable to breathe. The question had taken him completely by surprise.

"Few wizards even know about them," Magius added, "for they are the most closely guarded secret of our order. And yet, this kender talks of them quite glibly."

Raistlin struggled to think of an explanation, but he could not even devise a plausible lie.

"And then there is the matter of the fey jewel the lady wears." Magius rested his hand lightly on Raistlin's arm. "You and I need to have a long talk, Brother. But not here. Somewhere private."

He smiled when he said the words, but Raistlin saw no corresponding smile in the mage's blue eyes.

CHAPTER
EIGHT

athed in Lunitari's red light, Magius leaned his staff against
a tree, then he and Raistlin began to clear the ground, picking up sticks and branches and brushing aside dead leaves
left over from last autumn.

The moon's light was unusually bright. Raistlin wondered if the
goddess was aware of his sudden and unexpected return to the world
and, if so, what she made of it. He also wondered if the gods themselves were aware of the return of the Graygem to the world and
what they planned to do about it—if anything. They might be as
helpless as mortals in the face of Chaos. Not a reassuring thought.

"I believe the ground is clear enough now," said Magius.

He took hold of his staff and gave the command word, "*Shirak.*"
The crystal globe began to shine and he held out the staff to Raistlin.

"Hold the light so that I can see what I am doing," Magius instructed. "I need to draw a circle."

Raistlin hesitated, longing to hold the staff again, yet fearing to
wake painful memories.

Magius grinned at him. "You do not fear to touch it, do you,
Brother? After all, according to the kender, you once owned it."

Raistlin firmly grasped the staff. He knew every flaw, every tiny crack, every burl, every knot. He ran his hand over the staff, touching again the smooth grain of the wood, and held the light so that Magius could see. He used the toe of his boot to scrape a circle into the dirt.

"I see you admire my handiwork," said Magius, referring to the staff.

"The craftsmanship is truly very fine," Raistlin said. "How did you come by the staff?"

"I cut down the branch and carved it myself. I have the scars on my hand to prove it," Magius added ruefully. "But spilling a little blood was worth it. The staff has served me well in the past, and I am continually adding new magical powers."

Raistlin longed to ask about these powers. When Par-Salian had given him the staff following the Test, he told him it had belonged to the great wizard Magius and that it was magical, but he had not told him anything about its powers.

Books on artifacts had been useless, so most of what Raistlin had learned about the staff came through trial and error. He had always surmised that the staff could do much more than he had discovered and he longed to ask Magius. But Raistlin dared not appear too curious about the staff. Showing too much interest in another wizard's possessions was not only boorish and impolite, it might look suspicious.

"There," said Magius, straightening from his task. "The spell specifies a radius of ten feet. I trust five of us will fit inside. You stay here, while I fetch the others."

He reached out his hand for his staff, and Raistlin reluctantly handed it back, feeling as though he was letting go of a dearly loved friend.

He stood in the moonlit darkness after Magius had gone. Tas had brought up unwelcome memories that still reached for him out of the past like the skeletal hands of the Shoikan Grove, clawing at him, trying to drag him into pain and darkness and regret. Raistlin firmly trampled them down, and he had regained his composure by the time Magius returned with the others.

Magius indicated the circle and explained that they had to stand inside it.

"Not a toe, not even the hem of Lady Destina's skirt can be outside the circle," Magius warned them.

He took his place in the center of the circle and held the staff high so they could all see the crude drawing by its light.

Tas had apparently recovered from his reluctance to go back to the High Clerist's Tower, for he leaped into the circle and crowded close to Magius. Destina entered with trepidation, as though the circle might swallow her. Raistlin saw her reach involuntarily for the Graygem, hidden beneath her collar, but she stopped herself and clasped both hands together. Sturm stepped inside, grim-faced, his jaw clenched, his hand clasping the hilt of his sword. Huma took his place beside him and said something reassuring to him in a low voice. Raistlin entered last and took his place next to Destina.

Magius lowered the staff, then suddenly whipped around to grab hold of the kender.

"Drop it!" he ordered.

"Drop what?" Tas asked.

"What you have in your hand," said Magius.

Tas opened his palm and regarded with amazement a small rod of iron. "You must have lost it. What is it?"

"One of my spell components," said Magius.

He retrieved it and returned it to a pouch, then bent down to look the kender in the face. "The success of this magical spell depends on you, Tasslehoff Burrfoot."

"It does?" Tas asked, wide-eyed. "But I'm not a wizard. I wish I was, but Raistlin says the three moons would drop out of the sky the day kender became wizards."

"Here is what you must do to make the spell work," said Magius. "You must put your hands in your pockets and keep them there until I tell you to take them out. If you remove them while I am casting the magic, the spell could fail and it will be your fault."

"I won't let you down," Tas promised. He handed Destina his hoopak to hold, then balled his hands into fists and jammed them into his pockets. "Like that?"

"Excellent," said Magius with a wink at Raistlin. "Do any of you have questions before I start?"

Tas took his hand out of his pocket and raised it.

"Anyone other than the kender," said Magius.

Tas sighed and stuffed his hand back into his pocket.

"I have a question," said Sturm. "The High Clerist's Tower is immense. Where will your spell take us?"

"I am aiming for the wine cellar," Magius replied gravely.

"He's jesting," said Huma hurriedly, seeing Sturm frown.

"I am not sure that I am," Magius protested. "A goblet of cold apple wine sounds particularly refreshing. But since you object to the wine cellar, I will take us to the main entrance in the front of the tower, what is called Noble's Gate. We will make ourselves known to the gate guards so that they do not mistake us for the enemy and run their swords through us. Does that satisfy you?"

Sturm gave a grudging nod.

"And now, if everyone is ready, I must ask you to keep silent to allow me to concentrate."

He looked pointedly at Tas, who still had his hands in his pockets. Tas clamped his lips shut tightly so that nothing unexpected popped out.

Magius whispered a command too softly to hear, and the light of the staff faded away.

He gazed up through an opening in the trees into the darkening sky. A few stars were out. Solinari, the silver moon, was just rising, barely visible in the east. Lunitari shone above them, full and bright.

Magius shook out his long blond hair so that it fell loosely about his shoulders and gazed up at the red moon.

She must love him, Raistlin thought, for she seemed to smile down on him.

Magius parted his lips as though to drink in the radiance and raised his hands to beseech her.

"Lunitari, I ask your blessing this night as we travel the paths of magic. Walk with us as we seek the safety and sanctity of the High Clerist's Tower."

He turned to Raistlin to teach him the spell, as he had promised. "I must now envision the precise location where I intend to transport us. Do you understand?"

Raistlin nodded, astonished. Few mages would have taken the trouble to teach a new spell to a novice. Most guarded their spells jealously, keeping them secret. But Magius was generous with his time and his knowledge. His hero had not disappointed him.

Magius closed his eyes and began to recite the words to the spell. *"Triga bulan ber satuan/Seluran asil—"*

He spoke the words slowly and succinctly, in a low voice. Raistlin listened closely and repeated them silently to himself, hoping to be able to remember them in order to later record them in his spellbook. If they were stranded here, such a spell might be useful. He noted that Magius did not use any spell components or make any gestures. The spell must simply require the words of magic.

The red light of Lunitari surrounded Magius and illuminated the circle, shining so brightly they could all see each other clearly. Tas's eyes were wide with wonder, and he appeared to be exerting all his might to keep his hands in his pockets.

Destina had her hand at her throat, clasping the Graygem. Raistlin could not see even a faint glimmer of gray light. Perhaps the Graygem was loath to reveal itself in the presence of Lunitari. According to some legends, Reorx had crafted the Graygem as a gift for the goddess. Perhaps Chaos feared that if the gods recaptured it, they would ensure that it never again escaped.

The red glow grew so dazzling they were forced to close their eyes against the brilliance. Raistlin did not want to miss a single gesture Magius might make, and he kept his eyes open until they filled with tears and the pain was too much to bear.

"—Tempat samah terus-menarus/Walktun jalanil!"

As Magius spoke the final word of the spell, Raistlin felt the magic pluck him from the circle, rush him through the night with the wind at his back, then gently lower him onto solid ground. The red light of Lunitari disappeared. Raistlin opened his eyes, but the darkness was so deep he could see nothing.

"No one move," Magius warned. *"Shirak."*

The globe on the staff blazed with light illuminating a large rectangular entry hall. Before them was a double door made of black ironwood banded by steel plates. The doors were enormous. Five knights on horseback riding abreast could have ridden through the double doors with ease. The hall had no windows. They could see torches mounted on the walls, but no one had lit them.

The large main door was bolted shut. Two smaller ironwood doors led off to the east and the west, and they were also closed and barred. The hall was guarded by life-size marble statues of knights bearing the symbol of the Knights of the Crown on their shields, standing in the corners, keeping silent watch.

But the statues were the only ones on watch. No guards patrolled the gates.

"Welcome to the High Clerist's Tower," Magius said faintly and collapsed. He lay crumpled on the floor, his eyes closed. His staff fell beside him, its magical light still shining.

"What struck him down?" Sturm demanded, drawing his sword and searching for enemies.

"Put your sword away," said Raistlin. He knelt beside Magius and put his hand on the mage's neck. "The magic takes its toll."

"How is he?" Huma asked, concerned. He lowered the bag he was carrying to the floor and knelt down beside his friend.

"His life beat is strong. He is drained by all the spellcasting he has done this day," Raistlin replied.

Magius was already starting to stir, his eyelids fluttering.

"He needs rest, but he will be fine," said Raistlin. "I will stay with him. You should see to the others."

Reassured, Huma rose to his feet. "Is everyone else all right? Lady Destina?"

She managed a faint smile. Sturm gave a curt nod.

Huma looked around. "Where is the kender? Did we leave him behind?"

"That would be too much to hope for," said Magius weakly.

"I'm here!" Tas called, running into the hall. "I've been exploring and I know where we are! If you go down this hall and up those three stairs you'll come to . . ."

"What did we talk about?" Raistlin demanded.

"Uh . . . that is . . . What I meant to say was I *would* know where we are if I'd ever been to the High Clerist's Tower before. Which I haven't," Tas added. "At least not in the present that's really the past. I know I'm supposed to be watching my tongue, Raistlin. I've tried watching it, but every time I do, I go all cross-eyed." He stuck out his tongue and attempted to stare at it. "See?"

The halls were dark and silent. The kender's shrill voice echoed loudly and bounced off the walls.

"It's so quiet," said Destina, shivering. "Where is everyone?"

"I thought there were going to be knights," said Tas. "And food. Especially food."

"I wonder that myself," Huma said, mystified. "We stand at Noble's Gate, the main entry hall on the first level. The knights always post sentries on these doors; at least they have done so in the past. Given our unorthodox arrival, the guards should have immediately accosted us. Yet we see no one."

Magius reached out his hand to Raistlin. "Help me stand."

"Are you strong enough?" Raistlin asked.

"It appears I had better be," said Magius dryly.

Raistlin assisted the mage to his feet and handed him his staff. Magius walked slowly, using his staff for support. He was not shamming this time. He was weak and his footsteps unsteady. Raistlin remained near him in case he needed assistance.

"How are you feeling?" Huma asked his friend.

"As though I carried four humans and a kender on my back for twenty miles," Magius said testily.

He focused the light of the staff on the floor and pointed. "Look there. Muddy boot prints, both coming and going. Someone lost his gauntlet over there, and I see a broken buckle near Brightblade's foot. As for why there are no guards, judging by the signs, I would say the knights packed up and left."

"The knights would never abandon the High Clerist's Tower!" Sturm stated, angry at the accusation.

"Hush!" Destina warned. "Someone is coming."

They could all hear the sound of footfalls pounding down the corridor, drawing nearer. Huma and Sturm both drew their swords. Tas grabbed Goblinslayer and hurried to stand beside Destina.

Three knights entered the hall, accompanied by soldiers bearing torches. Two of the knights were young and wore the traditional mustaches of the knighthood; their breastplates bore the emblem of Knights of the Sword. The third man was clean-shaven with long, iron gray hair. He was wearing the breastplate of the Knights of the Crown and was the eldest of three, perhaps in his late fifties. His expression was stern and grave. Deep furrows of sorrow and care had eroded any trace of warmth from his face.

All three knights carried swords and were clearly expecting trouble. The oldest knight was clearly taken aback when he saw them—especially when he saw Destina and Tasslehoff. His puzzlement increased when he noticed Sturm wearing the armor of a Solamnic knight. Then his gaze took in Raistlin and Magius, and the knight's expression hardened. He gestured to the soldiers. The elder knight inspected the doors and found they were bolted.

"The gates are locked! How did you get in here?"

Tasslehoff raised his hand. "I know!"

"Hush!" Destina whispered.

Tas sighed and lowered his hand.

The knight gazed balefully at the strangers and motioned to his soldiers.

"Take them into custody! And be careful of those wizards! Especially the one with the metal skin." He stared at Raistlin in perplexity. "Damnedest thing I ever saw."

Raistlin could hardly blame the knight for distrusting them. Not only was he strange-looking, but they were all travel worn, disheveled, and spattered with goblin blood. Roving bands of outlaws would have appeared more presentable.

"Hold a moment, sir!" Huma said. "I believe I recognize you. You are Sir Titus Belgrave. I am Huma Feigaard. We met two years ago at the Knight's Council."

Titus blinked at him. "Now that I see you in the light, I do remember." He slowly lowered his sword. Glancing over his shoulder, he dismissed the soldiers but kept the two knights and told them to sheathe their weapons.

"These are my companions," said Huma. "My friend, Magius, a war wizard. He and I recently met Lady Destina Rosethorn and her escorts, Sturm Brightblade, Knight of the Crown, and Raistlin Majere, who is also a war wizard."

"Allow me to present Sir Richard Valthas and Sir Reginald Homesweld, both Knights of the Sword," said Titus. He frowned at Raistlin and Magius. "War wizards. I have never heard of such an animal. What do war wizards do, exactly?"

"Sneak people into locked towers," Magius replied.

Titus frowned, and Huma cast his friend an exasperated glance. "War wizards fight with magic instead of swords, Commander."

"The sentries reported hearing voices at Noble's Gate," said Titus. "I did not believe them at first. How did you break through our defenses?"

"Magius told you," said Tas eagerly. "He and I magicked us here. I helped and the moons didn't fall out of the sky. At least, the last time I looked they were still there."

Titus ignored the kender and turned to Raistlin and Magius. "Is he right? Did you use magic to break into the tower?"

"A simple journeying spell, sir," Magius explained modestly. "My companions and I were trapped in the forest with the red dragon's army between us and safety. I used my magic to carry us here, thereby avoiding disturbing the dragon."

Titus regarded him grimly. "You are telling me this spell you cast carried the lot of you through solid stone walls and bolted doors?"

"We walked the paths of magic, sir," said Magius. "On those paths, there are no walls, no doors, no locks."

"Could enemy wizards cast this spell?" Titus demanded.

"It would be risky," Magius replied. "If the wizards had never been inside the tower and had no idea where they were going, they could end up drowning in the bottom of a well or materializing inside a wall. That said, if enemy wizards were intent on entering, you could do nothing to stop them, so I would not waste my time worrying."

"I don't intend to," Titus said dourly. "I have all the worries I can handle at the moment. And which of you brought the kender?"

"We weren't introduced. I am Tasslehoff Burrfoot," said Tas, extending his hand.

Titus took a step backward. "Keep your distance, kender."

"Tasslehoff is my friend, Commander," said Destina.

"—and bodyguard," Tas added.

Titus eyed him dubiously. "Ordinarily kender aren't permitted in the tower, but I suppose I'll have to make an exception since you claim him, Lady Destina. But I expect you to take charge of him. I don't want him roaming about loose."

"I will, sir," said Destina, placing her hand on Tas's shoulder.

"He's very rude for a knight," Tas said to her in a loud whisper.

"How do you and your friends come to be here, Lady Destina?" Titus asked.

She was going to reply, but Sturm stepped forward to intervene.

"I understand you do not trust us, Commander Belgrave, and that is your right, for you are responsible for the defense of the tower. But we have answered your questions. Lady Destina is the daughter of a knight. She was attacked by goblins and barely escaped with her life. She is exhausted and requires rest."

"I require food," said Tas.

"And if you could direct Magius and me to the chambers of the High Clerist, sir, we must report for duty," Huma added.

"The High Clerist is not here," Titus said. "If you report to anyone, I suppose it would be me. I am in command. We make our quarters in the small fortress adjacent to the tower known as the Knight's Spur. We do not have room to house all of you there, but I will give orders to take you to the bedchambers on the sixth level of the tower. The rooms were recently occupied by those refugees who fled Palanthas. The kitchen in the tower is not in service. You may take your meals in the dining hall of the fortress with us. You apparently know about the dragon. Just so you are warned, the tower could come under attack any day."

He spoke calmly, but it seemed the calm of one who has lost all hope. The two younger knights who flanked him were attempting to put on a bold front, but they were haggard and clearly unnerved. Not surprising, Raistlin reflected, given that Immolatus had been flying overhead, tormenting them, filling their days with terror.

"Thank you, sir, those arrangements should be fine. As Sturm said, I am the daughter of a knight. I am not afraid," said Destina. "But what became of the refugees? Are any still here?"

Titus did not appear to hear her question, for he continued on. "As for the kender, he can bed down in the dungeons."

"I'm certain your dungeons are very nice, Commander," said Tas. "Any other time I'd be glad to visit them, especially since I didn't get to see them the last time I was here. But I'm traveling with Lady Destina and she needs me. I'm her bodyguard."

"My friends and I will keep an eye on Tas, sir," Destina offered.

"And we wizards will keep an eye on each other, so you don't have to lock us up either," said Magius.

"Good to know," said Titus dryly. "And now I was about to have my dinner. Will you join me, or would you prefer to go directly to your rooms?"

"Thank you, sir, but I am far too tired to eat," said Destina. "I would like to go to my room."

"I will also retire," said Magius. "I need to memorize my spells for the morrow and then I plan to sleep for the next hundred years."

Raistlin should have also gone to his room to memorize his spells, but he required information, so he accepted the commander's invitation to dine, as did Sturm and Huma.

"I'll come with you, too," Tas announced. "I'm extremely hungry. Will there be sausages?"

Titus sent Sir Valthas to escort Destina and Magius to the tower's sixth level. Before she left, Destina extended her hand to Sturm.

"Thank you for your care and kindness, sir," she said softly. "You have treated me far better than I deserve."

Sturm bowed over her hand but said nothing. Their guide accompanied Magius and Destina to a staircase that led to the tower's upper levels. Titus led the others through the High Clerist's Tower to the adjacent fort. Huma walked alongside the commander. Sturm was about to join them when Raistlin nudged him and pointed to Tas, who had veered off down a dark corridor.

Sturm, looking grim, nabbed the kender and marched him back.

"But I thought I saw a wraith," said Tas.

"You didn't," said Sturm.

"You don't know that," Tas said. "Do you recognize this part of the tower?"

Sturm shook his head. "I was not on this level."

"This was near where I found the dragon orb," said Tas. "Coming back here must be hard for you, Sturm. It's hard for me and I didn't die here."

"Dying was hard. But I began a new life in death," said Sturm.

"Are you sad you came back to this life?" Tas asked.

"The gods brought me here," said Sturm. "I do not question their wisdom."

"The gods didn't bring you," said Raistlin caustically. "Chaos brought you."

"I wish Chaos would bring me some sausages," said Tas with a wistful sigh.

Titus led them along a wide hallway that wound around the tower's interior, took them through several doors, and led into another hall. Tapestries portraying battle scenes covered the walls. Flags and banners hung from the ceiling. Marble statues seemed ghostly in the torchlight. They followed the hall until it ended at an iron gate guarded by two men-at-arms. They saluted Titus and opened the gate, allowing them entry, then swiftly closed the gate and barred it behind them.

Raistlin noticed the men-at-arms were wearing the same uniform that Tully had worn. Recalling his suspicions, he spoke to Titus.

"We encountered goblins raiding a village not far from here, Commander," Raistlin said. "I met one of your yeomen who was wounded in the assault—Mullen Tully. He said you sent him to the village to warn them about the dragon."

Titus grunted. "I hardly needed to warn anyone about the dragon. The beast made himself well known. Where is Tully now?"

"The villagers took him in. They will tend to his wounds. I found his story hard to believe."

"He deserted. He wouldn't be the first, nor likely the last," said Titus. "Though it sounds like he was luckier than most who fled. They likely ended up in the dragon's belly."

Halting, he turned to face the others.

"If you are wondering where you are, we are in the fortress known as the Knight's Spur," said Titus.

The fortress was a much smaller building, far less imposing than the tower. No tapestries hung on the stone walls. No statues watched them from the corners. Titus led them across a wide stone bridge that arched over a rushing stream far below.

"The fortress was built after the tower was completed, in order to strengthen Westgate Pass," Titus explained. "The aqueduct we just crossed runs beneath the fortress and provides water to both the Knight's Spur and the tower."

They entered a large chamber with a high ceiling hung with banners and lit by torches and braziers of charcoal. The hall was filled with cots lined up in neat rows. Soldiers sat on the cots, talking in low voices, or lay rolled up in blankets asleep.

"This was once the Knight's Council hall," said Titus. "We have turned it into a barracks. You see here the defenders of the High Clerist's Tower."

Huma regarded him in dismay. "Defenders! But . . . there can't be more than forty men here, Commander!"

"Forty-five men-at-arms and three knights, two of whom just won their spurs," said Titus. "Yet we must hold the tower against the Dark Queen, her dragons, and an army that numbers in the thousands."

"But where is the High Clerist?" Huma asked. "Where are the rest of the knights and the soldiers?"

"The High Clerist is dead, as are those knights who rode with him and all the refugees," Titus replied. He paused and added gravely, "Consider yourself fortunate, Sir Huma, that you and your war wizard came late, or you would have died with them."

"Paladine save us!" Huma said, shaken. "What happened?"

"A tale best told after you have dined, sir," said Titus somberly. "Otherwise, you will lose your appetite."

CHAPTER
NINE

The Knight's Spur was sparsely furnished. A large wooden
table in the dining hall did double duty, for trenchers, mugs,
and bowls had been shoved aside to make room for several
large maps. A few chairs were scattered about the table in a desultory
manner. A wrought-iron candle holder suspended over the table
provided light.

Titus cleared the table, rolling up the maps and placing them in
a tub that had been recruited as a map holder. He then gestured to
the chairs and invited the newcomers to be seated.

As they took their seats around the table, Tas hurried over to
gaze in delight at the tub filled with maps. He reached out his hand,
then apparently remembered his manners.

"May I look at your maps?" he asked Titus. "I collect maps. Or
rather I used to in the past that's now the future. Tanis always asked
to see my maps when he was trying to figure out where to go. They
were mostly right, even though one said Tarsis was by the sea when
it wasn't."

"The maps will keep him out of mischief, sir," Sturm added, seeing Titus frown. "I will search him before we leave."

Titus gave a grudging nod. Tas leaned his hoopak against a wall and picked out one of the maps. He spread it out on the floor and happily plopped down to study it, his elbows on his knees, his chin in his hands.

An elderly retainer appeared, emerging from the shadows. He scrutinized them intently from beneath shaggy white brows and scowled at the sight of Raistlin. His scowl deepened when he noticed Tasslehoff on the floor.

"We have guests, Will," Titus stated.

"I can see that for myself, sir," said Will. "I suppose they'll be wanting food and drink?"

"If you would be so good as to inform Cook," said Titus.

"Even the kender?" Will demanded.

"Even the kender," Titus replied gravely.

Will snorted, then marched off into the shadows.

"Will has been with my family for years," said Titus. "I urged him to return home when the war broke out, but he refused to leave."

"Given the small number of troops, I take it you have pulled back your forces from the tower to concentrate them here," said Sturm.

"I could hardly do otherwise, given the tower has sixteen floors. I do not have forces enough to man the battlements on even one level," said Titus. "The gods themselves must defend the High Clerist's Tower, if they've a mind to do so."

"About the High Clerist—" Huma began.

"After we eat," said Titus. "I need a mug of dwarf spirits to wash it down."

Will returned a short time later with a man who, judging by his apron, must be the cook. He brought freshly baked bread and a pot of venison stew, which he placed on the table. Will plunked down wooden trenchers and handed around pewter mugs, nearly tumbling over Tas in the process. He glared at the kender, snorted, and left. He came back carrying a pitcher of chilled ale and a jug of dwarf spirits, which he handed to Titus.

"We have other guests. Ask Sir Reginald to carry food to the lady and the wizard," said Titus. "I have given them rooms on the sixth level of the tower."

Will shook his head and left on his errand, muttering to himself.

"At least the men eat well," said Titus. "Armies march on their stomachs, as the Measure states."

He poured ale for Sturm and Huma. Raistlin took nothing but water. He had to memorize his spells tonight and he needed a clear head.

"We had laid in stores of food for hundreds," Titus continued. "Eat up, gentlemen, and then I'll explain everything."

Raistlin had not realized how hungry he was until he smelled the stew. In his past life, he had taken no pleasure in food. He ate only to sustain himself. He had often wondered if his lack of appetite had been due to his poor health or his disgust at his brother, Caramon, who ate with the manners of a starving wolf. Now Raistlin was surprised to find himself savoring the taste of the stew and even sopping up the gravy with the bread.

Tas paused in his perusal of the map to return to the table to eat.

"This stew is even better than sausages," he announced. "The map I found is very interesting. It was drawn long before the gods hurled the fiery mountain down and broke Ansalon apart. I saw maps like this when I was in Istar before the Cataclysm."

He finished one bowl, helped himself to another, and returned to the floor with the map.

"What is he talking about?" Titus asked. "What fiery mountain?"

"We have learned not to ask questions," said Raistlin. "He might answer them."

Titus smiled and shoved away his trencher. Will removed the dishes and poured the dwarf spirits for Titus. The others politely declined the potent liquor.

Titus took a healthy gulp, wiped his lips, and heaved a sigh.

"Do you know about the fall of Palanthas?"

"That soldier, Tully, told me," said Raistlin. "We did not know whether to believe him or not."

"Believe him," said Titus grimly. "Minotaur ships sailed into the Bay of Branchala. The minotaurs overwhelmed the city guard, who laid down their arms, then they took control of all the gatehouses and seized the palace of the Lord of Palanthas. They set fire to the Temple of Paladine and drove out or killed the clerics. They tried to enter the Great Library to set fire to it, too, but it seems that the god

Gilean stood up to them. According to the refugees, the windows and the doors of the Great Library vanished, leaving the minotaurs with no way to enter. They even tried to break through the marble walls, to no avail. Eventually they gave up."

"They won't let kender into the library, either," said Tas, looking up from his map. "I found a way through a window once, but I guess if there aren't any windows that wouldn't work."

"What of the Tower of High Sorcery?" Raistlin asked.

"The last I heard, it was still standing," Titus replied. "Not surprising. I doubt if even minotaur warriors could summon the courage needed to enter the haunted grove that surrounds it. I have no knowledge of the welfare of those inside the tower, although I have tried to find out."

Raistlin thought this interest in the tower odd from a man who had such disdain for magic-users. He, too, doubted if the minotaurs would be able to enter, then he wondered uneasily if the Shoikan Grove would permit him to reach the tower.

All the Towers of High Sorcery in Ansalon were guarded by magical forests, but the Shoikan Grove was the most powerful. Fear radiated from the grove, the terror so powerful that most people could not even venture near it. If a minotaur had managed to overcome his fear and enter, he would be attacked by trees dripping blood, skeletal hands reaching up from the ground, and spectral guardians whose claws could rip off heads.

The magic of the grove recognized only mages who had passed the Test and permitted them entry. Raistlin had passed the Test, but in a different lifetime. Once he had been master of the tower. Once the horrible trees had bowed to him. Now the grove might try to kill him.

"The Lord of Palanthas and members of the senate and their families and a swarm of other refugees managed to escape," Titus was saying. "They rode through the Westgate Pass and arrived here to bring us the news. A thousand knights and men-at-arms were here, having answered the High Clerist's summons to defend the High Clerist's Tower. But instead, the Lord of Palanthas begged the High Clerist to send his forces to Palanthas to retake the city.

"A few of us spoke out against such reckless action, including myself, saying it would leave the tower defenseless. But we were in the minority," said Titus with a shrug. "The High Clerist and the council were infuriated to hear about the burning of the Temple of Paladine. Such sacrilege must not go unpunished, they said."

Titus poured himself another mug of dwarf spirits. Raistlin wondered if history had happened this way. He had never heard this account of Palanthas falling to minotaurs, but that was not surprising, given how much knowledge had been lost during the Cataclysm.

"In truth, their pride was hurt," Titus said, resuming his story. "They considered minotaurs nothing more than dumb beasts, and those 'dumb beasts' had snatched their city out from under their noses. The High Clerist named me Master Warrior and left me here with two young knights and a handful of men-at-arms to guard the tower. They rode out in force, together with those refugees who had been driven from their homes and were determined to return. A small army of men, women, and children set out, bound for Palanthas."

Titus took another swallow of the fiery spirits.

"To be fair, neither the High Clerist nor any of the rest of us knew about the red dragon. All dragons had been banished to the Abyss at the end of the Second War and we had no way of knowing that any had escaped. The red dragon was waiting for them at Westgate Pass."

"Paladine save them," said Huma softly.

Titus nodded and took another drink. "I assume he tried. The High Clerist and his forces and the refugees had been gone about three days when the sentries saw the night sky in the east blaze with fire. I climbed the stairs to the High Lookout on the fifteenth level. I watched flames flare among the mountain peaks and I saw an enormous dragon, silhouetted against the flames. I knew then what had happened."

Titus fell silent, nursing the mug in his hands. Dwarf spirits were extremely potent, and he had consumed a fair amount. He did not appear to be drunk, however. The spirits seemed to only deepen his sorrow.

"That was a fortnight ago," Titus said at last. "We prepared the infirmary to receive survivors." He took another drink. "No one returned."

Huma stared at him, aghast. "All those people? Wiped out?"

"We first saw the red dragon when he appeared in the sky above the tower that night," said Titus. "He flew with impunity, trumpeting his triumph and spreading his dragonfear. Most of my men are stout of heart and managed to withstand it, but the fear took its toll. Several soldiers, like Tully, deserted. I cannot say I blame them. Since then, the dragon has been keeping watch on us, reminding us of his presence. As if we were likely to forget."

Titus shoved back the mug and replaced the cork in the jug of dwarf spirits. "And now we are the last bastion. When the High Clerist's Tower falls, Takhisis will rule all of Solamnia. Today Solamnia. Tomorrow the world."

"I had not heard the situation was this dire," Huma said, shocked.

"At the start of the war, the Dark Queen concentrated her forces on cities in the south," said Titus. "She summoned the other gods of evil to join in the fight. Thelgaard was the first to fall. Takhisis's consort, the minotaur god Sargonnas, and his forces took Palanthas. The ghostly armies of Chemosh, god of the undead, swept into Solanthas and the people succumbed to the terror."

"What of Vingaard Keep?" Huma asked. "The knights have a strong garrison there."

"The plague god, Morgion, brought death to Vingaard Keep," said Titus. "Bodies piled up in the streets. It is said that the Dark Queen's own soldiers refused to come near the place. She spread her forces thin at the start, but now she's had time to consolidate them and hurl all her strength against the High Clerist's Tower. And me with only a handful of men to defend it."

Titus rose to his feet. "The hour is late and morning comes early, as they say. I must make the rounds before I sleep. I bid you a good—"

A yell came from the direction of the kitchen, followed by a crash, as of pans hitting the stone floor, and accompanied by a shout of "Stop, thief!"

"I didn't do it!" Tas said quickly.

Titus was already running toward the kitchen, accompanied by Sturm and Huma. Tas grabbed his hoopak and raced after them, while Raistlin followed more slowly. As they came within sight of a door, it burst open and a woman ran out. She was not looking where she was going and barreled straight into Huma, nearly oversetting him.

He caught hold of her by the shoulders. She cried out in pain and Huma let go of her, startled. The woman sank to the floor, clutching her shoulder and moaning.

"Gwyneth!" Tas cried excitedly. "I found you!"

"It *is* you!" Huma said softly, awed.

The woman violently shook her head. Her braid had come undone and her hair tumbled around her shoulders in a shining cascade of silver.

"I know you! I saw you in the forest and I have been searching for you ever since," said Huma. "Searching for you all my life . . . Forgive me, Mistress. I did not mean to hurt you!"

The woman kept her head lowered, so they could not see her face. She was dressed in a green belted tunic with green leggings and brown slippers. A dark stain of blood was spreading over the tunic, beneath her hand.

"She has been wounded," said Huma, indicating the blood. "She needs treatment."

"We have no cleric," said Titus.

"Raistlin is a healer," said Sturm.

Raistlin was too disconcerted by what he was seeing when he looked at the woman to realize that Sturm had said something good about him. When he looked at this woman, he saw two faces. One was the face of an elf with silvery hair. The other was the face of a dragon with silver scales. The two faces blended, merged, separated, and blended again. Both faces had the same radiant eyes.

Raistlin remembered, shaken, the last time he had looked into such a face. Or rather, as Tas would say, the time in the future when he would look into the face of a human wizard and see the face of the dragon Immolatus.

"Then you must help her!" Huma said insistently.

Raistlin blinked and the woman's two faces resolved into that of an elf. Covering his hesitation with a cough, he started to approach her. Seeing him coming, she sprang to her feet and stumbled backward, placing her back against the wall and facing them defiantly.

"I can help you," Raistlin said. "Please, let me examine the wound."

"Don't touch me!" the woman cried, speaking Solamnic, though with an accent. "Don't come near me."

"I only want to tend to your injury," said Raistlin. He raised his hands to show her that he did not hold a weapon.

The woman shook her head. "I don't need your help. Leave me alone."

Will came out of the kitchen, accompanied by the irate cook. "I see you caught her, sir. Cook and I heard a rustling sound coming from the pantry. He thought it was a rat and went after it. The next thing we knew, this fiend sprang out. She knocked Cook flat and struck me in the chest. I went down hard on my butt, and when I made it to my feet, I chased after her. I almost caught her, but she tipped over the stew pot, spilling hot stew everywhere, and ran for the door."

Will walked over with a lantern and shone it in her face, causing her to squint against the light. "That's her. That's the thief."

"She's not a thief!" said Tas irately. "She's Gwyneth! My elf!"

The woman raised her head, blinking in the bright light. Her delicate beauty appeared to touch those gathered around her. She glanced at Huma, and her gaze lingered on him as she pressed her hand to her bleeding shoulder.

As for Huma, he could not take his eyes from her. Clearly, as he said, he knew her. Raistlin remembered the knight's insistence on trying to find her when they had first met, saying he had known an elf once before and Magius refuting him, claiming he had dreamed it. Raistlin made a mental note to question Magius.

Titus's expression darkened. "An elf! It seems we have caught another of the Dark Queen's spies."

"Gwyneth is not a spy!" Tas was indignant. "I know her and so does Destina. She helped us fight off goblins and she cleaned my face with elf spit and gave me a magical water jug that never runs dry, though the water does taste a little of turtle."

"Lady Destina did tell us that an elven woman had saved them," Sturm said, affirming the kender's story.

Titus was grim. "Then what was she doing hiding in the pantry?"

"Probably looking for sausages," said Tas.

Gwyneth stood with her back to the wall, her hand pressed against the wound. Her silver-green eyes shimmered in the torch-light.

Huma gazed at her, entranced. "I am truly sorry I hurt you, Gwyneth. I did not mean to. Please forgive me!"

Hearing the anguish in his voice, Gwyneth seemed to let go of doubt, of fear. She met his gaze, as he met hers, and she smiled as though in recognition.

"You became a knight," she said.

"I did," he replied. "Because of you."

Gwyneth shook her head. "I held the mirror so that you could see yourself. That was all."

She grimaced and bit her lip. Tears sparkled on her eyelashes.

"It seems you know this elf, Sir Huma?" Titus asked, frowning.

Huma hesitated. "The story is long and complicated, sir."

"I have no time for long and complicated stories," said Titus tersely. "She'll be spending the night in the dungeon. We will sort out this tangle in the morning, after I've had a chance to speak to Lady Destina. Now I had better go inspect the damage in the kitchen."

"I require a basin of water and cloth for bandages," Raistlin called after him.

Titus nodded and walked off, accompanied by Will and Cook, who was roundly swearing over the loss of his mincemeat pies.

Raistlin once again approached Gwyneth, and this time she permitted him to draw near.

"You are faint from loss of blood," said Raistlin. "You should sit down."

He started to assist her, but Huma was there before him. Gently taking Gwyneth's hand, he led her to a chair at the table.

"The blood has caused your tunic to adhere to the wound, and I need to remove it," said Raistlin once Gwyneth was seated. "This will hurt, I am afraid."

"Grip my hand," said Huma.

Gwyneth clasped his hand tightly and kept fast hold of him, as Raistlin slowly prized the blood-gummed cloth from the wound as gently as he could.

Raistlin inspected the injury. "She was wounded by an arrow."

"Did one of our soldiers do this to you?" Huma demanded.

Gwyneth shook her head. "Goblins." She flashed a sudden, defiant glance at those gathered around her. "I am *not* spying for the

Dark Queen! I came here to learn if you knights will fight the dragon or run away."

"We will fight to protect our homeland, as you would fight to protect yours," said Huma. "But you must know that. For you *do* know me, don't you, Gwyneth? You came to me in my hour of despair. I fell in love with you then and I have waited for you to return all my life."

"Leave me alone, I beg of you," Gwyneth said sadly. "We cannot be."

"You say 'We cannot be'!" said Huma, quick to grasp at the slightest hope. "What cannot be? Love? You and I? I have prayed to Paladine that I would find you, and he has led me to you."

Gwyneth shook her head, but she kept hold of his hand.

Tas sat down beside her. "Are you the white stag, Gwyneth? That's how you were wounded, wasn't it? I was wondering—"

"Stop bothering my patient!" Raistlin ordered. He had been thinking the same thing about the white stag and, by his grim look, so had Sturm.

"I wasn't being a bother," said Tas. "I was just wondering why the white stag was hiding in a pantry. That wasn't in the song, at least not that I remember."

Fortunately, Will returned at that moment, carrying a basin of water and several clean towels and placing them on the table. Raistlin dipped a cloth in water and dabbed it on Gwyneth's wound, washing away the dried blood.

Will observed the proceedings. "I have orders to escort the prisoner to the dungeon."

"Is that truly necessary?" Huma asked angrily.

"You heard the commander, sir," said Will.

"You may take your prisoner after I have finished treating her," Raistlin told him.

He bound the cloth around the wound and helped Gwyneth draw the tunic over her shoulder.

"I will prepare a potion to relieve the pain and prevent the wound from turning putrid," Raistlin told her.

"Thank you," Gwyneth said, as Huma assisted her to stand. "I hope Lady Destina has not suffered any ill effects from the fight with the goblins?"

"She is fine," Raistlin replied. "Only very tired."

Will stepped toward Gwyneth and started to bind her wrists with a length of rope.

"No need for that," Gwyneth said. "I am not a threat to you or any true knight. It is the Dragon Queen who puts these barriers between us."

Will looked irresolute, but he did not press the issue.

"Where are the dungeons?" Huma asked. "I will take her myself."

"The dungeons are in the tower on the ground level," said Will. He jingled a set of keys. "I have orders to see her locked up safe in a cell."

"I will come with you," stated Huma.

He gallantly offered Gwyneth his arm and, after a moment's hesitation, she slipped her arm through his.

Tas tried to be helpful. "I've never been to these dungeons, Gwyneth, but I'm sure they're very nice."

She smiled at Tas over her shoulder, from behind a shimmering curtain of silver hair. She looked back at Huma and said in a low voice, "You should know that I prayed to Paladine to keep you away."

"Then I am glad the god listened to me," Huma replied.

Will took a torch from the wall and led them to the bridge that would take them back across the aqueduct and into the tower. Raistlin, Sturm, and Tas remained in the dining hall. Raistlin guessed they were all thinking the same thing.

"She's the silver dragon from the song, isn't she?" Tas asked. "The one that was a woman and then changes into a white stag. I knew she reminded me of Silvara."

"Remind me of the song," said Raistlin.

"'The end of this journey was nothing but green and the promise of green that endured in the eyes of the woman before him,'" Sturm quoted. "Although the *Song of Huma* doesn't explain how Huma thinks he knows her, nor yet why she thinks she knows him."

"What do you see with those cursed eyes of yours?" he asked Raistlin. "You see all things aging and dying, or at least so you claim. Did you see an elf or a dragon?"

"I saw both," Raistlin replied. "I believe the kender is right, much as I hate to admit it. Gwyneth is a silver dragon who has taken the form of an elf. Dragon magic is very powerful."

When Raistlin had first encountered Immolatus, the red dragon was also in mortal form. Immolatus had disguised himself during the day and shifted back to his true form at night, when dragons did their hunting.

"So since she is the silver dragon, she and Huma are supposed to fall in love," said Tas.

"They both appear to be inclined in that direction," said Raistlin dryly.

"I just remembered something," said Sturm. "Silvara told us a story about Huma and the silver dragon. He fell in love with her in her elven form. She feared to tell him her secret—that she was a dragon. She thought he would no longer love her if he knew the truth. If we accept that Gwyneth is a silver dragon in disguise, she has now met Huma. He is clearly infatuated with her as an elf, though we have no way of knowing how she feels about him or how he will feel about her if he discovers she is a dragon."

Sturm frowned. "But if that is true, why would she risk coming to the tower, knowing she was certain to encounter Huma?"

"Immolatus," said Raistlin. "A silver dragon would know that the knights cannot fight such a powerful dragon without her help and that of the dragonlances."

"And Gwyneth knows where to find them," said Sturm. "Which means that as of now, we have not altered history."

"The River of Time appears to be flowing placidly in its banks. History is happening as it should, based on what little we know," Raistlin agreed.

Tasslehoff had been thinking through all this, apparently, because suddenly he regarded them in consternation.

"But what little we know is terrible!" Tas said.

"Why are you upset?" Raistlin asked. "We have not changed history."

"That's the point!" Tas said, distraught. "Huma and Gwyneth both die at the end of the song!"

"Their sacrifice is heroic," said Sturm. "They die fighting the Queen of Darkness and driving her back to the Abyss."

"They are not the only ones who will die in this war," said Raistlin. "Magius is doomed to death, as well. According to the lore among wizards, he was captured by the forces of the red dragon when he had no more magic to cast. They tortured him for information about the tower's defenses. When he refused to tell them, they killed him."

Tas regarded him in distress. "Magius dies, too? But I don't want the song to end that way!"

"You never cared before now," said Raistlin.

"Before now the song was just a song about people I didn't know," said Tas miserably. "But now I know Huma and Gwyneth and Magius, and I don't want them to die! I've seen too many of my friends die. Flint and Sturm . . ."

His face crumpled. Two tears traced trails through the grime on his cheeks. "I don't feel very good. I have a stomachache here." He put his hand over his heart. "I guess I'll go to bed."

"Sturm and I will come with you," said Raistlin, remembering their promise to Titus to keep an eye on him.

Sturm took a torch from the wall to light the way and they crossed the bridge that led to the High Clerist's Tower. Once there, he and Raistlin climbed the stairs to their bedchambers on the sixth floor, while Tas trailed disconsolately after them, dragging his hoopak so that it thumped on the stairs.

"So far, we have not altered time, at least as far as I can determine," said Sturm. "Unfortunately, we know little about the Third Dragon War. I never heard of the disastrous attack on the knights and the refugees at Westgate Pass. You don't think that could have been caused by the Graygem, do you?"

Raistlin shook his head. "The attack happened before we came. We need be concerned only about what happens after our arrival in this time. But with every moment that passes, we endanger the past. We need to take the Graygem away from here. Tomorrow I will speak to Magius. I will need his help if I am to acquire the Device of Time Journeying."

"What are you going to tell him?" Sturm asked.

"I do not know yet," said Raistlin.

By this time, they had reached the sixth level. The knight, Valthas, was standing at the entrance to the level, either placed there to guard them, to keep a watch on them, or both. He guided them to their rooms.

"Lady Destina's chamber is there," said Valthas, taking them down a hallway. "And the other wizard's room is there. Sir Huma will sleep here when he returns from escorting the elf to prison. I am to lock the kender in this chamber and give you the key, sir."

He escorted Tas into the room, shut the door, locked it, and then returned to his post. Neither Sturm nor Raistlin had the heart to tell the young knight that a lock would be no deterrent to Tasslehoff Burrfoot.

"Let us hope Tas is too despondent to do any irreparable damage before morning," Raistlin remarked.

Sturm was about to enter his room when Raistlin stopped him.

"I know what happened to you in your life. Don't you wonder what happened to me?"

"Not particularly," said Sturm. "I do not care."

He started to open the door.

"The evil you always believed of me came to pass," Raistlin continued relentlessly, determined to make his confession and get it over.

Sturm paused and looked back at him.

"I turned to darkness," Raistlin continued. "I sought power and attained it at the cost of my soul. I committed unspeakable crimes. Caramon tried to save me, and when he could not, he was grieved to the heart and tried to drown his pain in dwarf spirits. I nearly destroyed him. He proved stronger than I was, however. He was able to overcome temptation and make a good life for himself and his family. Yet even now, according to Tas, he remains loyal to me, his unworthy brother."

"Why are you telling me this?" Sturm demanded. "I never did like you, and this isn't helping."

Raistlin started to answer, then began coughing. Sturm waited until the fit ended.

"Tas knows the truth," Raistlin said, wiping blood from his lips. "He would have blurted it out sooner or later. Better I told you myself. I need you to trust me. Or at least make an effort to trust me."

Sturm's expression was grim. "Do you feel any remorse?"

Raistlin wondered. Did he feel any remorse? Or would he do what he had done again? When he didn't answer, Sturm shook his head, entered his room, and slammed the door shut without another word.

Raistlin was going to his room to study his spells when he noticed a light shining beneath Magius's door. He started to knock and found the door open. The room was small but comfortable, with a canopied bed, rugs on the floor, and two wooden chairs furnished with cushions.

Magius had fallen asleep in a chair, the light of the crystal atop the staff still blazing. The spellbook in his lap was open to the page he had been studying.

Raistlin closed the book, refusing to allow himself to look at the spells, and slipped it back into its carrying case. Finding a blanket, he covered Magius, then, touching the staff, he said softly, "*Dulak.*" The light of the crystal went out.

Raistlin returned to his own room, which was furnished exactly the same as Magius's, and shut the door. He mixed a potion to treat Gwyneth's wound from the herbs in his pouches and set it aside to give the ingredients the night to work. Sitting down on his bed with his own spellbook, he opened it and copied into it the words of the journeying spell.

He did not have that many spells to memorize and he was soon finished. Closing the book, he recalled the time in his life after his Test when he had been inordinately proud of these few simple spells.

Raistlin blew out the candle. Wrapping himself in the blanket, he lay down on the bed and stared into the empty darkness he knew so well.

CHAPTER
TEN

CR aistlin slept later than he had intended and woke feeling as
though his head was stuffed with wool. A pitcher of water
and a basin stood on the sideboard. He stripped off his
robes, poured cool water into the basin, plunged his face and head
into the water, and bathed as best he could. As he washed, he attempted to recall the spells he had memorized the night before. He
was pleased to see the words take shape in his mind and feel the
magic warm his blood.

He dressed and emerged from his room to find all quiet and Sir
Reginald on duty.

"Where is everyone?" Raistlin asked.

"The commander took the two knights to inspect the tower's
defenses," Sir Reginald replied. "Lady Destina is keeping to her
room."

"Is she all right?" Raistlin asked.

"I believe so. She has requested hot water for a bath. And the
other wizard, Magius, said something about finding breakfast."

"And the kender?" Raistlin asked.

"I haven't seen him," said Sir Reginald. "I assume he is still in his
room."

"You don't know many kender, do you?" said Raistlin.

"He is the only one I have met, thanks be to Paladine," said Sir Reginald. He suddenly looked worried. "Should I check to see if he is still there?"

"It would be advisable," said Raistlin dryly. "Though you are probably too late."

The young knight started to unlock the door and found it already unlocked. He opened it, looking alarmed, and peered inside. "He's gone!"

"I'll find him," said Raistlin.

He crossed the bridge to the Knight's Spur, but did not locate Tas. The gods only knew where he was. Raistlin found Magius in the dining hall, eating leftover stew.

"Good morning, Brother," said Magius cheerfully. "Will you have stew for breakfast?"

Raistlin felt his stomach turn at the thought. He politely declined and went to the kitchen for a pot of boiling water and to see if Tasslehoff was in the pantry. Cook reported that he had not seen the kender all morning, for which blessing he thanked the gods. Raistlin took the hot water back to the table. Removing the bag of herbs from his belt, he scattered them in the water to steep, as Caramon had always done. Raistlin swiftly banished the memory.

Magius wrinkled his nose. "What is that concoction you are drinking? It stinks to high heaven. I hope it tastes better than it smells."

"Quite the contrary," said Raistlin, sipping the tea with a grimace. "I have a question for you. How does Huma think he knows the elf woman, Gwyneth?"

"He's been talking about her again, hasn't he?" Magius shook his head.

"He met her last night," said Raistlin, and he described that night's adventures. "He claims he knows her, and she appeared to know him. She is currently being held in the dungeon."

"You astound me!" said Magius, amazed.

"What is the story?" Raistlin asked.

"I cannot believe this," said Magius. "The night before Huma was to be inducted into the knighthood, he kept vigil in the family chapel. He remained awake all night, on his knees in prayer to Paladine. During his vigil, Huma confessed to the god that he had doubts. He did not believe himself worthy of becoming a knight. He feared he would falter in battle or basely run away. An elven woman came to him. She had silver hair and green eyes and was clothed in silver raiment. She took hold of his hands and told him she had watched him from afar, and she knew him better than he knew himself. She told him he was honorable and courageous and noble. He would know fear, she said, but he would overcome it. He would fight bravely in righteous battle and win glory and renown for the knighthood. She kissed him on the brow and gave him the blessing of Paladine and vanished."

Magius finished off the stew and shoved the bowl to one side. "The woman was very real to him, as, of course, she would be, given that he had not slept or eaten anything for two days. I've tried to explain that he had been dreaming, but he won't listen to reason. Huma has been searching for her ever since. And now it seems he's found her."

Magius shook his head. "I suppose one could say that having searched for years for an elven woman, he would latch on to the first he came across. Still . . . she does fit the description."

"'She had been watching him from afar. . . .'" Raistlin repeated thoughtfully.

"I would like to meet her," said Magius.

"We will seek permission to visit her," said Raistlin as Tasslehoff came wandering into the room.

"Where have you been, kender?" Magius asked. "Ransacking the fortress?"

"I wasn't ransacking," said Tas. "I wasn't doing anything with sacks." He picked up the empty bowl, regarded it with interest, and absently started to drop it in his pouch. Magius rescued the and set it back on the table.

"I was on an Important Mission," Tas continued. "I was thinking about Gwyneth and she made me think about Silvara and she made me think about the dragon orb—"

"What did we talk about, Tas?" Raistlin said sternly.

"We talked about the . . . uh . . . thing I'm not supposed to talk about," said Tas. "So I went to see if *it* was where *it* was when I found *it* the last time that hasn't happened yet. If *it* was there, you see, I would have to tell Titus how to use *it* to fight the red dragon and I don't want to do that because there was all that blood and screaming. But *it* wasn't there. So I don't have to."

Tas heaved a glad sigh and picked up a spoon.

"I heard Cook say he fixed sausages," said Magius, taking away the spoon.

"Oh, good! I'm a lot hungrier now that I know *it* isn't here."

Tas dashed off toward the kitchen. Magius gazed after him thoughtfully, then turned to Raistlin.

"I believe this would be a good time for our talk, Brother."

"I agree," said Raistlin. "But not here."

Magius picked up his staff and the two climbed to the battlements on the top floor of the Knight's Spur. A soldier was walking back and forth, keeping watch. At the arrival of the two wizards, he retreated to the far end of the ramparts, either out of courtesy or distrust.

The roof of the fortress was flat and unremarkable, surrounded by a waist-high wall of gray stone. The western wall butted up against the side of a mountain. The eastern wall had been undergoing renovation to enclose it within the new curtain wall being built around the tower. Raistlin looked out over the wall to the south. The enemy's numbers had grown during the night, and more troops were arriving. He saw no sign of Immolatus this morning.

Magius leaned his staff against the wall and turned to face Raistlin.

"Rational people generally pay little heed to kender tales, and ordinarily I am one of them," said Magius. "But your kender's tales are the most intriguing I have ever heard. How does he know about dragon orbs? They were created by wizards during the Second Dragon War to defend the Towers of High Sorcery from attack by dragons, and they have been a closely held secret ever since. Few wizards know about them. A kender most assuredly would not!"

"I will answer your questions, though you may find my answers hard to believe," said Raistlin.

"I am listening," said Magius, folding his arms across his chest.

"In the future, centuries from now, Tasslehoff will find a dragon orb in the High Clerist's Tower. He and an elven woman named Laurana will use the orb to defeat the Dark Queen's dragons in what will be known as the War of the Lance. Tas knows this because he is from the future. Sturm, Destina, and I are all from the future, as well."

Magius laughed derisively. "You said I would find your story hard to believe, not preposterous! You do not seriously expect me to believe that you traveled through time, do you? Try again, Brother."

"And yet you yourself contemplated such a journey," Raistlin said quietly. "You planned to use the Device of Time Journeying to go back in time."

Magius gave a perceptible start. His laughter died. His blue eyes darkened to gray. "Go on with your tale, Brother. If nothing else, your story is amusing."

"Lady Destina used the Device to bring us to this time, although that was not her intention. She planned to transport Sturm to the High Clerist's Tower during our own time, but when she tried to leave, powerful magical forces collided. The Device of Time Journeying could not withstand the strain and blew apart. Now we are stranded here with no way to return unless we can find the Device."

"You said it blew apart," stated Magius.

"It was destroyed in the future, but I believe it exists here in this time. And you know where it is."

"I may or I may not," said Magius coolly. "This destructive magical force you talk about, does it have something to do with that fey jewel Lady Destina wears around her neck?"

"I will tell you all I know," said Raistlin, "but only on one condition. You cannot reveal what I say to Huma or to anyone else."

"Huma and I have no secrets from each other," Magius said.

"Nonsense," said Raistlin sharply. "Everyone has secrets. For example, did you tell him what happened to you during your Test in the Tower of High Sorcery?"

Magius was grim. "You know I did not. He would never understand. Very well. I promise I will not reveal your secret. You have my word as a brother wizard."

Raistlin was satisfied. "The jewel Destina wears is the Graygem of Gargath."

Raistlin expected him to scoff in derision, but Magius was grave.

"The Graygem . . ." Magius repeated in thoughtful tones. "Now I start to believe you, Brother."

"I am glad," said Raistlin, relieved. "Most people think the Graygem is a myth."

"I am not one of them. In my wild and misspent youth, I contemplated going on a quest to find it. I traveled to the Library of Palanthas to study it and realized then that finding the Graygem would be hopeless unless it wanted to be found. The lady tries to keep it hidden, but I caught a glimpse of it and I recognized it from the account in the book. 'The jewel is gray in color, constantly changing, never seeming the same from one moment to the next.' I should have realized the truth. How did she come by it?"

"Her story is her own and you must ask her," said Raistlin. "Sturm and I happened to land in the middle of it. But even without the presence of Chaos, there exists the danger that those of us who do not belong here could change history. The Graygem increases the danger tenfold or more. It is imperative I find the Device of Time Journeying and return us to our own time as swiftly as possible."

"And how did you find out I intended to use the Device?" asked Magius.

"According to Destina, her father came across an account of you and Huma written by some soldier who had served with you both. Destina learned about the Device from this account."

Magius was skeptical. "Why would anyone write about Huma and me?"

Raistlin stood in silence. The summer morning was chill from the wind coming down from the mountains. He shivered and put his hands in the sleeves of his robes.

"I cannot tell you," he said at last.

"You mean you *will not* tell me," said Magius, his voice hardening.

"You know I cannot reveal the future to you," said Raistlin.

"Because if I do not like what I hear, I might try to change it," said Magius. "Does something happen to Huma? If he suffers some dread fate and I can prevent it, I will do so. And the future be damned!"

"The Graygem contains the essence of Chaos," Raistlin explained. "We have only an imperfect knowledge of the past, based on song and legend. Consider this: In trying to save Huma from some dread fate, you might inadvertently be the cause of it."

Magius stood in thoughtful silence, then slowly nodded. "I think I am beginning to understand. But if you cannot reveal the future, at least tell me about this account Destina mentioned. You said it related to my past, which is over and gone. No harm can come of you telling me that much. And it would serve to prove your veracity."

"The soldier wrote that he overheard you and Huma talking one night. You told Huma you had discovered the existence of a device that could take you back in time. You wanted to use the device to go back to save Huma's sister, who had died."

Magius turned away from Raistlin. He leaned his elbows on the wall and looked out over the plains. He was not seeing the present; he was viewing his past.

"Greta," he said at last, the ache of loss in his voice. "Her name was Greta. She was Huma's younger sister. She was only seventeen when she died in a minor skirmish with roving hobgoblins at the manor house. A hob slashed Greta's arm with a spear. The wound was not deep. We even teased her about it. But by that night she was screaming in pain and burning up with fever. The family sent for a cleric of Kiri-Jolith, but the cleric was useless and so was the god. The cleric determined the spear tip was poisoned. By the next morning, Greta was dead."

"I am sorry," said Raistlin, though he knew the words were inadequate.

"I loved her dearly," said Magius. He caressed the silver ring on his finger. "We had been in love since we were children. I would have done anything to save her. I would have changed time to save her."

"The future be damned," Raistlin said.

Magius nodded. "I remember this conversation you say the soldier recorded, for it was the only time Huma and I ever quarreled. We were in camp late at night after some battle or other. I had learned about the Device during one of my visits to the Tower of High Sorcery in Palanthas. It was there and I knew I could easily steal it because the master of the tower was a dolt. He still is a dolt, by the way. Anyhow, Huma refused to allow me to use it. He said the danger that I could alter time was too great. He would not risk it, even to save his sister. I flew into a rage, but he was right, of course. I realized that when I had calmed down."

"Is the Device of Time Journeying still in the tower of Palanthas?"

"It was there five years ago," said Magius. "I have not been back there since. I avoid the tower if I can. The master does not like me."

Raistlin understood. Par-Salian, the master in his time, had not liked him, either.

"I must find the Device and return the four of us—and the Graygem—to our own time before Chaos does harm either in this time or our own," said Raistlin. "But as you and I both know, the minotaurs control the city of Palanthas. The magical portals would take us there. I know how to use them in my time, but each master regulates them differently."

"I have traveled to the tower using them, and I can take you there," said Magius. "But first tell me more about the Graygem. It is a powerful magical artifact, perhaps the most powerful in the world. A valuable prize for any wizard. Did you ever think of taking it for yourself?"

"The Graygem has chosen Destina and will not leave her. A goblin tried to steal it from her and the Graygem nearly burned off the creature's hand."

"Would you take it if you could?" Magius persisted.

"I would not," Raistlin said emphatically. "I could not endure the thought that Chaos might be dictating my actions. What about you?"

Magius shrugged. "I was once interested in it when I was young, but now that I am older, as you say, I prefer to control my own fate. The lady is welcome to keep her accursed jewel."

"Then will you help us?"

"I will take you to the tower on one condition. The wizards who created the orbs planned to use them to summon the dragons to the Tower of High Sorcery and then kill them with deadly spells. Was this how your kender friend used the dragon orb during the battle he mentioned?"

"I do not know, for I was not present," Raistlin replied. "I was fighting my own battles at the time. Why do you ask?"

"Because I am thinking of using the dragon orb to fight the red dragon," said Magius coolly.

"Commander Belgrave is like Sturm. He does not trust magic," said Raistlin. "He would never permit you to bring such a powerful and lethal artifact into the most holy site in Solamnia."

"What Commander Belgrave doesn't know won't hurt him," said Magius. "I have been developing this plan for a long time. It would be easy to smuggle the dragon orb inside the tower. After all, it seems your kender will find one in the future."

Of course! Raistlin suddenly knew the answer to a question that had long perplexed the wise: Tas had found a dragon orb in the High Clerist's Tower during the War of the Lance. By all accounts, the Measure adjured Solamnics most strongly to refrain from putting their trust in wizards. So how had the dragon orb come to be in the tower?

Magius had brought the dragon orb to the High Clerist's Tower during the Third Dragon War. He intended to use it to fight dragons, but he would die before he had a chance. Centuries later, Tas would find it, and the orb would help save Solamnia.

Good does indeed redeem its own, as the adage says, Raistlin reflected.

"You will assist me to find the Device of Time Journeying?" he asked.

"If you will help me obtain a dragon orb," said Magius.

"We have a bargain," Raistlin said, and the two shook hands.

Magius picked up his staff, and they walked back toward the stairs.

"I had a strange dream," said Magius. "I dreamed I was asleep in my room when you came in. I had fallen asleep over my studies, and you very kindly covered me with a blanket and doused the light of the crystal in the staff. You used the word, 'Dulak.' The magical word I assigned it. No one would know that except one who owned the staff. The kender was right about that, wasn't he?"

"In the future, after I take the Test in the tower, the master will give me your staff," said Raistlin. "It is—was—my most treasured possession."

"I am glad to know something of me lives on," said Magius. "One more question. You carry a knife concealed beneath your sleeve. The gods of magic do not permit wizards to carry bladed weapons. Has that also changed in the future?"

Raistlin placed his hand self-consciously on his arm, feeling the knife hidden beneath his sleeve.

"The legend goes that a wizard fighting in a battle used up all his spells and so was left defenseless. He was captured, tortured, and killed. In his memory, the gods of magic now permit mages to wear a small, bladed weapon."

"Quite a tragic tale," said Magius. "The bards must have everyone in tears when they sing of it."

"No one weeps," said Raistlin. "Few people care what happens to wizards."

"I guess some things never change," agreed Magius.

CHAPTER
ELEVEN

Magius and Raistlin were descending the tower stairs from the battlements when they encountered Titus Belgrave coming up.

He looked startled to see them. "I hope the commotion in the night did not disrupt your sleep."

"What commotion?" Magius asked. "I heard nothing."

"We caught another spy last night and he fought like a cornered kobold. He had stolen a uniform and tried to pass himself off as one of the men-at-arms. We might not have detected him if our army had been at full strength, but now there are so few of us the soldiers realized that he was not one of ours. They wrestled him to the floor and clapped him in irons."

"I assume you questioned him," said Raistlin. "What information did he provide?"

"None," said Titus. "He won't even tell us his name. A day or two languishing in the dungeon will loosen his tongue."

"The information this man knows could be of vital importance, Commander," said Magius. "My friend and I would be glad to pay him a visit. I am certain we can persuade him to talk."

"I am certain you could," said Titus dourly. "But the Measure prohibits the use of torture."

Magius flared in anger. "I said nothing about torture!"

Titus pushed past them, continuing up the stairs to the battlements. "If you want to do something constructive, find the kender."

Magius looked grimly after him. "He is like every other bucketheaded knight I've ever met. They always assume magic-users delight in inflicting pain."

"The exception being Huma," said Raistlin.

"I raised him right," said Magius, smiling. "Titus mentioned they caught a second spy. Did he mean Gywneth was the first?"

"So I assume," Raistlin answered.

"I should like to meet her," said Magius.

The two continued down to the bottom of the staircase and paused at the bridge that led from the fortress to the High Clerist's Tower.

"As a Solamnic war wizard, are you required to follow Titus's orders?" Raistlin asked abruptly.

"I am required to follow the Measure," said Magius. "Though I generally don't."

"Then perhaps you and I should pay a visit to the dungeons," Raistlin suggested. "I have an excuse. Gwyneth was wounded in a fight with goblins, and I promised I would take her a healing balm. You could meet her. And we could question this spy."

"And if we get caught," said Magius with a conspiratorial grin, "we can always say we were going to the wine cellar."

Raistlin retrieved the jar of balm from his room in the tower, and the two sought out the dungeons, which were located on the first floor on the tower's north side. This part of the tower had no windows, leaving it dark even by day, so Magius used the staff to light their way.

"Huma and I spent a great deal of time here when his parents made their annual pilgrimage. As you can imagine, the dungeons held a powerful attraction for us when we were boys," Magius said. "We were always hoping the knights would capture an ogre and lock him up. He would escape, of course, and Huma and I would be the heroes who captured him. Unfortunately, most of the prisoners in the dungeon were pilgrims overcome by a surfeit of wine or ecstasy."

He led Raistlin down a staircase. They turned right down a narrow hall that brought them to another hall that slanted off to the east and, finally, to the dungeons.

The prison cells in the High Clerist's Tower were clean and well-kept. The jailer sat at a desk in front of a locked cellblock gate made of iron bars. An iron-and-glass lantern hung from a hook on the wall above him. Additional lanterns lit the cellblock and they could see the cells through the bars, lined up in a row against the wall.

"Tas would approve," Raistlin remarked. "He is a connoisseur of dungeons, and this meets his standards."

The jailer had propped his chair at a precarious angle against the wall and was leaning back with his eyes closed. Hearing them talking, he rocked forward in his chair, opened his eyes, and glared at them accusingly.

"I wasn't asleep, if that's what you're thinking. What do you two want?" he demanded. "With all you people coming and going, I can't get a moment's rest."

"I would not have thought dungeons were so popular," said Magius.

The jailer snorted. "Yesterday I had to lock up an elven spy. Then the commander wakes me in the night to lock up a human spy. This morning I find a kender chatting with the elf. I have no idea how he got in the cellblock. When I asked him, he gave me some rigmarole about lockpicks being his birthright or some such thing. I had to chase him off and now Sir Huma is inside, talking with the elf."

"Huma is here?" Magius asked, startled.

"He's with the elf now," said the jailer, looking disapproving—a disapproval he extended to them with a scowl. "What do you two magic-users want?"

"We came to find out if that human spy you mentioned is a wizard in the service of the Dark Queen," said Magius. "We fear he could be planning to use evil magicks to destroy us."

"He doesn't look like a wizard," said the jailer, frowning. "He's not wearing robes like you two."

"He wouldn't," Raistlin said. "He would be in disguise, dressed in ordinary clothing."

The jailer was shocked. "You mean to tell me you wizards can look like normal folk? I thought you had to wear robes to . . . to warn people you were coming!"

"Like a bell on a cat?" Magius suggested, winking at Raistlin.

The jailer nodded. "Something like that. So how can you tell if he's a wizard?"

"He will smell funny to another wizard," said Magius gravely. "He could be extremely dangerous. You should remain with my colleague while I investigate. He will protect you if the wizard attacks."

The jailer took cover behind Raistlin and peered over his shoulder as Magius walked over to the cellblock gate.

Magius strolled back and forth, sniffing loudly, as the jailer watched him intently. Raistlin slid his hand into one of his pouches and drew out a pinch of sand. Magius sniffed again, and Raistlin threw the sand on the jailer and spoke the words of the sleep spell.

"Ast tasarak sinuralan krynawi."

The jailer's knees buckled and he started to keel over. Raistlin caught him and eased him to the floor, while Magius removed the keys from his belt. He opened the gate to the cellblock, and the two mages entered. The cellblock consisted of six prison cells. Each had an iron door with a small grate the jailer could use to keep watch on the prisoners inside.

Raistlin opened the grates, searching for Gwyneth, and found her in the fourth cell, sitting on her cot, wrapped in a blanket. She was talking with Huma, who was also seated on the cot, though at a decorous distance. The jailer had locked them inside, which was probably unnecessary. The two had eyes only for each other. They weren't going anywhere.

Raistlin started to rap on the door to announce his presence.

Magius stopped him. "No hurry," he said softly.

Huma was talking animatedly, describing a funny incident that had happened at a joust, when his horse had suddenly balked as he rode toward his opponent and tossed him head over heels.

"I landed on my back on the ground," said Huma, laughing. "My lance went one way, my shield the other. I was one massive bruise and so heavily encased in my armor I could not get up. I rolled about, helpless as an overturned turtle."

His eyes crinkled with laughter at the memory of his predicament, and Gwyneth laughed with him. Her eyes were alight with silver flame; her laughter was like the chiming of a silver bell. Impulsively, without truly being aware of what they did, each drew near the other.

"Iron to lodestone," Magius murmured. "I remember that feeling. Greta and I could speak without speaking."

"What happened?" Gwyneth was asking Huma.

"My squire had to come rescue me and he had to enlist help from a stable hand to pull me to my feet," said Huma. "I limped from the field covered in shame and ignominy and horse manure."

Gwyneth laughed until the tears ran down her cheeks, and Huma joined in, his own laughter deep and booming. The two stopped, out of breath, although perhaps not from the laughter. They leaned toward each other, their lips parted.

Magius loudly cleared his throat and Raistlin rapped on the door. "Forgive the interruption. I am here with the balm," he called.

"Your healer has come to treat your wound," Huma said, rising to his feet. "I will withdraw to give you some privacy. I am going to speak to Commander Belgrave to see if I can persuade him to release you."

"I have enjoyed our conversation," said Gwyneth, rising with him. She gave him her hand. Huma bowed to her and called for the jailer to release him.

"I have the keys," said Magius. "The jailer is currently indisposed."

Huma left the cell, leaving the door open for Raistlin to enter. Magius stopped his friend as he passed.

"I admit that I was wrong," Magius said. "It wasn't a dream. I am glad for you."

Huma smiled and looked back at Gwyneth. "I have found her. She has found me."

He went on his way and they heard him running up the stairs, singing like a youth. Magius remained standing in the doorway while Raistlin stepped inside.

He held up the clay jar. "I brought the balm for your wound as I promised. How are you this morning? Your visitor seems to have done more for you than any medicine."

"He came to see how they were treating me. He was only being polite," said Gwyneth, blushing.

Raistlin said nothing more and removed the bandages. The arrow wound was inflamed and must pain her, though she appeared far beyond feeling pain at the moment. Raistlin gently spread the balm over the wound.

Gwyneth regarded him in wonder. "That does help. Is it magic?"

"A mixture of comfrey and yarrow, which are standard for treating wounds, and a few ingredients of my own, none of which are magic," Raistlin replied. "Is there anything else I can do for you while I am here?"

"Thank you, no," said Gwyneth.

She leaned back against the wall and smiled wistfully, then sighed deeply. A tear glimmered on her cheek. She hurriedly brushed it away.

Raistlin shut the cell door and Magius locked it.

"She is certainly beautiful," he said when they were out of earshot. "Her hair shines like molten silver. I have never met an elf before. Do they all look like her?"

"No," said Raistlin. "She is special."

"Huma certainly thinks so," said Magius. "How do you think she feels about him?"

"She loves him," said Raistlin. "But for some reason she appears to be afraid of loving him."

"It's the mustaches," said Magius. "I keep telling him that women find them terrifying."

They discovered the other prisoner asleep on his cot. Magius opened the door to the cell and entered.

"*Shirak*," said Magius and the crystal globe on the staff began to glow.

The man's face was bruised and battered, his knuckles bloodied from his fight. But the jailer had treated him well, apparently, for he had fresh water to drink and they had fed him, to judge by the empty bowl outside the cell door. Magius shook the man by the shoulder. Startled, the prisoner jerked awake. He stared at Magius in alarm and started to yell for the jailer.

"*Tan-tago, musalah.*" Magius brushed his hand against the man's cheek. "You and I are now the best of friends and you will be glad to share with me all you know. What is your name?"

"Calaf," the man replied readily.

"Where are you from?"

"Sanction."

"That city is in the Khalkist Mountains," Magius said. "Not far from Neraka. Is Sanction now under control of the Dark Queen?"

"Most of western Ansalon is now under her control," said Calaf with a smirk. "Only Istar holds out, and their time will come."

"Who sent you to spy on us? Who is your commander?"

"Immolatus," Calaf replied.

"Who is that?" Magius asked.

"The red dragon. He is considering launching an attack on the tower himself. He ordered me to find out how many knights and soldiers are left to guard it. The dragon did not think there would be many left alive after the slaughter in Westgate Pass. He wiped them out to a man—or a woman. They tried to shield their children with their own bodies when the dragon breathed his fire on them. Needless to say, that didn't work."

Magius tightened his grip on his staff. His knuckles grew white with the effort to restrain himself. He managed to speak calmly, however.

"When does Immolatus plan to launch this attack against the tower?"

"He could attack it today if he wanted," Calaf boasted. "None of the knights' puny weapons can touch him. They hurled spears at him, but they shattered like twigs and he roasted the knights alive in their armor. You should have heard them scream! But he has orders to wait for Takhisis. She wants to be here to witness the downfall of the knights. Her Dark Majesty will be here soon—far sooner than you want. And then I'll listen to your screams!"

"You first, friend," said Magius.

Lifting the staff, he jabbed it into the man's groin. Calaf crumpled and sagged to the floor, clutching himself and moaning.

Magius eyed him with revulsion. "Finish interrogating the wretch if you want, Brother. I cannot stand the sight of him. I'll wait for you at the entrance."

After he was gone, Raistlin knelt down beside Calaf, who was still rocking back and forth in pain.

"Who else is spying for Immolatus?" Raistlin asked. "I know you are not the only spy he has planted in the fort. The dragon is more efficient than that."

Calaf gave a feeble shake of his head. "I don't know."

"But I am right," Raistlin persisted. "He has planted other spies."

Calaf nodded.

Raistlin drew closer. "Give me their names! Would one be Mullen Tully?"

"I don't know!" Calaf whimpered. "Leave me alone!"

Raistlin closed his hand over Calaf's wrist in a crushing grasp. "I am not a knight. I am not sworn to follow the Measure's laws against torture. I know a great many ways to inflict pain far worse than what you are suffering now! I once placed my fingers on a man's chest and burned five holes into his flesh. Tell me the names of these spies!"

Calaf stared at him in terror. "I don't know! I swear to you that's the truth. Do you think the dragon would be likely to tell me?"

Raistlin slowly released his grasp and stood up. Calaf spoke the truth. Immolatus was not likely to tell him. He did not trust anyone, not even his own Dark Queen.

Raistlin slammed the cell door shut. As he was leaving, he saw Gwyneth's face framed in the grate.

"Mage, stop a moment."

"Is something wrong?" Raistlin asked. "Are you still in pain?"

Gwyneth brushed aside his question as unimportant. "I overheard what that prisoner said about the knights and the human refugees, how they lacked weapons that could harm the dragon, and they died horribly. Is that true?"

Raistlin understood the import of her question and the reason she asked it, and he didn't know at first how to respond. Gwyneth knew where to find lances that would not *shatter like twigs* against the dragon's scales. Magical lances made of dragonmetal—forged by silver dragons, blessed by Paladine—were in her care. But if she brought them to the knights, she would have to reveal her true nature to Huma, the man she had come to love, who might well cease to love her when he knew the truth.

Raistlin could have given her a nudge, told her the knights were desperate, that their only hope lay in finding weapons better suited to fighting dragons. But he could see the agony in her eyes, and he decided against it. The decision had to be her own.

"I do not know, Lady," he replied. "I was not there."

"But it could be true," Gwyneth insisted.

"The commander told us he saw the dragon, he saw flames on the mountain. He waited to treat survivors, but none returned," said Raistlin.

Gwyneth turned away. As Raistlin left, he heard her pacing her cell.

Magius was waiting for him outside the cellblock. He shut the gate, locked it, and replaced the keys on the belt of the slumbering jailer. Raistlin prodded the man with the toe of his boot, waking him. The jailer sat up, startled.

"You were sleeping on duty," Magius said sternly. "I won't report you this time, but don't let it happen again."

They left the jailer blinking at them in confusion.

"Did you find out anything else?" Magius asked as they climbed the stairs.

"I asked if the dragon had planted more spies and if Calaf knew their names," Raistlin replied. "He said he didn't."

"Do you believe him?"

"He was in too much pain to lie," said Raistlin.

Magius grinned. "I admit I enjoyed that. Perhaps Commander Belgrave is right about us wizards, after all. And now I propose we stop by the wine cellar. I need to wash the foul taste from my mouth. After that, I will speak with the kender about the dragon orb."

"You realize Tas will tell you twelve different tales," Raistlin grumbled. "Six of which involve Uncle Trapspringer and the other six a woolly mammoth."

Magius laughed. "Do you know where to find him?"

"I doubt if even the gods know where to find Tasslehoff," said Raistlin. "But I would start with the kitchen."

CHAPTER
TWELVE

estina was in her bedchamber that morning, combing her
wet hair after a bath. Will had groused about the work
involved, but he had hauled in a metal tub, carried in
buckets of hot water, and provided soap. She had thanked him and
then cast a rueful glance at her bloodstained clothes.

"I do not know if I can bear to put these on again," she had said.

"Leave it to me," Will had replied.

Destina had luxuriated in the bath and washed off all traces of the
goblins' attack, though the lye soap almost took off her skin with it.
She felt immeasurably better and was attempting to scrub the goblin
blood off her jacket when she was interrupted by a knock on the door.

She wrapped herself in a blanket, clutching it close around her
neck to hide the Graygem, and opened the door to find Will standing there, holding a large wooden chest bound with leather straps.

"What is this?" Destina asked.

"A change of clothes," said Will. He did not ask her permission
but dragged the chest into her room. "They belonged to the lady
wife of the Lord Mayor of Palanthas. You are about the same size.
They'll likely fit."

He undid the leather straps and threw open the chest to reveal fine woolen clothes, linen chemises and other undergarments, all trimmed in lace, along with stockings and nightdresses. The clothes had clearly been hastily packed, probably by some frantic maid.

"The lady won't be needing them anymore," Will added gruffly. "Would be a shame to let them go to waste."

Destina drew back, holding the blanket tight around her neck, conscious of the Graygem.

"She died. . . ." Destina swallowed and couldn't finish.

"At Westgate Pass," said Will. "At least, so we have reason to believe."

"I couldn't possibly," said Destina, shaking her head.

"They're just clothes, my lady," said Will, his gruff voice softening. "Lady Olivia was generous and loving, a friend to all in need. If she was here, she would have given them to you herself. That's why I thought of it."

He shrugged. "But suit yourself. You best find some clothes, however. The commander wants to see you in his office immediately. The matter is urgent. I doubt you'll want to wear a blanket."

Will left, shutting the door behind him.

Destina looked at her own clothes, travel-stained, bloodstained. The hem of her skirt was stiff with dirt and mud. Her stockings were torn. A faint and comforting fragrance of lavender came from the trunk. She could almost hear the lady saying in brisk tones, "I have moved on, my dear. I have no need of such finery anymore. Be practical."

Destina knelt beside the chest and took out a skirt made of lamb's wool, dyed sky blue, and a matching jacket, finely tailored. The jacket had pewter buttons up the front and a pewter fastening known as a frog at the collar that would clasp it firmly around her neck.

Destina was admiring it when there came a knock at the door.

"Commander's waiting, my lady," Will called.

Destina sighed. As Will had said, she couldn't wear a blanket. She gave a soft thank you to the unknown lady, spread the clothes out on her bed, and hurriedly dressed.

Will gave her an approving look when she emerged. She accompanied him down the stairs and across the bridge to the Knight's

Spur. The commander's office was located on the ground level. Will knocked and opened the door.

"Lady Destina, sir," he said.

The commander's office was small and furnished only with necessities, and those were plain and practical. The walls were adorned with maps and nothing else. Titus was standing at a single, recessed, iron-barred window, gazing morosely out at the plains to the south. He turned as she entered.

"Thank you for coming, Lady Destina," Titus said, motioning her to a chair. "Will told me he brought you a change of clothes."

"I am most grateful to him," said Destina.

Titus nodded and moved on to business. "I understand that you know an elven woman who goes by the name of Gwyneth."

"I do know her," Destina said, mystified. "She came to our rescue when Tas and I were attacked by goblins. Why do you ask?"

"We caught her hiding in a pantry last night," Titus replied. "What do you know about her? Could she be working for the dragon?"

"Gwyneth saved our lives. I do not believe she is a spy for the dragon or anyone else," Destina said briskly. "Where is she? I want to speak to her!"

"I am holding her in the dungeons, and those are in the tower. I have no one I can spare to escort you," Titus replied. "And speaking of dungeons, you need to keep an eye on your kender. He was down in the cellblock, talking to the elf. If you don't, I will have no choice but to lock him up, as well."

"I will watch Tas," Destina promised. "But about Gwyneth—"

"I will take her situation under advisement. You will forgive me, my lady, but I have work to do," Titus added, taking up a sheaf of papers. "You should go find your kender."

Destina did not like being so summarily dismissed, but she reflected that perhaps Tas knew something about Gwyneth since he had been speaking with her. Destina left in search of him and found him in the dining hall, eating pudding she hoped to the gods he had not stolen.

"Here you are!" said Tas. "I was looking for you. You have new clothes. Those are very pretty. Where did you get them?"

But he didn't wait for her to answer. "It was very exciting last night! The cook found Gwyneth in the pantry and started chasing her. She ran out of the kitchen as Huma was running into the kitchen and she flew right into his arms. He caught her and she cried out and fell on the floor. She had an arrow wound in her shoulder just like the white stag! Huma couldn't do much except stare at her. I think he is enameled with her."

"Enamored," Destina corrected.

Tas nodded. "That's what I said. Anyway, I was visiting with her in the dungeons this morning, when the jailer caught me and asked me if I wanted a cell of my own. I thanked him for the offer but said maybe another time. I have too much Important Work to do to fix the song. I was thinking I could climb all the way to the top of the tower and maybe talk to the dragon. I could warn him that if he doesn't leave, he's going to get skewered with a dragonlance."

"I don't believe that would be a good idea," said Destina, alarmed. She tried to think of some way to distract him. "I was hoping you would show me the map you found last night. The one before the Cataclysm."

Tas happily rummaged around in the map tub and pulled out a map. He spread it on the table, and since it had a strong propensity to roll back up, he anchored it at the corners with an empty tarbean tea mug, a salt cellar, and two pewter candlesticks.

"Have you seen any of the others today?" Destina asked.

"I saw Raistlin and Magius go up to the battlements," said Tas. "Sturm and Huma walked across the bridge to the tower. First I thought I would go with Raistlin and Magius, especially if they were going to work some magic, so I started up the stairs to the battlements, but then I thought it would be more fun to go with Huma and Sturm and so I started to go to the tower. But by that time I was hungry again so I went to the kitchen."

"My father had old maps like this," said Destina, bending over it.

"It was drawn before the gods dropped the fiery mountain on Krynn and smashed it to smithereens. Do you know what a smithereen is? I've often wondered. I thought they might be people who lived in Smitherea, so I looked for it, but it's not on the map. The most interesting part of this map is Qualinesti. You can see before the Cataclysm it is right here next to Solamnia. No wonder Gwyneth is worried about the dragon attacking her people. And look at this!"

He pointed excitedly to a dot labeled *Gnomes.*

"That's likely the village Uncle Trapspringer visited when he helped the gnomes forge the dragonlances. I would really like to see it."

"Keep your voice down!" Destina warned. "We're not supposed to talk about dragonlances. It just says 'Gnomes.' Doesn't the village have a name?"

"Mapmakers don't put the gnome names on maps because the names are so long it would take up the entire map and likely spill over onto the back," Tas explained. "Most gnomes live in Mount Nevermind, which is over here to the west, but there are gnomes all over the world. They spread out when the gnomes went to Gargath Castle and knocked it down and went chasing after the—" Tas sneezed. "Drat! I thought I was over that!"

Tas looked up from his map as Magius and Raistlin entered the room. "Hullo, Magius! Hullo, Raistlin! Would you like to look at this interesting map?"

"Actually, we came looking for you, Master Burrfoot," said Magius.

"Are you sure?" Tas asked, dubious. "Because no one ever looks for me. Except for that one time when the Seekers thought I had stolen that golden statue of Belzor. I hadn't stolen it, you know. I think Belzor must have jumped into my pouch when I wasn't looking. I told them that, but they didn't believe me. They said the statue couldn't jump. I pointed out that if they thought Belzor was a god he could do anything he wanted, like jump into my pouch. But I guess they didn't have that much faith in him because they were going to lock me up—"

Magius looked around. "Where is the commander?"

"He was in his office the last I saw him," said Destina.

"Good. I want to hear some of the kender's stories and I don't want to be interrupted."

"Which story?" Tas asked eagerly. "Do you want to hear about the time I went to the Abyss to see Queen Takhisis and was chased by an angry demon? Or the time I put on a ring and accidentally turned into a mouse? Or how I found a woolly mammoth?"

"I want to hear your story about the dragon orb. How did you use it to defeat the evil dragons in the High Clerist's Tower?"

Destina cast a startled glance at Raistlin.

"Magius knows the truth," Raistlin told her. "He has promised to help me find the Device."

Destina wondered why, then, they were talking about dragon orbs. She didn't like to ask, however. And Tas, apparently, didn't want to answer.

He was sitting in silence, staring down at the map.

"You can tell him, Tas," Raistlin urged. "I won't turn you into a cricket."

"I'd rather be turned into a cricket," said Tas in a small voice. "I think you all should leave now. I'm busy saving the song."

He removed the mug and the candlesticks and the salt cellar from the map and began to vigorously roll it up.

"Please, Master Burrfoot," said Magius. "I would like to hear it."

Tas paused in the act of rolling up the map. "I'll tell you about the time I was a mouse. There was this wizard named Par-Salian. Raistlin knows him. Knew him. Will know him. Anyway—"

"I want to hear about the dragon orb," Magius said.

"I'll tell you about the time I smashed a dragon orb," Tas offered.

"You smashed a dragon orb?" Magius said, appalled. "Is this true? Why did you do such a terrible thing?"

"All these people—elves and humans—were arguing over this dragon orb they had found and I thought they were going to kill each other when we were supposed to be on the same side to fight the Dark Queen, so I picked it up and smashed it. And I wish I had smashed the one I found in the High Clerist's Tower!"

Tas dropped the map to the floor and plunked down in a chair. He gave a doleful sigh. "I know what Laurana and I did was good because we used the dragon orb to kill the Dark Queen's dragons who were going to kill us. But it was horrible with all the blood and the dragons screaming when the knights stabbed them to death. And then part of the tower collapsed and Laurana and I were nearly killed and Sturm *was* killed. . . ."

Tas was so upset he took the salt cellar out of his pouch and put it back on the table.

"Why did part of the tower collapse?" Magius asked.

"The dragons in the traps were flailing about and hitting the walls and the tower started to come apart," Tas explained.

"Traps?" Magius was puzzled. "What traps?"

"The dragon traps in the High Clerist's Tower," said Tas.

Magius frowned and glanced at Raistlin. "Is he telling the truth?"

"He is," Destina answered. "The Battle of the High Clerist's Tower is famous."

"Will be famous," Tas corrected. "It hasn't happened yet."

Magius shook his head. "I have been to every part of the tower and I have never seen a dragon trap. Will you show them to me?"

"No," said Tas. "I'm sorry, Magius. I don't like to disappoint you, because you did magic me here and you let me help cast the spell, which was a truly wonderful experience, but I can't ever go back into that horrible place where the dragons died. I'm not afraid. It's the memories. They make me feel sick inside."

Magius could see the kender was truly distressed, and he laid his hand gently on Tas's shoulder.

"I have unhappy memories of my own that I don't like to think about. I am truly sorry to have to ask you to remember what must have been a terrible experience, but the red dragon is going to attack us, and we need to know how to defeat him. Our lives depend on you. You will be a hero."

"I will?" Tas looked up at him, his eyes wide. "You mean I might be in a song? It would be called the *Song of Tasslehoff*?"

"I am certain the bards will sing of you," said Magius, hiding his smile.

"Then I guess I'll show you the dragon traps," said Tas heroically.

"Lead the way, Master Burrfoot," said Magius.

"You can call me Tas," said Tas. "Everybody does. Will you come with me, Destina?"

"Of course I will," she replied.

Tas picked up his hoopak, dropped one of the candlesticks in his pouch, and slowly walked off in the direction of the tower, his footsteps dragging. Magius accompanied him, staying at his side to make certain he didn't take a detour.

Raistlin fell into step alongside Destina, the two of them following behind.

"Why did you tell Magius the truth?" she asked.

"I had little choice," Raistlin replied. "He had already guessed much of it from listening to Tas."

"But isn't that dangerous? Does he know what will happen at this battle?"

"Do you take me for a fool?" Raistlin snapped. "I told him nothing about the future. Besides, none of us know for certain *what* will happen at the battle, do we, Lady? Given that Chaos has entered the picture."

Raistlin pulled his cowl over his head and thrust his hands into the sleeves of his robes. Destina clasped her hand around the Graygem and quickened her pace to walk alongside Tas, keeping her distance from Raistlin.

Tasslehoff led them across the bridge to the High Clerist's Tower. The halls were dark and deserted, just as they had been the night they arrived, and Magius spoke the magical word "*Shirak.*" The crystal on his staff blazed.

"Are you sure you want light?" Tas asked. "Wouldn't you rather see the traps in the dark?"

"No," said Magius.

Tas sighed. "The dragon traps are on the first floor. I guess you never noticed them because they don't look like traps. They look like walls with teeth. The traps are located right inside the front entrance, close to where you magicked us."

"Noble's Gate," said Magius.

"Do you remember the stairs we saw?" Tas continued. "If we had climbed up those stairs instead of going down the corridor, we would have walked right into the traps."

Tas stopped and pointed. "We go up these steps and through those doors."

"Wait a minute, kender," said Magius, holding the staff so that the light shone directly in Tas's eyes. "Are you telling me that these dragon death traps are through that door?"

Tas squinted in the bright light. "That's what I meant to say. Did the words come out wrong?"

"Stop playing games!" Magius said coldly. "Do you think this is a matter for jest? There are no dragon death traps or any other sort of trap on this level! You have been lying to us all this time."

"I don't lie!" said Tas indignantly. "Tika says lying is as bad as stealing. Tell him I'm telling the truth, Destina!"

"He is telling the truth, sir," Destina replied. "I was not present, but I have heard the accounts, and Raistlin can verify it, as can Sturm. The magic of the dragon orb lured the dragons into the death traps where the knights killed them."

Magius was grim. "I do not know what is going on but see for yourselves."

He led them up the three wide marble stairs to a hall with white marble walls. Two large ironwood doors banded in iron stood at the end of the hall. The golden emblem of the kingfisher was emblazoned on each door. Marble statues of knights flanked the doors as they had other places in the High Clerist's Tower. But unlike the others, these knights were not armed. Their marble hands were folded in prayer.

"But this is all wrong!" Tas gasped, his shrill voice echoing eerily through the chamber. "This door wasn't here! This was a portcullis that came down, smash, on the dragon's head. And this wall had sharp points like teeth so that the dragons couldn't turn around or back out. They could only thrash and scream as the knights killed them, and the floor was a river of blood and the walls shook and . . . and . . ."

Tas sobbed and hid his face in his hands. His slender shoulders heaved.

"Leave him alone!" Destina told Magius angrily, putting her arm around Tas. "He is telling the truth!"

Magius was mystified. "He certainly sounds as though he is, and you confirm it. But that cannot be."

He walked up to the double doors and gave them a push. The doors swung open silently on well-oiled hinges. Magius entered and raised the staff. The others followed and stared around in astonishment.

They stood beneath a vast rotunda. A domed ceiling, supported by slender marble columns, glittered with crystalline stars that sparkled in the magical light of the staff. Wooden pews were arranged in successive rows leading down to four altars that were lighted by candles.

The faint perfume of roses carried with it a sense of peace and tranquility.

"As you see, this is not a hall of death," said Magius. "This is a hall of life. The sacred Temple of the High Clerist."

CHAPTER
THIRTEEN

A hushed and reverent silence enveloped them as Destina and the others entered the temple. Words were carved in Solamnic above the entrance and Destina read them aloud.

The love and understanding of the gods enfolds you in a comforting embrace. Know that whatever mistakes you made, the gods love you and forgive you.

Destina felt the tumult in her soul ease, as if loving arms enveloped her, blessed and cherished her. The gods were with her, embracing and enfolding her, forgiving her, understanding her.

"The Temple of the High Clerist is dedicated to the patron gods of the Knights of Solamnia: Paladine, Kiri-Jolith, and Habakkuk, and the goddess Mishakal," Magius was saying. "You see the statues at the far end of the temple? Paladine stands in the center in the form of a platinum dragon with outstretched wings, either attacking or protecting. The flames of the four candles burning on his altar never die and never need replenishing.

"To his left, his consort, Mishakal, is portrayed as a woman holding a child in her arms, for she is the goddess of healing and the protector of children. Pilgrims often leave gifts of toys on her altar, which the priests distribute to the poor.

"Kiri-Jolith stands on Paladine's right. The god is represented as a bison, strong and powerful, the god of unity and honorable warfare. His twin brother, Habakkuk, is on Mishakal's left. His statue is a phoenix rising from the flames, newborn. He represents the promise of the spirit rising from death to embark on a new journey."

He glanced at Raistlin. "The god of magic Solinari is *not* represented in this temple, despite the fact that he is brother to Kiri-Jolith and Habakkuk."

"Not surprising," said Raistlin.

Tas was wandering around the pews, tapping on the floor with his hoopak and staring up at the ceiling. He came back to them, scratching his head.

"This is all very strange. I swear on my topknot that when I was here with Laurana, there were only walls with teeth!"

The kender's voice echoed among the stars. Two figures they had not previously noticed were standing at the altar of Kiri-Jolith and turned to look at them. The light of the candle shone on their armor, and Raistlin recognized Huma and Sturm.

Huma said something to Sturm, who turned and came forward to greet them. Huma remained standing at the altar, his head bowed.

"Magius, Huma would like you to join him at the altar," Sturm said as he approached.

"I don't suppose he plans to address my complaint about Solinari," said Magius.

"I don't believe so," said Sturm.

"A pity," said Magius, and he walked down the aisle to join his friend.

Sturm waited until Magius had moved out of earshot before speaking. "I heard what Tas said. He is right. When I was here, this chamber was a death trap, not a temple!"

"You see?" said Tas. "I was telling the truth! I don't think Magius believed me."

"Magius knows the truth?" Sturm asked, frowning.

"As much of it as he needs to know," said Raistlin. "I told you I would have to tell him."

Sturm shook his head and continued to gaze around the temple. "Why do you suppose the knights would tear down such a beautiful temple and replace it with death traps?"

"Perhaps the dragon's attack at Westgate Pass had something to do with it," said Raistlin. "The knights had learned that the gods could not protect them from dragons, and they had much better rely on death traps."

Sturm started to chastise Raistlin for speaking sacrilege, but he was interrupted by the arrival of Commander Belgrave and Will. The commander stopped. He seemed surprised to see them.

"Hullo, Commander!" Tas said, extending his hand.

Titus grunted at him and put his hand on the hilt of his sword. His expression was grim. "You're all here. Good. I need to speak to the lot of you."

He glanced at the altar where Huma and Magius were in conversation. "I do not like to interrupt their prayers, but this is a matter of urgency."

"You do not disturb us, Commander," said Huma, ascending the series of stairs that led to where they were standing. "How may we assist you?"

"Come outside," said Titus. "I see no need to trouble the gods with this matter."

Titus had entered through Knight's Gate, which led from the fortress into the temple. He led them out the front entrance, Noble's Gate, and into a courtyard surrounded by the half-completed curtain wall covered in scaffolding. The day was cool and overcast. Gray clouds shrouded the top of the High Clerist's Tower.

Titus turned his grim gaze on Magius and Raistlin.

"Will tells me that according to the jailer, you two spoke to the spy we captured, despite the fact that I explicitly ordered you not to do so. The prisoner complained that you mistreated him."

"We merely asked him a question or two," said Magius. "He answered quite readily, which I found rather disappointing. I had been looking forward to gouging out his eyes with a red-hot poker."

"He's jesting," said Huma.

Titus was not amused. "Did either of you wizards speak to the elf woman?"

"I did not," said Magius. "Although now I wish I had since it so clearly annoys you."

"I treated her wound," said Raistlin. "Naturally I asked how she was feeling. I trust that is not against the Measure."

Tasslehoff waved his hand. "I went to the dungeon to see Gwyneth. I had to ask her about the song because it's not going the way it's supposed to go. I told her how to fix it."

"Indeed. What did you tell her, kender?" Titus asked.

"You can call me Tas," said Tas. "Everyone does. The knights need weapons to fight the Dark Queen and I told Gwyneth they could find them in the gnome village where Uncle Trapspringer and the gnomes are forging the magical dragonlances. I told her she needs to go pick them up."

"I also visited her. Why are we being interrogated like common criminals, Commander?" Huma asked, growing angry.

Titus rubbed his jaw. "The elf woman has escaped. She is gone. I went down to release her and found the jailer locked in her cell."

"Escaped?" Huma repeated, disbelieving. "But that is not possible! How could she?"

"The commander suspects one of us helped her," said Magius.

"Is that true, Commander?" Huma asked.

"I do not think she grew wings and flew out," said Titus dryly.

"Gwyneth wouldn't need to grow wings, because she already has them," Tas offered helpfully.

Titus cast him a baleful look and shook his head.

"I went to visit her, Commander," Huma stated. "I opened her cell and went inside to make certain she was all right. The jailer locked me in. Gwyneth and I spoke . . . for a long time. She was there when I left."

Huma paused. "And now, you say, she is gone."

Titus studied him intently. Huma was clearly upset. Magius saw his friend's distress and drew Titus's attention to himself.

"If you doubt him, Commander, you can confirm his story with the jailer or the other prisoner."

"Sir Huma's word is all the assurance I need," said Titus. "But someone must have helped the elf escape."

"Gwyneth wouldn't need any help," said Tas, glad to be of assistance. "She's a silver dragon, which means she could fly away."

"I am sorry, Lady Destina," said Titus. "I gave your kender a chance, but he is the only one who could have released her. Take him to the dungeon, Will, and tell the jailer to keep watch on him."

"You can't lock him up! You have no reason. Tas is telling the truth!" Destina protested.

"That the woman is a silver dragon?" Titus snorted.

"What I meant, sir, is that Tas is telling the truth about not setting her free," said Destina stubbornly. "There must be another explanation."

"My decision stands," said Titus.

He bowed to her and walked off, heading west, back in the direction of the fortress. Will dragged Tas away, still protesting his innocence.

Magius rested his hand on Huma's arm. "I am sorry, my friend."

"I cannot believe Gwyneth fled," said Huma, anguished. "Perhaps it is my fault. Perhaps I said or did something that frightened her. I'm going to go speak to the jailer. Find out what he knows."

Huma hurried off to catch up with Will and Tasslehoff. Magius stood leaning on his staff, thoughtfully gazing after his friend.

"He is in pain, but perhaps it is for the best. There can be no future for a romance between a human and an elf. Can there? You are from the future. Perhaps you can enlighten me?"

Sturm looked grave. Destina touched the pewter fastening on her collar, then let her hand drop.

"You know we cannot," said Raistlin.

"Well, I tried," said Magius, smiling. "When should we leave for the tower, Brother? I must collect my spell components, but I will be ready after that."

"I have to talk to my friends, then gather my own spell components," said Raistlin.

"Meet me in my room when you are ready. I will wait for you there."

Magius crossed the courtyard, walking swiftly, his staff tapping on the paving stones.

"Tas doesn't belong in a cell," said Destina. "He is telling the truth!"

"Quite the irony, since it's probably one of the few times in his life he's ever done so," said Raistlin. "Leave him be, Lady. A dungeon is the best place for Tasslehoff. We know where he is, at least until the novelty of being locked up wears off. Hopefully I will have returned by then. I am traveling to Palanthas with Magius to obtain the Device."

"The city is in the hands of the minotaurs," Sturm pointed out. "You and Magius are both taking a great risk."

"We will be safe enough," Raistlin assured him. "Magical portals will take us directly to the tower. The moment I have the Device, I will return, so be prepared to depart, perhaps within the hour."

"But what do we tell Huma and Commander Belgrave?" Sturm asked. "We cannot simply disappear. That might cause further harm!"

"We will tell them the truth for a change," said Raistlin. "We are going home."

CHAPTER
FOURTEEN

Magius and Raistlin returned to their rooms in the High Clerist's Tower to collect spell components and other equipment they would need on their journey.

"Where should we cast the portal spell?" Raistlin asked. "We need someplace where we won't be disturbed."

"I was thinking we could use the library," said Magius. "When Huma and I visited the tower, I would go to there to study my spell-books. I can guarantee we won't be disturbed. It is located on the fourteenth floor."

"Fourteenth!" Raistlin repeated, aghast, thinking of the long climb.

Magius laughed. "You don't think I'm going to climb fourteen flights of stairs, do you? I am far too lazy. Take hold of my staff. It will carry us both."

As Raistlin grasped the staff, Magius spoke the word "*Bankat.*" At the command, the staff lifted them off the ground. They floated up the stairwell with as much ease as if they'd been made of smoke.

Raistlin sighed deeply. He had known that the staff would allow him to fall as lightly as a feather, but he had not known it could give him the power to fly. He wished to the gods that there was some way he could impart this knowledge to his future self. But if they escaped without having altered time, when he returned to the Raistlin in the Inn of the Last Home that autumn evening, he would have no memory of this encounter.

Arriving at the fourteenth level, Magius spoke to the staff— "*Aki*"—and they settled lightly to the floor. They arrived in pitch darkness and eerie silence. Magius lit the crystal on the staff.

"The tower's upper floors are considerably smaller than those below," said Magius, shining the light around. "This floor has only a few rooms, but, as you can see, they are sumptuous. The high-ranking priests lived on this level, including the High Clerist. They have their own private dining hall and bedchambers. The library is this way."

They entered a small rotunda adorned with a fresco that featured a knight flanked by two kingfishers flying through the heavens. The knight held the sun in his hands, shedding light on Solamnia, represented by a map done in mosaic tiles on the floor.

As Raistlin started to walk across it, Magius suddenly stopped him. "Look at the map!"

The tiles that formed the map were black, save for a patch of shining silver located in the center. Magius tapped the silver tiles with his staff.

"The High Clerist's Tower," said Magius. "This map was blessed by Kiri-Jolith. I have heard it said that in time of war, the god would reveal the positions of enemy forces. According to this, the dark tiles represent the Dark Queen. As you see, her forces occupy all of Solamnia except for this patch of ground. And we cannot withstand her might."

He glanced at Raistlin. "You are right. You and your friends need to leave."

The door to the library stood open. The room was semicircular, following the curve of the wall. Sunlight shone through mullioned windows on the north side. The library smelled pleasantly of leather and vellum. Bookshelves stood along the walls, extending from the floor to the ceiling. Students could sit at tables or at ink-spattered desks furnished with round holes to accommodate inkwells. Those who simply wanted to lose themselves in a book could relax in comfortable leather chairs.

Raistlin closed the door and cast a locking spell on it, while Magius shoved the furniture to one side to provide a bare space on one of the walls. The level was deserted but, as one does instinctively in a library, the two spoke softly.

"I always loved this place," said Magius, looking around with pleasure. "I felt at home here, amidst the books and silence."

The staff's light illuminated row after row of books bound in different colors of leather or cloth; some stamped with gold leaf, others simply plain.

"The knights encouraged everyone who lived and worked in the tower to use the library to improve their knowledge," said Magius. "The head librarian kept all neat and orderly. He knew every single volume and where it belonged—and the gods help you if you put a book back on the wrong shelf."

Magius sighed. "I do not like to think what will happen to the library if the tower falls. The Dark Queen prefers her subjects to live in ignorance. Knowledge is her foe."

"Time is also our foe," Raistlin said, ignoring Magius's attempt to gain information. "We should proceed with the spellcasting."

Magius smiled and removed an ornate key from a fob he wore on his belt. He held it to the light.

"What is the key for?" Raistlin asked curiously. "I never knew a key to be part of the portal spell."

"One could say this is the key to the front door of the Tower of High Sorcery in Palanthas," Magius replied. "The previous master gave keys to all of us who passed the Test. She encouraged us to return to the tower to study or simply spend time in the company of our fellow mages. Sadly, she died shortly after that.

"The current master—a White Robe named Snagsby—ended the policy. He gave keys only to members of the Conclave—one of the many little favors he did for them so they would elect him master. I have to give him credit," Magius added with a curl of his lip. "Snagsby is a skilled politician, even if he is a mediocre mage. Since I was not a member of the Conclave—nor do I ever want to be— Snagsby ordered me to return my key. When I refused to relinquish it, he forbade me from entering the tower without his permission. I told him in quite graphic detail what he could do with his permission, then I left. I haven't been back since."

"And how do we persuade this man who loathes you to give us a dragon orb *and* the Device of Time Journeying?" Raistlin asked, alarmed. "Do you have a plan?"

"I have something better than a plan," said Magius serenely. "I have luck."

He placed the key in the palm of his left hand, passed his right hand over it as he whispered words of magic beneath his breath. A portal opened like a window in the wall, permitting them to see inside an unfurnished chamber; austere, but elegant, with a floor formed of red, black, and white marble tiles.

"The entry foyer," said Magius, pleased. "You said you lived in this tower. Do you recognize it?"

Raistlin shook his head. "I lived in the tower years after a Black Robe wizard cursed it and then leaped off the top and impaled himself on the sharp finials of the iron fence below. His blood transformed the tower from the most beautiful of the five Towers of High Sorcery to the most hideous."

"Why would the man do such a mad thing?" Magius asked, shocked.

"A long story," said Raistlin. "I look forward to seeing the tower as it once was."

"I will enter first and hold the portal open for you. Be quick!"

As he started to take a step inside the portal, it slammed shut and disappeared, causing him to walk headlong into the wall. Magius rubbed his nose and swore. "Damn Snagsby to the Abyss and back!"

"What happened?" Raistlin asked. "Did the spell fail?"

"The fool Snagsby has sealed the portals shut!" said Magius. "Now no one can enter. I should have known the cowardly wretch would do something inane like this!"

"How do we get inside?" Raistlin asked in dismay.

"The old-fashioned way," Magius said grimly. "We must walk."

"But that means we will have to travel to an enemy-occupied city. And if we escape being captured by minotaurs, we must pass through the dread Shoikan Grove," Raistlin said.

"Not the most pleasant experience, but we have no choice if we want to obtain our objectives," Magius said. "Do not worry. The grove will let us pass."

"The grove will let *you* pass," Raistlin said grimly. "I have taken the Test, but I did so in my past, which is in the future and thus has not yet happened."

"An interesting point," said Magius. "Consider this: Lunitari knows you are here in this time. She must know, for she has granted you the ability to cast spells. In her eyes, you have passed the Test."

"True," said Raistlin, musing. "I had not thought of that."

"Since you have the sanction of the goddess, the grove should allow you to enter," Magius concluded.

"And if not, the grove will kill me," Raistlin said.

"The master will return your effects to your loved ones," Magius said in soothing tones. "He will even neatly fold your robes and cleanse out the blood."

Raistlin could not help but smile. "So how do we proceed? A journeying spell?"

"I think that would be the best," Magius agreed. "It won't take us into the grove, for its magic would block my magic. But I am familiar with a tavern that is not far from the tower. The tavern is is called the Night of the Rye. Clever, don't you think?"

Raistlin nodded, appreciating the word play on the Night of the Eye: the night when all three moons come together to form an eye in the heavens. Magic was most powerful on such nights.

"As you can guess by the name, the tavern used to be frequented by magic-users," Magius continued, using the staff to draw a circle in the dust on the floor. "It has now probably been taken over by minotaurs, but the alley across the street is generally deserted. Still, we should be prepared to make a run for it in case any minotaurs see us."

"Should I put my hands in my pockets?" Raistlin asked, stepping inside the circle.

Magius laughed and joined him. Composing himself, he spoke softly to the goddess.

"Lunitari, the times are dark, but I hope you can hear us and see us and grant us your blessing." Magius spoke the words to the spell. *"Triga bulan ber satuan/Seluran asil/Tempat samah terus-menarus/ Walktun jalanil!"*

The hand of the goddess whisked them over mountains, across the plains, and gently set them down in a rubbish-choked alley. The sun was shining brightly in the sky but the surrounding buildings cut off the light, leaving the alley in shadow. Magius and Raistlin stood frozen, not daring to move until they could take in their surroundings. They waited tensely for someone to yell or gasp or scream at the sight of two mages appearing out of nowhere. When no one did, they relaxed. The alley was deserted, except for the rats scavenging. among heaps of refuse.

"That is the tavern," said Magius, pointing.

They had a good view, for the tavern was directly opposite the alley on the other side of the street. The tavern seemed a welcoming place with ivy-covered walls, a thatched roof, and lead-paned windows. A garishly painted sign hanging over the entrance read *Night of the Rye* and featured the three moons forming a staring eye. The sign painter had added a sheaf of rye in the center of the black pupil, just in case anyone missed the pun.

The tavern was typical of neighborhood drinking establishments, where friends would gather every night to imbibe ale and share the news. But as they had feared, the only ones currently imbibing ale and sharing the news were the enemy.

Minotaurs had the heads of bulls and the lower bodies of humans. They stood twelve feet tall, with massive shoulders, chests, arms, and torsos. They were the favorite race of the god Sargonnas, consort of the Dark Queen, who loved them so much he chose a minotaur as his avatar.

They could hear raucous shouts and bellows coming from inside the tavern. A gigantic fist smashed through one of the windowpanes, and the next moment, the tavern door burst open and minotaurs flooded the street, waving mugs of ale, shouting and jeering.

Raistlin and Magius were close to the tower. Raistlin could see the trees of the grove and the tower rising above them. Their destination was only about a block away, but between them and the tower, the street was filled with drunken minotaurs.

"I wonder what all the bellowing is about," Raistlin said. "Perhaps they are leaving."

"Sadly, no. They are about to engage in some sort of contest," Magius answered. "And it looks as if we are going to have a front-row seat."

The minotaurs began forming a circle around two brutes who

were snarling and growling at each other. A third minotaur entered the ring and appeared to be laying down rules for the contest, ordering the combatants to remove the long, curved-bladed cutlasses both wore on their harnesses. He then pointed to their horns and scowled and shook his head.

"They're not being allowed to fight with weapons or use their horns," Magius explained in a low voice. "Minotaurs observe a strict code of honor. If they believe they have been insulted, they have the right to challenge their foe to a fight to avenge their honor. They are in many ways like the knights. They even worship Kiri-Jolith, as we do, and they honor the knights of Solamnia. They won't hesitate to kill a knight if they encounter one, but they will give him a chance to fight for his life. Which is more than they will do to any other human."

"Such as us," said Raistlin. "You know a lot about minotaurs."

"I encountered one in my Test," Magius replied. "Since then, I have made a study of them."

He said nothing more. Raistlin wondered suddenly if Huma had been part of Magius's Test, as Caramon had been part of his.

The two minotaurs clenched their fists and started circling each other, throwing jabs and feints, jeering and stomping their feet. The other minotaurs yelled encouragement and began placing bets. Silver coins flashed in the sunlight.

The combatants started pummeling each other, grappling with their arms and slugging each other in the snout. A single blow from the massive fists looked as though it could have knocked down a small building, but neither appeared to be suffering much damage.

The fight was, unfortunately, attracting attention. Word spread, and minotaurs began converging on the scene to witness it.

"We can't stay here," said Raistlin. "If one of them sees us, they'll stop fighting each other to attack us."

"Perhaps we could get in on the action," said Magius coolly. "I like the chap with the twisted horn." He drew a silver coin from his purse. "Let's go place a bet."

"Are you mad? You are going to get us killed!" Raistlin protested.

"Do you have a spell handy?" Magius asked. "It better be a good one."

Raistlin brought the words of a spell to his mind and recalled the gesture that accompanied it.

"Ready?" Magius asked.

Raistlin nodded.

Gripping his staff, Magius strolled calmly out of the alley. The minotaurs had their backs to him, watching the fight. Magius walked up to one and tapped him on the shoulder. The minotaur looked around.

Magius held up the silver coin. "Put this on the snout of that ugly fellow with the curly horn."

The minotaur blinked at the coin, then gave a roar that caused the other minotaurs to turn their heads.

"Run!" Magius shouted to Raistlin. "Make for the grove!"

Raistlin hiked up his robes and dashed down the street. He ran as fast as he could, for he guessed what was coming. When he deemed he was far enough away, he stopped running and turned around, not wanting to miss this sight though it could cost him his life.

Magius raised his staff high in the air, shouting words of magic. Multiple bolts of lightning streaked from the crystal ball, striking the minotaur, who howled and bellowed in pain. The air was redolent with the rank smell of burnt fur.

His spell cast, Magius broke into a run with several outraged minotaurs in hot pursuit.

"Your turn!" he shouted.

Raistlin readied his spell. The magic filled his mind and body, tingled in his blood. As Magius dashed past him, Raistlin shouted the words and spread his fingers.

"Kalith karan, tobaniskar!"

Flaming darts shot from his fingertips and blazed toward the minotaurs. He did not wait to see the results but turned and ran. Hearing shrieking, he assumed that at least some of the darts had hit their target.

He dashed after Magius, who glanced at him over his shoulder and grinned.

"Having fun?" he shouted.

Raistlin didn't have the breath to answer, but he realized he was having fun. He couldn't believe he was enjoying this madcap adventure, even as he ran for his life with a host of furious minotaurs chasing after him.

The dark shadows of the trees of the cursed Shoikan Grove loomed in front of them. Magius bolted into the grove and Raistlin plunged after, whispering a hasty prayer to Lunitari. He had taken only a few steps when thick and noisome darkness half blinded him and the first sickening wave of fear washed over him. Raistlin stumbled and nearly fell. Recalling the skeletal hands that would reach up from the ground to grab interlopers and drag them to their doom, he clutched desperately at a tree to keep from falling. A limb of the tree snaked down and tried to seize hold of him.

Raistlin snatched back his hand. The light of the crystal on the staff still burned defiantly. He staggered toward it and saw Magius crouched on his hands and knees.

"Once the grove recognizes us, the fear will pass," he said in a tight voice.

Either that, or I'll die of it! Raistlin thought.

The fear had hold of him, wringing every drop of courage from his heart. He could almost wish for death. Suddenly, thankfully, the grove eased its grip. He sagged to his knees, closed his eyes, and drew in deep gulps of air.

Magius rose and helped him to his feet. Raistlin managed a weak smile and mopped his face with his sleeve.

"Are the minotaurs still chasing us?" he gasped.

"They are standing on the outskirts of the grove. Let's watch. This should be entertaining," Magius remarked. He spoke lightly, but he was clearly still shaken.

The minotaurs knew the grove's evil reputation, and they were apparently debating what to do. Most shook their horned heads, shrugged, and walked off. Three remained, glowering at the forest and motioning, perhaps trying to goad one another into entering. At last one of them—either bolder or drunker than the others—drew his cutlass and strode into the shadows.

He had gone only a few feet when a tree branch swooped down and struck him on the head. The minotaur snarled in rage and struck back at the trunk of the tree, slashing it with his cutlass.

"Ah, that was a mistake," said Magius.

A massive limb dropped from the tree and landed with crushing force on top of the minotaur, completely burying him in leaves and branches. Figuring that was the end of their pursuer, Raistlin and Magius were about to turn away when they saw the minotaur crawl out from under the debris. He had lost a horn and was covered in blood, but he managed to limp back to his fellows before he collapsed. They picked him up and dragged him off. No other minotaurs dared enter the grove after that.

Raistlin and Magius ventured deeper into the forest. The tangle of branches and leaves blotted out the sunlight, turning day to ghastly night. They lost sight of the tower and had no idea where they were going. The air was foul and stank of blood and rotting leaves. Even the magical light of the staff grew weak and feeble, as though it were suffocating. They could see only a foot or so ahead of them. A tree root suddenly snaked out and tried to wrap itself around Magius's ankle.

"Stop it, damn you!" Magius cried. "We belong here!"

He struck his staff on the root and it released its grip. The grove relented. The branches of the twisted oak trees parted. The sun shone down on a gated fence made of twined silver and gold. The gate swung open and they could see the tower beyond: a large minaret flanked by two smaller ones. The walls of the three minarets were made of white marble striated with red. The spires at the tops were black marble.

The tower had been hideous to look upon when Raistlin had entered the gates. The sun had not shone on him, but then he had welcomed the darkness, embraced it. As he gazed up at the glistening white walls, he wondered if some part of him would remember this moment of sunlight when he next walked his dark path.

They came to an immense door made of ironwood. The door had no handle and no keyhole. The ironwood was covered in powerful, deadly warding runes, visible only to those who had the gift of magic. The symbols for the three moons were carved in the center: a white circle for Solinari, a red circle for Lunitari, and a dark circle for Nuitari.

Magius placed his hand, palm flat, against the symbol of Lunitari.

"I am Magius. I ask permission of the blessed goddess Lunitari to enter."

Raistlin approached the door. He had served all three gods during his lifetime, but he had felt closest to Lunitari. He placed his palm on the symbol of the red moon.

"I am Raistlin Majere. I ask permission of the blessed goddess Lunitari to enter."

The runes on the door flashed with blinding red light. The door opened, swinging silently inward.

Raistlin reflected that the last time he had entered as master.

This time, he was nobody.

CHAPTER
FIFTEEN

The tower's foyer was small, austere, and dark. Magius held up the staff, and its light shone on the floor made of blocks of white, red, and black marble with the symbol of the Eye emblazoned in gold. A spiral staircase led to the upper chambers. They heard the distant chiming of a bell announce their arrival.

"We are not permitted to advance farther without an escort," said Magius. "We must wait until an apprentice comes to fetch us."

They soon heard the footfalls of someone running down the stairs. A breathless and frightened-looking mage crouched at the end of the hall.

"Stop where you are!" The mage was holding a wand made of crystal, aimed directly at them. "Who are you and what do you want?"

Raistlin had no idea what the wand did, but he was not taking chances. He raised his hands, palms open, to show he was not a threat. Magius regarded the mage with disgust.

"Rodolfo, it's me, Magius! What do you mean by pointing that wand at me? You could blow my head off!"

Rodolfo stared at Magius intently, then lowered the wand, though he continued to regard them with suspicion.

"I am sorry I did not immediately recognize you, Magius, but it has been ten years," said Rodolfo stiffly. "We have all been on edge since the minotaurs arrived. Who is your companion?"

"Raistlin Majere, escort to the daughter of a knight who was forced to flee her home by the Dark Queen's armies."

"I am sorry for your lady, Brother," said Rodolfo curtly, "but many of us share a similar fate these days. Why have you come here, Magius? If you are seeking a safe haven, you will not find it here. The tower is under siege."

Magius stared at him in disbelief. "Under siege? Who is besieging you? We just saw the grove drop a tree branch the size of a house on a minotaur. They won't come near this place so long as the master remains here to defend it."

"I ask again, what do you want?" Rodolfo said, glowering.

"We need to speak to Snagsby," said Magius. "The matter is extremely urgent."

"*Master* Snagsby is not receiving visitors," said Rodolfo.

"I guessed as much when I tried to travel through the portals only to find he had closed them," said Magius.

"Then you should have taken the hint and stayed away. As it is, you have wasted your time. I bid you a safe journey home."

Rodolfo turned on his heel and started back toward the stairs. Magius pointed to the Eye on the floor, stepped on it, and motioned for Raistlin to join him. Magius tapped on the Eye with the staff, and the next instant Raistlin found himself standing alongside Magius in the center of a large and elegantly appointed chamber occupied by several apprentices in white robes, who were bustling about in frenzied activity. Some were draping cloth over the furniture, while others were rolling up the rugs or packing objects into chests, crates, and coffers. Still others were hurriedly pulling books off the shelves and stashing them in wooden crates.

They were so intent on their work that none appeared to take notice of their arrival.

"What in the Abyss is going on?" Magius wondered aloud.

As he and Raistlin watched in perplexity, two apprentices hurried into the room, one carrying what appeared to be a pair of spectacles and the other a cloak.

"I begin to understand. Those are magical artifacts," said Magius in a low voice to Raistlin. "Those two are the Goggles of Foefinding and the Vanisher Cloak."

The two apprentices handed over the artifacts to a third apprentice, who carefully lowered them into a large iron-banded chest. They were followed by a tall man in white robes who began inspecting the chests and criticizing the packing.

"That is Snagsby," said Magius.

At the sound of his voice, one of the apprentices saw them at last. She gave a gasp.

"We have visitors, Master."

Snagsby quickly turned. Raistlin recognized him as one with a politician's face, the sort that could be all things to all people and mean none of them. In this instance, the face was scowling.

"Magius! What are you doing here? You are not welcome."

"Master Snagsby," said Magius in dulcet tones, making a respectful bow. "It has been a long time since we met."

Snagsby was grim. "Not long enough as far as I am concerned. I sealed the portals to keep out visitors. I am far too busy to deal with you or your companion." He glared at Raistlin. "I don't know you. Who are you?"

Raistlin was about to reply when he was interrupted by Rodolfo, who came running into the room, panting for breath. "I am sorry, Master! I tried to stop them!"

"Stay here to escort them out," said Snagsby.

"Yes, Master," said Rodolfo. "This way, Brothers."

"I see you are packing, Master," said Magius, ignoring Rodolfo. "Are you going somewhere?"

"Due to the current crisis, my students and I are moving to the Tower of High Sorcery in Istar," Snagsby replied. "We are taking the most valuable artifacts with us."

"Who is staying to defend the tower?" Magius asked.

"No one," said Snagsby. "Far too dangerous."

"You cannot do this, Master!" said Magius angrily. "If you abandon the tower and leave no one to defend it, Takhisis will seize it!"

"Rodolfo, take these two out and make certain they stay out!" Snagsby whipped around to shout at an apprentice. "Be careful with those crystal gauntlets!"

Magius was breathing hard, holding his temper with difficulty. "Does the Conclave know you are deserting your post?"

"Since you are not a member, that is none of your business," Snagsby said curtly. He strode over to snatch a glass jar from the apprentice. "We don't pack the potions in with the scrolls! They might leak. The potions go in the hamper that is lined with straw. Must I do everything myself?"

Rodolfo plucked at Magius's sleeve.

Magius rounded on him. "Touch me again and I will change you into the toad you are!"

Rodolfo regarded Magius with enmity, but he took a step back.

All this while, Raistlin had been observing the artifacts, hoping he would see the Device of Time Journeying among them. Since the Device could be in pendant form, he kept particular watch on the jewelry, but he could not locate it.

He did notice one of the apprentices gingerly handling a crystal globe and nudged Magius with his elbow to draw his attention to it. Magius stared at it intently.

"That's it," he said softly. "The dragon orb! Do you see the Device?"

Raistlin shook his head.

They watched the apprentice carefully slide the dragon orb into a white velvet bag and gently lower it into a chest. Master Snagsby straightened from his work with the potions. Sighting Magius, he scowled.

"Why are you still here?" he asked sourly.

"We have just come from the High Clerist's Tower, where the knights intend to make a stand against the armies of the Dark Queen. As you must be aware, Master, the knights face a powerful red dragon known as Immolatus and they have no weapons that will stop him. I am here to ask you for the loan of the Orb of Dragonkind to aid us in battle."

Raistlin was watching the apprentice with the velvet bag. She had not been paying much attention to the conversation up to that point, but at the mention of the High Clerist's Tower, she raised her head in shock and concern. She was a young woman, about eighteen, with long, straight, dark hair. Her features reminded him of someone, though he could not imagine who.

"Out of the question," said Snagsby. "We are taking the orb to Istar, where it will be safe."

"The orb was not created to be kept safe," said Magius. "It was created to fight dragons!"

"To help *wizards* fight dragons, not knights," Snagsby stated. "Where were the knights when Palanthas was attacked? Hiding in their tower, that's where they were."

"They were riding to free Palanthas when they were attacked by the red dragon," said Magius in a low voice. His fists clenched. "Many hundreds of knights and refugees died in his flames."

The young apprentice put her hand to her mouth. The color drained from her face and she quickly rose to her feet.

"I can do nothing for you," Snagsby stated coldly. "You have my permission to bring up the matter at the next meeting of the Conclave. I bid you goodbye. Rodolfo, I gave you an order. Escort these gentlemen out."

"I have a question, Master," said Raistlin. "I am searching for the Device of Time Journeying. Do you know where it is?"

"Never heard of it," said Snagsby.

"You must have some knowledge of the Device, Master Snagsby," said Raistlin. "It is a rare and ancient artifact."

"I cannot keep track of all the artifacts on Krynn," said Snagsby snidely.

"I know for a fact you are familiar with the Device of Time Journeying, Master," said Magius. "You showed it to me that last time I was here. You were trying to impress me, then, as I recall, thinking to ingratiate yourself with my wealthy family until you discovered they had disowned me."

"I do not know what you are talking about," said Snagsby brusquely. "As for the Device, if it was here then, it is not here now. I know nothing about it. I am going to my laboratory to pack up my papers. I expect you to be gone when I return."

Snagsby stalked out of the room. Raistlin saw two of the apprentices glance at each other. One was the young woman who had reacted so strongly to their news of the attack at the pass. The other was a young man. They spoke softly together and then both turned to Raistlin.

"I am Anitra and this is Kelly. We know of the Device," the woman said. "The master is right, sir. It is not here. About a year ago, he dispatched it to the tower of Wayreth, saying the master of that tower had need of it. Kelly can tell you, for he carried it."

"Are you certain it was the Device of Time Journeying, sir?" Raistlin asked, tasting the bitterness of despair.

"I am truly sorry, Brother, for I can tell your need is desperate," said Kelly. "But I know for a fact the Device is not here. I carried it to Wayreth myself. Let Solinari be my witness."

"We could travel to Wayreth on the paths of magic," Magius suggested, only to see Anitra shake her head.

"The master of Wayreth has sealed off that tower for fear of attack, as well. You would not be able to enter."

"Besides, the tower can be found only by those the master invites to seek it," Raistlin said. "Otherwise, Wayreth Forest prevents entry."

Rodolfo confronted them. "Since you have no further business here, Magius, you should leave and take your friend with you. If you do not go at once, I will be forced to summon the wraiths."

"Return to your duties, Rodolfo. These brothers do not need an escort," said Anitra. "They know the way, and I could use your advice on where to pack the Goodberry Bracelet."

Rodolfo looked uncertain, clearly not trusting them.

"Please, Rodolfo," said Anitra. "I would not want to put it in the wrong place."

"Mind you don't trip on the stairs and break your neck," Rodolfo said to Magius.

He stalked off, going to inspect the chest. Anitra gave Magius an intense look. "Go," she mouthed, then added, "Trust me!" She turned away and went over to speak to Rodolfo.

Magius gazed after her, pondering, then said loudly, "Let us leave, Brother. There is nothing more we can do here."

He and Raistlin descended the stairs that wound around the tower's central shaft. Their number seemed endless. Magius caused the globe on his staff to shine in the dark stairwell, and they continued the long trek down.

"I am sorry you could not find the Device, Brother," he said.

Raistlin nodded, not trusting himself to speak.

"When the war is ended, we will petition the master on your behalf, obtain an invitation, and travel to Wayreth."

"That could take months or longer," said Raistlin. "It would be too late. Without the Device of Time Journeying, we are trapped here and so is the Graygem. Our very presence has already changed history to some extent. The longer we remain, the greater the odds that the Graygem will do irreparable damage. And what if the worst happens? What if Takhisis finds out the Graygem is here? She would stop at nothing to try to get her hands on it."

"You could take Lady Destina and the Graygem to a place of safety," Magius suggested.

"And what place on Krynn is safe?" Raistlin demanded. "If the High Clerist's Tower falls, Takhisis will rule all of Solamnia, and next, the world."

"I notice you say 'if,' Brother, and not 'when,'" said Magius coolly. "Am I right to assume that the High Clerist Tower will *not* fall? That Solamnia is saved?"

Raistlin cursed himself. He had been so upset he had not paid attention to what he was saying.

"You may assume what you like," Raistlin replied curtly. "Destina wears Chaos around her neck. If the knights held the tower then, they might lose it now. I know this much. Win *or* lose, if Takhisis acquires the Graygem, she will become so powerful that not even the other gods will be able to stop her. We cannot let that happen."

"Then we have one clear objective, Brother," said Magius. "We must prevent the Dark Queen from taking it."

They continued down the stairs in silence, each absorbed in his own dark thoughts, and both were intensely startled to see Anitra materialize on the stairs right in front of them. Raistlin had the words to a spell on his lips and Magius raised the staff.

"I mean no harm!" Anitra said.

Magius sighed in relief. "You scared the wits out of me, Sister! I thought you were one of Snagsby's wraiths."

"I did not mean to startle you," said Anitra, smiling. She held out a white velvet bag. "I wanted to give you the Orb of Dragon-kind. I heard you say you needed it to defend the High Clerist's Tower."

"That is what you meant when you spoke to me!" said Magius. "But I fear you risk a great deal, Sister. The master will be furious."

Anitra shrugged. "He won't realize it's missing until he reaches Istar."

"I am in your debt, Sister," said Magius, accepting the bag.

Anitra regarded him anxiously. "You know that you must first gain control of the orb before you can use it, and that is highly dangerous. The dragon inside the orb will try to seize control of you."

"So I have heard," said Magius. "I am prepared to risk it."

"I admire your courage." Anitra smiled. "Here is a book that contains information you will need regarding the orb."

Raistlin took the book, as Magius opened the velvet bag and peered inside. "I see nothing except a child's marble."

"The orb shrinks to protect itself," Anitra replied. "The book explains. I have to ask you a question, Brother, before you go. You said the knights were riding to retake Palanthas when the red dragon attacked and killed them."

"That is sadly true, Sister. They were escorting hundreds of refugees back to Palanthas when the dragon attacked. As far as we know, there were no survivors."

Anitra tried to speak and had to pause to clear her throat. "Are you aware . . . Was a knight named Titus Belgrave among those who died? I ask because he is my father."

"Commander Belgrave is your father!" Magius repeated, astonished.

"I am Anitra Belgrave. Why? Do you know him? Is he still alive?"

"Very much so," said Magius dryly. "He is now in command of the High Clerist's Tower. My friend and I are war wizards serving with him."

"I am so glad!" Anitra said, relieved. "Although I gather by your expression that my father is making life difficult for you. He does not have much use for wizards."

"That is true," Magius conceded. "I find his distrust strange, considering his own daughter is an apprentice mage."

"Father did not approve my choice of profession, but he respected me enough to allow me to pursue it," said Anitra.

"You should know that your father is concerned about you," said

Raistlin. "The commander mentioned that he had made efforts to find out if the tower and those within it were safe."

Anitra brightened. "Did he? I am glad." She glanced back up the stairs. "And now I must return to my work before the master misses me."

"Please, Sister, do you know anything at all about the Device of Time Journeying?" Raistlin asked desperately. "Is it possible your fellow apprentice is mistaken?"

Anitra shook her head. "I am sorry, Brother, but there can be no doubt."

"And you are certain the master has closed the tower?" Raistlin asked.

"Takhisis threatens the world, Brother," said Anitra gravely. "Not just our small portion of it."

Before she left, she handed each of them a butterfly charm made of silver. "These charms will take you safely through the grove. The master usually provides them to visitors, but he is so upset, he must have forgotten to give them to you."

"I am certain that must be the case," said Magius with a curl of his lip.

Anitra heard the contempt in his voice. "Master Snagsby is not a bad man, only a weak one. And do not fear that Takhisis will seize the Tower of High Sorcery, Brothers. We have not yet told the master, but my fellow apprentices and I do not plan to travel to Istar with him. We will remain to defend the tower."

"I honor your courage, Sister," said Magius, regarding her with admiration. "May the gods of magic fight at your side."

"And may they bless both of you and my father, whether he likes it or not," said Anitra. "Tell him I send my love and that, as he taught me, I will not abandon my duty."

She vanished as swiftly as she had come. Magius stood gazing after her a moment before continuing down the stairs.

"By Lunitari, I would stay and fight with her if I did not have to battle this damned dragon. A handful of apprentice magic-users left to confront the Dark Queen. How do you think they will fare? Few living creatures can brave the terror of the grove, but it will not stop Chemosh and his undead."

"Nuitari is more than a match for Chemosh," Raistlin replied. He knew something of the power of the god of the dark moon, having once served him. "The gods of magic will keep the tower safe as long as they can."

"Takhisis will first concentrate all her efforts on the High Clerist's Tower," said Magius somberly. "But if it falls, then I fear this must fall, too."

Raistlin felt his lungs start to burn. He began coughing and had to lean against the wall to keep from falling. Magius waited with him, observing him with grave concern. As the sound of his coughing echoed through the stairwell, Raistlin thought he saw eyes peering at him out of the darkness. Probably Snagsby's wraiths. At last, the spasm subsided, and he was able to draw a shuddering breath.

"Are you well enough to keep going?" Magius asked worriedly.

"I am as well as I will ever be," said Raistlin, wiping his lips. "Though I admit I am in no hurry to return to my friends. How can I tell them that I have failed to find the Device and we are trapped here to drown in the River of Time?"

They reached the bottom of the stairs. The door opened of its own accord, as though eager to usher them out. They did not have to brave the terrors of the grove, for Anitra's charm magically whisked them through the forest and deposited them safely on the street.

The sun was sliding into the west. The time was late afternoon, and the trees of the grove cast long shadows into the empty street. The citizens of Palanthas would be locked in their houses, afraid of venturing out, and the minotaurs were not likely to come near the grove for a long while. Raistlin and Magius walked the deserted street, keeping to the shadows.

"Wizards lead lonely lives, as you well know," Magius said. "Especially here in Solamnia, where we are regarded with suspicion and distrust. When I first started showing an inclination toward magic, my mother summoned a cleric of Mishakal to 'heal' me. When I saved my money to buy my first spellbook, my father found it and beat me. Huma was the only person who defended me. He fought my battles, but he never truly understood. He asked me before I took the Test how I could risk my life for the magic."

Magius smiled at Raistlin. "All this is my way of saying that I take pleasure in talking with someone who does understand me. This is very selfish of me, Brother, but I am a selfish sort of person. I am glad you will be staying."

Raistlin was pleased and touched. Like Magius, he had never had a friend who knew the warmth of the flame of the gods.

"I was more fortunate growing up," Raistlin said. "When my parents died, my older sister, Kitiara, took over raising us. She realized my twin brother, Caramon, and I would need some way to make a living. She taught Caramon to wield a sword, and she found a wizard who ran a mage school and persuaded him to take me on as a pupil."

"Your sister sounds like an extraordinary person," said Magius.

"She was," said Raistlin. "She ended up serving the Dark Queen."

Magius raised an eyebrow. "What of your brother?"

"Caramon is a good man, honest and true. He loved me better than I deserved. But, as you said, he never understood." Raistlin paused, then added quietly, "I am not certain I wanted him to."

Magius nodded in understanding. They both thrust their hands into the sleeves of their robes and continued on down the street. The tavern, the Night of the Rye, came into sight and they halted in the shadow of a building near the alley to survey the situation.

The contest in the street must have ended, for there were no minotaurs around and a large quantity of blood on the cobblestones. They could hear a raucous party going on inside the tavern, perhaps the victor celebrating.

"I wonder if I won any money?" Magius remarked. "I should step inside to inquire."

"I believe you are just mad enough to do it," said Raistlin.

Magius laughed. "I would if I did not have this dragon orb in my care."

They were about to continue on when they caught sight of a minotaur pounding down the street, coming their direction. For a moment, they feared he was coming after them, but he ran past them without a glance and barreled inside the tavern, nearly taking the door off its hinges. He bellowed an alarm, and the next moment, twenty or more drunken minotaurs bolted from the tavern, pushing and shoving. Those who could still walk staggered off as fast as they could manage. Others made the attempt but did not get far before they collapsed onto the street. Some had friends who assisted them to their feet. Others were left to lie where they had fallen.

"What is going on?" Raistlin asked.

"That brute warned them that a minotaur shore patrol is coming," said Magius. "Don't worry. They're not here to arrest us—but they will be if they see us, so we had better retreat to the alley."

Six minotaurs came marching down the street. They wore cutlasses on their harnesses and carried truncheons and clubs. Two entered the tavern and dragged out a human—probably the owner—in chains. The other four pursued the minotaurs who were either too drunk or too slow to escape. When they caught them, they beat them with their truncheons, then hauled them away. Before leaving, the minotaurs shut down the tavern, scrawled an X on the door, padlocked it, and then continued on their rounds.

"Minotaurs won't tolerate drunkenness," Magius explained. "Sargonnas teaches that it shows a lack of self-discipline. Fortunate for us, for now we can escape without being observed and take our grateful leave of Palanthas."

Magius cleared the trash from the alley and drew a circle on the pavement in the muck and he and Raistlin stepped inside. He cast the journeying spell, and they stood once again in the silent and deserted library of the High Clerist's Tower.

"Are you tired after our adventures?" Magius asked.

"Not particularly," said Raistlin.

"Good. Come with me to the High Lookout. The view is spectacular."

He held out the staff. Raistlin grasped it, and they rose up a narrow spiral staircase to the top floor of the High Clerist's Tower. Circular in shape, the High Lookout was open to the air. A wall designed to resemble a crown formed a decorative and protective barrier. A smaller tower, known as the Kingfisher's Nest, rose from the center.

"When I was here, sentries manned the High Lookout," Magius remarked. "I would guess the commander does not have men enough to post them."

Magius and Raistlin leaned their elbows on the wall and gazed out over the plains to the mountains beyond. Magius did not seem inclined to talk, and for his part, Raistlin was glad to remain silent, thinking about how he was going to break the news to his companions.

They watched the sun sink down into the mountains, leaving all but the afterglow. The sky above them was clear and dotted with faint stars. On the plains below, they could see what looked like countless orange stars shining luridly in the darkness—enemy bonfires.

"There are a great many more tonight than last night," Magius observed. "And there will be twice this number tomorrow night and more the next. At least we have the dragon orb. I have been considering how to use it. The wizards who created the orbs summoned evil dragons to the tower, then killed them with lethal magicks. I plan to do the same. I will stand here in the High Lookout, then command the orb to summon Immolatus and the rest of the Dark Queen's dragons, and I will kill them with my magic."

"You leave out one important point," said Raistlin. "Legions of powerful spellcasters used the dragon orbs when the dragons attacked the Tower of High Sorcery. There are only two of us—and the gods know how many dragons."

"Two of us. Are you saying you will fight at my side?" Magius asked, pleased.

"I will, as long as a good twenty feet separates us," Raistlin said. "I do not want to be in the range of your 'Sizzling Goblin.'"

Magius laughed. "I'll wager you fifty silver I hit the dragon with my first spell."

"A safe bet, since you know we have no hope of surviving this encounter," Raistlin retorted. "Like I said, we are vastly outnumbered."

"Perhaps you are right," said Magius quietly, gazing into the stars. "But imagine what it will feel like to summon the lightning from the clouds and hurl blazing bolts at our foe. And if we die, we will die with the glory of Lunitari shining down on us and the flame of the magic in our hearts. We will die with the magic burning in our blood!"

Raistlin did not trust himself to reply. For, according to history, Magius would not die the glorious death he envisioned. He would die a terrible death by torture in the dragon's camp. Raistlin wondered what would happen to history if Magius did not die. He was, after all, only a drop in the River of Time. History celebrated Huma, but only wizards remembered Magius. Whereas the world might remember him standing atop the High Lookout, hurling thunderbolts at a dragon.

"But first I must gain control of the dragon orb," Magius was saying. "I will return to my bedchamber with it, for I am not likely to be disturbed there. Do you know anything about controlling a dragon orb?"

Raistlin knew a great deal about the subject. The horrifying memories of his fight to control a dragon orb were tinged with mist, and he left them buried, shrouded in time.

"If I did know, my experience wouldn't help you," said Raistlin. "Each mage must fight this battle alone."

"I am not looking forward to it," Magius admitted. "As Anitra told us, it is said to be a terrifying ordeal. Meantime, we must keep the dragon orb a secret. We say nothing to anyone."

"As far as my friends are concerned, I went to the Tower of High Sorcery to seek the Device of Time Journeying and failed," Raistlin said.

Magius rested his hand on Raistlin's shoulder in silent commiseration. They left the High Lookout. The magic of the staff floated them down the stairs to the sixth floor.

"Thank you for accompanying me," said Magius. "I am sorry you did not find what you sought, but I enjoyed our adventure. Those minotaurs who tried to enter the grove are probably still running."

"They must be halfway to Mithas by now," Raistlin agreed, smiling.

"Good night, Brother."

Magius clasped Raistlin's hand, then entered his bedchamber and closed the door.

Raistlin went to his own room and lit the lantern. He knew he should go break the bad news to his friends, who must be waiting impatiently to hear. They would already be worried because he had been gone far longer than he had told them. But he was too tired to deal with their despair.

He had to first get over his own.

"After all," he reflected ruefully, "it's not as if I need to rush. None of us are going anywhere."

Someone—probably Destina—had been thoughtful enough to leave him a tray of food. He ate a little and drank some wine, then sat down to memorize his spells.

But the only words he could hear were those that had been spoken by Magius. He could picture both of them standing on top of the High Clerist's Tower bathed in Lunitari's blessed light, hurling flame and lightning as the dragons swooped down on them.

"To die with the magic burning in our blood . . ." Raistlin murmured.

CHAPTER
SIXTEEN

Tasslehoff was accustomed to spending the night in jail cells, and he had been glad to have a chance to see the prison cells in the High Clerist's Tower, since he had not seen them the last time he was here. He would have enjoyed them more if he had been viewing them from the outside, however, not the inside.

The dungeons were certainly everything he had expected. The cells were neat and clean. He had a fresh straw mattress on a cot, not the floor, and a blanket that didn't smell of cat pee. But he soon discovered that while this dungeon was certainly more comfortable than most, it was also more boring.

When he was locked up with his fellow kender, they had lots of fun dumping out their pouches, comparing interesting treasures, and hearing about one another's adventures. In this cell, he was alone. The iron door had a barred grate at the top, but he was so short that to see through the grate, he had to drag the cot to the door and stand on it, only to discover there wasn't anything to see except more iron doors with grates.

He tried talking to the jailer, but the jailer was in a bad mood. He'd been severely reprimanded by Will for letting the elf escape.

"At least she got out of this death trap," the jailer had said. "When the dragon gets here, the rest of us are going to die in this godforsaken place."

"If you'd just talk to the gnomes," Tas had shouted from his cell. "They have dragonlances!"

But neither man had paid any attention to him, or maybe they couldn't hear him. Then he had heard Will leave, and everything was quiet.

Tas sighed deeply. The jailer had taken away his pouches, so he didn't have anything to occupy his mind, and he began to think it was time to leave. Not only was the jail cell boring, it was preventing him from saving the song. Someone had to go find the dragonlances—and although he'd repeatedly told people where to look, none of them appeared to be interested in pursuing the matter.

The task fell to him.

A favorite kender saying is: "When the jail cells get boring, the bored get going."

Tas had foreseen that he might need a way out, and while the jailer had been trying to untangle the straps of the kender's pouches and pick up those Tas had dropped and take away pouches that Tas kept taking back, Tas had managed to slip his lockpicking tools out of a pouch and shove them down his socks.

Retrieving the tools, he selected one, inserted it into the lock, and heard the most satisfying sound in the world—the click of a lock opening.

Tas waited to leave until he saw the jailer walking past his cell, carrying a tray of food. While the jailer was opening the door to the other prisoner's cell, Tas sneaked out. He was tempted to snag at least a couple of his pouches, which were hanging on hooks on the wall, but then he heard the jailer returning.

To save time on long explanations about why he couldn't stay locked up when he had to save the song, Tas grabbed his hoopak and his magical turtle water jug, borrowed the jailer's lantern, and made a run for it. He didn't have to worry about retrieving Goblinslayer, which the jailer had locked in a cabinet, for he knew the knife would retrieve him.

Tas lighted the lantern and dashed up the stairs to the first floor of the High Clerist's Tower. He spent several moments getting lost, then finally located the way they'd come in, which Magius had called the Noble's Gate. The huge ironwood doors at the tower's entrance were bolted shut. That should not have been a problem, and Tas was mildly excited about the prospect of picking the lock until he realized with a sigh that it was a deadbolt, and no kender lockpick ever made could force it open. He had to find another way out.

He wandered about with the lantern and came across a room somewhere between Noble's Gate and another called Merchant's Gate that appeared promising. Gilt lettering on the door stated that it was named *Sacristy*.

The door to the room was locked, but the lock was so simple it was almost an insult. Tas opened the door and walked inside. He had lost track of time while in the jail cell, and he was disappointed when he peered out a window to find that night had arrived when he wasn't looking.

Nights were good times for adventures, but they also tended to be dark, which made it difficult to find one's way around. Tas was lucky this night, however, for he had the lantern and Solinari was shining brightly, so that once he managed to escape, he would be able to see where he was going.

The room was extremely interesting, for it contained beautiful robes hanging from pegs, a great many volumes of books, helms and other pieces of armor and weapons, wooden chests that were closed and locked, a desk, and a door that led outside. This door was not locked, rather to his disappointment, so all he had to do was push it open. He regretted he didn't have time to see what interesting things were inside the chests, but he had to save the song.

He had his new hoopak for the road and, patting his belt, he was glad to find Goblinslayer had not abandoned him. He wasn't particularly worried about being attacked by goblins or kobolds or hobgoblins. He was far more concerned about defending himself from the gnomes.

For while gnomes were the meekest, mildest people on the face of Krynn, there was no getting around the fact that—with the possible exception of dragons—gnomes were also the most dangerous. Gnomes didn't mean to be a danger to life and limb. They didn't harm people intentionally. They just had an unfortunate tendency to have accidents, not to mention mishaps, disasters, catastrophes, and calamities. If you happened to be in the vicinity during one of these accidents, it was not conducive to a long life, as Tanis would say.

According to legend, gnomes were a people originally called the Smiths whose skills in forging and inventing had led them to the worship of the forger god, Reorx. The god loved the Smiths and showered them with blessings. Unfortunately, the Smiths grew prideful and told Reorx to take a hike. That, understandably, angered the god. He cursed all gnomes with an insatiable desire to invent things and then added insult to injury by stating that none of their inventions would ever, under any circumstances, work.

Given this, Tas might have wondered about the ability of gnomes to invent the first dragonlances. But since Uncle Trapspringer was involved, Tas was confident that the Trapspringer genius would go far to overcome any gnomish deficiencies.

Tas enjoyed the outing. The night was fine, and the road that ran through the foothills across the plains was deserted. He could see the campfires of the red dragon's army, but those were east of him, and he was traveling west. The High Clerist's Tower was behind him and it looked very beautiful with the light of Solinari shining on it, as though it were made of silver.

He continued walking, and when he calculated he was far enough away from the tower that the commander wouldn't be likely to come after him, Tas sat down beneath a tree to rest his eyes. As always happened whenever he was resting his eyes, he fell asleep.

When he woke, it was morning. The sun was up. The birds were singing. The sunlight filtered through the branches of the trees, and a gentle breeze stirred the leaves. Tas took a drink from his magical water jug and ate some bread and meat he'd found on the jailer's desk and didn't think the jailer would miss, then continued on his way.

He soon encountered a perplexing dilemma. Reaching the top of a hill, he saw that the road branched off in two different directions. He didn't have the map with him, and he had no idea what road to take to find the gnome village. He sat down to rest and try to figure out which way to go.

He had just decided to take the road to the northwest when he heard a hubbub of voices coming from the far side of the hill. Tas's first instinct was to race to the top of the hill to see what was on the other side. His second was to recall that Tanis had often warned him to look before he leaped. Having found this to be sound advice in the past, Tas slipped stealthily through the brush until he reached the top of the hill and could see what was going on.

The voices didn't sound like goblin voices, though it was hard to tell, for there were a great many of them, and they were all talking at once. He could also hear other sounds: clanks, rumbles, clatters, clangs, whirs, belches, hissing, and the occasional whistle.

Reaching the top of the hill, he looked down to see an astonishing sight. A veritable army of gnomes stood clustered around what appeared to be an enormous contraption. A gigantic ballista, made of steel and as big as a tree, was bolted onto a large box that was also made of steel and as big as a smallish house.

The contraption was apparently meant to be propelled over the ground by a great many wheels, which were lined up in rows underneath. At least, Tas could see that was the plan, but the wheels weren't turning and the contraption wasn't moving despite the clouds of steam pouring out of a large tank affixed to the back.

Some of the gnomes were standing around the contraption, kicking the wheels, while several more gnomes were peering down at them from the window of a castle-like turret mounted at the front of the contraption. These gnomes were yelling at the gnomes kicking the wheels.

Tas grabbed his hoopak and ran down the hill to get a closer look.

"Hullo, there!" he yelled, waving his hoopak.

The gnomes stopped kicking at the wheels of the contraption and turned to stare at him. They then began a lengthy discussion about whether he was friend or foe, and if he was a foe what they should do about him, and if he wasn't, did it matter? This was followed by a show of hands, after which a gnome wearing a long leather apron over his shirt and breeches came to speak to him.

"We have decided you are a friend," said the gnome.

He was short and stocky with white hair and a soft, white, curly beard. He wore the usual look of harried intensity common to gnomes.

"I *am* a friend," said Tas, pleased. "My name is Tasslehoff Burr-foot."

The gnome made a bobbing bow and launched into his name, and Tas realized at once he'd made a dreadful mistake. Every gnome's name is a record of that particular gnome's family's history dating back to the Age of Dreams and could easily fill up several large leather-bound volumes. It would take this gnome probably a day and a half to get through it.

"Short version," said Tas hurriedly.

The gnome started off again, and Tas recalled that each gnome had three names: the long version, the shortened version of the long version, and the short version of the short version.

"The shortest short name," Tas specified.

"Knopple," said the gnome.

They shook hands. Tas regarded the contraption with admiration.

"That's a wonderful ballista, Knopple. I've never seen a ballista that big or made out of steel with all those gears and levers and those big pointy things on top."

"Youveneverseenaballistalikeitbecauseitsnotaballista," said Knopple, sounding peeved.

Tas had not been around gnomes in a long time and had forgotten that they talked extremely fast, especially when they were excited.

"I don't want to hurt your feelings, Knopple, but you need to slow down when you talk," said Tas. "I can't understand you when you smash all the words together."

Knopple heaved an exasperated sigh. His face was wrinkled up like a walnut, but that wasn't necessarily a sign of old age. Almost all gnome faces were wrinkled. Gnomes claimed the wrinkles came from deep thinking, but Tas considered it more likely the wrinkles came from scrunching up their faces to avoid being injured by the blasts.

"I said you've never seen a ballista like it because it's not a ballista," said Knopple.

"What is it?" Tas asked and instantly knew he'd made another mistake, because Knopple proudly launched into the name of the contraption.

"Therevolutionarysteampoweredbangbangboomhowitzerspear-
hurlerdragonkillerandaerialpyrotechnicdisplay—"

"Stop!" said Tas.

Knopple stopped.

"What does it do?" Tas asked.

"I was just telling you," said Knopple.

"I don't have a lot of time," Tas explained. "Some of my friends
are trapped inside the High Clerist's Tower about to be attacked by
a very fierce dragon and I need to save them and the song."

"Then this weapon is exactly what you're looking for," stated
Knopple, and all the gnomes standing around them broke into ap-
plause. "We are on our way to that very tower in order to save the
knights."

"With a ballista?" Tas asked, doubtful.

"It's not a ballista!" Knopple yelled.

"I beg your pardon," said Tas contritely. "What is it?"

"Thedragonspearpikejavelinbayonetharpoonboltcorkscrew-
lance—" Knopple began.

"A dragonlance!" Tas cried excitedly, understanding the first
word and the last. "I had always heard that you gnomes had invented
them, and I was on my way to your village to tell you the knights
really need them."

"Dragonlance," Knopple repeated several times, rolling the words
on his tongue.

He looked at his fellow gnomes. Several nodded their heads and
they began to discuss the new name. This took some time and another show of hands. Knopple turned to Tas.

"We consider that the term 'dragonlance' is simplistic, but it
does have a ring to it. Therefore, we have agreed to refer the new
name to the committee on Honorifics, Epithets, Labels, and Moni-
kers. You'll receive a memo."

Tas eyed the contraption dubiously. The dragonlance that was a
ballista that wasn't a ballista was indeed a fearsome-looking weapon.
The wooden shaft that was about the size of a tree sported a variety
of wicked-looking blades.

"The blades rotate," said Knopple, seeing Tas studying them.

"It's really a very remarkable weapon," said Tas. "But—and I
don't mean to hurt your feelings—it's not a dragonlance."

Knopple took offense. "How would you know what is or is not a dragonlance, since we are the ones who invented it and no one has ever seen one before?" He added with a snort, "Everyone's a critic."

Tas started to say he *had* seen a dragonlance before. He'd seen lots of dragonlances. But then it occurred to him that the dragonlances he had seen were in the future during the War of the Lance. Perhaps this was what dragonlances looked like in the time of Huma.

"How does it work?" Tas asked to mollify the irate gnome.

"That's the problem," said Knopple, his shoulders slumping. "At the moment, it doesn't."

The other gnomes shook their heads and went back to arguing and kicking the wheels.

"What is it *not* doing?" Tas asked.

"Anything," said Knopple, which wasn't much help.

Tas tried again. "What's it supposed to be doing?"

Knopple brightened, and gave Tas a tour of the contraption, proudly displaying the finer points.

"We made the dragonlance far more efficient than a ballista by removing the need for torsion prods and tension springs and replacing those with blasting caps and gunpowder."

Tas did his best to look impressed, though he had no idea what a torsion prod was, or a tension spring, or a blasting cap, for that matter.

"As you see here," Knopple continued, "the dragonlance has various spearheads which are interchangeable depending on the type of dragon. We have color-coded them for easy reference based on the type of dragon: fuchsia, lavender, puce, mauve, and mustard."

"I never heard of a mustard dragon," said Tas.

Knopple glared at him. "They're extremely ferocious, although not as ferocious as mauve. Do you want to know how this works or not?"

Tas would have liked to have heard more about puce and fuchsia dragons, but he didn't want to upset the gnome. "Please, go on. What does that big kettle do?"

"That is the boiler. It generates steam that turns the gears that drives the wheels that propel the machine across the ground. At least," he added, heaving a sigh, "that's the theory."

Tas could now see the problem. The boiler was furiously boiling and belching steam, but the wheels weren't turning. And he didn't think kicking them would be likely to help.

"Why don't you push it?" Tas asked.

Knopple's eyes widened to such an extent that his eyebrows nearly flew off his head.

"*Push* it!" he repeated in horror. "Did you say *push* it?"

The other gnomes were equally horrified, and one fainted dead away in shock at the very idea.

"The dragonlance travels under its own steam," said Knopple. "It is not meant to be *pushed*!" He said the word with an explosive emphasis.

"But there are more than enough of you," Tas pointed out. "And I'll be glad to help. If we all get behind it and put our shoulders into it—"

Two more gnomes fainted from shock, and Knopple had to sit down and lower his head between his knees. Tas shared some of the water from his magical turtle shell and patted Knopple on the back, and eventually he revived.

"We can't push it," he said weakly. "According to Professor Trapspringer . . ."

"Who?" Tas interrupted.

"Professor Trapspringer," Knopple repeated. "The professor was instrumental in the design and the development of this weapon, with particular emphasis on the pyrotechnic part of the invention. Not only will our weapon slay dragons, it puts on a spectacular aerial display in the process. He was quite adamant that on no account were we to push it. Or pull it, for that matter."

Tas had no idea what pyrotechnics were, but he knew better than to ask. He had more important concerns.

"Tell me about Professor Trapspringer. Is he still in your village? Could I meet him? We're related, you see. He's my uncle."

The gnomes regarded him with deep and profound sorrow. They all took off their hats, and Tas heard murmurs of "Sorry for your loss," "Regrettable incident," "Unfortunate accident," and "A pity he was standing so close. . . ."

All of which was soothing but of no help.

"Where is Uncle . . . I mean Professor Trapspringer?" Tas asked.

"Ah, that's the question," said Knopple sadly. "Only a few days ago, he was standing on that very platform about to launch what we will now call the dragonlance, at least until we hear back from committee, and the next he wasn't."

"Wasn't what?" Tas was confused.

"Standing on the platform," said Knopple. "We believed the explosion had something to do with his sudden disappearance, and thus we referred the matter to the committee on Safety in the Workplace Environment. Their initial findings were that he had been hoisted on his own petard."

"What's a petard?" Tas asked.

"We have no idea. That went back to committee," said Knopple.

Tas was sad to think that he had come so close to meeting Uncle Trapspringer and had apparently missed him by only a few days. Still, he was proud to think that Uncle Trapspringer had played a role in the invention of the dragonlance as kender history had recorded. He looked forward to informing Sturm and Raistlin, who had often spoken insultingly of Uncle Trapspringer. But first, he had to figure out how to haul the dragonlance to the High Clerist's Tower.

Tas didn't dare bring up pushing the contraption again, for they had just managed to revive the gnomes who had passed out. While he was thinking, Knopple and the gnomes went back to work.

They crawled under the device and inside it and on top of it. They unrolled large charts and diagrams and spread them on the ground and got into heated arguments, while others hammered and prodded and poked the contraption.

"Can I help?" Tas offered.

"Do you know anything about internal combustible engines?" Knopple asked.

"No," Tas admitted.

"How about carburetors?"

"Sorry," said Tas.

"Then what good are you?" Knopple demanded with a snort. He eyed the contraption. "I think we should disassemble it and start over."

"No!" Tas cried, alarmed. "I mean you can't. All this work for nothing? Let's have a show of hands! Who doesn't want to disassemble the dragonlance?"

The gnomes were about to vote when a whistle sounded.

"Breakfast!" Knopple shouted, and the gnomes all piled out of the contraption and quit kicking the wheels.

There appeared to be considerable consternation among them. After some discussion, one came to Knopple to report.

"We can't find the food. We seem to have left it behind. I blame the members of the Culinary and Knife Sharpening Committee, but they claim it's not their fault. They left it to a subcommittee, the Sous Chefs and Pastry Cooks, who deny all responsibility. We therefore suggest that a group be detailed to go bag a deer."

This received unanimous support. The gnomes invited Tas to go hunting with them, but as he watched them arm themselves with sinister-looking weapons they called "thundersticks," he decided that it would be conducive to a long life to politely decline the invitation.

Several gnomes traipsed off into the woods, and their departure was soon followed by the sounds of explosions and a couple of yelps of pain. The gnomes returned with what they called a deer, but which Tas could clearly see was a milk cow with a bell around her neck.

The cow was, fortunately, still alive and in better shape than many of the gnomes, who were bleeding profusely. Knopple summoned the Butchers, Bakers, and Candlestick Makers Committee and instructed them to carve up the deer. Tas felt called upon to point out their mistake.

"That's not a deer. It's a cow."

"No!" said Knopple, shocked. "Are you certain?"

"It's mooing," said Tas.

"It is too a deer!" several of the hunters shouted.

This resulted in a heated argument. The butchers were preparing to go to work on the cow when the irate farmer arrived carrying a pitchfork. He aimed it in a threatening manner at the gnomes and accused them of stealing his cow.

"You claim it is your cow and we claim it is our deer," said Knopple. "We are nothing if not fair-minded, and we will refer this matter to the Court of Law once we find it. The court went missing after the Great Blast of '33, and none of us have seen a lawyer since, though we continue to look. In the meantime, we will retain the contested animal as evidence."

The farmer went red in the face and began to jab at Knopple with the pitchfork. The other gnomes scattered while Knopple sought refuge underneath the wheels of the dragonlance.

"Come out from under there!" the farmer shouted, trying to skewer Knopple with the pitchfork.

Knopple rolled one way and the other, but Tas could see that sooner or later the pitchfork was going to win. He jumped on the contraption and, not knowing else to do, flipped a switch.

The dragonlance gave a great belch of steam. Whistles blew, gears clanked, pistons plunged, cranks cranked, and the wheels started to turn.

The dragonlance was on the move.

Both the cow and the farmer took one look at it and ran the other direction. Tas leaped off and managed to pull Knopple out from under the wheels mere seconds before the dragonlance would have rumbled over him.

"You did it!" Tas cried, throwing his arms around the gnome. "It works!"

"Well, of course it works," said Knopple testily. "What else did you expect?"

By now, the dragonlance had picked up speed and was rolling along at a pretty good clip. Knopple jumped onto the platform and Tas scrambled up beside him, then he and Knopple assisted the rest of the gnomes to climb on board.

Knopple took his place in the turret and called on Tas to join him. "Marvelous view from here!"

Tas climbed into the turret and looked at his surroundings.

"That large building you see over there is the High Clerist's Tower!" Tas said, forced to shout to be heard over the bells and whistles. "That's where the knights are trapped. You need to steer the dragonlance in that direction."

Knopple suddenly looked concerned.

Tas saw the gnome's eyebrows quiver, and he got a sinking feeling somewhere around his kneecaps.

"You *can* steer this, can't you?" he asked.

"Ah, as to that," said Knopple. "I believe I received a memo right before we started from the Committee on Steering Wheels, Drive Shafts, and Seat Belts."

The gnome fished about in his shirt, removed a piece of paper from his pocket, unfolded it, read it, folded it up, and put it back in his pocket.

"No," he said.

"No, what?" Tas asked uneasily. "What do you mean 'no'?"

"I mean no, we can't steer it," Knopple replied with a shrug. "The committee looked into it and didn't find the initial plan feasible and referred the matter back to committee for more work. We expect an updated memo any day now."

Tas looked out across the plains and saw hills and gullies and ravines and, very far in the distance, fires from the dragon's armies. They were headed away from the High Clerist's Tower and straight toward the enemy. Even Tas could see that was not going to be conducive to a long life.

"How do you stop this thing?" Tas shouted.

"Stop it!" Knopple glared at him, outraged. "We just got it started! Why would we want to stop it?"

Tas had no good answer to this without explaining about Tanis and conducivity—if that was a word. Knopple was standing in the turret of the dragonlance with the wind blowing through his few sparse hairs, grinning from one large ear to the other. The other gnomes were happily riding on the dragonlance, hooting and cheering, except for the three who had tumbled off when the wheels ran over a rock and were now running along frantically behind, trying to catch up.

The dragonlance thundered along, belching and whistling.

Tas decided to just enjoy the ride. "Where are we going?" he yelled.

"To find a dragon," Knopple yelled back.

CHAPTER
SEVENTEEN

The location of Silver Dragon Mountain was a secret known only to the metallic dragons. It stood in the Last Gaard range in Ergoth, shrouded by thick mists that rose from the boiling hot springs of Foghaven Vale below.

Dragon lore held that Paladine had brought forth metallic dragons at the beginning of time, lovingly crafting them from the streams of rare dragonmetal that flowed beneath the mountain. The god had created gold, silver, brass, bronze, and copper dragons and blessed them as they emerged gleaming from the shining pools of dragonmetal to walk the world and bring forth others of their kind.

All dragons make pilgrimages to Silver Dragon Mountain during their lifetimes. Gwyneth had flown there as a young hatchling in company with her sister, Silvara, and she knew how to find the mountain that was otherwise hidden in the mists.

She had left the High Clerist's Tower the previous day, having escaped from her prison cell with ease. She had opened the cell door with a touch of her hand, then cast a spell on the jailer and locked the slumbering man in her cell.

She had then hidden inside the deserted temple until Solinari had set, then, still in her elven form, she had slipped through the eastern gate and climbed up into the foothills. She had to make certain that Immolatus did not see her shift into her dragon form. She had chosen this time, well after midnight, because he hunted at night and she knew he would be asleep in his lair after gorging himself.

She found a wide patch of ground and lifted her head to the stars and let go of the magic that made her appear to be an elven woman. She spread her arms and they transformed into wings. She burst free from the weak and fragile mortal body and emerged in her dragon form, twenty-two feet in length, strong and powerful, sleek and graceful, covered by scales that shone silver in the lambent light of the stars.

Gwyneth could not take the time to revel in returning to her true form, for she was surrounded by danger. She listened intently and sniffed the air but heard only the sounds of the night animals going about their business. Lifting her wings, she took to the sky.

The flight to Silver Dragon Mountain was long, but she had a lot to think about, a lot to consider, to keep her occupied on the journey.

Gwyneth had been glad when the commander had ordered her to be locked up in a prison cell far below ground. She had been glad to be away from the man whose strong hands had been so gentle, whose eyes had been kind and filled with compassion when he had helped what he had thought was a white stag.

She had been glad to escape the man she had seen in the dream. When dragons dreamed, their spirits roamed the stars as they had before they were born. They were free, unfettered by flesh and bone. They could commune with the god who had created them: the Dragon Father, Paladine.

One night, not many years ago, Gwyneth had been drifting among the stars, when she had received a summons from Paladine. The god had taken her to a small, private chapel. A human male knelt there, praying to Paladine.

"His name is Huma and he is to be made a knight tomorrow if he chooses," Paladine had told her. "He is in every way worthy. He is noble and good, valiant and courageous. Yet he cannot find those qualities within himself. He doubts. He fears he will falter and fail."

"Why do you bring me here, Dragon Father?" Gwyneth had asked.

"He needs help. He stands upon a precipice and the world with him," Paladine had said.

"But what am I to do?" Gwyneth had asked, confused.

"Since you have your own fears and doubts, Daughter, I thought you would understand his," Paladine had said. "If you do not want to go to him, I understand."

"You think I fear the prophecy," Gwyneth had said. "I do not believe in something some daft old dragon nursemaid muttered over my sister, Silvara, and I as we lay curled up in our nest. 'Beware mortal men, Sisters, for they will be your doom.'"

Gwyneth snorted in disdain. "Both Silvara and I have chosen to live among mortals and assist them when we can, and neither of us has met our doom."

"And yet you have taken care never to grow close to any mortal," Paladine had said. "Ask yourself this question, Daughter. Do prophecies foretell our fate and thus we fulfill them, or do we fulfill them because we act on them and thus bring about our fate?"

Gwyneth had no answer to this riddle and she doubted the god did.

"This mortal needs your help, Daughter," Paladine had said before he left her. "If you choose to give it."

Gwyneth could have left the knight to his prayers, but the god's words rankled. Perhaps she did fear the prophecy, after all. She had studied the young man, liking what she saw. She had listened to him confess his doubts and his sorrow. She had heard his anguish and felt his pain, and her heart had misgiven her. She would not let fear stop her from giving help where it was needed. After all, she had thought, what was the harm? They were never likely to meet in this world.

Gwyneth had gone to Huma in the chapel. She had appeared before him in mortal form as an elven maiden. She had knelt beside him and taken hold of his hands, and she had helped him see into his heart, come to know his worth. She had often found herself thinking of him, wondering what had become of him, if he had fulfilled his promise. She had not expected to know the answer, but then she had seen him again in the forest near the High Clerist's Tower.

She had seen him, seen her doom. And she had seen his doom, as well, for the knights with their spears and arrows could not hope to defeat Immolatus and the Dark Queen.

Following the Second Dragon War, the metallic dragons had banished Takhisis and her evil dragons into the Abyss. They had then gone into self-imposed exile on the Isles of the Dragons, far to the north. Having suffered extensive casualties in the war, they had wanted only to live in peace, heal their wounds, and raise their young. The metallic dragons were content to leave the light of Krynn to the children of the gods.

But these dragons were not naïve. They knew Takhisis would never give up her desire to rule the world. And so the elders had asked for volunteers to walk among the children of the gods to keep watch and report the first signs that Takhisis had returned. Gwyneth and her sister, Silvara, were young and adventurous and bored with life on the Isles of the Dragons, where their elders lazed about and talked of past glory. They had eagerly volunteered.

At that same time, the dragons had also decided, after much contentious argument, to provide mortals with the weapons they needed to defend themselves against Takhisis and her hordes. A militant gold dragon named Sharpfang had conceived the idea that lances made from the sacred dragonmetal could be used to fight the dragons of Takhisis.

Dragon lore holds that Reorx himself forged the first dragonlance beneath Silver Dragon Mountain, using a silver arm and wielding a silver hammer. He gifted the lance to Paladine. The god called them dragonlances and told Reorx to bring dwarven smiths to the mountain to forge the rest. The dragonlances were to remain hidden and secret, to be given to mortals only if the need was dire—for although Reorx assured the dragons that the blessed lances could never be used to harm a metallic dragon, the metallics themselves were not so certain.

Gwyneth and Silvara had both decided to dwell among the long-lived elves, for the life span of dragons was also long, and they would fit more readily into elven society. In addition, the elven people worshipped Paladine. The Dark Queen was not able to easily lure them to her worship as she did humans, who often succumbed to her false promises.

The sisters had used their dragon magic to shift into elven bodies. Gwyneth had taken up residence among the Qualinesti, while Silvara had gone to live with the Kagonesti in Ergoth.

Years passed. Gwyneth had heard rumors that goblin armies were attacking Solamnia, but wars were commonplace among mortals, and she thought little of it. Then, last winter, Gwyneth had been hunting with a party of elves when she had felt a chill shadow of dread flow over her. She had looked into the sky and been horrified to see a red dragon flying with impunity among the clouds. She had immediately flown to the Isles of the Dragons to report to the Council of Elders.

"The pact with the Dark Queen is broken," Gwyneth had told them. "A red dragon named Immolatus has escaped the Abyss. Takhisis and the other evil gods have attacked Solamnia. If she establishes a base there, she can send her armies south to Qualinesti. If the elven nation falls, as I fear it must, the Dark Queen will rule the center of Ansalon. She can then attack Istar in the northwest and Ergoth in the east. We must act now to stop her."

The dragon elders had been opposed. "If we entered this war, it would quickly escalate. Takhisis would unleash her hordes on us, and the blood of dragons would once more fall like rain on Krynn."

Gwyneth had expected this argument, and she was prepared. "Then we should make provision for the children of the gods to defend themselves. We should give the Solamnic knights the dragonlances to drive Takhisis and her dragons back into the Abyss."

"You ask us to give humans the means to kill dragons," a gold had said sternly. "That puts us all in danger."

"The Knights of Solamnia do not pose a threat to us," Gwyneth had maintained.

"Humans fear all dragons," a silver had said. "They make no distinction between us and Immolatus."

"Then why did you forge the dragonlances?" Gwyneth had demanded angrily. "To assuage your guilt over leaving the children of the gods defenseless against the Dark Queen?"

The other dragons had been offended by her bluntness. They had reared their heads and flapped their wings and regarded her with ire.

"Do you trust these humans with your life?" a silver had countered.

Gwyneth had hesitated, then she had said uneasily, "I chose to live among the elves. I know so little of humans...."

The dragons had nodded their heads wisely, as though they had made their point.

"She fears the prophecy," a silver had added. "Perfectly understandable."

"I do not fear some silly prediction about a mortal being my doom!" Gwyneth had retorted angrily. "If I did, I would be hiding on this island with the rest of you! The truth is that I don't live with humans because I don't understand humans. They live such short and frantic lives. They are never content to sit and watch but must be up and doing. They have no steady, abiding faith. Humans are erratic and unpredictable. I do not know what to make of them."

That much had been true. But Gwyneth had not told the elders about the dream of the man with the noble bearing and gentle eyes, or that she secretly found something fascinating about the few humans she had met. She had come to grudgingly admire their stubborn courage and how they refused to give up, fighting on even when defeat was inevitable, willing to sacrifice their short lives for the sake of others.

The dragons had retired to make their decision regarding the dragonlances. Gwyneth had known all along what the decision would be, but she was still disappointed when she received it.

"We deem the danger to ourselves too great," said a gold dragon. "The dragonlances will remain hidden in Silver Dragon Mountain. The humans have many thousands of soldiers and knights to fight their battles. They have other weapons. We fought the last war. Let the mortals fight this one."

Gwyneth had been forced to accept their decision, even though she had believed it was the wrong one. She had returned to Solamnia to find that the situation was dire. Immolatus and his armies were camped in front of the High Clerist's Tower, waiting only for Takhisis to complete the downfall of Solamnia.

Gwyneth had been planning to return to Qualinesti to warn the elves and then make one last attempt to persuade the elders to re-

lease the dragonlances. Her plan had been overthrown when she had
encountered a human wearing the Graystone, a kender who couldn't
keep quiet, and the knight she had seen in her dreams.

Gwyneth had been uncertain what to do. Her first impulse was
to flee. She had an excuse. She should report back to the dragons, tell
them of the return of the Graystone, but the flight to the Dragon
Isles was long and she was reluctant to leave the Graystone unpro-
tected. And then she heard about the slaughter at Westgate Pass.
The humans had no weapons that could fight a powerful red dragon
such as Immolatus.

She could not let Huma or any of the other bold, illogical, gallant humans who were bravely prepared to fight the dragon give
their lives for a hopeless cause. She could not let Solamnia fall.
Above all, she could not let the Graystone fall into the hands of
Takhisis.

Gwyneth reached a decision. She would fly to Silver Dragon
Mountain and bring the dragonlances to the knights herself.

When she entered Foghaven Vale, the mists parted for her, and
she could see Silver Dragon Mountain and the enormous cavern
where the dragonlances were hidden. But she did not immediately
enter. She crouched amid the foothills at the base of the mountain,
working up the courage.

The elder dragons would be outraged with her for defying their
command, and she would face punishment. She didn't know what
form the punishment would take. She had never heard of a dragon
defying the elders. She thought about the prophecy that some ad-
dled old gold dragon had spoken when she and her sister had barely
emerged from their shells. And though she didn't believe in it, she
wondered if this is what the prophecy meant by saying humans
would be her doom.

She looked up at the peak of Silver Dragon Mountain and almost lost her nerve. But she could still hear Calaf's laugh as he described how Immolatus had burned the humans alive and mocked
their "puny" weapons. She heard Huma's words.

You truly do not know us, Gwyneth, if you think we would run from
danger. We will fight to protect our homeland, as you would fight to pro-
tect yours.

The cavern was located about halfway up the mountain. Gwyneth made up her mind. She flew to the entrance, which was wide enough that she could land inside. To reach the main chamber, she had to traverse a narrow passage and she was forced to fold her wings close to her body, duck her head, and crawl the rest of the way.

The main chamber contained a large molten pool of dragonmetal that shimmered with silver light. The stalactites and stalagmites surrounding it gleamed with silver radiance.

Gwyneth crept inside. Once they had finished their task, the dwarven craftsmen had hidden the dragonlances in a small chamber off the main one. They had wrapped the dragonlances in soft sheepskin to keep them safe. They had been well paid for their work. The dragons had sent them back to the dwarven kingdom with chests of gold and jewels, though they never afterward knew how they had come by their wealth, for Reorx had erased all memory of their work from their minds.

The little chamber was pitch dark. Even with her night vision, Gwyneth had difficulty locating the bundles. The dwarves had crafted two sizes of dragonlances: the footman's lance and the mounted dragonlance. The footman's lance was eight feet long, designed to be wielded by hand. The mounted lance was sixteen feet and intended to be attached to the saddle of a warhorse.

Gwyneth selected a bundle of twenty footman's lances. She debated taking the mounted lances, but the knights had lost all their horses in their ill-fated ride to save Palanthas. She decided at last to take two mounted lances, figuring it would be better to have them than to regret that she had not taken them.

After wrapping them in sheepskin, she returned to the main chamber, clutching the lances in her foreclaw. The sun was rising and Gwyneth did not want to return to the tower during the hours of daylight. The day would come when she would have to reveal herself to Immolatus, but not yet.

"For on that day, I will have to reveal myself to Huma," Gwyneth said softly.

BOOK
TWO

CHAPTER
EIGHTEEN

Although Justarius and Dalamar were far from the travelers lost in the River of Time, the wizards nonetheless had Destina and the others very much on their minds. They had contacted a member of the Conclave, the wizard Bertold, who lived in Solanthas, and asked him to find a woman called Alice Ranniker.

Bertold had been highly alarmed. "What do you want with her?" he had demanded in a panicked-sounding voice.

"We understand that she lives in Solanthas. We just need to know where she resides," Justarius had replied.

"I don't have to go to her house in person, do I?" Bertold had asked.

"Not at all," said Dalamar in a soothing tone. "We would prefer you didn't. Once you have provided us with the knowledge of where she lives, we will take care of the rest."

"Very well, Masters," said Bertold in a tone that said quite plainly he thought they were mad.

He had soon contacted them with the terse message: "I have found her."

The ancient Solamnic city of Solanthas dated back to the time of Vinas Solamnus. Located near the Vingaard River on some of the most fertile land in Ansalon, the city had started as a small farming community and still had its roots in agriculture. The Solanthas farmers market was the largest in Ansalon, and the people took pride in the fact that their food fed a nation.

Unlike Palanthas, which had been laid out in concentric circles by noted architects, Solanthas had sprouted up like a weed. Random buildings had erupted along streets that went every which way. It was said that only those born and bred in Solanthas could find their way around. Visitors were encouraged to hire guides, for without them they were soon hopelessly lost.

Bertold was a white-robed wizard who dwelled in a newer house in the city's central district. As Justarius confided to Dalamar, the only hope they had of reaching his house was by traveling directly there on the paths of magic.

Bertold was finishing his morning tarbean tea and reading a book when he was startled by the sight of the two archmages materializing in his library. He gave them both an effusive welcome and invited them into the kitchen to sit down to breakfast.

"I take it you found Alice Ranniker," Justarius said. "How do you know her?"

"Alice was my pupil," said Bertold, brewing more tea. "You haven't accepted her for the Test, have you, Master?"

"No, no," said Justarius hurriedly. "She did not qualify."

"Thank the gods!" said Bertold. "I should never have accepted her as a student, but her father was a friend of mine, and I took her as a favor to him. Alice is intensely interested in magic, and she works extremely hard, but she finds it difficult to concentrate. She cannot memorize even the simplest spells. The words slide from her mind as though coated with oil. That said, she is a remarkably talented mechanic. She recalibrated my measuring scale, repaired all my clocks, and fixed the flue in the chimney which had been smoking for years."

Dalamar and Justarius exchanged glances.

"We would like to meet this young woman," said Dalamar. "Can you tell us where she lives?"

"I can provide directions," said Bertold. "What is your business with Alice?"

"If you could just give us directions," said Justarius.

Bertold appeared disappointed, for he was understandably curious as to why two powerful archmages had traveled all this distance to speak to his failed pupil. He knew better than to insist, however.

"Alice's cottage is not in the city, but it is still difficult to find. It is located on a lane about a mile south of Granary Road and is screened by thick fir trees. You can't see it until you are almost on it. Just keep walking down the lane until you think you'll never find it, at which point you'll find it. You'll know it by the thatched roof, the forge out back, the perpetual cloud of smoke in the air, and the mechanical water well in the front yard."

Dalamar and Justarius thanked him and accepted his offer to walk with them as far as Granary Road. He indicated the lane, which began at the outskirts of the city.

"The gods go with you," he said in ominous tones, as though to imply the gods wouldn't be helpful, and hurriedly took his leave.

The lane was lined with fields of wheat that seemed never to end but stretched on and on to the heavens. Dalamar and Justarius followed the lane, and at the point when they began to think that Bertold had given them the wrong directions and they would find the Abyss sooner than the cottage, they came to the stand of fir trees and heard sounds of clanging, hammering, and banging.

They followed the noise to the small cottage with the thatched roof as described, and the mechanical water well—a series of small buckets attached to a chain that traveled down into a hole and emerged filled with water to be met by a mechanical "hand" that tipped each bucket, spilling its contents into a trough. The water flowed from the trough through a sluice, which led to the forge. Smoke and soot drifted through the air. The grass was black. Justarius frowned at the soot falling onto his red robes.

"You are lucky yours are already black," he grumbled to Dalamar.

They walked toward the sound of hammering, which was emanating from a large building made of stone. Aware that they would never be heard if they announced their arrival, they walked inside.

A short and stocky young woman with her hair wrapped in a scarf and some sort of helm over her head glanced at them through a glass panel in the helm and continued with her work. Dalamar presumed she was Alice Ranniker.

She was dressed in a rough calico shirt, leather breeches, leather apron, heavy leather gloves, and thick boots. She stood over an anvil, using a large hammer to beat a piece of red-hot metal into submission. The helm apparently protected her face from the heat and the sparks flying from the hammer.

Alice plunged the metal into a tub of water connected to a barrel that was in turn connected to the sluice that brought the water in from the well. The water hissed, sending up clouds of steam. She took the cooled metal out of the water, laid it aside, and removed her helm to regard her two visitors with frank curiosity.

"Hullo," she said, smiling, completely unconscious of the soot and grime on her face. "I'm Alice Ranniker. Who are you?"

"I am Justarius, master of the tower of Wayreth," said Justarius with dignity. "This is my colleague, Dalamar, master of the tower of Palanthas."

"Bless my gears and garters!" Alice gasped. Pulling off the gloves, she hurried forward to greet them. "Merciful moons of magic, this is such an honor! No, no. Don't come into the forge," she warned hastily. "You'll get your fine robes dirty. We'll talk in the house. Such an honor!"

She took off the leather apron and, with flustered courtesy, herded them into the small cottage and deposited them in a minuscule parlor. Every piece of furniture was covered with soot. Justarius and Dalamar eyed the chairs askance and chose to stand.

Alice excused herself, saying she needed to go wash up and change clothes. She returned a short time later minus the scarf, looking clean and neat in a sprigged dress, with her brown hair bound in a single braid wrapped around her head.

She was built like a blacksmith, with large shoulders and well-muscled arms. Dalamar judged she could have probably picked him up, heaved him over her shoulder, and walked off with him. She had bright eyes and an infectious smile.

"Have you come to invite me to take the Test?" she asked excitedly.

"I am afraid not, Mistress Ranniker," said Justarius. "We are here on a far more important mission."

Alice looked crushed at first, but her disappointment faded when

Dalamar brought forth the black velvet bag and asked if there was somewhere he could display the contents.

"My laboratory," said Alice proudly.

She hustled them out of the parlor and into the laboratory, which apparently doubled as the kitchen, for it contained a large marble table covered with magical runes and soup stains. Dirty plates and cutlery jostled with bottles, test tubes, and sheaves of paper with diagrams of various outlandish-looking and fantastical machines. A fire burned in the fireplace, where a mechanical hand was slowly turning a chicken roasting on a mechanical spit.

"Would you like to stay for dinner?" Alice asked.

Justarius glanced at the test tubes and the dirty plates. "Thank you, Mistress Alice, but I am on a restricted diet."

"Suit yourself," said Alice. "Make yourself comfortable. Sit on that stool. You can prop your crutch against the fireplace."

She cleared a space on the table with a sweep of her arm, sending plates and tubes crashing to the floor. Dalamar emptied the contents of the bag onto the table. He did not tell her what it was, for he wanted to see her reaction.

Alice bent to study the debris. "I can see it's magical, or at least it was at one time. Are the pieces trapped or may I safely touch them?"

"You may touch them," said Dalamar, giving her credit for having the sense to ask.

Alice picked up the rod and studied it from both ends. She held the orbs in her palms and seemed to weigh them. Rummaging about the remaining contents on the table, she located a jeweler's glass and put it on her eye to examine the jewels. She picked up one of the faceplates that formed the pendant and peered at it in the sunlight, then took the chain and swung it back and forth. Removing the jeweler's glass from her eye, she said, "Excuse me," and disappeared into another room. She returned carrying a large leather-bound book and thumped it down on the table.

"My great-great-great-grandfather Ranniker's *Book of Artifacts*," she said proudly.

Opening the book, she carefully turned the pages until she found what she sought, then shifted the book so they could see and pointed to an entry: *Device of Time Journeying.*

"This is or was the famous Device," she stated. "Forged on the Anvil of Time during the Age of Dreams by person or persons unknown, it is one of a kind. There will never be another."

She shook her head sadly. "What did you gents do to it? Run it through a meat grinder?"

Justarius glowered in anger and Dalamar hastily intervened.

"What happened to it is not relevant, Mistress. As you can see, it no longer works. We know you cannot build another one, but we were hoping you could repair this one so that it would once more be functional."

Alice looked at the diagram in the book, then back at the pieces on the table. She picked up the rod and screwed one of the orbs onto the end, then lifted the chain and attached it. She placed the faceplate on the table and began fitting some of the smaller jewels into the settings. Dalamar noted her touch was surprisingly delicate as she handled the tiny objects.

"It's been broken before now, hasn't it?" she said abruptly.

Justarius acknowledged that it had.

"Did a gnome repair it?" she asked.

"So I was told," said Justarius.

"Thought so. Some of the repairs are gnomish work. You can always tell."

"Can you fix it, Mistress Ranniker?" Dalamar asked.

"No," said Alice, straightening. "Sorry."

"Are you certain?" Justarius asked, dismayed.

"Too many bits and pieces are missing. For example, you need four small screws to hold the rod in place and there's only one screw here. These four sapphires go here, here, here, and here, but, as you see, that leaves two empty slots. I could make replacement parts, including the jewels, but your biggest problem is that the magic's drained clean out of it."

Justarius sank down in a chair with a bleak sigh. Dalamar began to gather up the pieces to place them back in the bag.

"Now, gentlemen, don't look so glum," said Alice cheerfully. "I can't fix this Device of Time Journeying, but I might be able to make a new one using the old parts, and I can refill the tank, so to speak."

"What does that mean?" Dalamar asked.

"Add the magic," said Alice.

"You can make a new device that will transport people through time?" Justarius asked, clarifying.

"It wouldn't be much of a Device of Time Journeying if it didn't transport people through time, now would it?" Alice asked with a snort. "I can build a newer one and, not only that, I can make it better. Much simpler to operate."

She pointed to the page in the book and grimaced in disgust. "Look at this long poem you have to memorize. It doesn't even rhyme! And notice how the chain drops down. Unless you manipulate the Device in a certain way, the chain can get tangled and you're sunk. Plus the description says it limits the number of people who can travel. I can fix that, too."

"I have no doubt you can construct such a device, Mistress, but who would supply the magic needed to operate it?" Justarius asked doubtfully.

"I will, of course," said Alice, looking amazed that they would even ask.

"Forgive us for doubting you, Mistress," said Dalamar gently, "but we have spoken to your teacher, and he said you had only the most rudimentary skills in magic. Yet the Device's magic will have to be extremely powerful. It would require a wizard who has both mechanical as well as the arcane knowledge to infuse it into the Device. Not even I could work such magic."

Alice rubbed her nose. "It's an odd thing. I can't cast a fireball spell to save my life; the words I'm supposed to say jiggle around in my head and come out upside down and wrong end foremost. But when it comes to forging steel or making new pieces for a clock or anything that involves working with my hands, the magic flows from my brain into my fingers like the water through that sluice."

She gestured to the front yard. "My well out there is powered by magic. The bellows in the forge are magic. All the lights in the house are magic. That spit cooking the chicken—magic."

Justarius exchanged glances with Dalamar, who gave a nod.

"Very well, Mistress," Justarius said. "How long will it take you to make a new Device? Time is of the essence."

Alice grinned. "Time is of the essence. Ha! Time-travel joke! That's a good one."

"This is not a matter for jest, Mistress," said Justarius sternly.

"I gathered that," said Alice. "Whatever's happened, you gents must be in one hell of a pickle barrel." She thought things over. "Come back in five days. Be here at noon sharp. I'll have the Device for you then. Leave those pieces there. I'll need the remains of the old one."

Justarius frowned. "What for?"

"To construct a new one, of course," said Alice. "This was forged on the Anvil of Time, not your local blacksmith's."

Justarius hesistated. "The Device is so rare—"

"What choice do we have?" Dalamar asked.

Justarius sighed. "Very well, Mistress Ranniker. We will return in five days at noon. What do you charge for the work?"

"I'll need money enough to cover the cost of materials. Throw in a visit to the Tower of High Sorcery in Palanthas and we'll call it even."

Dalamar envisioned Alice Ranniker roaming about his tower, and he shuddered. "I am afraid that is not possible—"

"What choice do we have?" Justarius reminded him, jabbing him with his elbow.

"You will be most welcome," said Dalamar.

Alice glowed with delight and clapped her hands.

"Raistlin was my hero, and I've always longed to see the Shoikan Grove! Dodging the skeletal hands coming up out of the ground. The trees that bleed real blood. And the Live Ones he created."

"Those pitiful creatures are no longer there," said Dalamar coldly.

"Oh, well." Alice looked disappointed for a moment, then soon cheered up. She grabbed a sheet of blank paper and a pen and began making sketches. She waved her hand. "You gents know the way out."

The two mages left the house. The last they saw of Alice, she was bent over the table, working on her diagram, oblivious to the fact that the chicken was being burnt to a crisp. The two walked past the well with its dripping, clattering, and clanking buckets, and entered the fir-tree-lined lane. They walked in silence down the lane until they were out of sight of the cottage, then stopped in the shadows of the trees to confer.

"What do you think?" Dalamar asked.

"That I would dearly love to get my hands on Ranniker's artifact book," said Justarius wistfully. "Did you see the pages as she flipped through them? Someone had made handwritten notes, and I'll wager it was Ranniker himself!"

"I meant about Alice making a new Device," said Dalamar.

"I do not know what to think. As you say, what choice do we have?" Justarius shook his head. "But we must be prepared to act, on the off chance she is successful. We need to choose someone to send back in time to rescue those trapped there."

"The most obvious candidate is the aesthetic, Brother Kairn. He knows those involved and he is familiar with the Third Dragon War, for he has made a study of it. Most important, he has traveled through time before, and he understands the perils."

Justarius nodded in approval. "A wise choice. Talk to Astinus and obtain his permission."

Both stood in silence a moment, then Justarius asked the question both had been thinking.

"If this journey proves successful and Brother Kairn manages to bring Lady Destina and the Graygem back through time, what do we do with the damn thing?"

"We will have to consult the gods of magic," Dalamar replied. "They know it is loose in the world, but I have not told them where it is."

"That will be a conversation I dread having," said Justarius.

Each mage prepared to cast the spells that would whisk them instantly back to their respective towers.

"I will meet you and Brother Kairn here in five days," said Justarius as he stepped through the portal he had created.

"Noon sharp," said Dalamar.

CHAPTER
NINETEEN

On his return to Palanthas, Dalamar was astonished to find Bertrem waiting in the entrance hall of his tower, keeping as near to the door as possible. Bertrem was mopping his face and looking nervously at two Black Robes who were in attendance. Dalamar was intensely curious to know what had brought Astinus's trusted assistant to his tower, but he would not forgo the responsibilities of a host.

"Has no one offered to make our guest comfortable, offered him food and drink?" Dalamar asked, displeased.

"We did, but he declined, Master," replied one of the Black Robes. "He refuses to stir from that spot."

Bertrem greeted Dalamar with obvious relief. "The master is expecting you. I will take you at once."

Dalamar would have preferred to rest, change his robes, have something to eat and drink, and spend time quietly reflecting on his journey. But the very fact that Bertrem had made the journey to the Tower of High Sorcery, a place he feared above all others, indicated that the matter was urgent. Dalamar gave all but a few of the spell components he had taken with him into the care of his apprentices and indicated to Bertrem that he was ready.

When they arrived at the Library of Palanthas, Bertrem led him to the private entrance. He ushered him inside Astinus's office, announced his name, then left him standing in front of the master's desk. Astinus did not look up from his work, but he did make a slight gesture toward a chair near the door.

Dalamar placed the chair in front of the desk and sat down. Astinus continued to write. Dalamar thrust his hands into the sleeves of his robes and waited.

Elves are a patient people. Their life span is long, and they see no need to rush toward the inevitable end. Dalamar watched the scratching of the pen across the paper and, by way of amusing himself, tried to make out the words, although he was forced to read them upside-down.

Astinus reached the end of a sheet of paper and added it to the growing pile on his desk. He drew forth a blank sheet, dipped his pen in the ink, and wrote even as he talked.

"Is it your belief, Dalamar Argent, that Alice Ranniker is capable of repairing and improving the Device of Time Journeying?"

Dalamar was not surprised to find that Astinus knew about their meeting. He was considerably surprised, however, that Astinus had deigned to ask his opinion.

"Let us say I do not believe so much as hope," Dalamar replied.

Astinus gave a barely perceptible nod. "You would like to speak to Brother Kairn, to see if he would be willing to travel back in time, provided Mistress Ranniker succeeds in her endeavors."

"Brother Kairn is the obvious choice, sir," Dalamar replied. "He is familiar with traveling through time. He knows the risks involved, and he is an expert on the Third Dragon War."

"I am certain Brother Kairn will be eager to assist," said Astinus. "He blames himself for the destruction of the Device, and he is desperate to find some way to rescue those stranded. In addition, I believe he has developed feelings for the young woman, Destina Rosethorn."

"I trust his feelings for her will not complicate matters," Dalamar said.

Astinus stopped writing and, for the first time, looked directly at Dalamar.

"Brother Kairn is one of *my* aesthetics, Master. You may be certain he will do his duty."

"I beg your pardon, sir," said Dalamar. "I did not intend any disparagement."

Astinus grunted and resumed his writing. Dalamar waited, but after several moments of hearing nothing except the pen scratch, he concluded that the meeting was over. He rose, bowed in respect, and departed. He found Bertrem waiting outside the door. The aesthetic spoke before Dalamar could open his mouth.

"I have summoned Brother Kairn. He will meet you in the common room."

"Were you eavesdropping, Bertrem?" Dalamar asked, pretending to be offended.

"Certainly not, sir!" Bertrem said, shocked. "The master told me prior to your coming that you would want to speak to him."

"I was teasing, Bertrem. Tell me about Brother Kairn," said Dalamar as they walked.

"I do not engage in gossip, Master," said Bertrem with a lofty air.

"I am thinking of asking Brother Kairn to undertake a delicate assignment," Dalamar explained. "I need to know if he is qualified. Where does he come from? What is his background?"

Bertrem seemed to find this explanation sufficient.

"Kairn Uth Tsartolhelm is the son of a Solamnic family who can proudly trace their ancestors back to before the Cataclysm. His father was a Knight of the Crown, as were his father and grandfather. The family expected Brother Kairn to enter the knighthood, but he preferred books to swords. He was admitted to the order of aesthetics at the age of sixteen. His chosen field of study is the Third Dragon War."

"Thank you, Brother," said Dalamar. "That is all I need to know."

The common room in the Great Library was one of the few places where people were permitted to speak above a whisper without fear of disturbing the work of the aesthetics. Dalamar sat at a table while Bertrem went to fetch the monk. The room was pleasant. Midafternoon sunlight streamed through the open windows. A cool breeze wafted inside.

Dalamar was grateful to see that he was the only visitor, for he wanted to keep their talk private. Bertrem returned with Brother Kairn in such a short period of time that Dalamar could almost assume the young aesthetic had been expecting him. Bertrem left the two together and said he would keep everyone else out.

Kairn was a young man, perhaps mid-twenties, and comely in appearance, with close-cropped black curly hair and brown eyes— although those eyes were now red-rimmed with fatigue, his handsome face drawn and haggard.

He sat down opposite Dalamar.

"Did you find a way to fix the Device?" he asked eagerly.

"We have been told by an expert that the Device is broken beyond repair—" Dalamar began.

Kairn sagged in his chair and lowered his head in his hands.

"This is my fault!" he said wretchedly.

"Lady Destina Rosethorn is the one at fault," said Dalamar sharply. "You were trying to help her. But I did not come to assign blame. What is done is done, and we must determine how to undo it. I require your help, Brother."

Kairn raised his head. "Anything, sir! I will do anything!"

"Would you be willing to go back in time to rescue those stranded there?"

"I would leave now, this instant, if I could!" said Kairn fervently. "But you said the Device was broken."

"Justarius and I took the remnants to a young woman named Alice Ranniker, who is related to the famous maker of magical artifacts. She could not fix the old Device. She did, however, offer to craft a new one."

"Do you think that is possible?" Kairn asked, sounding both hopeful and dubious.

"Mistress Ranniker is something of an eccentric, but Justarius and I were both impressed with her," said Dalamar. "If she does succeed in making a new Device of Time Journeying, we believe you should be the one to go back in time. Astinus has granted his permission."

"I will be glad to go, sir!" Kairn said, jumping to his feet.

"Take a moment to consider, Brother," Dalamar admonished. "This journey will be fraught with peril. You are going back to a time of war. You have no idea what you will find or what dangers you will face. You will be using an untested and extremely powerful magical device."

Kairn sat back down. "I understand the risks, sir."

"I doubt you understand the biggest risk," said Dalamar dryly.

"The Graygem of Gargath. Lady Destina still possesses it. Or rather, the Graygem possesses her."

"I have not forgotten about it, sir. I have been doing research on the Graygem, as well as on the Third Dragon War." Kairn made a helpless gesture. "I felt I had to do something."

Dalamar glanced around the common room. The two of them were the only people there, but he still lowered his voice.

"I will tell you a secret I have not told anyone, not even Justarius. When I first discovered that Lady Destina had acquired the Gray-gem, I informed the gods of magic. They suspected that Reorx was involved, since he had been the god to originally trap Chaos inside the Graygem. Lunitari wrung a confession from him. When Reorx heard that the lady had found the Graygem, he intended to take the Graygem from her and keep it himself. He lured her to his forge and there made a setting to hold it. But either by accident or by Chaos's design, Reorx nicked the Graygem with his hammer. The crack was tiny, and he claims he managed to seal it, but the possibility exists that Chaos might be seeping out of this crack."

"What does that mean, sir?" Kairn asked, perplexed.

"Chaos may change history simply to create chaos," Dalamar replied. "When I asked the gods what would happen if the Graygem disrupted time, Lunitari replied that the resulting disaster would make the Cataclysm seem like a gentle summer's rain. Your knowl-edge of the history of the period will serve you well. Take note of any change or disruption."

"I will do my best, sir," said Kairn.

Dalamar was satisfied. "We are to meet Mistress Ranniker at her home in Solanthas in five days' time at noon. You have no objection to traveling the paths of magic, do you?"

"None at all, sir," said Kairn. "I will continue my studies and be ready."

FIVE DAYS LATER, half an hour before noon, Dalamar and Kairn emerged from the magical portal at the end the fir-tree-lined lane near Alice's house and found Justarius waiting for them. Dalamar introduced Kairn.

"What is in your pack, Brother?" Justarius asked, observing the rucksack Kairn carried on his back.

"A change of clothing, sir," Kairn replied. "I have brought robes that are brown in color and made of the same cloth as those worn by the aesthetics of that time period. I have also brought several pairs of dry socks—always important when traveling. My shoes are similar to those worn in that era. Unfortunately, I could not find an exact match."

"You did not bring any books about the Third Dragon War, did you? We could not risk having those fall into the wrong hands."

"Of course not, sir," said Kairn, offended. "I carry my knowledge in my head."

"Forgive me for doubting your expertise in this matter, Brother, but we dare not leave anything to chance," said Justarius.

The three proceeded down the lane to the cottage, walking slowly to accommodate Justarius. When they reached the cottage, Dalamar noticed that the forge fire was not burning. He could not hear any sounds of hammering or banging. The house and grounds were quiet, except for the clanking of the buckets and the sound of water splashing into the barrel. Admittedly, they were early—the sun had not yet reached its zenith—but all were impatient.

Justarius knocked at the front door, calling Alice's name and announcing their presence.

"Come in!" she shouted. "I'm in the laboratory!"

They made their way to the laboratory and found Alice seated at the large stone table in almost exactly the same place they had left her five days ago. The table was empty save for a single object that they could not see, for she had covered it with a dish towel.

"I thought you eager beavers might be early," she said, grinning. She eyed Kairn curiously. "I see you brought a monk along. Did you come to pray for me, Brother? Not necessary, I assure you. All is well."

Dalamar introduced Kairn, explaining, "We have asked Brother Kairn to be the person to travel back in time."

"Good to meet you, Mister Monk," said Alice, shaking hands.

As Kairn stared about in wonder, Dalamar noted that the mechanical hand that turned the spit in the fireplace was not at work today, but another mechanical hand holding a large spoon was stirring something in a kettle. A strong smell of lye soap pervaded the room.

"Today's laundry day," Alice explained.

"Were you successful, Mistress?" Justarius asked. "Did you make a new Device of Time Journeying?"

"Of course!" Alice said calmly. "I never undertake anything unless I plan to succeed at it. Gather around the table, gents and monk."

She waited until they were settled and she was certain she had their full attention. She whisked off the dishtowel with a flourish, revealing a globe made of silver inlaid with gold and dotted with jewels set in patterns.

"I give you the newer and improved Device of Time Journeying," Alice said.

The globe was about the size of a loaf of bread and perfectly round. It rested on a small wooden stand that kept it from rolling off the table.

"It is beautiful," said Dalamar. "A work of art."

"Thank you, sir," said Alice. "I melted down the original and used some of the metal to make this one."

Justarius stared at her in horror. "You *melted* the Device of Time Journeying?"

"It was useless the way it was," Alice pointed out. "And I couldn't make the new Device without the old one. I needed to use the metal of the original, just as I used the jewels."

"It was ancient!" said Justarius, seething. "A treasure!"

"But it didn't work," Alice said, sounding puzzled.

Justarius could not speak for fury. He could only glare at her in outraged disbelief.

"I think I have a few of the leftover cogs and wheels and screws if you'd like to have them," said Alice. "They're probably in the dustbin."

"Perhaps you would explain to us how this new Device works, Mistress," Dalamar suggested, hoping that would give Justarius time to calm himself.

Alice shrugged, clearly not understanding the problem. "As you see, gents, the new Device is quite simple in design. No chains or rods or orbs. I did include a poem the operator has to recite as a safety precaution, so no unauthorized person can use it. A simple code would have worked just as well, but I thought it would be nice to make it a poem as an homage to the original. It's not nearly as complicated, though."

"The patterns of the jewels seem familiar," said Kairn, studying them.

"The constellations," said Alice. "Each represents one of the gods of Krynn. This is the constellation of the dragon Paladine, and this is the bison head of Kiri-Jolith, and this is the five-headed dragon of Takhisis. The gods of magic are also present in the form of three moons: one of diamonds, one of rubies, and one of obsidian."

Dalamar started to touch the globe, but Alice snatched up the Device, held it out of his reach, and wagged her finger at him.

"Who knows where your hands have been? I can't have your magicks interfering with mine. No offense, of course, sir."

"I take none, Mistress," said Dalamar, not daring to look at Justarius. "Perfectly reasonable."

"Good. I need to make one more test, and I thought you gents would like to be present to witness it. Sit down and make yourselves comfortable. This might take a while."

They sat down. Justarius leaned his crutch against the table.

Alice placed her soot-stained hand on the top of the globe, closed her eyes, whispered something, then added, "'And with a poem that almost rhymes, now I travel back in time.'"

She and the Device both vanished.

Kairn gasped and jumped to his feet. Justarius cast Dalamar a grim glance. "Now what do we do?"

"Wait for her to return," said Dalamar.

Justarius snorted. Kairn slowly sat back down.

The three waited in silence, listening to various mechanical objects whir, buzz, clank, and clatter. An enormous clock ticked away the minutes. One of its hands held a hammer, and when it reached the hour, the clock struck a bell.

Alice returned, materializing in the kitchen.

"I'm back!" she announced unnecessarily.

"Did it work?" Dalamar asked tensely. "Did you travel through time?"

"Of course it worked!" said Alice with an indignant look. "I said it would, didn't I?"

She was holding the globe in one hand and a large book in the other.

"I went to visit great-great-great-grandfather Ranniker. I've always wanted to meet him. He and I had a nice chat about artifacts. Did you know he made a clock that could give people a glimpse of the future?"

Dalamar and Justarius exchanged startled glances.

"We know about the clock," said Dalamar.

"Do you have it? I'd love to see it," said Alice.

"I regret to say it has been destroyed," said Dalamar.

"That's a pity," said Alice. "Maybe I'll make another one. He gave me a few pointers. Speaking of artifacts, Ranniker sent this to you, Master."

She placed the book she was holding on the table in front of Justarius.

"Ranniker's *Book of Artifacts*," he stated, reading the title.

"Not just *any* book of artifacts," said Alice triumphantly. "Ranniker's own book. I saw how much you admired the one I had. This is an early edition, mind you. He had just written the updated version, which is why he said I could have this one."

Justarius gazed at the book in awe. He touched the leather cover with trembling hands and gently and reverently opened it to the flyleaf. Dalamar read the signature: *Ranniker.*

Justarius slowly turned the pages.

"This is his handwriting! I recognize it. Ranniker always wrote in block capital letters."

"I figured you'd require proof that my Device works," said Alice complacently. "Well, there you have it. You two gents can leave now. Mister Monk and I have work to do. I have to teach him how to use the Device."

"We intend to stay, Mistress," said Justarius.

"Suit yourself," said Alice. "This could take days. I'm not letting this young man go unless I'm sure he can get there and back safely. You two can sleep in the forge. And I think I have some leftover chicken stew. . . ."

"Perhaps we should stay just long enough to hear how it works," Dalamar suggested to Justarius.

Apparently the thought of sleeping in the forge was too much for Justarius, for he grumblingly agreed.

Alice placed the globe in front of Kairn.

"Here you are, Mister Monk. This is now yours," Alice said. "Listen to me carefully."

Kairn appeared to suddenly realize the enormity of the task he had agreed to undertake, for his jaw tightened and he drew in a deep breath.

"I am listening, Mistress."

Alice sat down beside him. "You must put your hand on the globe—anywhere is fine. And all those intending to travel with you must also touch the globe. You state aloud the name of the place you want to visit and provide the date and the time. The more specific, the better."

"I would appreciate it, Mistress, if you would clarify your instructions," said Kairn. "Considering the importance of my mission, I want to make certain I understand completely what I must do."

Alice appeared pleased and gave him a laudatory pat on his shoulder. "Good for you, Mister Monk. So let's suppose you want to study the War of the Lance. You could say, 'Take me to the War of the Lance' and it would take you to the war. But if you don't specify the date and the place and the time, the Device could take you anywhere from the Blood Sea of Istar to the Dark Queen's Temple in Neraka."

Kairn nodded to indicate he understood.

"You should therefore try to narrow it down. For example, you could say 'Take me to Solamnia during the War of the Lance,' but that still covers quite a bit of territory. What you should say is 'Take me to the High Clerist's Tower, Solamnia, 352 AC, the month of Fierswelt, noon on the seventh day, Knight's Entrance.'"

"And then what do I do?" Kairn asked.

"Once you state where you want to go and when, you recite the little poem, which is simple enough for a child to remember, and off you travel. Swoosh!"

Kairn regarded her in admiration. "Your work is amazing, Mistress Ranniker!"

Alice was clearly pleased. "I included one feature from the original Device which I considered made a lot of sense. No matter what happens, if someone steals it or you drop it down a well, the globe will always come back to you. You don't need to fuss over it. The globe is pretty much indestructible. You can carry it in your rucksack without fear of damage. If a jewel falls out, just stick it back in. You can take this with you to make repairs."

She handed Kairn a corked vial filled with a viscous liquid.

"What is that?" Justarius demanded. "A magical elixir of some sort?"

Alice gave him a funny look. "Glue."

She stood up. "That's it, gents. Mister Monk and I will spend a day or two making practice runs so that he gets the hang of it. Any questions?"

"Can he bring back everyone?" Justarius asked.

"All those who traveled back in time can return with him," she said. "In fact, they must. He can't leave anyone behind. What is it they always say? Never split the party. It's all or none."

"What if one of them has died?" Dalamar asked.

"Then you're screwed," said Alice. "You better hope they've had sense enough to take care of themselves. If you bring them back here together, then they were never there. Leave them back there and they were never here." She gave a shrug. "Either way, the River keeps flowing. But if you split them up piecemeal, leave two back there and bring two back here . . ."

"Then we risk changing history," said Dalamar.

"Splitting the party could be done," said Alice cautiously. "But only *in extremis,* as you scholarly types say. It means 'on the point of death.' If you must, you must, but I wouldn't advise it. Oh, and I forgot to mention that you have the ability to come back by yourself, Mister Monk. In fact, you'll have to return whether you succeed or not. I don't suppose Astinus wants you gallivanting through time."

"All of us who travel back into the past take vows to return to our own time, Mistress," Kairn said.

"So that's cleared up," said Alice. "And now, my laundry's about finished. Mister Monk and I have work to do, and I'm sure you gents have somewhere important to be."

"I have one more question, Mistress Alice," said Dalamar, as they rose to take their leave. "What would happen if the Device were to come into contact with another extraordinarily powerful artifact?"

"What artifact did you have in mind?" Alice asked, giving him a shrewd look.

"The Graygem of Gargath."

Alice had singed off most of her eyebrows, but she raised what little she had left.

"Well now. I wasn't expecting *that*," she said and rubbed her nose. "Are you saying the Graygem is mixed up in all this?"

"We believe so," said Dalamar.

"That could change things. But I don't know much about the Graygem. Let's see what Grandpa Ranniker had to say about it."

She opened the book and after some searching located the page.

"Ranniker notes the various legends surrounding the making of the Graygem and includes scholarly speculation as to whether it truly exists or is a myth.

"He writes: 'The fact that it has not been seen in thousands of years leads most of the wise to conclude it was a myth, but I am not so certain. We have read too many detailed accounts from those who claimed to have seen it. These accounts come from different races and different parts of the known world, yet all agree in their descriptions of the gem. All of them state that it is difficult to study, for it glows with an unsettling gray light and is constantly changing its shape. The wise consider the Graygem to be the most dangerous artifact known to man, for it holds Chaos. But I don't believe Chaos is as clever as it thinks it is.'"

"An odd statement to make," said Justarius, frowning.

"Ranniker was an odd duck," said Alice. "As for the Graygem, I have no idea how it might affect the magic of the Device. In other words, Mister Monk is on his own. But if it is as dangerous as Ranniker says, I take back my comment on splitting the party. All bets are off. You should just hope you can rescue the survivors."

"Gilean save us!" Kairn murmured, shaken.

Alice patted his hand. "Don't worry, Mister Monk. Keep the faith, as you religious types say. Any other questions, gentlemen? If not, Mister Monk and I have work to do."

"I demand to stay," said Justarius stubbornly.

"Up to you," said Alice. "There's the laundry basket. The clothes-line is outside. You can hang my drawers out to dry while you wait."

Justarius glowered. Then he picked up the precious book of arti-facts, muttered his thanks, and reached for his crutch.

"Godspeed, Brother Kairn," said Dalamar, grasping the monk's hand.

"I appreciate your trust in me, sir," said Kairn. He looked unhap-pily after Justarius, who was limping to the door. "I fear I have an-gered him."

"He is afraid," said Dalamar. "We both are. Take the time you need for study, Brother, but don't take too long. The river is rising. Contact me immediately upon your return."

Alice accompanied Dalamar and Justarius to the door and stood on the stoop to watch them walk down the lane, undoubtedly mak-ing certain the two wizards were actually leaving.

"I could fit you with a mechanical leg, Mister Mage," she called after Justarius. "It would take a little getting used to, as the leg could have a tendency to walk away on its own. . . ."

Justarius pretended he had not heard her and quickened his pace. Once they were past the well with its rotating buckets and out of sight of the house, he said feelingly, "The gods help that young man!"

"Mistress Ranniker is a little strange, but I am impressed with the Device she created," said Dalamar.

"Odd that she brought up Ranniker's Clock," Justarius said.

"I was thinking the same," said Dalamar. "I still remember the terrible future I saw when I entered the clock. That blue-skinned creature breaking open the Graygem and unleashing Chaos. Magic gone from the world. Alien dragons holding mankind in the grip of terror."

"Ungar committed criminal folly when he sent Lady Destina after the Graygem in some scheme to profit off what he had wit-nessed," said Justarius. "For all we know, in his attempt to prevent the terrible future he saw from happening, the wretch may well have precipitated it."

The two arrived at the end of the lane. They both looked back in the direction of the cottage. All was quiet, save for the distant clanking of the magical mechanical water well.

"I approve your choice of Brother Kairn," said Justarius. "He seems sensible and courageous. And from what you say, he is knowledgeable regarding the history of the era. But he will need all his wisdom and courage, for he has no idea what awaits him."

"That is what frightens me," said Dalamar.

CHAPTER

TWENTY

Destina had waited all day for Raistlin and Magius to return from the Tower of High Sorcery. She had nothing to do except worry. She considered visiting Tas in the dungeons of the tower, but she had no idea where they were located, and she didn't want to ask, for she knew how the commander would react. She was afraid she would get lost searching for them on her own.

Magius and Raistlin had not returned by suppertime and Destina knew something had gone wrong. She had returned to her room and tried to stay awake, hoping to hear news. She had lost hope as the night wore on with no sign of Raistlin or Magius. Eventually, worn out and despondent, she had fallen asleep.

Destina woke early the next morning from a dream about Kairn she had never meant to have. The dream had seemed very real. He had reached out his hands to her, but when she had tried to take them, he had vanished.

The bell chimed the hour of seven. She quickly dressed and hurried across the bridge to the Knight's Spur, hoping to hear news.

The only person at the table was Will, eating his breakfast.

"Have you seen either Raistlin or Magius this morning?" Destina asked.

"Thank the gods, no," Will said dourly. "Will you have some porridge, Lady? I can have Cook bring another bowl."

"Thank you, but I am not hungry," said Destina. "I did not sleep well. I am going for a walk on the battlements to clear my head. If Raistlin comes, will you tell him where to find me?"

Will promised he would do so.

She climbed the stairs to the battlements at the top of the Knight's Spur and looked out on the plains below where the tents of the dragonarmy were sprouting like hideous toadstools.

More enemy troops were arriving daily, marching from the east, the west, and the south. All of Solamnia was now under the Dark Queen's control. The knights could only watch the numbers swell and wait for the day when the enemy's horns blared the attack and brought death to the High Clerist's Tower. The sight was unnerving, and Destina was about to return to the dining hall when she was joined by Commander Belgrave.

He leaned on the wall and gazed out at the enemy.

"Look at them, strolling about their camp without a care in the world, knowing full well we can't touch them. And their numbers are still relatively small."

Destina looked out at the tents. Most were small, gray or brown in color, but she saw two rows of red tents, each tent flying a flag the color of flame.

"Those red ones belong to an elite mercenary force," Titus explained. "I suppose we should count ourselves honored that Immolatus has hired them to fight us. He treats them well, though he expects to get his money's worth. They had better be prepared to shed their life's blood for the cause."

"Who is housed in that large tent, the one with the red and black stripes?" Destina asked.

"That is the dragon's command tent."

"I thought dragons slept in lairs," said Destina, trying to imagine the enormous dragon in a small tent.

"Ordinarily they do. Your friend Raistlin seems to know something about this dragon and, according to him, Immolatus only goes to his lair at night. During the day, he shifts into human form in order to meet with his officers and keep an eye on his troops. Or like the elf woman. According to your kender, she's a dragon, as well." Titus gave a wry smile.

"When will the red dragon and his armies attack, do you think?" Destina asked, trying to keep her voice from shaking.

"Immolatus won't strike on his own. He will wait until Her Dark Majesty arrives, and she's apparently in no hurry," said Titus. "According to scouting reports, she's within two days' ride of the tower. Her troops number in the thousands, and she has blue dragons and the undead among her ranks, as well as humans, goblins, kobolds, ogres, and any others who worship her. Not to mention the mercenaries who are simply in this war for the spoils."

Titus turned to face Destina, his expression grave. "I was coming to find you, Lady. Those two wizard friends of yours should use their magic to transport you and the kender to a place of safety. And they can transport themselves along with you. I don't need war wizards. When it comes to fighting, I prefer cold, hard steel."

"I will speak to them," said Destina.

"Just so you know, Lady Destina, that wasn't a request," said Titus. "That was an order. And now I'd best be getting back to my duties. I bid you good day."

He descended the stairs, leaving her alone.

The morning was cool with a cloudless blue sky and a gentle breeze. Destina paced back and forth, wondering what they would do if they were stranded here in time. She was not worried as much about herself as she was the Graygem. She could not allow Takhisis to get hold of it.

"She can't take it if she doesn't know it's here," Destina reasoned. "Perhaps it would be better if we left before she finds out."

She heard footfalls on the stairs and hoped it was Raistlin coming in search of her. She turned hopefully, only to be be disappointed to see a soldier emerge from the stairwell.

"I was told I would find you up here, Lady Destina," he said.

He spoke familiarly, as though he knew her, yet Destina could not place him.

"Did Commander Belgrave send you?" she asked.

"You don't recognize me?" the soldier said. "Not surprising. I was not at my best the last time you saw me. I am Yeoman Mullen Tully. I was wounded when the goblins attacked that village. You saved my life."

"Oh, of course!" said Destina, remembering. "But I did very little. It was Raistlin who tended to your wounds. I heard the villagers say they had a cleric that could heal you. I am pleased to see you up and about."

He smiled at her, and there was something in his smile that made her uneasy. She did not want to be alone with him. Yet he stood between her and the stairs.

"It is good to see you, Yeoman," Destina said coolly. "The wind is starting to grow chilly. If you will excuse me, I believe I will go inside."

Destina was trying to edge around him, when he suddenly sprang at her. He grabbed hold of the collar of her jacket and ripped it open, and seized the Graygem.

Gray light flared. Tully gave a sharp cry and snatched his hand away. He stared at the reddening blotch on his palm and the blisters on his fingers and wrung his hand in pain. He scowled at her, muttered a foul imprecation, then shoved past her and ran down the stairs.

Destina stared after him, horrified by the suddenness and shock of the attack. She waited on the battlements until she could no longer hear his footfalls, then hurried back across the bridge to the tower and up the stairs to her room. She locked the door, splashed cold water on her face, and tried to calm her fast-beating heart. She had to tell someone about Tully, that he knew about the Graygem and had attempted to take it. She should tell Raistlin, but he was not around—at least she had not seen him. She decided to seek out Sturm.

A knock on the door alarmed her.

"Who is there?" she called out sharply, making no move to open it.

"Commander Belgrave would like to speak to you, my lady," Will called.

Destina sighed deeply. She made certain the Graygem was hidden beneath the collar of her jacket, then opened the door.

"Do you know where I can find Sturm Brightblade?" she asked.

"I do not, my lady, but perhaps Commander Belgrave will know."

Will escorted her back to the Knight's Spur and led her to the commander's office, where he announced her before ushering her inside.

"Lady Destina Rosethorn, sir."

"Come in, my lady," said Titus.

Destina entered the office and saw a man wearing the gray robes and cowl of a monk seated in a chair in a corner. His wrists were shackled, and a guard stood beside him, his hand on his sword hilt. A rucksack lay at his feet, along with a quarterstaff.

"Who is this?" Destina asked, startled.

"I am hoping you can tell me, my lady," said Titus grimly.

The monk had been sitting with his head bowed, but at the sound of Destina's voice, he raised his head and rose to his feet, alarming the soldier, who drew his sword.

The monk paid no heed to him. He had eyes only for her. A ray of sunlight shining through the window touched his face, and Destina stared at him in paralyzing shock.

"He says his name is Kairn and he claims to be a monk from the Great Library," Titus was saying. "He says you know him and can vouch for him. I am beginning to think you know everyone in Solamnia, Lady Destina."

Destina could not move. She could not breathe. She could not answer. All she could think was that Kairn could not possibly be here. He was far away—centuries away!

She staggered and reached out her hand to steady herself on the back of a chair.

"Destina!" Kairn said in concern and took a step toward her, but the guard dragged him back. Titus shouted for Will.

"Lady Destina is ill! Fetch some wine," Titus ordered when the retainer appeared. "Sit down, my lady."

Destina paid no attention to him. Kairn was the only person in the room who mattered, and he couldn't possibly be in the room.

"Are you . . . real?" she faltered. "Am I . . . still dreaming?"

"I am sorry, Destina!" said Kairn. I did not mean to cause you such distress. But you must have known I would come back for you!"

He reached out his shackled hands to her as he had reached out to her in the dream. Destina touched him, and he was real. He was flesh and blood. She had no idea how or why he was here. That didn't matter. She flung her arms around him and held him close, shackles and all.

Kairn could not return her embrace due to the manacles, but he whispered, "I have come to take you home."

Destina clung to him, not wanting to let him go. She looked up into his eyes. "I am so glad! But how . . . The Device was destroyed. . . ."

"Hush!" Kairn whispered. He cast a glance at his rucksack. "Say nothing more!"

"I see you do know this man," said Titus dryly.

Destina nodded and reluctantly released her hold.

"I know Brother Kairn from the Great Library," Destina said confusedly, feeling her face grow warm.

"I have been assisting Lady Destina with her studies," Kairn added.

Titus looked from one to the other. "Well, he's not a spy, whatever else he may be. Remove the manacles."

Will produced a key and unlocked the manacles. Kairn rubbed his wrists and smiled uncertainly at Destina, who suddenly found it difficult to look at him after she had just flung herself into his arms.

"Sit down," Titus ordered, gesturing to two chairs in front of his desk. "Both of you."

He regarded them grimly.

"I want to know the truth about what is going on. I've seen the looks you and your companions exchange when you think I'm not watching, Lady Destina. I've seen how all of you go out of your way to muzzle the kender."

"Tas says . . . such nonsense," Destina murmured.

"Does he?" Titus demanded. "Or do you stop his mouth because he's telling the truth?"

Destina lowered her eyes and kept silent.

Titus gestured at Kairn. "And now this monk arrives, telling some harebrained tale about having traveled here on Astinus's orders to take notes on a battle that none of us are likely to survive—

including him. And he's a bit vague on how he managed to make his way safely through enemy lines. According to him, the goblins didn't slit his throat because he's a librarian!"

Kairn shifted uncomfortably in his chair and Destina stared down at her hands. She didn't know what to say. Fortunately, she was saved from responding by someone beating on the door.

"Commander, sir!"

"Now what?" Titus muttered.

The jailer hurried inside the room.

"The kender, Burrfoot, has escaped, sir."

Titus rubbed his hand over his jaw. "I was thinking it was about time. I'm surprised he stayed this long. Go find him and lock him up again. And this time, chain him to the wall."

"He's not in the tower, sir," the jailer clarified. "Looks like he crawled out a window in the sacristy. We found it open and a desk shoved underneath it."

Titus shrugged. "Then he's goblin fodder. I can't help him."

"We have to find him!" Kairn said urgently, and he cast a significant look at Destina.

"Tas talked a lot about going to see the gnomes," Destina said, stricken.

"Gnomes?" Titus repeated.

"I had no idea he would run off. I won't go back home without him, sir!" Destina said and rose determinedly from the chair. "I will search for him."

"It's not safe, Destina," Kairn said, jumping to his feet. "I will go."

"No one is going anywhere!" Titus roared and slammed his fist on the desk. "Don't you people realize we're surrounded by the enemy in the middle of a damn war?" He glared at them. "Sit down!"

Destina and Kairn sank back into their chairs.

Titus looked at Destina. "What did the kender mean about going to see gnomes?"

"He showed me their village on the map. He talked a lot about the gnomes, but . . . I'm afraid I wasn't paying attention."

"There *is* a gnome village about twenty miles from here, though I'm sorry to say it's likely a goblin village now," said Titus.

"Isn't there something we can do to find him, sir?" Kairn asked.

"I can't spare any of my men. Ask your wizard friends," Titus suggested. "They might be of some help. Maybe they have a locate kender spell."

"I don't believe Raistlin and Magius are here either, sir," Destina said. "Raistlin said something about the two of them traveling to Palanthas...."

"Palanthas?" Titus exploded. "Do you lot think you are all on a kender wanderlust?"

He stood up, shoving his chair back with such force it crashed into the wall.

"Will, come with me." Titus glared at Kairn and Destina. "You two stay here!"

He slammed out of the office, and they heard his angry footfalls in the hall. Destina and Kairn sat quite still, afraid to move or speak. When all was quiet, Kairn went to the door, opened it a crack, and looked out.

"No one is there," he reported. "We can talk freely." He came to sit by Destina. "Why did Magius and Raistlin go to Palanthas?"

"To obtain the Device of Time Journeying," said Destina. "It blew apart—"

"In my hands," said Kairn, grimacing. "But since the Device was destroyed, why did Raistlin think it might be in Palanthas?"

"Raistlin reasoned that even though it had been destroyed in our time, it would still exist in this one," Destina explained. "He and Magius went to the Tower of High Sorcery to find it. They were only supposed to be gone a short time, but I haven't seen either of them this morning and I fear something has gone wrong. But you said you came to take us home! Were you able to repair the Device?"

"Not even Justarius could fix it," said Kairn. "He found a young woman skilled in making artifacts, and she constructed a new Device from the bits and pieces of the old one. I have it with me in the rucksack."

"I am surprised the commander didn't search it," said Destina. "He obviously doesn't trust you."

"He did look through it," said Kairn. "Fortunately, Dalamar cast a spell on the rucksack, so that if someone looks inside, they will see only a change of clothing. We can leave, but only if we are all together. Alice specified that 'all must go or none.' So we need to find Tasslehoff. You said he went to look for gnomes?"

"He kept talking about how Uncle Trapspringer and the gnomes invented the dragonlance. I think he may have gone to find out if that was true."

"But why would he go in search of dragonlances?" Kairn asked, bewildered. "History records the battle will start on Bakukal, the sixteenth day of the month of Palesvelt. By my calculations, that's the day after tomorrow. Huma will take up the dragonlance and ride the silver dragon to battle and save Solamnia."

Destina shook her head. "He cannot take up the dragonlance because they are not here. No one has ever even heard of them."

"Gilean save us!" Kairn rose distractedly to his feet and began to pace the room. "Perhaps this is why the pages of the book were blank!"

"What book? What do you mean?" Destina asked, frightened.

"After the Device blew up, Astinus held a meeting to discuss the possibility that the Graygem had gone back in time to the Third Dragon War. He sent me to fetch the record he had made of this period, but the pages he had written then were blank. Since then, I have been studying the history of the Third Dragon War so that I could bring you and the others back—and the Graygem."

Destina clasped hold of it. The jewel was uncomfortably warm in her grasp.

"How did you know I possess it?" she asked.

"Dalamar knew you were wearing it. He told us at the meeting. I came back to find you and the others and prevent the Graygem from changing time. Does anyone else know about it?"

"Tasslehoff and Sturm both know," said Destina. "Raistlin saw the jewel and figured out what it was. And, just now, a man named Mullen Tully tried to steal it from me. The Graygem stopped him; it burned his hand when he touched it."

"Who is this Tully?" Kairn asked.

"He is supposedly a soldier serving in the tower, but I don't trust him and neither does Raistlin." Destina shivered. "He thought he was a deserter, and so did Commander Belgrave when we mentioned him."

"Where is this Tully now?" Kairn asked, troubled.

"I don't know," said Destina. "I was going to tell Sturm and ask him to keep watch for him. And Gwyneth also knows about the Graygem. She cast a spell on Tas that keeps him from talking about it. She warned me that if Takhisis found out, she would try to seize it. And if the Dark Queen joined forces with Chaos . . ."

Destina gave a despairing sigh. "I have made such a mess of everything! I have put us all in danger and I have no idea how to set it right—or if I even can!"

Kairn sat down and pressed her hand in comfort. He sat quietly, thinking. "I believe you may have more help than you know. Tell me about Gwyneth."

"She claims to be an elf, but she does not look like any elf I have ever seen," said Destina. "She has silver hair and a silvery tint to her skin, and she possesses extraordinary powers of magic. Tas says she reminds him of Silvara, who was apparently a silver dragon. He believes Gwyneth is the silver dragon in the song who fell in love with Huma."

Kairn was about to reply, but Destina heard a sound outside the door—a strange sound, as if someone were struggling to draw breath. She squeezed his hand in warning.

Fearing it was Tully, Destina rose quickly and flung open the door. No one was there, but she heard footsteps receding. She closed the door and sat back down.

They listened, but the sound was not repeated.

"We were speaking of Gwyneth," she said.

"Tas is right. Gwyneth *is* the silver dragon," Kairn said, keeping his voice low. "She was Silvara's sister. And since Gwyneth is here, then that is good. All is well. She knows where to find the dragon-lances. She loves Huma and she will fight at his side."

"Gwyneth has disappeared," said Destina, sighing.

Kairn was shocked. "But she has to be here! She and Huma will defeat Takhisis!"

"She is gone." Destina shook her head. "The commander thought she was a spy and locked her in the dungeons. She escaped and now she has vanished. If she loved Huma, why would she leave?"

Kairn was troubled. "I think I might know. Gwyneth spent many years among the Qualinesti and they consider her one of their own. An elven legend says there was a prophecy given when Gwyneth and Silvara were born. The prophecy foretold that mortals would be the cause of their doom. Perhaps she fled to escape that fate."

Destina sighed. "All I know is that the silver dragon is gone. The knights are outnumbered thousands to one. They have no dragon-lances and, without them, they cannot hope to defeat the Dark Queen. Solamnia will fall. History will change and the fault is mine."

"Do not lose faith, Destina," said Kairn. "Paladine and the other gods are with us still."

"Are they?" Destina asked hopelessly, clasping the Graygem. "Or have they fled, as well?"

CHAPTER
TWENTY-ONE

Magius had been too weary the night of his return from the Tower of High Sorcery to attempt to control the dragon orb. He had memorized his spells but refused the temptation to even look inside the white velvet bag on his nightstand. He had lain down in his bed, though he found it difficult to sleep. In his dreams, the orb called to him.

He rose early after a restless night. No one else was awake and he was hungry from missing dinner. Going to the kitchen, he rummaged through the pantry and found a meat pie. He cut himself a portion and carried it back to his room, along with a jug filled with apple wine.

As he ate the pie and sipped the wine, he read the small book about the orb Anitra had given him. It had been written by one of the wizards who had helped create the dragon orbs. They had crafted five orbs, trapping a different evil dragon inside each orb. Magius thought of the wondrous magic involved in the creation and he was still appalled to think that the kender had deliberately destroyed one.

He was hoping the book would describe the secret of their creation, but the author stated that out of respect for those who had

MARGARET WEIS AND TRACY HICKMAN

given their lives in the attempt, the Conclave had decreed that the secret would never be revealed. The book did, however, describe how a wizard could take control of the orb and force the dragon trapped inside to obey the mage's will.

The book explained that the orbs could take on the characteristics of the dragons trapped inside, and cautioned that the imprisoned dragon would try every means possible to thwart the wizard. The book concluded with this stern warning: *If the wizard fails to gain control of the dragon, the dragon will gain control of the wizard.*

Magius studied the words to the spell, then laid aside the book. He took the marble-sized orb from the bag and placed it on the silver stand that had come with it. He drew back his hands and waited.

The orb gleamed in the light of the lamp, and Magius could see a red miasma moving about sluggishly inside. According to the book, the red color meant that a red dragon was trapped in the orb. Magius was skeptical. He could not begin to imagine how those wizards had trapped a red dragon inside a crystal globe. The feat seemed impossible. But then he reminded himself that he could hurl fireballs and float through the air.

"I do the impossible every day," he muttered.

He stared intently at the orb and saw the red miasma inside the globe start to swirl. The orb began to grow in size, although Magius had the uneasy impression that it was not growing. He was shrinking. He was careful not to touch it, not until he was ready to try to take control.

The red color swirled a little faster, the orb grew larger, and now he could see eyes inside. The eyes gazed at him and he saw the malevolence and hatred in them. He understood the dire fate that awaited him should the dragon break free.

Magius felt his stomach tighten. His mouth was dry and his palms were damp. The dragon invaded his mind, promising him everything he had ever wanted—if he would only surrender.

"Give yourself to me," said the red dragon, "and I will tell you the secrets of the universe. All knowledge will be yours. All power. All wealth. Whatever you want you can have."

The dragon's eyes became Greta's eyes. She smiled at him from the red miasma. She held out her hands to him.

Take my hands, beloved, Greta pleaded with him. *Bring me back from the realm of death.*

Greta reached out to him. Magius knew this was a trap and he held still, keeping his hands flat on the table. Suddenly her hands changed into red-scaled claws, their talons stained with blood. The claws seemed to lunge out of the orb and try to seize hold of him.

Magius jumped from his chair and drew back. He was shaking, sweating, and chilled.

Ast bilak moiparalan/Suh akvlar tantangusar—the words to the spell he would use to seize control of the orb. Magius repeated them over and over, reciting the spell in his head, not saying the words aloud. Not giving them power. Not yet. Not until he was ready.

He looked at the orb. The claws had disappeared. The eyes were laughing at him.

"Cast your puny spell," the dragon taunted him. "I will sink my claws into your flesh, crush your bones, drag out your heart and devour it. Then I will consume your soul!"

Magius was angry now. He sat back down at the table and placed his hand firmly on the orb. The eyes of the red dragon gleamed, as though looking forward to the battle. Magius drew in a breath, about to recite the words of magic.

Someone knocked on his door, breaking his concentration. He tried to cling to the words of magic, but they slid through his fingers like quicksilver and he lost them.

"I left orders I was not to be disturbed!" Magius shouted furiously. "Go away! Leave me alone!"

"I am sorry, Magius!" Huma called. "I know I am never supposed to interrupt your magic, but I *have* to talk to you. I . . . I am desperate."

Magius heard the anguish in his friend's voice and he sighed. His concentration was shattered anyway. He took his hands from the orb and flung a cloth over it. He waited a moment to catch his breath and stop trembling, then rose and walked over to unlock the door and open it.

Magius thought at first Huma had been wounded. His face was haggard, his eyes shadowed. He staggered and had to brace himself against the door.

"My friend! What is wrong?" Magius asked, alarmed. "Come in and sit down before you fall."

Huma entered the room and sank down in a chair.

"Are you hurt?" Magius asked, looking for signs of blood on his clothes. "Has the battle started? I didn't hear anything—"

"No, no!" Huma said. "I have no physical injury. The wound is deeper. In my soul. Gwyneth . . ." He swallowed and lowered his head to his hands.

Magius poured his friend a cup of wine, then drew up a chair and sat down beside him.

"What has she done to cause you such pain?"

Huma drank a sip of wine without seeming to know what he was drinking. He started to set the cup down and almost dropped it. Magius quickly took the cup from him.

"I have a question," said Huma. "Is it possible for a dragon to take the form of a mortal?"

"Those who have made a study of dragons believe that red dragons, as well as gold and silver dragons, have this ability," Magius replied.

"Silver dragons . . ." Huma repeated in a low voice.

Magius suddenly guessed the truth. "Gwyneth is a silver dragon!"

"How do you know?" Huma asked, startled.

"I am astonished I did not realize this before now. The question is, how did you find out?" Magius asked.

"A monk from the Great Library came to the tower. He and Lady Destina were in the commander's office—"

"Wait! Stop. A monk? From Palanthas?" Magius was incredulous. "How did he get here?"

"Let me finish!" Huma said desperately. "Forget the monk. He is not important. Or at least not to me. I overheard him and Lady Destina talking. I did not mean to eavesdrop. Brightblade and I were walking past the office when we heard them. They were talking about Gwyneth. . . ."

Huma shook his head. "I admit that when I heard what they were saying, I stopped to listen. I know I acted dishonorably, but I could not help it."

"They say eavesdroppers never hear good of themselves. You have been suitably punished. So what did you hear them say?" Magius asked.

"They spoke of her as a silver dragon. I would have laughed and paid no heed, but I could see from Sturm's appalled expression that he, too, had heard them."

"Did you confront him?"

"He said—and rightly so—that if Gwyneth was a silver dragon, it was up to her to tell me or not, as she chose," Huma replied. "The secret was hers, and he could not in honor reveal it."

"What you knights need is less honor and more common sense," Magius said testily. "He could see plainly you were falling in love with her and he should have warned you. What did you do?"

"First tell me the truth, Magius," said Huma. "Do you believe Gwyneth is a silver dragon?"

"It would explain a great deal about her," Magius admitted. "Her extraordinary skills in magic, for example. How she appeared to you during your vigil, though not necessarily why."

"She came to me to reassure me," said Huma. "And now she has vanished and I fear she has gone because of me. I made no secret of my feelings for her. She could see I was falling in love with her, and I believe she fled because she was afraid that if I knew the truth, I would hate her, revile her—"

"Well, don't you?" Magius demanded. "And if you don't, why not? She duped you, my friend! She deceived you."

Huma stood up and flung back his chair. His eyes flashed in rare anger. He clenched his fists, and Magius thought for a moment he might strike him. Huma mastered himself with a great effort. Turning on his heel, he opened the door and started to walk out.

Magius sprang after him and seized hold of him.

"Huma, I am sorry! Forgive my hasty words."

Huma halted, but he was breathing heavily and he did not turn around. Magius drew him back inside the room and shut the door.

"Come, sit down, my friend. Drink some wine."

Huma sat back down, but he did not touch the wine. He stared at the cup as though he had no idea what it was.

"Talk to me," said Magius. "You would not be human if you did not feel a sense of betrayal!"

"When I first heard Lady Destina speak of Gwyneth as a silver dragon, it was as if my heart shattered," Huma admitted. "Although not because I had learned the truth. I was upset to think she did not love and trust me enough to tell me."

Magius gave a rueful smile. "Really, my friend, you have to stop being so noble and honorable. You make the rest of us look bad."

Huma shook his head. "And now she is gone. Perhaps she is in danger because of me."

"We do not know why Gwyneth fled," Magius pointed out. "If she is a silver dragon, perhaps she realized she was falling in love with you. She knows you better than I do, apparently. She knows you would embrace her, forgive her, love her. The possibility exists that she left to spare you both heartache."

Huma regarded him intently. "Go on. What do you mean?"

"Consider what it would be like for a dragon to fall in love with a mortal," said Magius. "Gwyneth knows there can be no happy ending for the two of you, only heartbreak and despair. Mortal lives are brief. You will die and she will live the centuries alone with only the memory—and the pain. Trust me. I know something of that myself."

Huma reached out to grasp his hand.

"Paladine strike me, I am a selfish wretch! I come to you to ease my sorrow, never thinking of your own."

Magius smiled. "Greta waits for me in Paladine's marble halls and someday I will join her. Although if Paladine refuses to permit wizards to enter, I may have to sneak in through the back door."

"You will jest on your deathbed!" Huma chided him.

"Which may not be far off," Magius observed.

"I know I have little hope of surviving this battle," said Huma more somberly. "I am prepared to face death. But I would dearly like to speak to Gwyneth, just one more time. I want to tell her that I know the truth and assure her of my love."

"She may yet return. We may be wrong about her, and she is an elf and no more a dragon than you are. Although some Solamnics would consider it better to fall in love with a dragon than an elf."

Magius hesitated, then added, "If she does return, there is a way you can discover the truth. According to the wise, a dragon disguised as a mortal will always cast a dragon's shadow. Look at her in direct sunlight and see what her shadow reveals."

"I have no need," said Huma. "Your wise counsel has cleared my thoughts. If Gwyneth wants me to know her secret, she will tell me. I pray only for her return to me."

"Lift your glass, then," said Magius. "The poet says 'The warmth of love's memory is better than the chill of never having loved.' I do not know that I entirely agree with him. Therefore I say we toast the hanging of all poets."

Huma smiled and sipped his wine. He glanced at the spellbooks on the table.

"I should take my leave and allow you to study."

Magius remembered the terrible eyes in the dragon orb. "Do not rush off. Help me finish this apple wine. This is the last of it and I do not intend to leave a drop for Takhisis."

Magius gulped down the wine, then poured himself another glass. "And do not despair, my friend. You are quite the catch. Any dragon would be lucky to have you."

CHAPTER
TWENTY-TWO

R aistlin slept late that day, later than he had intended. He wondered immediately on waking if Magius had succeeded in taking control of the dragon orb, and he lingered in his room, hoping Magius would come tell him. He heard nothing from his friend, however, and eventually left his room and crept to Magius's door. Raistlin started to knock, then found it unlocked, with no warding spells. He considered that unsettling, and he quickly opened the door and stepped inside.

Magius was dressed, but had apparently gone back to bed, for he slept in his clothes. Raistlin saw two mugs and an empy jug of cider on the table and assumed Magius must have had a visitor. The small book containing information about the dragon orb lay on the table. He had flung his arm over his eyes to keep out the morning light. His sleep appeared peaceful and easy. Raistlin saw a lump on the table covered with a cloth and knew immediately that was the dragon orb.

Raistlin drew near it and thought how easy it would be to take it.

The wizards had created several dragon orbs, and he remembered his own, its image glistening through the mists of time. He could feel the cold crystal beneath his hands and see the eyes of the green dragon, Cyan Bloodbane, staring at him with hatred. He could hear the dragon's voice taunting him. But the last time, the final time, the voice in the orb belonged to Takhisis, as she caught hold of him and tried to ensnare him.

The memory of the fear, the panic, the horror swept over him. He shuddered; yet, even through the terror, he reached for the orb.

"Try your luck," the dragon whispered in his ear. "Try your skill! Think of the power I could give you!"

Skill! Raistlin sneered at himself. He could number the spells he knew on one hand and he was considering trying to master a dragon orb!

Magius stirred in his sleep and rolled over with a deep sigh. Raistlin thrust his hands into the sleeves of his robes to avoid temptation and fled the room, softly shutting the door to let his friend sleep.

He knocked on Sturm's door, but he was not in his room. Destina was not in hers. He had to give them the bad news, that they were trapped here, and he could not put it off any longer. He was entering the dining hall in the Knight's Spur, wondering how to tell them, when he felt the familiar burning pain in his lungs. This coughing spell was going to be a bad one.

He pressed his handkerchief to his lips. He was dimly aware of Sturm and Destina and someone else, a stranger. Raistlin drew out the bag of herbs and laid it on the table, then collapsed into a chair and doubled over, his handkerchief pressed to his mouth.

Sturm knew what needed to be done. He went to the kitchen for boiling water and a mug. On his return, he picked up the bag of herbs, shook some into the mug, and added the hot water.

"Don't make a habit of this," he said, placing the mug in front of Raistlin. "I am not your brother."

Raistlin grabbed the mug with both hands and gulped the hot tea, burning his mouth. The pain in his chest began to ease. He stopped coughing and was finally able to draw a breath.

Raistlin looked at those sitting around the table. He was surprised none of them asked him about the Device. He was about to admit his failure when he noted with astonishment that the stranger was a monk, an aesthetic from the Great Library.

236   MARGARET WEIS AND TRACY HICKMAN

Raistlin sipped his tea and studied the monk, thinking he had seen him before.

"How do I know you?"

"I am Brother Kairn. I was with Destina and Tasslehoff in the Inn of the Last Home the night . . ." He glanced at Destina and did not finish.

Raistlin remembered. "The night the lady decided to upend our lives." He suddenly realized what he was saying. "A night that is centuries in the future. How did you get here? Were you able to repair the Device?"

"Unfortunately, the original Device had suffered too much damage," Kairn said. "I was just telling Sturm and Destina what happened. Alice Ranniker, a descendant of a famous artifact-maker, constructed a new Device of Time Journeying out of fragments of the old one. Astinus sent me back in time to find you and the others and bring you home."

Raistlin raised an eyebrow. "Forgive me for seeming to doubt you, Brother, but how did you know where and when to look?"

"I knew you were here in this time because I found a record from the Third Dragon War that named Sturm Brightblade among the knights who fought at the battle. You were listed as a war wizard, along with Magius."

"Then if Sturm and I are mentioned in past records, doesn't that mean we have changed time?" Raistlin asked.

"If you have done nothing to drastically alter time while you are here, Astinus believes that when I bring the four of you back to your respective times, the original timeline will be restored. Your names will fade from the records of the Third Dragon War and you will pick up your lives from the night they were disrupted. You and Sturm will both go back to the Inn of the Last Home with no memory of what happened here, because you were never here. The River of Time will resume flowing as it should and wash away all traces of your presence."

"I am glad to hear Astinus corroborates my theory of time travel," Raistlin remarked. "What does Astinus say about the Graygem?"

Kairn was grave. "We must remove it from this pivotal point in time as swiftly as possible."

"I have no idea what the two of you are talking about," said Sturm. "What do you mean that I won't remember being here?"

"I would explain it to you, but we have no time and you won't remember it anyway," said Raistlin. "I suggest you take us back now, this moment, Brother."

Kairn sighed deeply. Sturm looked exceedingly grim and Destina was downcast and unhappy.

"What is wrong?" Raistlin asked sharply. "We have the ability to go back home." He looked around the group at the table and answered his own question. "Where is Tasslehoff?"

"He escaped from his cell," said Sturm. "We think he has gone to find the gnomes."

"Gnomes?" Raistlin repeated, astounded. "Why would he go in search of gnomes?"

"Tas wanted to fix the *Song of Huma*," said Destina. "He told me that Uncle Trapspringer and the gnomes had invented the dragonlance. He kept talking about it, and he showed me a gnome village he found on the map. I am afraid I did not take him seriously. But I never imagined he would run off!"

"We cannot go back without him," said Kairn.

Raistlin sighed. "And where is this village?"

"About twenty miles east," Sturm replied. "The Dark Queen's army controls all the land to the east, so we must assume the village is held by the enemy."

"Then we must also assume Tas is dead," said Raistlin. "We will have to go back without him. Or at least, the lady must go back."

"Tas isn't dead! He can't be! And I won't leave without him," said Destina firmly. "I brought him here. He is my responsibility."

"You have a far greater responsibility, Lady—the Graygem," Raistlin said acerbically. "You should leave now before anyone else discovers that you are wearing it."

"Too late," said Sturm. "That soldier, Tully, already knows about it. He tried to take it from her."

"He must have heard us talking about it when we thought he was unconscious," said Destina. "But he didn't succeed. The Graygem burned his hand, and he fled."

Raistlin was grave. "Yet he knows about it, and now he knows where it is. The prisoner, Calaf, told me Immolatus has planted spies. Tully must be one of them. He risked coming back here to find the Graygem. And if he is spying for Immolatus, then we must assume that the dragon now knows about the Graygem. You *must* go back now with Brother Kairn, Destina. The rest of us will stay here to search for Tas. The monk can return to fetch us."

"But I can't leave! Not without knowing what has happened to Tas," Destina protested.

"You have no choice, Lady Destina," said Raistlin bitingly. "You may have already changed the future of the world. I trust you don't want to destroy it!"

Destina flinched and lowered her head.

"You have no right to speak to her like that!" Kairn said angrily. "Besides, the argument is moot. We must all go back or none of us can go back. The maker of the Device made that clear to me."

"But what if something happened to one of us?" Sturm argued.

"I asked Alice the same question myself. To use her own colorful language: We are 'screwed,'" said Kairn unhappily. "She said if I must, I must, but she wouldn't advise it. Although, when I asked her about the Graygem, she said 'all bets are off' and told me I should 'bring back the survivors.'"

Raistlin smiled grimly.

"We have to find Tas," Destina insisted.

Sturm gave a helpless shrug. "I would not even know where to start looking. He could be anywhere."

"To give the kender credit, he is good at getting himself into trouble, but he's also good at getting himself out of it," Raistlin said grudgingly. "If anyone could survive being caught behind enemy lines in the middle of an epic battle, it's Tasslehoff Burrfoot."

Sturm smiled faintly. "For once, you and I agree. And if Tas is alive, he will do his best to return for his prized possessions. He took his hoopak, but he left all his pouches behind."

"Then I will speak to Commander Belgrave," said Destina, rising from the table. "We should at least alert the guards to keep watch for him. Will you come with me, Brother Kairn? I may need your help convincing the commander to let Tas back inside."

"I am not certain how much help I will be," said Kairn doubtfully. "The commander still more than half suspects *I* am a spy. But I will gladly come with you."

He and Destina walked away together, talking quietly, their hands almost, but not quite, touching. Sturm and Raistlin sat alone at the table.

"The lady is fortunate that monks of Gilean are not required to take vows of celibacy," Raistlin remarked dryly, observing the two. "I believe they are even permitted to marry."

"We are a long way from celebrating a wedding," said Sturm.

Raistlin drank his tea. The food had grown cold, but he had no appetite anyway. Although the morning sun was shining brightly outside the fortress, the interior rooms were dark and cool. Three candles in the center of the table were there to provide light. Two had already burned out and the third was failing.

"I take it you did not find the the original Device?" Sturm asked abruptly.

"It is in the tower of Wayreth," said Raistlin wearily. "Our trip to Palanthas was not entirely wasted, however. Magius brought back a dragon orb. He will not live to use it, but at least it will be here in the future for Tasslehoff to find."

"If there *is* a future," said Sturm. "Or one that we would recognize." He slowly rose to his feet. "I promised the commander and Huma I would join them to discuss plans for the tower's defense."

"Has Gwyneth returned with the dragonlances?" Raistlin asked.

"Not that I have heard," said Sturm.

Raistlin gave a sardonic smile. "Then that should be a brief conversation. By the way, I have been meaning to ask you. They say we should never meet our heroes, for they will be sure to disappoint us. You have met and fought alongside Huma, a man you long revered. What has that been like? Are you disappointed?"

Sturm paused to consider. "What did Tas say? 'Before now the song was just a song about people I didn't know.' Huma is not what I imagined him to be. He is a man, as I am, and his most trusted friend is a magic-user."

"Reprehensible," Raistlin murmured.

"Huma makes light of honor and appears to regard the Measure more as guidelines than as laws by which one must live. But he does believe in the oath. 'My honor is my life.' In fact, I would say that one sentence defines him."

"So are you disappointed?" Raistlin asked.

"No," Sturm replied. "I may have lost a hero, but I have found a friend. What about you? Magius was your hero."

"I have found both a hero and a friend," said Raistlin.

"You must find it hard, knowing as you do that Magius is destined to die a terrible death," said Sturm.

You have no idea, Raistlin thought. "By the way," he added as Sturm started to leave, "when you see Belgrave, tell him that Magius and I met his daughter, Anitra."

Sturm was surprised. "I didn't even know he had a daughter. How did you meet her?"

"She is an apprentice mage, studying magic in the Tower of High Sorcery in Palanthas," Raistlin explained. "The master has fled the tower, which leaves it open to attack. Anitra and her friends plan to remain to defend it against Takhisis. She is a brave and courageous young woman. Tell Commander Belgrave he can be very proud of her. She sends her love to him."

Sturm agreed to carry the message and left to find Commander Belgrave.

Raistlin sat alone in the dining hall. The last candle flamed, guttered, and went out.

CHAPTER
TWENTY-THREE

Gwyneth left Silver Dragon Mountain when the sun was in its zenith. She planned to arrive at the High Clerist's Tower after sunset to avoid being seen. The sun's afterglow filled the sky when she arrived, but the tower itself was shrouded in darkness. She landed among the foothills west of the tower, far from the dragon's armies, which were camped to the east. Dropping the bundle of lances on the ground, Gwyneth quickly shifted into her elven form.

The commander did not have enough men to guard all the entrances to the tower, and he had given orders that all the gates were to remain closed and bolted. Gwyneth used her magic to release the bolt and pushed open the steel-banded doors. She picked up the bundle of dragonlances—they were now far heavier for the elf than they had been for the dragon—and hauled them inside. She closed and locked the doors, then carried the lances into the Temple of the High Clerist.

The temple was shadowy and deserted, restfully quiet after her journey. Gwyneth lowered the lances to the floor, then sank into one of the wooden pews, hoping the peace and serenity would ease the pain in her heart, as the mage's balm had eased the pain of the flesh.

She let her thoughts go to the time she and Huma had spent together inside her prison cell. She heard again every word and saw the small lines around his eyes crinkle when he laughed. She had not been able to keep from laughing with him, and in that moment, as their hands touched and they had almost kissed, she admitted to herself that she had fallen in love with him.

She remembered and she let herself dream of being mortal, of loving him, holding him in the night, growing old with him, walking with him into eternity. The dream lasted only a brief moment, then she firmly banished it.

For the dream was foolish. It only made reality more painful. As the prophecy foretold, her love would be her doom. Huma must never know the truth, that he had fallen in love with a dragon. Let him think Gwyneth had run away.

And let her be the one to suffer. Let her be the one to live the long and empty years of her life with only the memory of his noble, gallant face; the warmth of his blue-gray eyes; his gentle touch.

Gwyneth planned to leave the dragonlances on the altar of Paladine, the Dragon Father, for Huma to find when he came to pray. He would think the lances were a miracle, a gift from the god. He would never know they came from a silver dragon who had broken the laws of her people to bring them to him.

Then Gwyneth the elf would depart, never to return, and Gwyneth the silver dragon would appear. She would fight alongside the knights as they carried the shining dragonlances into battle. The silver dragon would guard them, protect them, and, with the help of the gods, she and the knights would drive Takhisis and her dragons back into the Abyss.

She resolutely picked up the lances, still wrapped in sheepskin, and carried them to Paladine's altar. Lowering the bundle to the floor, she looked into the face of the marble statue of the platinum dragon. The light of the four candles burned steadily, unwavering as the god's love.

"Perhaps I have done wrong to bring the knights the dragonlances, Father. My people opposed it, but I could not let the knights fight this battle alone, without hope of victory."

The god was present. She could see the light of the candles reflected in the eyes and his outspread wings seemed to enfold her, embrace her.

"You have chosen as I hoped you would choose, Daughter," said the Dragon Father. "Your people living isolated and alone on the Dragon Isles are the ones in the wrong. They have abandoned the world and the mortals out of fear. And, because your people failed in their watch, Takhisis and her evil dragons were able to return. You and your sister had the courage to live in the world, be a part of it. I can make your dream a reality."

"You will grant me my wish to become a mortal woman," said Gwyneth.

"You have only to ask me," said the Dragon Father.

Gwyneth already knew her answer, though the words came wet with tears.

"Huma does not need the love of a mortal woman, Dragon Father," said Gwyneth. "He needs the might of a silver dragon."

"The dragonlances are magical and formidable weapons. But remember, Daughter, the most powerful weapon you possess against evil is love."

The light in the eyes of the statue faded. The light of the four candles on the altar continued to burn steadily.

Gwyneth wiped away her tears. She picked up the heavy bundle of dragonlances, intending to lift them onto the altar, but her strength failed her. The dragonlances fell to the floor with a clattering crash that shattered the silence and seemed to reverberate throughout heaven.

"You came back," said Huma.

He must have been sitting quietly on the pews in the darkness, for she had not known he was there. A whisper of air, stirred by the gentle wings of a god, brushed her cheek, wet with tears.

"Take up the candle from the altar and hold it so that the light shines directly on me," Gwyneth said. "Look at the shadow the light casts on the altar and see the truth."

Huma did as she told him. He lifted one of the candles and held it high. His gaze shifted to the altar behind her. He would see her shadow. The shadow of a dragon.

She braced herself for his anger, his shock, his repudiation.

"Tell me what you see," said Gwyneth harshly.

"I see my own true love," said Huma.

He flung the candle to the stone floor and gathered her into his embrace.

She tried to push him away. "You cannot love me!" she cried brokenly.

Huma kissed her lips and her eyes, and slowly she relaxed and rested her head against his chest. He kissed away her tears and then he let her go to kneel before her, at the altar of Paladine. He clasped her hand.

"I call upon the gods to witness my vow," Huma said. "As my honor is my life, you are my life and my honor. Before Paladine, I pledge both to you."

Huma removed a ring he wore on the little finger of his right hand and regarded it fondly. "This ring is my dearest possession, for my sister, Greta, gave it to me. I ask you to accept this ring as a pledge of my love."

He kissed the ring and held it out to her. "I stood on the High Lookout, keeping watch for you, praying to Paladine that you would return to me. I saw the fire of the setting sun shine on your silver wings and blaze on your silver scales."

He opened his palm to reveal a silver scale, glistening like a tear in the light of the candles, in the eyes of the god.

"I know you, Gwyneth. And I love you."

She accepted his ring and slipped it onto her finger, then put her arms around him. The two held each other close for long, blessed moments, and standing before the altar of Paladine, they pledged their love, each for the other.

The prophecy foretold she would fall in love with a mortal and he would be her doom. Gwyneth knew the truth. Huma's love was not her doom. His love was her salvation.

Huma picked up the bundle and drew out the dragonlances. He gazed at them with admiration, tested their balance and their weight, and smiled with pleasure, then placed them, one by one, on the altar. The candles burned with a holy radiance. The dragonlances shone silver in the hallowed light.

Gwyneth and Huma left the temple together, holding fast to each other, and walked into the quiet, sacred night, glittering with stars.

CHAPTER
TWENTY-FOUR

The red dragon, Immolatus, sat alone behind his desk in his command tent. He was almost always alone, for he preferred his own company to that of mortals. He loathed mortals. He tolerated them only because the fools were always willing to fight and die for his cause—or at least for his gold.

He was in a foul mood because he detested having to take on the form of a mortal, because then they considered him their equal. They would drop by to chat or ask stupid questions or urge him to drink some foul liquid known as dwarf spirits, which was like drinking molten lava.

Above all, he hated having to shrink his magnificent, powerful, shining, red-scaled body into the weak, soft, squishy flesh of a human. Immolatus compensated by making himself as like a dragon as he could in human form. Immolatus the human had fiery red-orange skin and teeth sharpened like fangs. He wore specially crafted burnished red armor and a helm with a red crest. He hoped that when the mortals looked at him, they would know they were looking at a red dragon. But his efforts were in vain. The mortals weren't terrified of the human like they were of the dragon.

Immolatus recalled with pleasure the battle at Westgate Pass, when he had ambushed the humans trying to return to Palanthas. He still relished the screams of the dying knights as he roasted them alive in their armor and smelled their flesh sizzling and their blood boiling, not to mention the other humans fleeing in panic as though they had thought they had some hope of escape.

He had been highly amused by their attempts to kill him with swords that broke and spears that bounced off his scaly hide. The fools would have done more damage throwing rocks at him, for at least a rock stood some chance of putting out an eye. As it was, he had killed the knights to a man and then feasted on their pack mules and horses.

After that victory, he had been prepared to attack the tower. He had made his plans. He would fly over the walls, spewing fire. He would batter the topmost spire with blows from his tail and send it crashing to the ground. He would then proceed to dismantle the tower stone by stone, and when the humans ran from him in terror, he would pick them off at his leisure and devour them.

Delightful thoughts, charming daydreams, but they were only daydreams. His plans had been thwarted. He had been looking forward to destroying the tower, but now he could not knock down so much as a flying buttress.

He had received orders this morning from Takhisis, delivered by messenger.

"Her Dark and Glorious Majesty has heard rumors that you intend to attack the High Clerist's Tower and destroy it. Queen Takhisis has decided to make the tower her base of operations while she is in the world and she does not want it damaged. When she launches her attack, you will fly over the tower and terrorize the humans with debilitating dragonfear. But you will not dislodge a single stone."

Immolatus had sullenly agreed to obey her command. The gigantic red dragon was powerful, but the thought of incurring the Dark Queen's wrath shriveled his belly and doused his fire.

A knock on the post of his tent roused Immolatus from his dreams of destruction. He gave a gruff snarl, which was his way of warning the visitor that he better have a damn good reason for disturbing him.

A guard peered nervously inside the tent. "That spy is here to see you, Lord."

Immolatus snarled again. "Which spy?"

"Mullen Tully."

"What does he want?"

"He says he has important information you need to hear, Lord," said the guard.

Immolatus snarled a third time, and Tully entered. The command tent was furnished with a desk and a single chair. Since Immolatus occupied the only chair, Tully was forced to stand. The dragon glared at his visitor.

"Why do you bother me, you worthless piece of goblin dung?"

"You recall, Lord, that I told you about the conversation I overheard between the mage and Lady Destina?" said Tully. "How they spoke about the Graygem of Gargath?"

"This ridiculous tale again?" Immolatus roared. "I don't have time to waste on such blatherings. Get out!"

Tully blenched but held his ground. "It is not ridiculous, Lord. The lady wears the Graygem on a chain around her neck. I know because I saw it. I touched it! Look at this!" He held out his blistered hand. "It nearly burned off my fingers! I swear by Her Dark Majesty that I speak the truth."

Immolatus eyed him. Tully was a greedy, slithering snake of a human who was not above lying if he thought he could profit from it. But there was a note of truth in the wretch's voice that interested the dragon, though he had no intention of letting Tully know.

"This from a man who managed to get himself beaten to a pulp by goblins," said Immolatus disdainfully. "You were delirious."

"The beating wasn't my fault, Lord," Tully said sullenly. "Someone should have warned me there were goblin raiding parties in the area. But I heard what I heard."

"Pah! You wouldn't know the Graygem from a goat turd!"

"I did some investigating, Lord. I spoke to a cleric of Takhisis in our own army and asked her what she knew about the Graygem," said Tully. "She told me the gem is gray in color. So is the gem the lady wears—"

"Probably just smoky quartz," said Immolatus dismissively. He was fond of treasure and knew his gemstones.

"The gem is strange to look at," Tully continued. "It constantly changes shape—round one moment, square the next, oblong the next, and so on. The cleric said as much, and that's exactly what I saw. I tell you it is the Graygem, Lord!"

Immolatus considered the information. Tully was not all that bright and he had no imagination, so it was unlikely he would make up such an outlandish tale. Perhaps Tully really had found the Graygem of Gargath. Immolatus felt a thrill tingle through his human flesh.

"On the off chance that you know what you are talking about, you weren't stupid enough to tell the cleric that you found the Graygem, were you?" Immolatus asked. "If you did, she's probably already blabbed to Takhisis."

"I came straight to you, Lord!" said Tully. "You're the only one who knows."

Immolatus tried to decide what to do. Tully did well enough as a spy, skulking about, peeping through windows and listening at keyholes. But he would be no match for the Graygem—if that's what it was—or this formidable Lady Destina, who was apparently bold enough to wear the accursed jewel around her neck.

"Tell me everything you know about the Destina woman," said Immolatus. "She's living inside the tower. Where does she sleep? Who are her companions?"

Tully described the conversation he'd overheard between Destina and the red-robed wizard, concluding with what he had learned when he had returned to the tower. "Her bedchamber and those of her companions are on the tower's sixth floor."

He drew a crude diagram and indicated the locations of the various rooms. "A guard is posted here. Day and night."

Immolatus glanced at the diagram, then waved his hand. "You're dismissed. Remain in camp. I might have need of you."

"But what about the Graygem?" Tully asked, disappointed. "Do you want me to fetch it for you?"

"You whined that it nearly burned off your hand," Immolatus said with a sneer.

"I could wrap the jewel in a handkerchief," said Tully.

"A handkerchief!" Immolatus snorted. "I will take care of the Graygem. You obey orders. Relieve me of your odious presence."

Tully lingered. "The Graygem must be worth a lot of money, Lord. I should at least get a finder's fee."

"I promise that you will get exactly what you deserve," said Immolatus.

Tully clearly did not find that overly reassuring, but Immolatus snarled at him, and he sidled out of the tent.

Immolatus sat behind his desk and wondered if he truly could be so fortunate as to have come across the most valuable, elusive, powerful gem in existence. Every dragon worth his treasure hoard coveted the Graygem of Gargath, and Immolatus was no exception. He pictured adding the gem to his collection. Its gray color would be a pleasing, startling contrast to the rubies and emeralds and sparkling diamonds.

"I have to be careful," Immolatus muttered. "Takhisis would give three of her five heads to obtain the power of Chaos. With the Graygem, she could get rid of the other gods and take over. Whereas, if I had the Graygem, I could get rid of Takhisis."

The dragon smiled fondly. "No more ordering me about. No more crawling on my belly. If I had the Graygem, Takhisis would be forced to come crawling to me!"

He indulged himself in this fantasy until he recalled the Dark Queen's volatile and vengeful nature. If she discovered that he'd stolen the Graygem and then kept it for himself, her five heads would tear him apart. Immolatus was saved by a happy thought.

"If she finds out I have it, I can always say I was going to surprise her with it as a gift!"

The problem settled to his satisfaction, he shouted for the guard.

"Tell Captain I want to see him," said Immolatus.

The guard hesitated. "Which captain, Lord? There are several."

"*The* Captain, you dolt. The commander of the Gudlose. And tell him to bring his wizard."

The Gudlose were a group of human mercenaries who came from a land somewhere beyond the Khalkist Mountains. They were highly skilled in warfare, and they sold their swords only to those who could afford the very best. The unit's name, Gudlose, meant "the godless ones." They did not worship any god or pledge allegiance to any nation. They obeyed no laws except their own; they swore loyalty only to one another.

Immolatus had first heard about them from the god Sargonnas, who had brought them to fight alongside his minotaur army in

Palanthas. Immolatus had observed them in action at the battle against the knights in the Westgate Pass, and he had been impressed by their skill and ruthless ferocity. He had hired them on the spot.

The leader, known only as Captain, entered the tent. Captain did not salute or bow but stood with his hand on the hilt of his sword, waiting to hear why he had been summoned. Immolatus did not know the man's true name or the true names of anyone belonging to the Gudlose. They were known by their specialties: Scrounger, Neckbreaker, Butcher, Garrote, and Knife.

They were the tallest humans Immolatus had ever encountered. They looked alike, with ice-blue eyes and blond hair that they wore in long braids down their backs. They spoke their own language, as well as camp talk, and kept to themselves. They did not permit anyone to enter their camp on pain of death and had slit the throat of a drunken soldier who had mistakenly wandered into the area. They had impaled his body on a tree in the center of their camp to serve as a warning to others.

"Where is your wizard?" Immolatus demanded.

"She is coming," said Captain.

A woman entered the tent. She did not wear traditional wizard's robes but was dressed the same as the men in leather trousers, boots, and a long, belted leather tunic over chain mail. She was as tall as Captain and was known by the improbable name of Mother.

The two Gudlose regarded him in silence, waiting.

"I need you to abduct someone," said Immolatus. "You will have to break inside the tower. I have here a diagram—"

"Put away your diagram, Dragon," said Captain. "You need us to get inside the tower. We will get inside the tower. Who is the target?"

"I'll explain in a moment, but first I must ask Mother a question. What do you know about the Graygem of Gargath?"

"Nothing," said Mother, dismissive.

Immolatus was startled and also skeptical. "But you must know something. You are a wizard and the Graygem is the most powerful magical artifact in the world!"

"I have no use for magical artifacts," said Mother with a curl of her lip.

"But this one is famous," Immolatus stated. "The god Reorx trapped Chaos inside it!"

"The very reason I do not trust artifacts," said Mother. She added as an afterthought. "Or gods either, for that matter."

Immolatus was displeased. "You say you don't believe in magical artifacts, but I need a skilled wizard! I have no use for those who merely play at being wizards."

"Do you insult us, Dragon?" Captain asked in dangerously quiet tones.

"I'm paying the bills," said Immolatus. "I want to see what I'm getting for my money."

Mother pointed her finger at the dragon's desk and spoke a single word.

The desk disintegrated and Immolatus found himself sitting in a pile of kindling.

"Need any more proof, Dragon?" Mother asked.

Immolatus kicked away broken pieces of his desk and wondered what to do. He needed a wizard with knowledge of the Graygem and particularly its powers, but perhaps it wouldn't be such a great idea to tell this dangerous bunch too much about it. They might want it for themselves.

Immolatus recalled Tully mentioning that a red-robed mage was one of the lady's companions. Presumably this mage would know all there was to know about the Graygem.

Captain broke in on his thoughts. "We grow weary standing here, Dragon. Either tell us what you want or let us go."

"I want you to abduct a woman named Destina Rosethorn, who is currently residing in the High Clerist's Tower, and bring her to me. I want her alive," Immolatus emphasized. "You should be aware that this woman is in possession of the Graygem of Gargath."

"Done," said Captain.

"That is not all," said Immolatus. "Since Mother knows nothing about the Graygem, I need a wizard who does. A red-robed wizard is part of this woman's entourage. Bring him to me—alive, as well. They all reside on the sixth floor of the tower, but they spend most of their time in the fortress known as the Knight's Spur. I can show you on the map—"

"We know it," Captain said. He glanced at Mother and the two conferred in their own language. He turned back to Immolatus. "Since you want these people alive, we will need a diversion to draw the knights and men-at-arms away from their posts. If we have to fight them, the captives might be harmed."

"Nothing easier. You will have your diversion," said Immolatus.

"And you will have your captives and this Graygem," said Captain.

"Good. You are dismissed," said Immolatus.

But Captain did not leave. His blue eyes glinting, he clenched his hand over the hilt of his sword and leaned close to Immolatus, so close his breath touched the dragon's cheek. "Do not ever insult us again, Dragon! You pay well. But not that well."

Captain straightened. Mother snapped her fingers and the two of them vanished.

Immolatus sat amid the pile of kindling and seethed. How dare they? No one spoke to him that way! He was sorely tempted to change into his dragon form and roast the lot of them, just to teach them some manners. But he had already paid them and he might as well get his money's worth.

After they brought him the Graygem, then he could roast them.

CHAPTER
TWENTY-FIVE

Huma had fallen asleep holding Gwyneth in his arms. She lay awake beside him, resting her head on his shoulder and watching over him, the guardian of his slumber. She would protect his peaceful sleep as long as she could, for she knew with aching sorrow that when the Dark Queen attacked, he would have no rest unless it was eternal.

Whatever he was dreaming must be pleasant, for he smiled and his hold on her tightened. Gwyneth knew happiness as she had not known in her hundreds of years of life. She would have been content to lie beside him, listen to his even, tranquil breathing, and feel the beating of his heart for all her years.

Her happiness did not last beyond a few moments. She had fallen into a doze when she was awakened by the sound of immense leathery wings rising and falling, and the acrid smell of sulphurous breath.

"Immolatus!" Gwyneth whispered, shocked.

Huma stirred uneasily in his sleep. "What?"

"Hush, beloved, nothing," said Gwyneth.

He smiled and murmured her name, and then sank back into

deep slumber. Gwyneth gently kissed him on the brow, then hurriedly put on her clothes and slipped out of the bedchamber into the hallway.

All was quiet in the High Clerist's Tower. The watchman called four of the clock, an hour before dawn, and all seemed well.

Gwyneth ran down the stairs to the fourth level and out onto the battlements. She first looked to the south, fearing to see the Dark Queen's armies were launching the assault. But no horns blared. The campfires burned low. The enemy slumbered.

Movement caught her eye and, looking up, she saw Immolatus. His great bulk blotted out the starlight. Flames flickered from the dragon's teeth. Sulphurous smoke curled from his nostrils. He was alone and he was flying directly toward the High Clerist's Tower.

As Gwyneth started to run back inside to sound the alarm, Immolatus gave a roar that seemed to shake the tower. He soared over the outer curtain wall and swooped down into the courtyard in front of Noble's Gate. The dragon sucked in a huge breath, then breathed a jet of flame on the steel-banded double doors and pulled up out of his dive to avoid crashing into the tower.

The doors were made of rare black ironwood and were impervious to flaming arrows, firebrands, and other incendiary weapons—including a dragon's fiery breath. The dragon's initial onslaught did little damage.

Gwyneth waited tensely for other dragons to follow, join in the assault. But none came and she was perplexed. Immolatus appeared to be acting on his own. His assault on the gate would make sense if the Dark Queen's armies were massed behind him. Immolatus would destroy the gate to allow thousands of ogres and goblins, hobgoblins and kobolds to rush inside.

But no goblins were out there in the night, thirsting for blood, brandishing their swords and howling. Takhisis was not here to watch his assault and smile on him.

The dragon's roaring had awakened everyone in the tower and in the adjacent fortress. Lights flared in windows. Drums sounded the alarm.

Immolatus paid no heed. He circled in the air above the courtyard, then made another dive and blasted the doors again. The steel bands began to glow, and the dragon hovered near the gate and breathed flame on the doors a third time, then struck the doors with a massive front claw.

The doors shuddered, but they held. Frustrated, Immolatus breathed yet another jet of flame. The steel burned white hot, and Gwyneth could smell smoke and see the ironwood starting to smolder.

Men were shouting that the battle had started. Gwyneth knew Huma would be awake and worried about her. She ran from the battlements and hurried back to their chamber, where she found him struggling to drag his chain mail shirt over his head.

She assisted him and he smiled in relief to see her safe.

"Battle at last!" he said, elated. "Help me buckle on my breast-plate."

Gwyneth shook her head as she tugged on the leather straps. "The enemy troops are asleep in their tents and Takhisis is nowhere in sight. Immolatus is on a rampage by himself."

The dragon howled and they could feel the walls of the tower shake as he battered them with his claws and his tail.

"What can be his objective?" Huma wondered.

"He appears to be trying to destroy Noble's Gate," said Gwyneth. "Gain entrance to the tower."

Huma paused in the act of strapping on his sword. "His objective is to destroy the gods!"

Gywneth understood and was appalled. "He's going to attack the Temple!"

Huma laughed like a child opening gifts on Yule. "And we will be waiting for him! The Measure says, 'Evil devours its own.' He has brought destruction on himself. The dragonlances are in the temple. We will stop him there!"

Huma buckled his sword around his waist and put on his helm. "We should check on our friends, although I am surprised I do not hear them stirring. The dragon's roaring is loud enough to wake the dead."

Gwyneth took a torch from the wall as Huma knocked on Sturm's door and called to him. There was no answer. Gwyneth checked on Destina and found her room empty, as was Raistlin's. A light shone beneath Magius's door. Gwyneth started to knock, but Huma stopped her.

"He may be preparing to cast some dread magic and he would not thank us for interrupting his concentration. The others have probably already left to join the commander and his forces at the Knight's Spur."

"Should we go to them?" Gwyneth asked. "We could tell the commander that he needs to bring his troops to defend the temple."

Huma thought what to do. "Belgrave will require time to gather his forces. We are here. We cannot wait for him. Come with me. I know a back way into the temple."

He guided her down a large, dark hall lined with columns that led to the north end of the sixth floor. Gwyneth carried the torch and its light shone on beautiful wall tapestries featuring motifs of kingfishers, roses, crowns, and swords. When they reached the end of the hall, Huma drew back a tapestry to reveal a door that opened onto a narrow staircase.

"The Order of Clerists' private staircase. It leads down into the temple, so they can make their way to the altars at their leisure, without having to deal with the riffraff," he explained. "No one else was permitted to use them. Magius and Greta and I had come with my father on one of his pilgrimages. We went exploring one night, after he'd gone to sleep, and found this staircase. We decided to see where it led. Unfortunately, one of the clerics caught us. My father was furious, and Magius and my sister and I got into no end of trouble!"

Huma laughed at the memory. His color was heightened; his eyes shone. He was eager, exhilarated, looking forward to the fight.

The staircase was narrow and steeply pitched. They had to descend with care. They could still hear the dragon raging, but his roars were muffled by the stone walls. Every so often, they felt the walls shake.

"Tell me all you know about Immolatus," Huma said. "How does he fight?"

"The first weapon he will use against you is dragonfear, and it is terrible," said Gwyneth. "I have seen stalwart warriors fall to their knees, quaking in panic. Pray to Paladine to give you strength to overcome it."

"*You* will give me strength," said Huma, smiling at her and squeezing her hand. "What are his other weapons?"

"His most lethal is his fiery breath," Gwyneth replied. "I saw him breathe fire on the steel bands of the ironwood door, and the metal glowed red hot. His breath is his strength but also his weakness. After he breathes a fiery blast, Immolatus must wait a short time for the fire in his belly to rekindle. Not long—perhaps the span of thirty heartbeats. But during that time you could strike."

"Thirty heartbeats," Huma repeated. "I will remember."

"Stop a moment," said Gwyneth. "I need to speak to you."

Huma was on the step below. He looked up at her.

"I must change into my true form to fight Immolatus," Gwyneth said. "I must change into a dragon."

She could see herself reflected in his eyes; the torchlight shining on her silver hair. His love for her shone in his eyes brighter than the flame. Huma took her hand that wore his ring and brought it to his lips.

"We will fight together," he said. "Steel and silver."

Gwyneth kissed him and her last doubt vanished.

CHAPTER
TWENTY-SIX

aistlin had been awake all night, waiting to hear what had
become of Tasslehoff. Commander Belgrave had promised
Destina he would alert his men to keep watch for the kender.
The moment he arrived and they were once more all together, Kairn
was planning to take them back to their own time. But midnight was
now long past. Dawn was approaching and still no sign of the kender.

"The commander asked me again when you and Magius were
going to work your magic to take us to a place of safety," Destina
said. "I told him I would not go anywhere without Tas."

"Apparently, none of us can go anywhere without Tas," said
Raistlin caustically.

He heard the watchman call four of the clock and rose to his
feet. "I am going to retire. Let me know if you hear word."

"I will come with you," said Sturm, taking a torch from the wall.
"I would like to speak with Huma. No one has seen him all day."

"Kairn and I will wait up a little longer," said Destina. "Tas might
still come and he would look for me here first."

"He would look for the pantry first," Raistlin remarked to Sturm
as they left.

They crossed the bridge to the High Clerist's Tower, walking in silence, each absorbed in his own thoughts. Arriving at the tower, they climbed the stairs that led to their rooms on the sixth floor.

"What will you do if Tas doesn't come back before the battle?" Sturm asked abruptly.

"We have two days to wait for him," said Raistlin. "Brother Kairn says the battle will not start until the day after tomorrow."

"But if he doesn't return?" Sturm persisted.

"I will cast a sleep spell on Lady Destina and tell Brother Kairn to take her and the Graygem back to Astinus. I will remain here to wait for the kender. I find myself reluctant to say this, but Tasslehoff Burrfoot is as important to the future as you are," said Raistlin. At that moment, they heard a ferocious roar and the walls of the stairwell shook. Sturm slipped on a stair and nearly dropped the torch. Raistlin braced himself with his back pressed flat against the wall.

"The dragon is attacking the tower!" Sturm exclaimed. "The battle must have started!"

"But that is not possible," Raistlin argued. "It's the wrong time!"

"Apparently, someone forgot to tell Immolatus," said Sturm.

The dragon roared again, and again struck the walls.

"We can see what is happening from the parapet on the sixth floor," said Sturm.

They hurried up the stairs and made their way through the dark and deserted hall to the parapet. Looking down from the wall, they could see the dragon setting fire to Noble's Gate. Flames lit the night as the dragon blasted the ironwood and smoke drifted through the sultry air.

The dragon was alone. No troops massed behind him, brandishing their weapons, eager to rush in for the kill.

"This is all wrong!" Raistlin said grimly. "I know the history of Immolatus, for I will meet him in the future. He attacks the tower with his army, for he wants to seize it himself. The knights strike him with dragonlances during the battle and he is critically wounded. He ends up denouncing the Dark Queen and flees the battle. He never attacked the tower on his own. Unless . . ."

Raistlin paused, thinking.

"Unless what?" Sturm prompted him.

"Unless Magius used the dragon orb to summon him," said Raistlin, chilled.

"But you said Magius would die before he could use the orb," Sturm argued.

"So long as history does not change! And we cannot be sure of that, for even now Destina sits in the fortress, wearing the Graygem around her neck," Raistlin returned.

Horns blared, and they could hear drums beating.

"Commander Belgrave summons the knights to battle," said Sturm. "I must fetch my helm and my sword."

"And I must find Magius," Raistlin said.

They left the parapet, returning to the central hall. Sturm was in the lead, carrying the torch. He came to a sudden halt and held up a warding hand, stopping Raistlin.

"Don't move!" Sturm cautioned him.

"What is it?" Raistlin asked, peering over his shoulder.

In answer, Sturm pointed to a body on the floor.

Raistlin edged closer and saw a man lying in a pool of blood that was black in the torchlight. He wore armor, and Raistlin recognized the young knight Sir Richard. His eyes were wide in death, and his mouth gaped in a cry he had never had a chance to utter.

Raistlin could see the man was dead, but he felt compelled to stoop beside him to feel for the life pulse in the neck. As he did so, the head wobbled unnaturally.

"He has been garroted," Raistlin said, rising to his feet. "The killer knew his business. He wrapped a length of wire around the neck and twisted it, exerting such force he almost severed the head from the body. This happened recently. The body is still warm."

Sturm pointed to bloody footprints on the floor. "There was more than one intruder. The footprints continue down the hall, leading toward our bedchambers."

"Toward one bedchamber—Destina's," said Raistlin, observing the footprints. "These people are here to steal the Graygem! The dragon's attack on the tower could be a diversion. The blood is fresh. These intruders are still here. We need to find Destina before they do!"

"We left her and Brother Kairn in the dining hall in the fortress," said Sturm. "I will look for her there."

"I will check her chamber for intruders," said Raistlin.

Sturm headed back down the stairs at a run. Raistlin took a torch from the wall and hurried to Destina's room. She had left the door unlocked. Raistlin opened it and saw the chamber empty. Turning around, he almost bumped into Magius.

"What is going on?" Magius asked, yawning. "I was sound asleep when I heard a roar and felt the walls shake. Damn near knocked me out of bed. Has the battle started?"

"The dragon is attacking the tower," Raistlin replied, studying Magius intently. "I thought perhaps you might have summoned him with the dragon orb."

Magius gave an incredulous laugh. "Are you mad? Or do you think I am?"

"No, but I had to ask," said Raistlin. "It appears that Immolatus sent agents to steal the Graygem. They killed one of the knights. Fortunately, Destina was not in her room. She is with Brother Kairn in the fortress. Sturm has gone to warn her."

The dragon's roaring grew louder, and a sudden booming crash shook the building and sent dust and debris cascading down around them.

"What a stroke of luck! We will fight Immolatus now!" Magius said eagerly, his eyes gleaming. "What spells do you have prepared, Brother? I have several in mind that are suitable for battling a dragon. I need to return to my room to fetch my spell components and a very special scroll."

Raistlin reflected bitterly on his few spells, none of them very powerful and few of them deadly. Magius must have known what he was thinking, for he clapped Raistlin on the shoulder.

"You will cast the spell on the scroll. It is one of my own creation. The spell will give you the power to lift a large and heavy object—such as a boulder—and hurl it at the dragon."

Magius was so excited, he ran back to his room. Raistlin followed more slowly. This was all wrong. Immolatus had attacked the tower during the Third Dragon War, but only in company with the Dark Queen, not on his own. He had been defeated by knights armed with dragonlances, not by Magius, who had not fought him, because he had been captured and killed. Raistlin would fight Immolatus, but not here, not now. They would meet in a distant future.

Immolatus had attacked the tower on this night because of the

Graygem. The intruders had come for the Graygem. Had history gone awry? Were they too late to save the song? If so, he might have the chance to stand beside Magius and do battle with a dragon, a chance to die with the magic burning in his blood.

"A chance to die a hero," Raistlin murmured. "My name will be celebrated, not reviled."

As he entered Magius's room, his eyes were drawn to the dragon orb resting on its stand. The orb glistened red, gently swirling. The eyes in the orb looked back at him, watching him. Magius paused in the act of removing a scroll from an ornate scroll case and saw where Raistlin was looking.

"You should hide the dragon orb," said Raistlin.

"A good idea!" said Magius. "These thieves might be here for the Graygem, but they would not be averse to stealing the orb if they found it. I could cast the apport spell. I won't know where I send it, but I can always retrieve it simply by reversing the spell. What do you think?"

"I think . . . I should tell you the truth," said Raistlin slowly.

Magius was puzzled. "The truth? What truth?"

"The wizard I told you about," said Raistlin. "The one who could no longer cast spells and was captured and tortured to death. According to lore, that was you."

"Me?" Magius was startled a moment. Then he began to laugh. "Ah, I see. This is some sort of jest. Hardly the time—"

"No jest," said Raistlin. "I don't know when you will be captured or how or where. As of now, I don't even know if you *will* be captured. I don't know if the myth is true or if it is false and you grow old and die in your sleep. But I could not live with myself if I did not warn you."

Magius saw he was serious. "Even though by telling me you risk changing the future?"

Raistlin gave a faint smile. "What is it you said? The future be damned."

"I see," said Magius. He added, frowning, "So what would you have me do to avoid my fate? Crawl under the bed and hide? How long should I cower there? A day? Two days? A year?"

Raistlin shook his head, unable to answer.

Magius saw his friend's anguish and rested his hand on his shoulder. "I thank you for telling me, Brother, but you know I cannot live my life in fear. If we stop living because we fear death, then we have already died."

The words sounded familiar to Raistlin, but he could not remember where he had heard them. He knew, of course, that they were true.

"Do not say a word to Huma!" Magius added. "I understand now why you were so reluctant to reveal what you knew about the future. If Huma found out I had been captured, he would do something noble and stupid to save me. And now, if you will keep watch to see that I am not disturbed, I will dispatch the dragon orb to some unknown location."

Magius slipped the dragon orb into the velvet bag, then ran his hand over it, murmuring the words of magic. Raistlin stood at the door and gazed into the darkness. It would remain hidden, gathering dust, until the day far into the future when Tasslehoff would find it. Unless that future no longer existed.

"The spell is cast," Magius reported. "The orb is with the gods."

"True," Raistlin said. "Far truer than you know. Where should we fight the dragon?"

"We will attack it from the High Lookout," said Magius. "We will have the high ground, so to speak."

He picked up his staff and spoke the word, "*Shirak*."

The globe burst into light illuminating a stranger who materialized out of the darkness, almost in front of them. A woman stood at his side. Raistlin blinked, startled.

"I believe we have found our intruders," said Magius coolly.

The man and the woman were both tall, fair, and blond. Both wore leather armor. The man carried a sword. The woman did not have a weapon, only a coil of braided rope attached to her belt. A faint sweet, sickening smell clung to her, as of a clover mingled with the noxious odor of rotten eggs.

"She's a magic-user!" Raistlin warned as he thrust his hand into his pouch.

Before he could speak or even think the words of the spell, the woman extended her hands. Bolts of black lightning streaked from her fingertips. The bolt struck Raistlin in the chest and sizzled through his body like boiling oil. He collapsed, writhing in pain.

Magius stood protectively over him. He raised his staff and shouted a command that sent a beam of white-hot light shooting from the crystal. The man deflected the beam with his sword and it struck the wall, blowing out a chunk of stone.

"The dragon told us to bring one of the wizards and we have two," stated the man. "Take your pick, Mother."

"I like the older one, Captain."

She removed the rope of braided grass from her belt and flung it at Magius. The rope uncoiled like a striking snake and wrapped around him with blinding speed, binding his arms and legs. Sharp thorns sprang from the braided grasses, piercing his robes, puncturing his flesh.

Raistlin could only watch helplessly as Magius tried to free himself. The rope's grasp grew tighter the more he struggled, the thorns jabbing deeper into his body. He sank to his knees. Blood flowed from myriad puncture wounds, staining the marble. But Magius still managed to keep hold of his staff, though it was now slippery and wet with his own blood.

"What about this one?" the man asked, prodding Raistlin with the toe of his boot.

"He is young and useless," said the woman. "Not worth the effort."

"Then kill him," said the man. "I will go make certain the woman and this jewel are not here."

He walked down the hall, heading straight toward Destina's bedchamber.

The woman squatted down beside Raistlin. She slid her hand beneath his head and dug her fingernails into the base of his skull.

Raistlin felt his feet tingle and then they went numb. He could not move them. The paralysis spread to his legs and from there crept up his body, moving into his arms and his chest. He shifted his head, trying to free himself, but she placed her hand on his forehead, holding him fast.

"My magic feeds off your pain," she told him. "I grow stronger the more you fight to stay alive. When the paralysis reaches your chest, you will not be able to breathe, and then you will die. Death is so much easier."

The woman stood up and called down the hall after the man. "Did you find her?"

"She is not in her room," the man reported.

Raistlin tried to draw a breath, but his body was now almost completely paralyzed. He struggled for air, then felt something touch his hand. He shifted his eyes to see Magius sliding his staff across the floor toward him.

The movement caused the thorns to pierce deeper into Magius's arms. The pain must have been excruciating, but he clenched his jaw and did not cry out. He touched Raistlin with the staff and whispered words of magic. His fingers brushed against Raistlin's. The globe on the staff glimmered briefly, then flickered out.

Raistlin felt the paralysis lift. His lungs expanded, drawing in air. He could breathe, wiggle his fingers, and shift his legs. He dared not move, however, or the woman would realize he'd broken free of the spell.

Beside him, Magius gasped in agony as the tiniest movement drove the thorns deeper. The stone floor was smeared red with his blood, and Raistlin realized in heartbreaking despair that he could do nothing to save him. He could not fight this woman. She was right. He was young and useless.

Captain returned. Walking over to the stairwell, he shouted down to someone below.

"Send Garrote and Bonebreaker with the litter. We have the wizard."

The two were speaking camp talk, the language of mercenaries, but with a strange accent, one that Raistlin did not recognize. They were not paying any attention to him and he half opened his eyes to see, though he was careful not to move and kept his breathing soft and shallow.

Two more mercenaries arrived, carrying a crude litter made of skins stretched over wooden poles. One of them carried a coil of wire on his belt and Raistlin guessed that he was the one they called Garrote, taking his name from his terrible skill. The other one with massive arms and enormous hands must be Bonebreaker.

"We found the woman, Captain," Garrote reported. "She's in the dining hall in the fortress along with a monk. We left Butcher to keep an eye on them. What are your orders?"

"Mother and I will deal with the woman. You and Bonecrusher take this wizard back to camp." Captain cast a dispassionate glance at Magius.

The two men bent to pick him up, then snatched away their hands with cries of pain.

"You trying to kill us, Mother?" Bonecrusher snarled. "Get rid of the damn thorns, will you?"

Mother smiled, then made a swift gesture. The thorns receded, but the braided rope remained, binding Magius tightly. He was sweating and shivering and covered in blood. He shuddered. His eyes closed; his head lolled.

Captain frowned. "What is wrong with him?"

"He has passed out from the pain," Mother replied.

"He's of no use to the dragon dead!" Captain warned. "Immolatus wants him to provide information about this jewel."

"I'll keep him alive so long as he's useful," said Mother complacently. "Though I doubt he'll thank me."

As the two men roughly rolled Magius onto the litter, one of them gestured to the staff lying on the floor in Magius's blood.

"Do you want this thing? It looks to be magic."

Captain cast a questioning glance at Mother.

"I have no need for it," she replied. "But we can always sell it."

She reached for the staff and Raistlin flicked his hand; the knife in its thong on his wrist slid into his hand. He grasped it and waited tensely for the magic in the staff to shatter the bones in her hand or blind her with dazzling light, then he would attack.

But the staff might as well have been an ordinary wooden walking staff, for it did nothing. It meekly allowed Mother to pick it up, and she tossed it contemptuously on top of Magius's body.

The two mercenaries carried the litter down the stairs. Magius lay unconscious. One arm dangled over the edge of the litter. Blood rolled down his arm and dripped from his fingers. The staff rested protectively across his chest, and Raistlin suddenly understood why it had not attacked. It would not leave Magius.

"What do we do with this other wizard, Mother?" Captain asked.

Raistlin lay with his eyes closed, holding his breath, not moving.

"He is dead," Mother replied.

Captain frowned and bent nearer. "Are you sure?"

"Do you doubt me, Captain?" Mother demanded, an edge to her voice.

Captain straightened. "No, Mother, of course not. If you say he is dead, he is dead."

Raistlin hoped they would leave, go with the others. But Captain and Mother were apparently in no hurry, for they were engaged in discussing the Graygem.

"I have been thinking about this jewel," said Captain. "The dragon sets great store by it. It occurred to me that if he wants it this badly, so will others. Takhisis arrives soon. I propose we keep this jewel and sell it to the highest bidder."

"An excellent idea, Captain," said Mother. "And now, if you are ready, I will take us to the fortress."

She put her hand on his shoulder and the two vanished.

Raistlin sucked in a deep breath and tried to calm his fast-beating heart and regain his strength. He could hear the dragon bellowing, smashing stones, and breathing fire. Commander Belgrave and his troops would be running toward the perceived threat and away from the true danger.

Raistlin returned his knife to the leather thong, then shoved himself to his feet. Taking a torch from the wall, he started down the stairs. He could hear, far below him, the two men with the litter swearing as they tried to carry their burden down the spiral stairs. A distant bell chimed five times, marking the hour.

Raistlin looked at the drops of blood gleaming in the torchlight, and tears of rage and grief blurred his vision. He supposed he should be grateful. Apparently they had not changed history. If the River of Time flowed as it was meant to flow, Magius would die an agonizing death.

"I was not here then," said Raistlin. "But I am here now."

CHAPTER
TWENTY-SEVEN

Destina and Kairn remained in the dining hall after Raistlin and Sturm had left, waiting for Tas. Will had joined them not long after and he had grumbled when Destina asked him to light torches and bring fresh candles.

"When Tas returns, I want him to see the light and know we are here," Destina said.

Will did as she'd asked, but he muttered about going to all this trouble "for some dang kender." He took a seat at the opposite end of the table, undoubtedly keeping an eye on Kairn, for Commander Belgrave had made it clear he did not trust the monk.

The hour was late, approaching midnight, and Destina was growing increasingly worried about Tas. Kairn was trying valiantly to stay awake, but Destina could see he was tired. She caught him yawning when he thought she wasn't looking.

"The hour is late, Kairn," Destina said to him. "The commander gave you a room in the tower. Get some sleep. I will wait here for Tas."

"I am only a little sleepy," said Kairn. He glanced at Will and lowered his voice. "I should remain here. When Tas returns, we will need to wake the others and go back. We should not stay a moment longer than is needful."

Destina gave a wan smile. "I am glad you said 'when' he returns, not 'if.'"

"He will come back," said Kairn, and he clasped his hand over hers, and felt something sharp prick his skin. "Ouch!" He drew back his hand and saw a tiny spot of blood.

"What is wrong?" Destina asked.

"That ring you are wearing on your little finger," Kairn said, more amused than hurt. "I think it bit me."

"Bit you?" Destina repeated, puzzled.

"Look," said Kairn, and he displayed his wound.

"How strange," said Destina. "The ring was a gift from my mother. She was a cleric of the goddess Chislev. She said the goddess had blessed the ring, and if I was ever lost, she would guide me."

The ring was very simple, made of gold, adorned with a single emerald. Destina held up her hand and watched the small emerald wink and sparkle in the candlelight. The green made her think of newborn leaves, shining in the spring sun. The emerald's steady green flame seemed restful and comforting compared to the strange glaring light of the Graygem.

"Perhaps Chislev is trying to get our attention," said Kairn, smiling. "Tell me about your mother."

"Her name is Atieno and she left me on my own after my father died," said Destina, gently touching the ring. "I was resentful, at first. But now I realize she was trying to help me find my own way. What is it the Measure says? 'Children cannot learn to walk on their own if you cling to their hands.'"

"In my case, I was the one who left to stand on my own. My father could never understand why I was content to read about battles rather than fight them," Kairn said.

Will snorted in disgust, as though he agreed with Kairn's father. Then suddenly the retainer cocked his head and jumped to his feet.

"Don't you hear that?" he demanded.

"I hear thunder," said Kairn. "A storm must be brewing."

"Pish-tosh, the sky was clear as Mishakal's bright eyes when I made my rounds," said Will. "That's not thunder. That's the dragon!"

The fortress had no windows, so Destina could not see what was happening. But she could now hear drums beating and the sound of soldiers clattering down the stairs from the rooms on the third level where they slept.

"What is going on?" Will shouted at one as the soldiers came dashing past.

"The dragon is attacking the High Clerist's Tower!" the soldier shouted back and ran off.

"The battle must have started!" Will said eagerly.

Drawing his sword, he grabbed a torch and started to dash after the soldier. Then, seeming to remember his duty, he glanced back at Destina and Kairn, who had risen in alarm.

"You two stay here!" Will ordered. "You'll be safe enough."

The fortress's thick walls muffled the sound of the dragon's roaring. They could hear men shouting and Commander Belgrave's bellowed orders echoing through the corridors.

"This can't be happening!" Kairn said, shaken and confused. "This is wrong, all wrong!"

"What do you mean?" Destina faltered, although she feared she knew.

"According to history, the battle does not start until the day after tomorrow," said Kairn.

"So the Graygem has changed history—" Destina began.

"If that is true, Mother," said a voice from the darkness, "then this jewel is more valuable than we first thought."

Three people materialized out of the darkness—two men and a woman, all similar in appearance with fair hair worn in braids and dressed in leather and chain mail. The two men carried swords and wore knives at their belts. The woman alone was not armed. Her eyes were a startling blue, so cold that the torchlight could not warm them.

"Do you believe them, Mother?" the man asked.

"A mere bauble could never be so powerful, Captain," the woman replied, adding in disparaging tones, "but if the dragon believes it, we can double our asking price."

Kairn grabbed hold of his quarterstaff, which he had leaned against the wall, and took his place beside Destina. "Do you know these people?"

"I have never seen them before," said Destina. "Who are you? What do you want?"

"We have come for the jewel you call the Graygem," said Captain.

Destina longed to put out her hand to touch it, but she dared not, knowing she would draw attention to it.

"I have nothing for you," she told them. "Go away and leave us in peace."

"We will leave when we have the Graygem," said the woman. "Butcher, hand me a torch."

The second man took down a torch from the wall and held it out to her. The woman plucked a handful of flame, held the fire in her palm as though it were nothing but a snowball, then flung the fiery ball at Destina.

Kairn lifted his quarterstaff and struck at the flame. The blazing orange ball dropped to the floor and fizzled out.

"Gilean, guide my hand!" Kairn cried. Swinging his staff, he leaped at the two men. He swept the legs out from under Captain, then whipped the staff around to slam Butcher in the face. Captain picked himself up, but Butcher lay in a heap on the floor.

"Who is Gilean?" Captain asked, seemingly unperturbed.

"Some god, I think," said Mother and she extended her right hand.

Five vipers flowed from her fingers and landed on the floor. The vipers slithered toward Kairn. He slashed at them with his staff, only to have the vipers coil around it. He flung it away, but other vipers wrapped around his legs, tongues flicking from their mouths. Kairn fell, helpless, to the floor.

The vipers reared their heads, hissing at him.

"The vipers are poisonous," said Mother. "Give us the jewel known as the Graygem or watch the monk die."

Mother spoke a word, and the vipers raised their heads, preparing to strike.

Destina was shaking, but not with fear. She was shaking with determination and resolve. She would not let them harm Kairn. Too many had been hurt because of her. She remembered Raistlin saying that the Graygem would look after her.

"Then do it!" she ordered it, grimly.

She took hold of the Graygem and felt the little emerald ring tighten around her finger, as it had done when she had been lost in the dwarven kingdom.

Chislev . . . trying to get her attention.

Destina yanked on the chain, and the clasp, forged by Reorx, gave way. She held the Graygem in her hand for an instant—long enough to see its glow strengthen and feel its warmth on her skin. But it did not burn her. She flung it at the intruders.

The Graygem landed on the floor in their midst. It lay there, seemingly subdued, its gray light faintly pulsing.

Mother bent to pick it up.

The Graygem brightened and darkened. It grew smaller and larger, wider and narrower. Mother hesitated and drew back. The gray light brightened dimly.

"Why do you hesitate?" Captain asked. "It is only an ugly rock."

"It is dangerous!" Destina warned. "More dangerous than the dragon. More dangerous than Takhisis herself."

Mother laughed in contempt, reached down, and picked up the Graygem.

The blast was so weak, it did not disturb a grain of dust, yet it was powerful enough to fling Destina back against the wall.

She slumped to the floor, stunned and dazed. She tried to see, but the darkness was too bright. Gradually her vision cleared. She recoiled in horror.

Mother and Captain and Butcher were dead. Blood ran from their ears and their mouths. Their staring eyes were wide with terror, their mouths open in silent screams of agony. In the center of the gruesome circle of death, the Graygem shone with a faint, smug, gray light.

Destina shuddered and crawled over to Kairn, hoping he had not been hurt in the blast. He was still unconscious, but alive. The vipers had disappeared.

"Kairn!" Destina cried urgently, grasping his hand.

He stirred and opened his eyes and blinked at her. "What happened?"

"I am not sure," she said shakily. "Are you all right?"

"I am. . . . I think," said Kairn. He sat up and reached for his staff. "Those people—"

"They are dead," said Destina, swallowing. "The Graygem killed them."

She helped Kairn to his feet and he stood staring at the bodies in horrified disbelief.

"They came for the Graygem," Destina continued in a low voice. "They were going to kill you. I had no other weapon, but I remembered Raistlin saying it would take care of me, so I took it off and threw it at them."

The Graygem lay on the floor, pulsing with a faint gray light. Destina put her hand to her throat and the sudden realization dawned on her.

She was free of it.

CHAPTER
TWENTY-EIGHT

Huma and Gwyneth ran down the staircase to the ground floor as Immolatus continued his assault on the tower. Smoke from the burning ironwood spiraled up the stairwell, burning their lungs and making it difficult to see. They groped their way to the bottom and came to a door marked with the symbol of Kiri-Jolith.

"Where does this lead?" Gwyneth asked.

"To the altars of the gods," Huma replied softly. "We can take cover behind Paladine's statue."

Judging by the sound, the dragon had succeeded in battering a hole in the wall and was trying to force his way inside the temple. The doors would not stop him for long.

Gwyneth thrust the torch she carried into a bucket of sand, dousing the flame, as Huma pushed the door open a crack. He peered through it and motioned for Gwyneth to join him.

They could see Immolatus silhouetted against a backdrop of fire. He could not yet enter the temple, for he was too large to fit through the aperture he had created. He was having to batter down more of the wall.

"The gods are with us," Huma said, pressing Gwyneth's hand.

They slipped inside the temple and crouched behind the altar of Kiri-Jolith.

The altars of the gods formed a semicircle with Paladine in the center. Mishakal, as his consort, was on his left, standing beside Habakkuk, and Kiri-Jolith was on his right. The three white candles that stood on the altar of Paladine burned steadily and did not waver.

"The gods guide our way," said Huma softly. "Wait here!"

He placed his hand on the statue of Kiri-Jolith, invoking the god's aid, then swiftly and silently made his way to the altar of Paladine. The dragonlances shone with a silvery radiance in the candlelight. Huma took hold of one. Grasping it tightly, he stood before the altar and waited.

Immolatus struck the wall a massive blow and stones cascaded down around him. He kicked aside the rubble and lumbered into the temple, wreathed in clouds of smoke. Chunks of stone clung to his back. He shook them off. When he was inside the rotunda, he almost purred in relief, stretching out and rising to his full height.

Immolatus was about thirty feet long, his red-scaled body enormous and ungainly. Two horns sprouted from his head and bony protrusions thrust out from his jaws. Small eyes gleamed beneath an overhanging brow. He kept his leathery wings folded at his side, for they could extend forty-five feet and would hamper his movements. His heavy tail trailed across the floor and out the hole in the wall.

He roared defiance, savoring the moment of his triumph.

"Cower before my might, Paladine! You can do nothing stop me!"

Immolatus crashed into the temple. His horns brushed the ceiling. The wooden pews snapped beneath his feet. Then he suddenly stiffened and stopped. His eyes narrowed so that they almost disappeared. He sniffed like a dog, his head swinging this way and back.

"I might have known this foul place would be crawling with vermin!" he snarled. "I smell you, human!"

The dragon continued searching and then his lips curled back from his fangs in a hideous grin. "I see you now! Cowering in Paladine's shadow. That weak and sniveling god cannot protect you!" Immolatus snorted and smoke gushed from his nostrils. "He can't even protect his own temple!"

Huma walked out from behind the altar, holding the dragon-lance in his hand. The lance shone with silver radiance. The light of the three candles was reflected in his armor.

"Let us see how brave you are, human," said Immolatus.

Dragonfear rolled off him and seemed to spread like a pall throughout the temple.

Huma shuddered. The hand holding the lance was white-knuckled. His face, visible beneath his helm, was pale. But although he trembled, he stood steadfast before the altar, his unwavering gaze on the dragon.

Immolatus scowled and Gwyneth could sense the dragon's uncertainty. He was accustomed to mortals fleeing in terror before him. He could see this mortal was afraid, yet the mortal defied him, holding a weapon that seemed to shine with the light of the gods.

Immolatus eyed this strange weapon. He had clearly never seen anything like it. He did not appear to fear it; no weapon forged by mortal hands had ever harmed the red dragon. Yet something about this silvery, gleaming lance seemed to unnerve him.

The dragon glanced around the temple and his tongue flicked out from between his fangs. Gwyneth had the impression that Immolatus was starting to regret his reckless decision to enter the temple. He had not expected resistance and now he was confined in a small space with no easy way out. Gwyneth could feel the anger of the gods, and perhaps Immolatus could feel it, too, for he suddenly sucked in an enormous breath. Flames crackled from nostrils.

"Huma! Take cover!" Gwyneth gasped, frightened.

She need not have feared. Huma remembered her warning about the dragon's fiery breath and he dropped to the floor, sheltering behind the altar of Paladine, still clutching the dragonlance.

Immolatus blasted the statue of Paladine, sending waves of fire washing over the altar. The flames instantly melted the candles and incinerated the altar cloth, reducing it to ashes. The heat was so intense that cracks began to form in the marble. Immolatus struck the statue with a foreclaw and it split apart. The head of the platinum dragon crashed to the floor, and the dragonlances that had been on the altar disappeared beneath the ruin.

Huma had steadfastly maintained that Paladine would protect

him. Gwyneth could not see him amid the ruin and she prayed his faith was justified. She shed her mortal body and shifted back into her true form. Breaking free of the magic and the confinement of mortal flesh, she expanded and grew and gathered her strength.

Immolatus continued to belch fire at the statue until he was forced to stop for lack of air. Satisified he had destroyed his foe, he took the opportunity to rest after his exertions, confident that no mortal could have survived his attack. He was surprised beyond measure to see Huma rise unscathed from the rubble. The dragon-lance gleamed silver in the light of the flames, making Huma seem surrounded by hallowed light.

Immolatus squinted and blinked, as though the bright light was painful.

"I cooked those other poor fools who threatened me with tooth-picks," he sneered. "I will do the same to you."

As he sucked in another huge breath and prepared to breathe it out in a blast of fire that would incinerate everything it touched, Gwyneth rose to her full height and spread her silver wings. She was yet a young dragon, only about twenty-two feet in length. Sleek and slender, graceful and powerful, she confronted Immolatus.

The red dragon gaped at her, so stunned that he choked on his own fiery breath and began to hack and cough. Gwyneth opened her jaws and breathed a blast of frost as cold and bitter as the winter winds off the peak of Silver Dragon Mountain.

The frigid blast froze Immolatus, stopping his breathing and chilling him to the heart. Ice rimed his scales and frost coated his eyes. Half-blinded, the dragon lashed out in rage. One claw toppled the statue of Mishakal. He shattered the statue of Kiri-Jolith with his tail and smashed the phoenix statue of Habakkuk.

"Strike now, my love!" Gwyneth called.

Huma hurled the dragonlance with all his strength and struck Immolatus in his chest. Blood gushed from the wound and ran down the dragon's red scales in a torrent. Immolatus stared down at the lance sticking out from his scales like a pin feather. He seemed amazed at first and then he howled in pain and fury. He tried to yank out the lance with his claw, but when he touched it, the lance sizzled like a thunderbolt, and he howled again. Frantic with pain, he clamped his teeth over the dragonlance, dragged it out, and hurled it from him.

"The knight wounded you with a dragonlance, Immolatus," Gwyneth told him. "Forged by the god Reorx, made of the sacred dragonmetal, the dragonlance can do what no ordinary weapon can do—pierce your foul hide. Fly back to your evil Queen and warn her that all the Knights of Solamnia are armed with dragonlances, and if she attacks the Tower of the High Clerist, she does so at her peril!"

Immolatus was too furious to pay heed to her. He wanted this knight dead. He opened his jaws and lunged at Huma, intending to seize him and tear him asunder.

Huma had armed himself with another dragonlance, but he didn't have time to throw it before Immolatus was on top of him. The dragon slashed at him with his massive foreclaws, trying to rip apart the knight who had inflicted such terrible pain on him.

Huma scrambled backward, tripped over the rubble of the broken statues, and fell before the dragon's furious onslaught. Gwyneth attacked, slamming into Immolatus, striking him in the flank and pummeling him with a flurry of wing attacks.

Immolatus staggered beneath her fury and briefly retreated, giving Huma time to regain his feet. Immolatus was now faced with two formidable foes. He slashed at Gwyneth with his claws and, when she tried to evade his talons, he whipped his tail around and struck her in the spine, smashing her into the floor.

Immolatus loomed over her, snarling and slavering. Gwyneth waited until he was close, then lashed at him with her claws, ripping his belly, tearing through scales and flesh. Blood spewed, maddening Immolatus. He opened his mouth and lunged at her, intending to crush her head in his jaws.

Huma saw her peril and thrust the dragonlance into the dragon's thigh. Huma put all his weight behind the blow and drove the lance deep. Immolatus shrieked and flailed about in agony and rage. He rounded on Huma, and the knight disappeared beneath the dragon's crushing body, then Immolatus turned on Gwyneth, who was struggling to regain her feet.

Immolatus sank his fangs into her shoulder. Gwyneth could feel her bones snapping in the grip of the powerful jaws. Pain radiated from her shoulder and her wing dragged on the floor, useless.

Immolatus released his grip, but only so that he could get a better hold and tear out her throat. Gwyneth tried to draw in a breath to blast him with frost, but she could not breathe for the pain and the despair, for she feared Huma was dead. She was preparing to join him in death when she saw him stagger to his feet.

Blood ran down his face. His armor was crushed and mangled. The dragonlances gleamed faintly beneath the rubble of the altar, but he would have to dig them out from the ruins. He would never reach them in time. He drew his sword. The blade was broken, yet he faced the dragon.

"Foul wyrm!" A stentorian shout sounded from the front of the temple. "Fight me if you dare!"

Commander Belgrave stood alone in the entrance, holding his sword. Immolatus, moving ponderously, shifted his bulk to confront this new foe.

Huma gave a ragged shout and began running toward Belgrave. "The lance, Commander! On the floor in front of you!"

Titus saw the lance on the floor where Immolatus had flung it, black with the dragon's blood. He snatched it up and ran at the dragon. He drove the lance into the red-scaled flank, hoping to strike a killing blow to the heart. The lance ripped through the dragon's wing and shattered his ribs but missed the death blow. Immolatus howled and sank his teeth into Titus. The dragon picked him up and shook him like a dog shakes a rat, then spat him out. The broken body landed at Huma's feet.

"You are next," said Immolatus.

Huma was covered in blood and obviously in pain himself. He threw away his broken sword and knelt at the side of his fallen commander, placing his hand on his neck, feeling for the life beat.

"The commander is still alive," he told Gwyneth. "I will not leave him to die alone."

"And I will not leave you," Gwyneth said softly.

She could continue her fight against Immolatus, but she was crippled and weak from loss of blood, and in the end, the red dragon would destroy her.

Gwyneth changed into the elf woman and knelt at Huma's side. Her left shoulder was crushed and bloody, and her left arm dangled uselessly. She clasped Huma's hand in her one good hand. He put his arm around her and drew her near. They had no weapon but their love.

Immolatus sucked in a breath, prepared to incinerate these foes who had inflicted such terrible pain on him. A single ray of white light shone from the three candles on the broken altar. The dragon flung up his foreclaws, as though to blot out the light that seemed to pierce him like another lance. But he could not blot it out; he could not escape it. His lethal breath fizzled into a moan of rage and anguish.

A woman dressed in shimmering blue appeared beside Gwyneth and Huma. The woman placed her hand on them and Gwyneth felt her pain ease at the blessed touch.

Half-mad with pain, Immolatus collapsed onto his belly. Unable to put weight on his injured leg, the dragon was forced to crawl ignominiously out of the temple. He limped through the shattered gate and into the courtyard, where he managed, after a couple of failed attempts, to take to the air. He flew off, his torn wing flapping feebly, his crippled leg dangling beneath him. His blood fell like gruesome rain.

Gwyneth remembered Paladine's words. *Your most powerful weapon against evil is love.*

She had not understood the Dragon Father then. She understood now.

"Why did he flee?" Huma asked in wonder. "He could have killed us all."

"But he could not kill the gods," said Gwyneth.

CHAPTER
TWENTY-NINE

A bell chimed five times, marking the hour. Huma was surprised to see dawn breaking in the west. It seemed to him that he had been fighting for days. He turned his attention to Titus, who lay gravely wounded. He looked up to see soldiers picking their way through the rubble at the entrance to the temple. They could not meet his eyes, but gathered, shamefaced, around the body of their fallen commander. Huma suddenly understood. They had fled, prey to dragonfear, leaving their commander to fight alone.

Titus had regained consciousness. He saw them and a smile flickered on his lips. Will, the commander's retainer, tore off his helm and flung it from him, then sagged down on his knees.

"Forgive me, Commander!" Will said brokenly. "I turned tail and ran—"

He choked and could not continue.

"You showed . . . more sense than I did, old friend." Titus shifted his head, searching. "The light is fading. I cannot see. Where is Sir Huma?"

"I am here, Commander," said Huma, taking hold of his hand.

Titus gripped him tightly. "The fight is not ended and I will not be here to finish it. I name you . . . commander. . . ."

"I will take command, but only until you are able to resume your duties, sir," said Huma. "You will soon be well."

Titus faintly smiled. "The Measure forbids lying. . . ."

His face contorted in pain. Blood gushed from his mouth, yet he refused to give up. He struggled to draw breath.

Huma clasped the dying man's hand to his chest. Tears crept down his cheeks. "Your watch has ended, sir. Go to your rest."

Titus drew a final, shuddering breath, gave a deep sigh, and closed his eyes. He did not draw breath again.

Huma kissed the bloodstained forehead and folded the lifeless hands across his chest.

The young knight, Sir Reginald, gave a broken sob and covered his face with his hands. "He would be ashamed of me! I am not fit to be a knight!"

Huma rose wearily to his feet. His armor was wet with blood—his own, the dragon's, and the commander's. He placed a comforting hand on the shoulder of the young knight and then turned to face those who had gathered around the fallen.

"I know what it is to feel the dragonfear, to see your death in the beast's eyes," Huma told them. "The gods stood with me and gave me strength. They will stand with you. As the commander said, the fight is not finished. The final battle is yet to come."

He picked up the dragonlance that Titus had been holding and raised it high. "The gods have given us these weapons—dragonlances—forged by Reorx and blessed by Paladine. We will fight on, and though we may fall, in the end, we will prevail!"

Sir Reginald smiled, taking heart. Some of the soldiers cheered.

Will wiped his eyes and stood up. "With your permission, sir, I would like to prepare my commander for his final rest."

"Granted," said Huma. "Sir Reginald, select six men to form a guard of honor to escort the body of Commander Belgrave to the Chamber of Paladine, the sepulcher below the tower. Those on guard, return to your posts. The rest of you start to clear away this rubble."

The men would feel better with work to do. Sir Reginald brought him a basin of water and Will began to cleanse the blood from Titus's face.

"He is at peace," said Gwyneth. "Paladine walks with him."

Huma nodded and slumped down, exhausted, on a broken block of marble.

Sir Reginald handed him a water skin. "We saw a silver dragon, sir. The men are wondering if the good dragons have come to join the battle."

Huma smiled at Gwyneth. "One of them has."

Reginald looked puzzled, but seeing that Huma was not going to explain, he left to tend to his duties. Huma put his hand to his eyes, which were gummed with blood, and rubbed them.

"Look who comes!" Gwyneth said to him.

Huma opened his eyes and saw a red-robed wizard walking toward them. He was accompanied by one of the soldiers.

"This wizard says he needs to speak to you, sir," said the soldier, sounding disapproving. "He claims the matter is urgent."

Raistlin had his cowl pulled low, leaving his face in shadow. He kept his hands in his sleeves. He approached Huma, who rose to greet him.

"If you and Magius have come to join the fight, you are late," said Huma, smiling. "Where is Magius? It is not like him to miss out on the action."

Raistlin drew back his hood. He was grave and wan.

"What has happened?" Huma asked, his smile vanishing, his voice taut. "Where is Magius?"

"I have bad news, sir. Magius has been captured and taken prisoner, sir," Raistlin replied.

Huma stared at him in dismay. "What? How? That is not possible! Who has taken him? Where?"

Raistlin was about to reply, but before he could speak, he staggered and almost fell. Gwyneth put her arm around him and eased him down onto the chunk of broken stone.

"Are you hurt?" she asked.

Raistlin shook his head. "I am fine. Let me speak to Huma. I cannot stay long."

"At least rest and drink some water and take a moment to recover," said Gwyneth.

Huma waited impatiently until Raistlin had taken a sip of water and moistened his lips. "Where is Magius?"

"He was captured by agents of Immolatus," said Raistlin. He looked at Gwyneth. "The dragon knows about the Graygem. His agents went to the fortress in search of Destina—"

Gwyneth was alarmed. "Immolatus must not get hold of the Graystone! Did they find her?"

"Sturm knew about the danger and went to warn her. He and the monk will guard her." Raistlin gave a sardonic smile. "Oddly enough, so will the Graygem."

"You are talking in riddles!" Huma said angrily. "The Graygem is a myth! What does it have to do with Magius?"

"The Graystone is not a myth," said Gwyneth in a low voice. "It is all too real and Lady Destina wears it on a chain around her neck."

"You knew this! Magius knew this! Why did no one tell me?" Huma demanded, angrily.

"We hoped to return home, to take the Graygem back with us before anyone else found out," said Raistlin. "Unfortunately, our plans to leave immediately fell through. The Graygem remains here and it is in peril, for now Immolatus knows where to find it. My guess is that he knew he would need a wizard to provide him with information about the Graygem. That is why they captured him alive. They have taken him to the dragon's camp. I came to tell you."

Huma reached for his sword, only to remember that it was broken and he had left it in the temple. He picked up Commander Belgrave's sword and thrust it into his belt. "Where is Sir Reginald? Tell him he is in charge in my absence."

"Where are you going?" Gwyneth asked.

"To rescue my friend," said Huma shortly.

"Stop! Think what you are doing!" Gwyneth said firmly, seizing hold of him. "You promised Commander Belgrave as he lay dying that you would take command. The Dark Queen's armies are within a day's march of the tower. The dragon is wounded, but he is not dead. Your men look to you for leadership. You cannot abandon your duties!"

"I cannot abandon my friend!" Huma said savagely. "I know what the dragon will do to him! I cannot let him die!"

"I will go," said Raistlin. "Magius is my friend, as well."

Huma made an impatient gesture. "I mean no offense, Majere,

but you are a wizard and not very skilled at that. You cannot save Magius with a bit of bat dung."

"And you cannot save him with steel, Commander," Raistlin returned grimly. "Entering the enemy camp will not require the Oath and the Measure. It will require deceit and guile. And, as it happens, I am adept at both."

Huma shook his head in anguish.

"I will accompany the mage," Gwyneth offered.

"Your place is with Huma, Lady," said Raistlin. "He will need you in the final battle."

"He is right," said Huma. "I cannot lose both of you."

He put his hand to his eyes. Tears crept from beneath his fingers.

"Magius is a war wizard, sir," Raistlin said. "He is willing to give his life for his country. He may be a mage, not a knight, but his honor is his life. If you abandon your duty in order to save him, you will dishonor him, and he would never forgive you."

Huma gave a rueful smile. "I should never hear the end of it." His tears were wet on his cheeks. He swallowed and gripped Raistlin's hand. "Tell Magius I could not come because . . . because I have better things to do than save his sorry ass!"

"I will, sir," said Raistlin.

Huma hastily turned away and was almost immediately accosted by men asking for orders. He gave them in a calm and steady manner, then went off to inspect the damage done to Noble's Gate. Gwyneth lingered behind.

"Does Magius know anything about the Graystone?" she asked.

"I almost wish he did," Raistlin replied. "They might kill him quicker. But he knows nothing. They took the wrong wizard. They should have taken me."

"And knowing they will kill you if you are captured, you still risk your life to try to save him," said Gwyneth.

Raistlin looked at her, his strange eyes intense. "I risk more than that, Lady. But I cannot let him die."

He turned on his heel and walked swiftly away.

Gwyneth gazed after him, thoughtful and uneasy.

CHAPTER
THIRTY

Destina stared at the Graygem lying on the floor in a pool of blood, surrounded by the bodies of those it had just killed. She put her hand to her throat.

"I am free of it," she said softly.

Except she wasn't. She and the Graygem both knew it.

"Lady Destina!" a voice called, and she heard the sounds of someone approaching, moving in haste. Kairn raised his quarterstaff, but Destina shook her head.

"I know that voice. He is a friend."

Sturm appeared in the doorway and stopped to regard them in concern.

"Thank the gods you are safe, Lady! I heard the most terrible screams—"

His gaze went to the bodies and to the Graygem, pulsing with light in the center of the carnage. His eyes widened in shock. He looked back at Destina. "What happened?"

"I am not sure," Destina faltered. "These people appeared out of nowhere. They told me to hand over the Graygem. The woman was some sort of magic-user. She conjured up vipers and threated to kill

Kairn. I remembered Raistlin saying the Graygem would take care of me and so I broke the chain and threw it at them . . . and the next thing I knew, they were all dead."

Sturm was perplexed. "I do not doubt your word, Lady, but you claimed you could not touch the Graygem. You said it burned your hand."

"Raistlin told me I needed to gain control of it," Destina said. "I didn't believe him. I didn't think that was possible. But in that moment, when I feared they might harm Kairn, I *knew* the Graygem would do my bidding. I didn't intend for it to kill anyone. I just wanted to frighten those people, to make them leave. I even warned that horrible woman not to touch it. But she didn't listen."

"Destina is telling the truth, sir," Kairn affirmed. "You should not doubt her. She saved my life."

"She saved both your lives," said Sturm. "Raistlin believes these people were agents of the dragon. Somehow he found out you had the Graygem and he sent his agents here to steal it."

"Tully knows I have it. He tried to take it from me," said Destina. "He could be working for the dragon."

"Then I would watch for him, Lady," said Sturm. "He tried to take it once and he may try again. These people deal in death. They killed Sir Richard as he stood guard."

"More death! Because of me!" Destina said, despairing.

"Not because of you, Destina," said Kairn. "The blame lies with Chaos."

Sturm was grim. "And now you are free of the Graygem, Lady. I say we leave the accursed jewel behind."

Destina was tempted. She could turn her back on it, leave it lying on the blood-covered floor, and walk away. Kairn would take her home. If she still had a home . . . if there was still a future.

"I wish I could," Destina said, sighing. "But I cannot."

She gestured to the gruesome scene. "Picture what the Dark Queen could do with the Graygem if it fell into her hands. Tully knows I have it. Her red dragon knows I have it. Takhisis will soon know I have it and I must do what I can to guard it. The burden is mine. I chose it willingly."

She walked over to the Graygem that was still attached to the chain Reorx had forged for it and, reaching down, she resolutely picked it up. The Graygem sparkled with a dull radiance, bearing no trace of the blood of its victims. But as Destina walked away from the corpses, she noticed she left bloody footprints on the floor.

She returned to the table, holding the Graygem in her hand. Destina drew in a deep breath and let it out in a sigh, then draped the golden chain around her neck and fastened the clasp. The Graygem nestled into her throat, warm and smug.

She grasped hold of the jewel and felt its warmth increase until it grew too hot to hold. She quickly let go.

Kairn was watching her with mingled sorrow and admiration. "When we return, we will talk to Astinus and find a way to rid you of this burden."

Destina gave him a reassuring smile, as though she believed him.

"We must report this to Commander Belgrave," said Sturm.

"Commander Belgrave is dead," said Raistlin, emerging from the darkness. He cast a dispassionate glance at the bodies. "Thus do the gods punish unbelievers."

"What happened to the commander?" Sturm demanded.

"He died fighting the dragon. Immolatus attacked the temple as a diversion so his agents could steal the Graygem. He imagined he would be perfectly safe, but he encountered a valiant knight holding a dragonlance, and a silver dragon in her wrath and glory. Immolatus was severely wounded and, like the great coward he is, he fled for his life."

"Gwyneth returned to Huma and brought the knights the dragonlances, which they used to wound Immolatus. It would seem we have not changed history," Destina said, sounding confused. "But according to Kairn, the fight didn't happen until the day of the last battle. And that is yet to come. So I *have* changed history."

"You take far too much credit to yourself, Lady," said Raistlin.

He grimaced and began to cough. He dabbed his lips with his handkerchief and eyed the Graygem at her throat.

"We are the tools of Chaos. It twists right into wrong. When we succeed, we fail. The dragon took Magius captive. He intends to force him to reveal information on the Graygem. They have taken him back to the dragon's camp. At least his death will be historically accurate," Raistlin added, with a scathing glance at Kairn.

"I am sorry, sir, but Magius has to die," said Kairn unhappily.

"No, he doesn't, Brother," said Raistlin. "Because I will not let Chaos win. I am going to save him."

"You are going to get yourself killed!" Sturm said grimly.

"Would that be such a great loss, Sturm Brightblade?" Raistlin asked. "I told you of the evil I will do in my life. The harm I will do to Caramon and countless others. The future will be better if I am not in it. Besides, I promised Huma I would save his friend. Should I break my word to him?"

"If you have made a promise, you must fufill it," said Sturm. "I am coming with you."

Raistlin gave an ungracious shrug. "Suit yourself. I do not have time to argue."

He thrust his hands into his sleeves and walked off, disappearing into the darkness.

Kairn gazed after him helplessly. "He cannot do this! You must try to stop him!"

"We are walking into an enemy camp, Brother," said Sturm wryly. "The dragon will undoubtedly stop us both. If we are not back by sunset, take Destina and the Graygem and Tas—if he shows up—to your own time. You will be centuries away and, with the help of the gods, the Dark Queen will not be able to find you.

"The knights are going to abandon the fortress and move all their forces into the High Clerist's Tower. You and Destina should seek refuge there. You will be safer there, especially if this Tully is searching for you. The gods walk with you."

Sturm took one of the torches and hurried after Raistlin. After he was gone, Kairn sank down in a chair.

"Alice told me that since the Graygem was involved, I should 'bring back the survivors,'" he said in despondent tones. "But I never thought I might be faced with that possibility."

Destina sat down beside him. She could offer no words of comfort, for there seemed to be no comfort in this world.

The Knight's Spur was silent with the stillness of death. The stench of blood mingled with the smell of melted candle wax and the smoke of the flickering torches. Destina realized that she and Kairn could be the only people here.

"Sturm says the tower is safer than the fortress and that might be true," said Destina. "But if Tully is searching for me, he would look for me in the tower. The Graygem would be safer here in the fortress. And I can wait for Tas."

Kairn took hold of the quarterstaff, picked up the rucksack, and rose to his feet. He held out his hand to her. "Then we should wait for him in the pantry. As Raistlin said, that's where Tas would go first."

Destina was grateful, glad to leave this hall of death.

"We should not stay too much longer," Kairn said, as they were walking down the deserted corridor toward the kitchen. "When the battle starts, the enemy will overrun the fortress."

"And we don't know when the battle will start, do we?" said Destina, clasping the Graygem.

Kairn was silent, wanting to be reassuring, yet unable to lie.

"No," he admitted. "We do not."

CHAPTER
THIRTY-ONE

I mmolatus had never known such agony. The wounds inflicted by the accursed knight and his horrible lance were inflamed and oozing blood. The silver had burned him with frost. His foes had broken his bones and torn his wing. The pain of his injuries struck deep to his very soul.

He had limped back to his camp instead of his lair, because he could not fly far and the camp was closer. Once there, he decided to remain in his dragon form, unable to bear the thought of enduring the further humiliation of shifting into a mortal body after his ignominious defeat.

Everyone in camp stared in shock to see the dragon land heavily on the ground, covered in blood. Immolatus glared at them, daring them to say anything.

"Fetch a cleric," he growled.

As guards scrambled to obey him, Immolatus crawled into his tent and collapsed, groaning in pain. Some fool called six of the clock and all was well. Immolatus wanted to roast him.

The guards soon returned with the cleric of Takhisis. She examined the dragon's wounds. Gingerly poking at one, she snatched her hand away.

"You are god-cursed," she stated. "Her Dark Majesty can do nothing to help you."

"Then what good is she?" Immolatus snarled. "I nearly get myself killed on her orders and she won't lift a finger to help me!"

"Her Dark Majesty did not order you to attack the temple," said the cleric coldly. "Your orders were to wait for her arrival. You brought this on yourself, Dragon."

After she had gone, Immolatus rolled over on his side and gnashed his teeth. He was particularly outraged because he had attacked the temple as a diversion, to give the Gudlose the opportunity to steal the Graygem. He had thought to have some fun, kill some knights, wreck their temple. He had been shocked beyond belief to encounter humans who did not fear him, gods who defied him, and—adding insult to injury—a silver dragon.

This same silver dragon had been trailing him for months, spying on him, reporting his every move to his foes, the metallic dragons. He'd actually viewed the silver's spying as a compliment. It only showed how much the metallics feared him.

Immolatus had certainly not expected the silver to attack him. Nor had he expected the knights to have forged those accursed weapons that had inflicted such terrible harm.

The dragon lay in his tent suffering and feeling very sorry for himself when the guard announced one of the Gudlose wanted to speak to him. Someone named Garrote.

Perhaps this was good news for a change. Immolatus lifted his head as the man entered. "Did you find the Graygem?"

"We captured a wizard as you ordered," said Garrote, "and brought him back to camp. What should we do with him?"

"What about the Graygem?" Immolatus demanded, scowling.

"Captain and Mother and the others are going after it," said Garrote. "Captain ordered Bonecrusher and me to return with the wizard. What should we do with him?"

Immolatus sank back down. "Find out what he knows about the Graygem."

"He hasn't been very talkative up to now," said Garrote.

"Then teach him what will happen if he doesn't cooperate!" said Immolatus. "Just don't damage him beyond repair. Once I have the

Graygem, I will speak with him myself and I can't do that if you fools kill him."

Garrote departed. Immolatus groaned and suffered and waited with impatience for Captain to bring him the Graygem. But the hours passed and Captain didn't arrive. Immolatus began to grow concerned. Perhaps the blasted Gudlose had betrayed him and kept the Graygem for themselves.

The dragon fell into a fitful doze that afternoon, probably from loss of blood. He was awakened by the guard announcing a visitor. Immolatus eagerly reared his head, expecting to see Captain.

What he saw was Mullen Tully.

"Where is Captain?" Immolatus demanded angrily. "Where is Mother? Where is my Graygem?"

"I have bad news, my lord," said Tully. "The Captain and Mother are dead."

"Dead? Impossible!" Immolatus snorted in disbelief. "They are the best! Invincible!"

"And dead," said Tully. He wiped his forehead with his sleeve.

Immolatus was bewildered. "Who killed them?"

"The Graygem," said Tully in a low voice. "I saw it with my own eyes, Lord! I was there."

"Where?" Immolatus demanded.

"In the Knight's Spur," said Tully. "I was keeping an eye on the Graygem."

Immolatus reared up his head, fixing Tully with a baleful glare. "You appear to be very interested in this jewel."

"It's worth a lot of money," said Tully.

Immolatus grunted. "What happened?"

"Like I told you, I tried to take it from Lady Destina, but the damn thing nearly burned my hand off. I figured she'd report me or tell her friends about me, and so I laid low, covered my face with my helmet, and waited to catch her alone. I would have had her, but you had to send those damn assassins to find her!"

"Given that you had botched the job once, I thought it best to hire professionals," said Immolatus.

"Yeah, well, your professionals now have blood running out of their eye sockets!" said Tully. "I had finally cornered Lady Destina in the fortress. She was with some monk, but the two were alone. I figured the monk wouldn't be a problem, and I was going to kill him and capture her, but the Gudlose beat me to it. Captain told her to give them the Graygem and she gave it to him, all right. She took it off and threw it at them and . . . I don't know what happened after that. It's hard to explain. What I do know is that Captain and Mother and Butcher are dead. It must have scrambled their brains because there was blood and gunk leaking out of their skulls."

"Never mind them! What about the Graygem?" Immolatus asked impatiently. "Where is it?"

"I didn't stay to find out," said Tully. "After I saw what it did to Captain and Mother, I left."

Immolatus shifted his massive bulk, trying to find a position that eased the pain.

"You are telling me this Graygem has the power to kill the best mercenaries money can buy, and yet some human woman wears it around her neck!" Immolatus seethed with anger and disbelief. "How is that possible?"

"I don't know," Tully returned sullenly. "Ask that wizard you captured. All I know is that I'm not going anywhere near it!"

Immolatus wanted the Graygem now more than ever. He deserved it, after all he had suffered. But he could not go after it himself, not in this state. Much as he hated the thought, he had to rely on mortals. He groaned and rolled over again.

"At the back of my tent is a large chest made of gold and silver," he said. "Inside you'll find a two-handed greatsword. Bring the sword to me."

Tully hesitated. "I've worked for you for a long time, Lord, and I know you always put magical warding spells on your treasure chests. It might blow off my head!"

"I will remove the spells, but just on that one chest," said Immolatus. "Don't go trying to open any of the others or you will end up a blob of smoldering flesh."

Tully returned carrying the sword and its nondescript leather scabbard. The greatsword was forged of steel. The hilt was set with five jewels made to look like five eyes: an emerald, a ruby, a sapphire, a white diamond, and a black diamond. Tully regarded it admiringly.

"It is a thing of beauty. How did you come by it?"

"The ogres crafted this greatsword during the Age of Dreams as a gift for Takhisis," said Immolatus. "I took a fancy to it, and she gave it to me. I call it Deathdealer because the blade is enchanted. One strike to the head or the heart of a metallic dragon and the sword will always kill. As for mortals, the blade pierces armor and glides through flesh and bone with ease."

Tully smiled in appreciation. "Who are you going to kill, Lord?"

"Not me, you fool!" Immolatus snapped. "You are going to slay that accursed silver dragon and her blasted knight, and when they are dead, you will kill the mortal wearing the Graygem and bring it to me."

Tully was incredulous. "Me? Kill a silver dragon? I am loyal to you, my lord, but I will not be of any use to you dead!"

"Stop blathering," Immolatus growled. "I told you the sword will always deal death."

"If I hit the head or the heart. What happens if I miss?" Tully asked.

"I wouldn't know," said Immolatus, sneering. "I never miss."

"The sword looks too heavy and unwieldy for me to use," Tully complained. "Don't you have another that's smaller?"

"The ogres have been using a straw dummy for target practice," said Immolatus with a hiss. "I'm sure a real live dummy, such as yourself, would make a nice change for them."

Tully blanched. He hefted the sword and swung it experimentally.

"It's not as heavy as it looks," he admitted grudgingly. "Very well. I'll do the job. I'll kill the silver dragon and any knight I can find, but I won't go near the Graygem."

Immolatus shot a blast of flame in Tully's general direction. Tully flinched and ducked, but his eyes glinted in anger. Immolatus realized a bit belatedly that Tully was the one holding the magical sword.

The dragon fumed, but he backed down. "If you're too scared to bring me the Graygem, then bring me the woman's corpse and I'll take it off her body myself. The damn jewel won't dare harm me."

Tully looked as though he did not share this opinion, but he had won, so he didn't argue. He thrust the sword into its leather scabbard, slung it over his shoulder, bowed to the dragon, and left.

Immolatus lay down and groaned. He comforted himself with thoughts of the Graygem. The more he heard about its powers, the more it intrigued him.

It had slain those who called themselves the Godless. He wondered if it could slay a god. He wondered if it could slay Takhisis.

CHAPTER
THIRTY-TWO

Raistlin heard Sturm running after him, but he kept walking, his robes rustling around his legs.

"You know what you are doing is wrong," said Sturm, catching up with him.

"Such considerations never stopped me in the past," Raistlin retorted. "Chaos is playing with us, watching us scurry about in terror, afraid to spit lest we change history. I have been thinking. Perhaps history doesn't care if Magius survives. The river might continue to flow just as well with him as without him."

"You don't know that," said Sturm.

"I know that I will not let Magius die!" said Raistlin with a flash of anger.

He and Sturm descended the stairs that led to the first floor of the Knight's Spur. When they reached the bottom, Raistlin turned to confront Sturm.

"You should not come with me," said Raistlin. "You should stay with the others."

"And what happens to the others if you get yourself killed? We cannot return to our time without you," said Sturm.

Raistlin continued, walking down a corridor that led to the front entrance. Sturm walked at his side.

"You don't want to return, do you?" Raistlin asked abruptly.

Sturm was troubled. "How can I run off and abandon Huma and Gwyneth and these men to their fate? Huma will need every sword to defend the tower. He trusts me and respects me. I would not have him think I am a coward who basely fled on the eve of battle."

"You heard Brother Kairn talking about time travel," said Raistlin. "If we do not change history—"

"Which you are about to do," Sturm said, interrupting.

Raistlin ignored him. "If we leave without having done anything to *drastically* alter time while we are here, the history will be restored. Huma and Gwyneth will defeat Takhisis, the bards will sing the song, and the river flows on. Our names will fade from the records of the Third Dragon War, and you and I will pick up our lives from the night of our reunion with no memory of what happened here— because we were never here. Thus Huma won't disparage you for being a coward, because he will have never met you."

"And I will have never met him," said Sturm in a low voice. "If we go back, all these moments will be lost, for I will not remember."

And I will have no memory of Magius, Raistlin thought. No memory of his sardonic smile, his caustic wit. No memory of that mad dash through the streets of Palanthas being chased by raging minotaurs, or sharing the joy of feeling the magic burn in the blood.

"Then explain to me this," said Sturm. "When I first encountered Huma, we did not meet as strangers. I felt as though I knew him. We were comfortable together as old and familiar friends. How is that possible if I had no memory of him?"

"He was your hero for so long, you gave him life," Raistlin said.

Sturm shook his head, not satisfied with the explanation. Raistlin wasn't satisfied with it, either. He had felt the same, as if he and Magius had been long-time friends.

"Or perhaps the heart remembers what the head does not," Raistlin added quietly, almost to himself.

"Why do you believe saving Magius from death will have no effect on history?" Sturm asked.

Raistlin shrugged. "I am not sure what I believe or if I even care. All I know is that I must try to save my friend."

He and Sturm continued down the corridor together, side by side, in silence and rare understanding. Raistlin suddenly found Sturm's presence irritating.

"You should go back, keep watch on Destina and the Graygem."

"She has Brother Kairn," said Sturm. "I am coming with you. I will help you save Magius, if I can."

Raistlin was touched and pleased, though he took care not to reveal it.

"Then you must get rid of your armor," Raistlin told him. "I cannot walk into the dragon's camp in company with a Knight of Solamnia. I don't suppose you would cut off your mustaches?"

"I would sooner cut my throat," said Sturm. "I dislike skulking about like a thief. Such deceitful practices are dishonorable and prohibited by the Measure. Still," he added with a faint smile, "I concede that wearing armor on such a mission would be unwise. But I must leave it somewhere safe. This armor is my legacy and means more to me than my life."

"You could leave it in Commander Belgrave's quarters," Raistlin suggested. "No one will go in there now that he is dead and the Knight's Spur has been abandoned."

They turned their footsteps in the direction of the officer's quarters. Torches flickered on the walls, but they did not light the darkness, only filled it with shadows.

The door to Titus's bedchamber stood open, as though he had rushed out the moment he had heard the dragon attacking and not taken time to lock the door behind him.

Sturm entered the dead man's quarters with reverent respect, commending his soul to Paladine. Raistlin looked around curiously. The room was small, neat, and sparsely furnished with a desk, two chairs, a camp cot, and a wooden chest. The desk was covered with papers, neatly stacked and arranged in different piles.

Sturm divested himself of his cuirass, his gauntlets and greaves, and his helm, and placed them in a wooden chest where the commander had probably kept his armor. Sturm retained his sword and the chain mail he wore over his shirt. He found a helm with a visor he could lower to hide his face.

Raistlin approved the use of the helm but eyed Sturm's sword with displeasure.

"Your scabbard is decorated with kingfishers and roses. Leave your sword here and take one of the commander's."

Sturm placed his hand protectively on the hilt.

"I am a Brightblade, named in honor of this sword. I will not leave it behind under any circumstances."

Raistlin was about to argue, then considered that he had won a victory with the armor. "Very well. Cover it with a cloak. If anyone questions it, tell them you looted it from the corpse of a dead knight."

"And what about you entering the enemy camp in those red robes?" Sturm asked. "Shouldn't you be wearing black?"

"And where am I likely to find black robes in the High Clerist's Tower?" Raistlin demanded. "I will cover my robes with a cloak."

He had worn the red color of Lunitari since he had taken the Test in the Tower of High Sorcery. The red had been his reward, as well as his chastisement, for they denoted his ambition, his thirst for power, his willingness to stop at nothing to achieve his goals. Including sacrifing his own brother.

"It seems we all have our legacies," Sturm remarked.

Raistlin scowled, but he had to admit that Sturm was right, and he irritably began to strip off his robes. Sturm dug out a leather tunic for him to wear over his breeches and a capuchin to conceal his golden skin and hourglass eyes. Raistlin tied the belt that held his spell components around the tunic and wrapped himself in a cloak to conceal them. Sturm flung a cloak over his own shoulders and draped it so that the folds covered his sword.

They reached the front gate of the fortress about an hour after sunrise. The gate was closed and no one was guarding it. The sentries must have left their posts to defend the High Clerist's Tower. Sturm lifted the bar and pushed open the heavy doors.

"You might as well leave it open," said Raistlin. "The gates at the High Clerist's Tower did not stop the dragon or his agents. They will not stop the Dark Queen."

"I will not make it easy for her," said Sturm and he closed the doors behind them.

"What about Tas?" Raistlin asked. "He might come back."

"Locked gates won't stop him, either," said Sturm dryly.

A ramp led from the entrance to the ground. They paused at the top to look out across the plains at the enemy encampment. Smoke was rising from the cookfires and they could see men and goblins milling about.

They followed the stream that flowed into the plains, taking care to keep to the cover of the brush. Raistlin studied the camp as they approached. The various races—humans, goblins, hobgoblins, ogres, and kobolds—had each set up their own camp. None of them trusted the others. Hobgoblins despised goblins. Ogres hated kobolds. The humans detested ogres. But they were all loyal to their Dark Queen and would fight together and die together at her command.

The dragon had posted humans on sentry duty, probably considering them the best of a bad lot. They had no fear of coming under attack. They already outnumbered the knights and their army was growing by the hour. The sentries were playing at dice.

Raistlin had no difficulty finding the tent belonging to Immolatus. It was the largest in the camp and flying a red flag, not the black flag with the symbol of the Dark Queen. He pointed it out to Sturm.

"Do you think the dragon is in there?" Sturm asked. "You seem to know him."

"He was badly wounded and probably wouldn't have the strength or the desire to shift into human form," said Raistlin. "He always did feel it degraded him. He has likely hidden himself away to heal. Hopefully, that is the case, and we don't have to worry about encountering him."

"Just a few thousand of his troops," Sturm said grimly. "Do you have a plan or do we stroll into camp and demand to know where they are holding Magius?"

"My plan is for you to keep quiet and let me to do the talking!" Raistlin returned. "We must see what transpires. We should enter now before the camp is fully awake."

Sturm halted him. "Wait! Look there! They're about to have visitors."

He pointed to an enormous half-ogre mounted on a draft horse that was riding toward the camp. The half-ogre was not as tall as an ogre, but he had the same massive shoulders, greenish-brown skin, and tusks that protruded from his lower jaw. He was dressed in black robes trimmed in gold, and wore a steel helm on his head and a huge mace in a harness slung across his back.

He must be someone important, Raistlin thought—or someone who considered himself important, for he was accompanied by a retinue of ten ogre guards, marching behind him on foot.

"He is wearing black robes," said Sturm. "Is he a wizard?"

"The gods of magic do not permit their wizards to carry such weapons as that mace," Raistlin replied. "He must be a cleric of Takhisis, and a high-ranking one to judge by the fact that he travels with an escort."

The cleric and his guards halted on the outskirts of the dragon's camp. The half-ogre ponderously dismounted from his horse. The human sentries had stopped their game to observe him. He glared at them, his jaw thrust out, and stated in a loud bellow, "I am Mortuga, High Cleric of Her Majesty, Queen Takhisis. I am here as an emissary from Her Majesty to speak to the dragon Immolatus. Let him be informed of my arrival."

The sentries looked startled at this demand. They held a brief conference, then one of them hurried off to report to their superiors.

"I would guess that no one wants to tell this cleric that the dragon managed to get himself skewered by dragonlances," said Raistlin.

Three half-dressed officers, accompanied by a a few sleepy camp followers, emerged from their tents. After speaking to the sentry, a grim-looking officer walked over to confer with the cleric. A group of onlookers gathered around to watch and listen. Raistlin motioned to Sturm and they drew near.

"Welcome, Holy One," said the officer. "I understand you want to see Immolatus. The dragon is indisposed. He will meet with you tomorrow."

"I will meet him with now. Where is he?" Mortuga demanded, thrusting out his lower jaw as he glared down at the human in anger.

"Immolatus is in his tent, Holy One," said the officer nervously. "He has given orders he is not to be disturbed."

Mortuga glowered. "The dragon should have been on hand to greet me! I am Her Dark Majesty's emissary. Takhisis will not be pleased. Inform him I am here. I will wait in that tent."

The tent belonged to the officers. They glanced at one another, but none of them dared challenge him.

"These are my bodyguards." Mortuga indicated the ogres with a wave of his hand. "See to it that they are provided with meat and drink and anything else they require."

Mortuga tossed the reins of his horse at the officer and lumbered into the tent. His ogre escorts strode into camp, grabbing food and anything else they wanted.

"I have an idea," said Raistlin. "You will act as my bodyguard. Keep near me, but not too near, as though you fear getting too close to me. Lower the visor on your helm to hide your face, and follow my lead."

Raistlin pulled the hood of his capuchin low over his head. Assuming a furtive demeanor, he slunk into the camp. Sturm walked at his back, keeping about five paces behind, his hand on the hilt of his sword.

Raistlin approached the two officers who were arguing over what to do.

"I say we tell that cleric the truth," said one. "Tell him that Immolatus disobeyed the Dark Queen's orders and damn near got himself killed."

"Let Immolatus tell him," said the other. "It's the dragon's fault we're in this mess."

The officer caught sight of Raistlin and Sturm and eyed them suspiciously. "Who in the Abyss are you two?"

Raistlin started to reply and was seized with a fit of coughing. He made a show of pulling out his handkerchief and pressing it over his mouth. Drawing it back as the coughing eased, he made certain both men could see that it was stained with blood.

"Here, now, you don't have the plague, do you?" one asked, edging away.

"I might," said Raistlin with an unpleasant smile. He lowered his hood, allowing them to see his face, his golden skin and his strange eyes. "I am a cleric of Morgion."

The officers exchanged frightened glances. Morgion was the god of disease and decay—the most feared of all the dark gods with the possible exception of Takhisis herself. Morgion did not have many clerics, for almost no one wanted to serve him.

"Keep your distance!" one of the officers ordered, drawing his sword. "What do you want?"

"The god I serve, Morgion, has been informed that you are holding a red-robed wizard captive. He has tasked me with bringing this mage to him for questioning, provided he is still alive."

He coughed again—a hacking cough, spitting up blood. The officers backed away several more steps.

"Judging by his screams, he's still alive," said one.

"We have orders to hold him for the dragon to question," the other added. "What does Morgion want with this mage anyway?"

"I am not in the god's confidence," said Raistlin in humble tones. "Perhaps you would care to ask Morgion yourselves. He is traveling with Her Dark Majesty. I can make arrangements. . . ."

"No, no, that's not necessary!" the officer said hastily. He pointed at several tents. "The mage is the prisoner of a bunch who call themselves the Gudlose. Fetch him yourself if you want him. None of us will go near those brutes. They don't take kindly to visitors."

Raistlin pulled his hood low to keep his face in shadow as he walked toward the tents. Sturm walked behind him, guarding his back. Glancing over his shoulder, Raistlin saw the officers gesturing at them and people regarding them with fear and disgust.

"Word is spreading," said Sturm.

"Good," Raistlin replied. "That means they will leave us alone."

As they drew nearer the camp of the Gudlose, Raistlin saw a man pacing back and forth in front of the tents.

Raistlin halted and motioned to Sturm to join him. "I recognize that man. He is one of the Gudlose known as Bonecrusher. He and his companion carried Magius back to camp."

As Raistlin watched, another assassin emerged from the tent.

"He is Garrote," said Raistlin in an undertone. "He is the one who murdered Sir Richard."

Garrote yawned and looked around the camp. He had taken off the leather armor and was wearing only a shirt. It was covered in wet blood, still fresh, and it clung to his skin.

"Aren't Captain and Mother back yet?" Garrote asked.

"No, and I don't like it," said Bonecrusher. "Something's gone wrong. How's that wizard? He's been quiet a long time. You didn't kill him like you did the last captive, did you? You know you have a tendency to get carried away with your work."

"He blacked out. I'll revive him, and he'll be yelling again soon enough. I came to get something to eat."

"Did he tell you anything?"

Garrote shook his head. "He thinks he's tough, but I've just started on him."

Sturm lifted his visor to get a better view. He looked very grim. "What is your plan?" he asked.

"You take one and I'll take the other," said Raistlin.

Sturm silently nodded and quietly slid his sword from its scabbard.

Raistlin raised his hands and aimed his magic at Garrote. *"Kalith karan, tobaniskar!"*

Darts of white flame shot from his fingers and struck Garrote in the chest. The magical darts burned his bloodstained clothes to ashes in an instant and seared into his flesh. He gave a strangled scream and collapsed, clutching at his chest, writhing in agony.

Bonecrusher saw his companion fall and stared at him in shock, then he caught sight of Sturm bearing down on him. Bonecrusher drew his sword and leaped at him, aiming a savage blow at the knight's head. Sturm ducked the wild swing and drove his sword through the leather armor and into the man's gut, almost to the hilt. Sturm yanked the sword free. Blood gushed from the wound and Bonecrusher crumpled.

Sturm examined the two men. "Both dead," he reported.

Raistlin flicked his wrist and the hidden dagger slid from its thong and into his hand. He walked toward the tent where they were holding Magius.

"There might be another guard. Let me go first," Sturm said softly.

He raised the tent flap and crept inside, holding his sword. Raistlin followed with the dagger. The stench of blood was overpowering. Flies buzzed and Raistlin could hear rasping breathing and a low, pain-filled moan.

Magius lay on his side, his body hunched, his breathing shallow. His face was bruised and bloodied. They had stripped his robes to his waist, and Raistlin could see the bloody marks left by brutal beatings on his chest and back. They had twisted and broken his fingers. His eyes were closed.

"You go to him," said Sturm, his voice harsh with pity. "I will keep watch."

He went to the front of the tent and opened the flap slightly, letting in fresh air and gray morning sunlight. Taking off his helm, he blinked his eyes and wiped them with the back of his hand.

Raistlin trembled with rage and the desperate need to keep his emotions in check. He thought at first Magius was asleep and he was loath to wake him to pain and suffering, but it was only a matter of time before someone found the bodies of the two Gudlose.

"Magius . . ." Raistlin said softly.

His eyes flickered open. He rolled over with agonizing effort. His split and cracked lips formed a single word.

"Water . . ."

"I will fetch it," said Raistlin.

He turned back to the entrance and was startled to see Sturm holding a tin cup in his hand. Sturm sat down beside Magius and lifted him gently in his arms, then touched the cup to his swollen lips.

Magius took a couple of swallows and seemed to revive. He recognized Raistlin and gave a faint smile. "I should have hidden beneath the bed."

Raistlin knelt beside him. "We have come to take you away from here."

"I thank you, Brother, but you wasted a trip. They made certain . . . I would not escape."

Magius gestured with his mangled hand and Raistlin saw that they had smashed both his legs. Splinters of bones protruded through the flesh. Flies were clustered on the wounds, feasting on the blood.

"Then I will carry you," said Raistlin through gritted teeth.

Magius shuddered. Blood trickled from his mouth. "They asked me about the Graygem. I told them nothing. Because I knew nothing."

He made an attempt at a laugh, but that ended in a gasp of pain. He closed his eyes a moment, then reached out his maltreated hand to Raistlin. "My staff . . . They took it from me. . . ."

"I will find it," Raistlin said, grasping his hand.

"I give it to you," said Magius. "Now ... and in the future."

He shifted his fading gaze to Sturm, who had been patiently holding him all this time.

"Huma, my friend, what are you doing here?" said Magius, gently chiding. "Shouldn't you be saving us from the Dark Queen?"

Sturm cast Raistlin a questioning glance.

"The shadows of death cloud his vision," Raistlin replied. "He sees a knight and mistakes you for Huma."

Sturm swallowed, then said with forced cheerfulness, "I told Takhisis that she must wait my pleasure. I cannot fight without you at my side, my friend."

"That's going to be difficult ... since I am dying." Magius choked. Blood frothed on his lips. He struggled to speak. "Do not grieve, dear friend. ... Death validates our lives. Without death ... we did not live."

Magius drew in a gasping breath. He stiffened, then cried out, shuddered, and died in Sturm's arms. As his head lolled, a sardonic smile touched his lips, as though he found death a source of infinite amusement.

Sturm held Magius a moment, then gently laid down the body with a whispered prayer. Traces of tears glimmered on his cheeks. The tears themselves were lost in the long mustaches. He rose to his feet.

"Magius died a warrior's death, and so I will tell Huma," Sturm said gruffly. "I will wait for you outside."

Raistlin remained behind to say a silent farewell to the man who had been his friend; who would be, throughout time, his only friend. Kneeling beside the body, he closed the blue eyes, composed the broken hands over his breast, and cleansed the blood from his face. Having prepared his friend for his final journey, Raistlin took off his cloak and covered the body. Then, swallowing his grief, he left the tent and closed and tied shut the flap.

Raistlin walked a short distance away, turned around, and raised his hands. The words to the spell came unbidden to his lips, a spell he knew in his heart, if not in his head.

"*Ast kiranann Soth-aran/Suh kali Jalaran!*" Raistlin cried.

A blazing ball of fire appeared in his hand. He hurled the fireball with all the strength of his rage and his grief at the tent. The magical fire blazed into an inferno that engulfed the tent, and it became a funeral pyre. The flames leaped high. It seemed they must touch heaven.

To die with the magic burning in the blood.

"Go with the gods, my friend," said Raistlin.

CHAPTER
THIRTY-THREE

Raistlin stood watching the fire, not moving even as the black smoke billowed around him and the heat of the flames scorched his face.

"We need to get out of here!" Sturm prodded him, choking on the smoke. "These flames can be seen for miles."

Raistlin saw a few idlers standing around, watching the fire, but no one was rushing to put out the blaze. Most people turned away with dark looks and vindictive grins. Raistlin recalled the officer saying no one would go near the camp of the Gudlose.

But then Raistlin saw in alarm that the fire was spreading, snaking through the grass toward the nearby tents. He took his handkerchief from his pocket and tied it over his nose and mouth.

"What are you doing?" Sturm demanded.

"I have to find his staff," said Raistlin, his voice muffled. "I promised him. Keep watch while I look for it."

"You had better hurry before this entire camp goes up in flames," Sturm advised.

Raistlin ran to the adjacent tent, thinking that would be the most logical place to hide the staff until they had time to dispose of it. The fire had already set the tent's canvas ablaze, as well as one of the posts. He sucked in a deep breath and ran inside.

The fire was spreading quickly. Ashes and red-hot cinders and bits of flaming canvas rained down from the ceiling, setting more fires. The tent was filled with smoke, the fumes thick and noxious. A tent post crashed down, taking part of the canvas with it. Smoke stung Raistlin's eyes and he blinked, trying to see. He could not hold his breath much longer.

"Lunitari!" Raistlin prayed desperately. "You loved him. Help me find his staff!"

He stumbled over a cot hidden by the smoke and caught sight of a flicker of light. At first he thought it was a spark from the fire, and then he recognized the light from the crystal of the staff. It had been carelessly thrown on a cot. He grabbed hold of the staff and ran from the tent as it started to collapse around him.

Safely outside, he tore off the handkerchief and gulped in air. It reeked of smoke, but seemed sweet as springtime to him. He rubbed his eyes to rid them of the ashes and then doubled over, coughing until he retched.

He held fast to the staff, remembering Magius telling him how he had carved it himself. *I have the scars on my hand to prove it, but spilling a little blood was worth it.* Raistlin closed his eyes and pressed his forehead against the cool crystal for a brief moment.

"Raistlin," said Sturm. "We need to leave."

Raistlin nodded, coughing in the smoke. The tent where Magius had died had been utterly consumed by fire. The ashes drifted up to heaven on a faint, whispering wind.

Sturm began brushing off glowing embers that had fallen onto Raistlin's robes.

"Do you have any idea how we get out of here?" Raistlin asked.

"By following the river, we avoid walking through the camp. We cross the bridge, slip into the forest, and make our way back to the tower," Sturm replied.

Raistlin pulled down the hood of his capuchin. Sturm put on his helm and lowered the visor. The Gudlose had made their camp on the riverbank, a prime location for it gave them easy access to water. Sturm and Raistlin followed the river, heading north toward the tower. The plan seemed a good one, for no one paid any attention to them.

The distance was long and their pace was slow, for Raistlin was weary from his spellcasting, and it was close to midday when they finally reached a part of the river that flowed through a deep chasm. They should have crossed the bridge here.

They both halted, staring in dismay at the rushing water and the charred and blackened wreckage of what had once been the bridge.

"Immolatus must have set fire to it! But why would he destroy it?" Raistlin asked.

"Either to stop the knights from attacking his camp or keep his own forces from fleeing into the hills," Sturm said.

"Probably both," Raistlin said grimly. "We have no choice but to retrace our steps. The only way back to the tower is through the camp."

"What about that magic spell Magius used to take us to the tower?" Sturm asked. "Do you know it?"

"The journeying spell. So now you're willing to rely on my magic," Raistlin said.

"I was thinking you could use it to save yourself," said Sturm. "I didn't say I would go with you."

Raistlin couldn't help but smile. "Would you really like me to stop here in the middle of the dragon's camp and trace a circle on the ground with the staff, and then stand inside it and start invoking the gods of magic? I imagine I would draw quite a crowd."

He shrugged. "We're not accomplishing anything standing here. Let us go."

As he and Sturm started back toward the camp, Raistlin saw people milling about and heard them talking excitedly. Judging by what he overheard, he gathered that Immolatus was going to be meeting with the Dark Queen's cleric, Mortuga, the half-ogre.

Rumors of the encounter had flown from camp to camp. Goblins and hobgoblins came running from their camps farther to the south. Ogres and kobolds hung about on the outskirts, watching in anticipation, glad for any break in the routine.

Mortuga was standing in front of his tent with his arms akimbo, waiting impatiently. His ogre escort flanked him. He appeared to be growing increasingly annoyed and started toward the dragon's tent, as though he would barge inside. He was stopped by the dragon's soldiers, who did not draw their swords but placed their hands on the hilts.

Mortuga sullenly ordered his escort to stand down.

"We should take this opportunity to slip out," said Raistlin.

They joined the throng eager for the entertainment to begin. Judging by the talk, people were speculating on whether Mortuga would survive the encounter with the dragon. Money was exchanging hands, with most betting on the dragon. Raistlin smiled. If Magius had been here, he would have probably placed a bet.

Mortuga began loudly complaining about being kept waiting. His ogres appeared disdainful of the dragon's soldiers. They watched the ogres balefully and slid their swords half out of their scabbards.

Raistlin and Sturm threaded their way through the onlookers. They had almost reached the outskirts of the camp when Sturm came to a sudden halt.

"Keep your head down!" he warned Raistlin. "Mortuga is looking directly at you!"

Raistlin ducked his head, but it was too late. Mortuga had seen him—or rather, he had seen the staff, for he was pointing an accusing finger. "I smell the foul stink of Nuitari! That man is a wizard. He has blood on his hands and he carries a staff of evil magic! Seize him!"

But none of the soldiers, either human or ogre, moved. They eyed Raistlin uneasily, none willing to lay their hands on a wizard who was covered in blood and carried a magical staff.

"What's going on?" Sturm demanded in a whisper. "Nuitari is the son of Takhisis! I thought he was on her side!"

"Nuitari is on his own side," said Raistlin.

He had to think swiftly—decide what to do. He could no longer pretend to be a cleric of Morgion. Mortuga, a true cleric, would easily penetrate that ruse.

"Cowards! I see I must deal with the foul creature myself," Mortuga snarled. "Speak, Servant of the Unseen Moon! Why do you walk among us with evil intent?"

"You mistake me for someone else, Holy One," Raistlin replied.

"I am not a wizard. This staff is not magic. It is just an ordinary walking stick."

Mortuga snorted. "An ordinary walking stick topped with a dragon's claw holding a crystal!" His eyes narrowed dangerously. "If it is so ordinary, as you claim, you will not mind giving it to me. I have taken a fancy to it. I may permit you to live in return."

"The staff is mine, Holy One," Raistlin said respectfully, but firmly. "I need it to aid my steps."

Mortuga swelled in anger. His tusks quivered. He turned to his ogres. "Seize him and the staff!"

The ogres were apparently reassured by Raistlin's announcement that he was not a wizard. The ogres carried maces on their backs and swords at their sides, but seeing that they only had to deal with humans, they didn't even bother to draw their weapons. Two ogres approached Raistlin and Sturm, flexing their gigantic hands.

"I will not give up the staff," Raistlin said to Sturm. "You should take this chance to escape."

"And go where without you?" Sturm demanded.

He drew his sword and Raistlin gripped the staff.

The ogres closed in on them. Sturm jabbed at the closest one with his sword. The ogre sneered, knocked the sword from his hand, and struck Sturm in the head with his fist. The blow dented Sturm's helm and drove him to the ground. Sturm managed to stagger to his feet, but he shook his head muzzily, half-stunned.

Raistlin raised the staff, but before he could say a word of command, an ogre grabbed hold of the staff and yanked it from his hand. The ogre immediately gave a pain-filled shriek and flung the staff to the ground.

Raistlin looked down to see that the staff had sprouted wicked-looking black thorns. The ogre was plucking thorns from his flesh and glaring at the staff in fury.

"Why do you wait? Fetch me the staff!" Mortuga ordered the ogre.

"Fetch it yourself," the ogre snarled and walked off, wringing his hand.

Mortuga raised his hairy hand to the heavens. "I call upon Takhisis. Smite this evil wizard—"

"Oh, shut up, Mortuga," said Immolatus irritably.

The dragon emerged from his tent. He was still limping, his wounds still bleeding. He was in obvious pain and a foul mood.

"Leave the wizard alone. He serves me."

Mortuga glared at the dragon. His curved tusks thrust so far forward they almost touched his forehead. "So you are reduced to hiring Nuitari scum. Her Majesty will not be pleased. I have already sent a messenger to tell her that you disobeyed her orders, attacked the High Clerist's Tower on your own, and got yourself nearly killed in the process!"

Immolatus rumbled deep in his chest. Smoke gushed from his nostrils and he spat a glob of fire at Mortuga. The glob did not hit the half-ogre. It landed a short distance away, setting fire to the grass. Immolatus was just blustering, and Mortuga knew it.

"You dare not lay a claw on me, Dragon. I warned Her Majesty that she should not trust you with such an important mission, but for some reason she thinks well of you. She will heed my warning now!"

Mortuga walked over to the staff that was still lying on the ground at Raistlin's feet. The cleric raised his hands in supplication.

"Queen Takhisis! I call upon you to bless this staff that I may use it for your glory!"

The thorns vanished. It seemed an ordinary walking stick.

"I warn you," said Raistlin softly. "Do not touch it."

Mortuga sneered and took hold of the staff.

The crystal in the dragon's claw blazed red as the red moon, then went black as the dark moon. Streaks of lightning, white as the white moon, shot from the staff and struck Mortuga in the chest.

The lightning blast lifted the half-ogre off his feet. He sailed backward and landed with a thud. His hands were charred black. His eyes bulged and smoke rose from his fine clerical garb. He was probably dead before he hit the ground. No one spoke. No one came near him.

Immolatus snorted flame and chuckled. "A staff like that could come in handy. Bring it to me, wizard."

Raistlin picked up the staff and gripped it tightly. "I will not part with it."

Sturm stood at his side, holding his sword.

Immolatus eyed them both. "A sack of gold to anyone who brings me their heads!"

Humans and ogres hesitated, but the thought of the dragon's gold overcame their fear. Humans and ogres began forming a circle of steel around them, from which they could not escape.

Sturm slashed at any who dared venture close. Raistlin swung his staff in a blazing arc.

The soldiers kept coming, the circle tightening.

"At least you won't die at the High Clerist's Tower," said Raistlin.

"And you won't end up in the Abyss," Sturm returned.

"Kill them!" yelled Immolatus.

An inhuman, heart-stopping shriek split the air, followed by a loud whistle, followed by another shriek. A mechanical contraption thundered into view. It was topped by a castle-like turret mounted on a platform made of steel. Clouds of steam belched out of a large tank in the rear and a fearsome-looking weapon that resembled a gigantic ballista shook and rattled as the machine rumbled over the ground.

The sight of the contraption had a paralyzing effect on the crowd, who had obviously never seen anything like it. This included Immolatus, whose jaw hung open in amazement.

The contraption rolled toward them, shrieking and whistling. Raistlin could see people standing in the turret. One was a gnome, grinning ecstatically. The other was Tasslehoff, jumping up and down and flourishing his hoopak.

"We've found Tas," said Sturm.

"And he found the gnomes," said Raistlin.

Gnomes were riding on the platform, clinging to the machine, and more were running frantically alongside, waving their arms and shouting for the contraption to stop. The contraption kept going, however, bounding over boulders, lurching and jouncing and sending gnomes flying in all directions. These unfortunates picked themselves up and joined their fellows in pursuit.

"Look out!" Tas was yelling, waving his hoopak to part the crowd. "Look out! Dragonlance coming through! Make way! Make way!"

The contraption climbed a ridge, reached the top, teetered on the brink for a moment as though trying to make up its mind, then plunged down the slope, belching and whistling and picking up speed. It was heading straight for the dragon's tent.

Immolatus howled. "Don't just stand there, fools! Stop it!"

Soldiers grabbed their bows and started firing arrows at it. Some hurled spears. The ogres plucked flaming logs from the campfires and hurled them at the machine.

The few gnomes who had managed to continue riding the machine saw arrows and burning lumber flying at them and jumped off. Tas ducked down inside the turret, but the gnome standing next to him smiled and waved, as though to an admiring crowd.

"I'm Knopple!" he was shouting. "Lead designer of the dragonlance. Patent pending!"

"Tasslehoff Burrfoot!" Sturm bellowed.

Tas saw him and yelled back excitedly. "Oh, hullo, Sturm! Hullo, Raistlin! Look! I brought the dragonlance!"

Raistlin gripped Sturm and pointed.

"Tell Tas to look out! It's on fire!"

Flaming logs had landed near a tank leaking some sort of dark, viscous liquid. The flames began eagerly lapping up the liquid and were spreading rapidly.

"Tas!" Sturm yelled. "You're on fire!"

Tas looked down to see the flames crawling toward several barrels that were strapped to the back of the contraption. Two of the barrels had split open and were spilling a black powdery substance. Tas appeared concerned and tugged on the sleeve of the gnome standing on the turret with him.

"Knopple, we're on fire!" Tas yelled over the whistling and the shrieking.

Knopple didn't appear to hear him. He was gazing at the dragon, his eyes shining with triumph. The dragonlance towered over him, its multiple heads rattling and shaking. Knopple reached for a lever on the side of the turret.

"Tas! Jump!" Sturm roared at him.

Tas was coughing in the smoke. The bottom of the turret had caught fire. Tas shook hands with Knopple, climbed out of the turret, dropped down to the platform, and flung himself off the contraption just as Knopple pulled the lever.

With a scream like a thousand banshees, the dragonlance blasted off, leaving the contraption and soaring into the air. The various razor-sharp blades whirled, flashing in the sunlight. The dragonlance flew straight at Immolatus, sailed over the dragon's head, lopped off one of his horns, and kept going.

The dragonlance seemed to have developed of a life of its own, for it traveled through the air as far as the eye could see, with no apparent intention of ever coming down.

Knopple watched his dragonlance disappear in dismay. Climbing from the turret, he jumped off the platform, landed on the ground, and chased after it. The contraption rolled on. The flames had spread to the wheels and up into the turret.

Sturm helped Tas to his feet.

"We've been searching for the dragon for days. The dragonlance is his Life Quest." Tas gazed after Knopple. "I hope he catches it."

"Tas, what is that black powder in those barrels?" Raistlin asked urgently.

"They put it in their thundersticks to make them thunder," Tas explained. "There are a whole lot of barrels, including some strapped underneath the platform that you can't see. Uncle Trapspringer—"

"Never mind Uncle Trapspringer!" Raistlin gasped. "Take cover!"

Sturm grabbed Tas and hauled him to a nearby ravine. Raistlin ran after them, and the three slithered down the sides of the ravine and landed at the bottom, where they were joined by three gnomes.

"As I was saying, Uncle Trapspring—" Tas began.

The explosion split the ground. An enormous cloud of smoke and flame, ashes and debris mushroomed into the air, accompanied by whistling rockets, blazing comets, and spectacular starbursts. Raistlin flung his arms over his head and hugged the ground as shards of steel, rocks, splintered tent posts, and flaming chunks of canvas rained down on them.

Eventually, debris stopped falling and an eerie silence settled over the plains. Raistlin sat up slowly and warily, half expecting something else to blow up.

The gnomes looked a little dazed, but being accustomed to things blowing up unexpectedly, they shook themselves off and cleaned the dirt out of their beards. Sturm was coughing and covered in dust and debris, but he indicated that he was not injured. Tas felt to make certain his topknot was still on his head, then he crawled up the side of the ravine and peered over the edge.

"Hoo boy!" Tas said, awed.

Raistlin and Sturm joined him and stared in appalled silence at a gigantic crater in the ground. Smoke boiled up from the bottom. Debris and ashes fell like black rain from the sky. The dragon's army was gone, obliterated in the blast. Immolatus alone survived.

The dragon's head was covered in blood from the wound left by the dragonlance when it had lopped off a horn. Immolatus crouched among the rocks, blinked the blood from his eyes, and surveyed the destruction of his army in stunned disbelief.

"Thank the gods," said Sturm.

"Thank Uncle Trapspringer," Raistlin remarked.

Sturm smiled. "Tas will never let us forget this."

"With luck, he won't remember," said Raistlin.

He and Sturm dropped back down into the bottom of the ravine, where they found Tas consoling the gnomes.

"I'm really sorry your dragonlance blew up."

The three gnomes sighed.

"Backtothedrawingboard," said one.

"Referittocommittee," said another.

The third jotted down a few notes, then said they had to be going. The gnomes shook hands with Tas.

"Itsbeenapleasurelookforwardtoseeingyouagaindontbeastranger."

The gnomes climbed out of the ravine and traipsed off, traveling east, in the direction of their village.

"Are you all right?" Raistlin asked Tas.

"Oh, yes. Just disappointed," Tas said sadly. "Knopple was taking the dragonlance to Huma to save the song, but now it's been blown to smithereens. I'm still not sure what a smithereen is, but I'd say it pretty well describes what's left. I guess we better go tell Huma."

Tas was starting to climb out of the ravine when they heard horns blaring across the plains in a defiant paean. Raistlin hurriedly pulled Tas back down into cover.

"What is it?" Tas asked.

"The Dark Queen and her forces have arrived," said Sturm.

Takhisis was present in human form, wearing night blue armor and riding on a blue dragon at the head of her troops. Her vast armies spread across the plains, marching toward the High Clerist's Tower. Her dragons flew above them.

Takhisis was taking her time, savoring the moment of her triumph. Her forces had driven the knights into their last refuge, the High Clerist's Tower, and now they were trapped. The minotaur armies of Sargonnas were marching east, unopposed, through Westgate Pass as Takhisis's force approached from the south and west. Her dragons ruled the skies.

"We need to get back to the tower before we are cut off," said Sturm urgently.

But before they could leave, a rider in chain mail, wearing a tabbard with the emblem of the Dark Queen blazoned on the front, came galloping toward them. The three hunkered down at the bottom of the ravine. Sturm clamped hold of Tas.

"Don't move!' he whispered.

Raistlin readied a spell but the rider rode right past without seeing them. The rider had raised the visor of his black helm and was regarding the smoke in frowning puzzlement. He spurred his horse and reached the crater—all that was left of Immolatus's army. The messenger was so stunned at the sight of the destruction, he did not immediately notice the dragon. Immolatus painfully heaved himself out from among the rocks to confront him.

The messenger wrenched his shocked gaze away from the sight of the destruction and looked at Immolatus, only to find the sight of the dragon, covered in blood, equally shocking.

"What happened?" the messenger asked, shaken.

"Just say what you came to say," Immolatus growled.

The messenger pulled himself together. "Great Immolatus, Her Majesty, Queen Takhisis, has received information that you are in possession of a rare and powerful artifact known as the Graygem of Gargath. Her Majesty wants to know why you keep such a treasure for yourself when by rights it belongs to your Queen."

Immolatus shifted his gaze from the messenger to look at what had once been his army. He drew in a breath and let it out in a gush of smoke. He gestured with his claw, indicating the blood oozing from his wounds, the crater in the middle of the plains, the rising smoke of destruction.

"This is the work of the Graygem of Gargath."

The messenger obviously didn't believe him. He shifted impatiently in his saddle. "What do I tell Her Majesty?"

Immolatus glowered at him, then sagged and let out his breath in a rasping cough. "Tell her the Graygem is in the High Clerist's Tower. I sent Mullen Tully after it and if your Queen is lucky, he might bring it to her. I think it far more likely the wretch will keep it for himself."

The messenger looked alarmed at this news but he had yet to finish with Immolatus.

"You need to make preperations for battle, Dragon. Her Majesty orders you to lead the assault on the tower."

"She does, does she?" snarled Immolatus. He reared up to full height and roared. "Tell that bitch that I quit! I'll see her in the Abyss."

The dragon flapped his wings and after a few failed tries, managed to struggle into the air. He limped off, leaving a trail of blood behind. The messenger stared after him in consternation, then, shaking his head, he turned his horse's head and rode off. He was not in a hurry, probably wondering how to bring his vengeful queen the bad news.

"Takhisis knows about the Graygem," said Raistlin grimly. "Tully is on his way to the High Clerist's Tower to find it, and once that messenger tells Takhisis, she will go to the tower in search of it."

"But that means Destina is in danger!" Tas said worriedly.

"The world is in danger if the Dark Queen gets hold of the Graygem," said Raistlin. Holding fast to the staff, he scrambled out of the gully. "But you are right. We need to find Brother Kairn and Destina and take our leave of this place."

"First we must tell Huma about Magius," Sturm reminded him.

Raistlin glanced at the staff and gave an inward sigh. "Tell Huma we failed."

"Is Magius . . ." Tas swallowed. "Did he die?"

"He died a hero," said Sturm, placing his hand on the kender's shoulder.

"Then he should really be part of the song," said Tas firmly.

"Bards don't write songs about wizards," said Raistlin.

They started the long walk back. Immolatus had fled, returning to the Abyss to nurse his wounds. The Dark Queen and her armies were drawing near.

"The day is late. The sun is sinking behind the mountains," said Sturm. "It will not be safe to travel after dark. We should find someplace to lay low and rest until morning."

"We cannot afford to rest. We must keep going," said Raistlin. "You are exhausted. The danger is too great!"

Yet even as he spoke, he staggered and almost fell. Sturm steadied him with a hand on his arm.

"You are exhausted. The danger will be even greater if we blunder into the arms of the enemy in the darkness," Sturm said.

"And I could really use some sleep," said Tasslehoff, yawning. "I'd like to stay awake to save the song, but my eyes keep closing and that makes it hard to see."

Raistlin felt the familiar burning sensation in his chest and began to cough. The spell was not a bad one. He pressed his handkerchief over his mouth to muffle the cough and it soon subsided. But every goblin within miles would hear him if they drew too close to the enemy lines.

"Very well, we will rest, but I will take first watch," said Raistlin, daring Sturm to argue.

Sturm smiled faintly. "Wake me at midnight."

They found a depression beneath an overhanging shelf of rock and settled down for the night. Tasslehoff curled up and was immediately asleep. Sturm lay awake, his hands beneath his head, his expression somber. Perhaps he was dreading what he would have to say to Huma. Eventually his eyes closed and he slept.

Raistlin sat with his back against cold stone, keeping his hand on the staff of Magius. He watched black clouds shot with purple lightning mass in the east. Thunder rumbled, shaking the ground. The setting sun still shone on the High Clerist's Tower, gilding the spires with gold. But the boiling clouds were fast approaching. They would soon swallow up the sun and plunge the tower into darkness.

CHAPTER
THIRTY-FOUR

T he bell chimed six times, the start of a new day.

Destina and Kairn had waited in the kitchen of the deserted fortress for Tas. They had dozed fitfully in uncomfortable chairs and made a breakfast of bread and meat, and he had still not returned.

"We should go back to the tower," said Destina at last. "That man, Tully, is searching for the Graygem, and he knows I am carrying it. We need to warn the knights that he is an agent of the dragon, urge them to be on their guard."

"Tas will know where to find us," said Kairn.

Destina carried one of the torches, and they walked through the dark halls. The fortress was quiet and deserted, yet it did not feel abandoned. Perhaps the spirit of Titus Belgrave, its commander, remained, true to his duty.

"Do you think the dragon will attack again?" Destina asked.

"According to history, Immolatus was so badly wounded by the dragonlances that he fled back to the Abyss," Kairn replied. "If so, the Dark Queen would lose one of her most formidable allies and that would greatly benefit the knights."

"You sound more hopeful," said Destina.

"The River of Time has taken many unexpected twists and turns, but perhaps it is still flowing as it should," Kairn replied. "We must trust in the gods."

Destina touched the little ring of Chislev and clasped hold of it instead of the Graygem.

The morning sun was shining, but a storm was brewing in the east and they hurried across the bridge, hoping to reach shelter before it broke. They intended to enter the tower by Noble's Gate and were shocked to see the devastation caused by Immolatus.

A work crew was trying to clear away the rubble prior to the battle, but they had a difficult, perhaps impossible, task. The dragon had set fire to the ironwood doors and torn them from their hinges. The huge doors lay in the courtyard, still smoldering. The men had to work around them, for likely only a dragon could shift them.

Destina and Kairn picked their way through the rubble, walking carefully among the smashed blocks and shattered stone. Holes gaped in the walls, and they could see that the once beautiful temple of the High Clerist was in ruins. The shattered statues of the gods littered the floor. Their altars were cracked, charred, and blackened. Smoke clouded the air. Blood stained the marble.

"History is different, yet essentially the same," said Kairn. "Immolatus destroyed the temple, although he did so during the battle. The knights did not rebuild it. When they saw the terrible destruction the dragon had inflicted, they replaced the temple with the dragon traps that Laurana and Tas would use during the War of the Lance to destroy the dragons. Four candles still burn on the broken altar of Paladine. The dragonlances lie in the ruins of the altar, but they shine with a holy light. The River of Time continues to flow."

The Graygem had gone dark, as though displeased. Destina saw the little emerald in Chislev's ring gleam with its own small light.

"We have to leave this time," said Destina. Her worried gaze went to the storm clouds. "Every moment we stay, the danger increases."

The interment ceremony for Commander Belgrave had just concluded. Soldiers filed out of the ruined temple. They stood talking in low voices amidst the debris that filled the courtyard, eyeing the approaching storm with dread. The advancing clouds had blotted out the sun. Day grew dark as night and so did the spirits of those left to defend the tower. A flash of lightning lit the courtyard, illuminating the scene for an instant, and then all was dark again. The flames of the torches wavered in the wind.

Destina heard one soldier say to another, "I wonder if anyone will be left to bury us?"

Will happened to be standing nearby and overheard. He walked over to the soldier.

"Take off your helm," Will ordered.

The soldier looked startled, but he took off his helm.

Will smacked him on the side of his head.

The soldier blinked and put his hand to his cheek. "What was that for?"

"For being a damned poltroon!" Will swore at him. "I thank the gods Commander Belgrave didn't live long enough to hear such cowardly bleating. Now go about your duties!"

The soldier slunk off, rubbing his head.

Destina walked over to Will and extended her hand. "I was sorry to hear about the commander. He was a good and valiant man."

"He was that, Lady Destina," said Will huskily.

"I need to ask you a question," said Destina. "Do you know a yeoman named Mullen Tully? I am looking for him. Have you seen him?"

"I know him," said Will. "Commander Belgrave thought he deserted. I heard he was back, telling some tale of being attacked by goblins. But if he is back, I haven't set eyes on him. Why do you ask?"

"We have reason to believe he is an agent for the dragon Immolatus," Kairn explained.

"So he was really a spy, huh?" Will muttered, clenching his hand over the hilt of sword. "Then I hope I'm the one who gets my hands on him. I have to go back to the fortress now to take care of some last business of the commander's, but don't worry, Lady. I'll spread the word. If we find him, we'll clap him in irons."

Will sounded confident as he left, but Destina was discouraged. She searched for Tully among the soldiers, trying to see their faces illuminated by flashes of lightning, only to lose sight of them in the gloom. Many of the soldiers were wearing helms and that made identifying them more difficult.

"This search is hopeless!" Destina said to Kairn. "Tully could be any one of these men and I would never know!"

The rumbling of thunder was almost continuous. Lightning forked among the clouds. During one bright flash, she saw Sir Reginald supervising the work to remove the wreckage of the gate and went to speak to him.

He smiled in relief to see her. "I am glad you are safe, my lady. How may I serve you?"

She explained about Tully to Sir Reginald.

"I have not seen him, but we will find him, my lady."

"I am hoping my companions, Raistlin and Sturm and the kender, Tasslehoff Burrfoot, will soon return," said Destina. "I was going to meet them in the temple but that's obviously not possible."

"I suggest you wait for them in the Knight's Chapel," said Sir Reginald. "I will send the knight and the mage, but the kender should go back to the dungeons."

"I will keep watch on Tas," Destina said. "Please, sir! He is my friend, and he has been very loyal to me."

"I will send him to find you if I see him," said Sir Reginald, relenting. "The Knight's Chapel is on the second floor. Use those stairs to the right. The chapel is at the end of the hall. Take one of those torches with you to light the way."

Kairn took a torch from the wall, and he and Destina climbed the stairs to the second floor. This part of the tower smelled of smoke but had not suffered any damage. They followed the knight's directions and came to a double door made of polished oak engraved with the symbols of the knighthood: the kingfisher, the rose, and the crown. Kairn gave the door a gentle shove and it readily opened.

Walls made of rosewood extended up into a vaulted ceiling. The pews in the nave were also made of rosewood. A marble altar graced the chancel and stained glass windows lined the walls. Located in the tower's interior, the windows were illuminated by some hidden source of light and filled the chapel with soft jewel-like radiance. The delicate scent of roses perfumed the air.

Destina looked around with pleasure, entranced by the chapel's delicate beauty.

"The Knight's Chapel was not open to the public," Kairn said, placing the torch in a sconce on the wall. "It was intended for the knights' private worship, away from the droves of pilgrims that crowded the temple."

Destina sat down in one of the pews near the chapel's entrance. She tried to find comfort in a divine presence, but she was uneasy. The Graygem had seemed subdued when they had first arrived at the temple, but now she could feel the jewel growing unpleasantly warm against her skin.

"I hope the others return soon, for we are not safe, even here," Destina said. "But I have been thinking, and we must decide what to do if they do not. Sturm and Raistlin could be dead. Tas is still lost and we have no way to find him."

"Let us not borrow trouble," said Kairn, sitting down beside her. "All will be well."

"You don't know that," said Destina sharply.

Kairn was startled by her tone. She clasped her hands together, trying to find the courage to say what she needed to say. "You told me you took a vow to return to your own time. You must promise me that you will go back, even if I cannot come with you."

She pointed to the rucksack at his feet, containing the Device of Time Journeying.

"You cannot ask that of me, Destina," said Kairn. "How could I go back and leave you behind, never to see you again? I have come to love you. I cannot lose you when I have only just found you."

Destina rose from the pew and walked down the aisle to the altar. No candles stood on the altar, but someone had left a bouquet of roses, now faded and withered. Destina gently touched the flowers and the petals crumbled to dust beneath her fingers.

"I am walking a dark path, Kairn. I deliberately chose this path with my eyes open. I acted willfully and selfishly, and I have caused terrible harm. I do not deserve your love. I cannot love you when I hate and despise myself."

"If we are laying blame, the fault is as much mine," Kairn said, joining her at the altar. "My mistakes compounded yours."

Destina scarcely heard him. "I hope I will be able to undo what I have done, Kairn. I will try, though it costs me my life. But if I fail, you *must* go back alone to tell Astinus. They say he is a god. Perhaps he can find a way to mend what I have broken. Promise me!"

"There is no need for me to make such a promise. All will be well," Kairn repeated. "The knights have the dragonlances. Huma and Gwyneth are together."

Destina shook her head. "And what if Raistlin saves Magius? Or what if Raistlin and Sturm are killed trying to save him? What if something terrible has happened to Tas? You must go back to tell Astinus!"

Kairn reached out to hold her, comfort her. She backed away.

"Promise me, Kairn. Here, in the presence of the gods."

Kairn placed his hand on the altar, careful not to disturb the withered roses. "By Gilean's Book, I promise, Destina."

Destina gave a sigh. He took her in his arms then and they held fast to each other. She leaned her head against Kairn's shoulder and he put his arm around her. Destina knew she should be strong and stand on her own, but she was tired of being strong, tired of being lonely. At least for the moment, she let herself relax and rest against his chest, feel the beating of his heart.

The walls muffled the thunder, and she couldn't see the lightning.

CHAPTER
THIRTY-FIVE

Sturm had wakened Tas and Raistlin at first light that morning. They stole through the forest, making their way back to the High Clerist's Tower under cover of the gloom of the approaching storm. Sturm walked with his sword drawn. Tas held fast to Goblinslayer and Raistlin had a spell on his lips in case they were attacked. Fortunately, the enemy forces were yet some distance away on the plains, and they were able to return to the tower without incident.

Sturm opened the massive gate in the curtain wall, and they breathed easier once they were inside and the gate closed behind them. They hurried to the Knight's Spur, planning to go first to Commander Belgrave's office to recover their belongings.

"I'll come with you," Tas offered. "You might need me to open the door in case it's locked."

"We left it unlocked," said Raistlin. But upon reaching the office, they found the door locked and heard the sounds of someone moving about inside. Tas was thrilled and was pulling out his lockpicking tools when Sturm disappointed him by simply knocking.

"Who is there?" a voice called.

"Sturm Brightblade and Raistlin Majere."

"You forgot me!" Tas said.

"No, he didn't," said Raistlin. "Go wait for us down the hall."

Will opened the door. His eyes were red, his face streaked with tears. He grunted when he saw Sturm and Raistlin and scowled at Tas, who had stayed with them, undoubtedly thinking Raistlin meant someone else should go wait down the hall.

Tas offered his hand to Will.

"I was sorry to hear about Commander Belgrave even if he did put me in the dungeons. They are very nice dungeons, by the way, and I was sad to leave, but I had to save the song."

Will ignored Tas's hand and his condolences. He eyed Sturm and Raistlin and frowned.

"I see you helped yourself to the commander's clothes. Lord Huma said you were going to try to rescue that wizard. Did you save him?"

"No," said Raistlin quietly. "We did not."

Will grunted. "You two can come in, but the kender's not setting foot in here."

"Keep watch, will you, Tas?" said Sturm. "We won't be long."

Tas sighed and then dutifully posted himself at the end of the hall and began humming a song to keep himself company.

Sturm and Raistlin entered the office and Will closed the door behind them. Lightning flashed in the windows and thunder cracked. The room was stifling hot and they soon saw why. Will had built a fire in the grate.

"I am destroying the commander's papers," he explained. "He gave orders that if he fell, I was to burn them. There are some here that should not end up in the hands of the enemy."

"Takhisis and her army are within a day's ride," said Sturm.

"I saw them," Will stated. "You'll forgive me if I keep on with my work."

Returning to his seat, he began reading through the papers on the desk. He tossed some into the fire and set others to one side, muttering to himself that he would give them to Lord Huma. At one point, he picked up a letter that had been carefully folded and sealed. Raistlin saw a charm fall out of the letter—the same butterfly charm Anitra had given him and Magius.

Will cast a puzzled glance at the butterfly, noted the address, then slipped the letter into an inner pocket of his leather vest.

"Titus wrote this to his daughter," he said gruffly. "I'll take it to her myself if I survive. Someone will find it on my body if I don't."

He held it, gazed down at it. "He loved her, you know. Even if she was a wizard. He was proud of her. He just couldn't tell her."

"She knew he loved her, as she loved him," said Raistlin. "The butterfly is a charm that will allow you to safely pass through the Shoikan Grove."

Will grunted and put the charm in his pocket along with the letter. He went on with his work, feeding papers to the flames and watching as they curled up and dwindled to ashes.

Raistlin stripped off the leather tunic he had worn in place of his robes. He started to lay the tunic aside, then noticed it was stained with Magius's blood. He rested his hand on it, felt the blood still wet.

Will glanced at him. "Bloodstains, huh? I'm used to them. Fold the clothes and place them on the chair."

Sturm removed his armor from the wooden chest and began to put on his breastplate.

"Do you know where we can find Lady Destina?" he asked.

Will watched Sturm struggle with the straps, then he rose from his task and came over to assist him.

"I saw her in front of the temple," Will said as he unfastened the buckles with an expert hand. "She told me about that man, Tully, working for the dragon. I've been keeping an eye out for him and I've passed the word to the rest of the men. We'll soon catch the wretch."

Raistlin thought of the immensity of the High Clerist's Tower with its sixteen floors and vast number of rooms. Tully could be hiding anywhere. He exchanged glances with Sturm and guessed by his grim expression that the knight must be thinking the same.

Will returned to sit down at the desk and continue sorting through papers. Sturm and Raistlin finished dressing and prepared to take their leave.

"Shut the door behind you," said Will, not looking up. "And make sure you take the kender with you."

They left Will bent over the flames and shut the door.

Outside in the hall, they found Tas peering into the darkness and jabbing at it with his hoopak. Catching sight of them, he ran to meet them.

"I'm glad you're here! A lot of knights marched past me into the tower and I was going to say hello to them and introduce myself, but then I noticed that they were all pale and shimmery and I could see right through them," Tas said excitedly. "Do you think they were wraiths? I've been looking for wraiths."

"It is said that the spirits of true knights will return to defend the tower if is attacked," said Sturm. "Perhaps these were the spirits of those who died at Westgate Pass."

"Then let us hope they fight better dead than they did alive," Raistlin remarked.

The storm was increasing in intensity as they left the Knight's Spur. The wind whipped Raistlin's robes. Tas held fast to his topknot to make certain it didn't blow away. Lightning lit the sky and Raistlin watched it blaze around the High Lookout where he and Magius had planned to attack the dragons. He lowered his gaze, keeping it firmly fixed on where he was going.

They went first to Noble's Gate, hoping to find Huma. The wind was strengthening. The hour was midday, the sun at its zenith, yet the sky grew darker. The wind hissed among the wreckage, forcing the workmen to abandon their efforts to try to remove the rubble. Sir Reginald had taken shelter inside what remained of Noble's Gate. He greeted them and motioned for them to join him.

"Lady Destina has been worried about you," said Sir Reginald. "She will be glad to see you are safe. She warned us about the agent of the dragon. We have been keeping watch for him, but no one has seen him."

"We will join her, but first we must speak to Lord Huma," Raistlin said. "The matter is urgent."

"Lord Huma is in the temple," Sir Reginald replied. "Lady Destina and Brother Kairn are in the Knight's Chapel. It's on the second floor, almost right above us."

"We could send Tas to find Destina while you and I speak to Huma," Sturm suggested.

"You don't have to worry. I'll keep watch for that bad man, Tully," said Tas. "I'm her bodyguard."

"Tell Lady Destina and Brother Kairn to meet us in the temple," said Raistlin. "Go straight to the chapel! No side trips!"

"I promise!" said Tas.

"Not so fast," said Sir Reginald, catching hold of Tas. "I have orders to confiscate all weapons. Hand over your knife."

"But Sturm has his sword and you're not stopping him," Tas protested.

"Brightblade is a knight," said Sir Reginald. "Hand over the knife."

"You can constipate Goblinslayer, but it will only come right back to me," Tas told him. "So why not just let me keep it and save all that trouble?"

"The knife either stays here or you do," said Sir Reginald. "You can keep the stick."

"It's not a stick!" Tas said, mortally offended. "It's a hoopak!"

"Do as he says, Tas," Raistlin ordered impatiently. "We don't have time to argue!"

Tas heaved a doleful sigh and handed over Goblinslayer. "It's magical, so don't be surprised if it disappears. I was in the Abyss once—"

"Go find Lady Destina," said Sturm, giving Tas a prod in the back.

"Which staircase do I take?" Tas asked.

Sir Reginald pointed and Tas dashed off. Sir Reginald thrust the kender's knife into his belt and excused himself, saying he needed to return to his duties.

"Do you think we have changed time?" Sturm asked. "Thus far, all has happened as history recorded."

"No, it hasn't," said Raistlin. "Immolatus attacked the tower because of the Graygem. He sent his agents to steal the Graygem. He questioned Magius about the Graygem. Takhisis herself now seeks the Graygem. Events turned out the right way, but for the wrong reasons. All things revolve around Chaos."

"The gods save us if the Dark Queen captures it," said Sturm.

"The gods won't be able to save us," said Raistlin. "They will be too busy trying to save themselves."

CHAPTER
THIRTY-SIX

Destina and Kairn were sitting in the chapel, both silent—
a restful quiet that seemed a balm to the soul—when their
peace was shattered by a shrill voice.

"Destina! Brother Kairn! Where are you?"

"Tas! We're here, in the chapel!" Destina answered. Overwhelmed with relief, she sprang to her feet and hurried to the door.

"Where's the chapel? Oh, there! I found you and Brother Kairn!"
Tas came running down the hall toward them.

"I am so glad you are back, Tas!" said Destina. "I was worried
about you. I feared you were lost."

"I wasn't lost," said Tas. "I knew where I was the whole time.
Hullo, Brother Kairn. Sturm says you've come to take us home.
That's an awfully nice rucksack you're carrying. I had to leave my
pouches in the jail, which means I had to put all the interesting
things I've found into my pockets and they're starting to weigh me
down. I bet there are a lot of interesting things in that rucksack.
Maybe I could look through it sometime."

"Nothing too interesting. Just a change of clothes and dry socks,"
said Kairn, slinging his rucksack over his shoulder and tightening
his grip on it. "Where are Sturm and Raistlin? Are they safe?"

"They have gone to talk to Huma," said Tasslehoff. "They sent me to tell you and Destina we're supposed to meet them in the temple."

They left the chapel, retracing their steps to the staircase that would take them down to the temple.

"It was very sad," Tas continued with a doleful sigh. "Raistlin and Sturm tried to save Magius, but he died anyway and I couldn't save the song either. I was going to bring Huma the dragonlance, but it blew up. Although the explosion did scare off the dragon, so maybe that counts."

"What do you mean the dragonlance blew up?" Destina asked, thinking this was one of Tas's tales.

"I'm not sure *how* it blew up," said Tas. "The explosion might have had something to do with the kegs of the powder the gnomes were going to use for pyrotechnics. That's a big word I found out means 'fireworks,' and Raistlin said there must have been some magic mixed in there, as well, because Uncle Trapspringer always did like magic—"

"Gnomes!" Kairn repeated, coming to a halt. "What gnomes?"

"The gnomes who made the dragonlance," Tas explained. "It didn't look at all like the dragonlances I've seen because it belched and whistled and rolled along on wheels. But I figured maybe that's what the dragonlances looked like back in Huma's time. It wasn't in the song, either, but that's because the poet likely couldn't find words that rhyme with 'gnome.'"

"Are you saying a gnomish device blew up in the dragon's camp?" said Kairn, sounding agitated.

"It was more of a contraption than a device, but all that's left of the dragon's army is a big hole in the ground," said Tas, "so I guess I'm saying it blew up the camp. Do you have a stomachache, Brother Kairn? You look a little queasy."

"Kairn, what is wrong?" Destina asked anxiously.

"According to the historical account, the gnomes invented a machine designed to kill dragons," said Kairn. "They planned to bring the machine to the High Clerist's Tower to help the knights battle the Dark Queen, but the machine broke down on the way. The gnomes never arrived at the High Clerist's Tower."

"The dragonlance *did* break down, but I fixed it," Tas said proudly.

"You fixed it!" Kairn gasped.

"I had to save Knopple from the farmer who was trying to skewer him," Tas explained. "I happened to be standing next to a switch on the machine, so I flipped it. The dragonlance gave a lurch and a whistle and started rolling along. I pulled Knopple out from under the wheels, and off we went looking for a dragon and we found the dragon's camp and rolled into it and that's when the dragonlance caught fire and exploded. It was all very exciting, although I still didn't get to meet Uncle Trapspringer."

"Gilean save us!" Kairn exclaimed, aghast.

"I know," said Tas sadly. "After coming all this way . . ."

"Tas, you changed history!" said Kairn, shaken. "You made the machine work!"

CHAPTER
THIRTY-SEVEN

As Raistlin and Sturm entered the temple, they paused just inside the ruins of the entryway to look around, allow their eyes to adjust to the darkness, and reflect on the sorrowful task that lay ahead of them. The candles on the broken altar continued to burn, but their flames flickered uneasily in the storm wind that blew through the cracks in the walls, trying to extinguish them. The glittering stars in the dome had vanished, shrouded in smoke. The silver dragonlances shone with bright defiance.

Huma and Gwyneth stood together before Paladine's altar, enveloped in the candlelight that gleamed on Huma's armor and glistened on Gwyneth's silver hair.

Raistlin walked down the aisle, making no sound, except for the soft rustling of his robes. Sturm followed a little behind, moving slowly, his hand pressed on his sword to keep it from rattling. Yet Gwyneth heard them. She glanced in their direction and said something to Huma. He turned with a welcoming smile, a hopeful look.

"*Shirak*," said Raistlin softly.

The crystal held in the dragon's claw on the staff glowed faintly. Huma trembled visibly and put his hand on the altar to steady himself.

"He is dead," he said in a low voice.

"I grieve to tell you, Lord, that Sturm and I failed in our efforts to save him," said Raistlin.

"Then it wasn't a dream," said Huma. "I was hoping it was a dream!"

He drew in a shuddering breath. "Magius came to me as I stood here before the altar. I felt a touch on my shoulder and I turned to see him and my sister as clearly as I see you. They embraced, their arms around each other, together at last. Magius said, 'I am with Greta now, dear friend. We wait only for you to join us, then together we will take our final journey.' He gave that mocking smile of his. 'Do not be long. You know how I hate to be kept waiting. And bring a jug of that apple wine. . . .'"

He took off his helm, bowed his head, and put his hand to his eyes. Gwyneth drew near. He clasped her hand tightly and brought it to his lips.

"Magius died nobly, sir," said Sturm. "A warrior's death."

Huma looked up at them. His expression was grim.

"How did he die?" he asked. "Did the fiends torture him?"

Sturm hesitated. He could not in honor tell a lie, but he was reluctant to reveal the dreadful truth.

Raistlin understood and answered for him. "Magius died at peace, sir."

But Huma heard the unspoken words and clenched his fist in anger. "I should have gone to save him! At least, I could have been with him at the end."

"In a way you were, sir," said Raistlin gently. "Sturm held him as he took his last breath. Magius thought he was you."

"We avenged his death, Lord," Sturm added, resting his hand on the hilt of his sword. "Those who took his life paid for it with their own."

Huma gazed at them, the tears standing in his eyes. He seemed to understand, for he came over to them and clasped their hands, first Raistlin's, then Sturm's. His grip was firm, but his hands were cold and Raistlin felt them tremble.

"You risked your lives to save him. Paladine's blessing be upon you both," Huma said.

"We also bring good news that will perhaps ease your sorrow, Lord," said Sturm. "The army of the red dragon was wiped out in an explosion. The dragon himself has returned to the Abyss."

"Immolatus has fled?" Gwyneth said in amazement.

"The dragon suffered from the wounds you gave him and those inflicted by the dragonlances," said Raistlin. "He had no more stomach for the fight."

Huma nodded absently, his thoughts still on his friend.

"What of Magius . . . His body . . . ?"

"The gods of magic sent their holy fire to consume his remains," said Raistlin.

Huma nodded and gave a wan smile. "I see you carry his staff, Majere. I am glad. Magius would have wanted his legacy to live on."

"His courage and his loyalty to the knight who was his friend will be celebrated through the ages, sir," Raistlin said. "You may be certain of that."

Huma reached out his hand to gently touch the staff.

"Your work is finished, Magius," he said to the dead. "But ours is not. Wait for Gwyneth and me. We will not be long."

As he spoke, the staff's light dimmed, as though in response. Outside the temple, the wind howled and beat against the walls as though it would batter them down. Thunder shook the tower's foundations.

Huma drew in a deep breath and put aside his grief. He spoke briskly.

"I am glad you are here, Brightblade. I was going to send for you. The battle will soon be joined. Gwyneth and I plan to fly to confront the Dark Queen and her dragons in the air. I need someone I trust on the ground to lead the defense of the tower.

"Sturm Brightblade, I would like to name you commander, place you in charge of the defense. I can think of no one I trust more. Majere, I hope you will take Magius's place as my war wizard. He would have wanted that."

Sturm was staring at Huma in shock. He struggled to speak, to tell Huma that he thanked him for his trust in him, but that he could not accept it. For he would not be here. But the words were too bitter to pass his lips and he stood in silent anguish.

Raistlin gripped the staff so tightly his hand ached. He was sensitive to every flaw, every whorl, every knot in the wood. The spells he had memorized were pitifully few and not particularly powerful, but he had the Staff of Magius and it was imbued with the spirit of the man who had created it, the greatest wizard of all time.

He pictured himself going into battle, his staff blazing with fire, lightning streaking from the crystal, destroying his foes.

To die with the magic burning in your blood . . . A better, a nobler death than he would know in the future.

"We must confer with our companions," said Raistlin. "We left word for them to meet us in the temple."

"Of course," said Huma. "You will find us here."

Sturm and Raistlin left them and walked down the aisle toward Noble's Gate. The lights of the candles did not penetrate far into the darkness beneath the temple's dome. They had to rely on the light of Magius's staff to guide their steps, a single star in the deepening night.

"It occurs to me that if you and I stayed, we might well survive the battle," Raistlin said as they walked. "After Huma defeats the Dark Queen and drives her and her dragons back into the Abyss, her armies crumble. Huma and Gwyneth die, that is true, but because of their sacrifice, many of the defenders of the High Clerist's Tower survived. As commander of this victorious battle, you might live to be an honored member of the knighthood, telling your grandchildren tales of valor. I would take Magius's place as war wizard. My name would be celebrated and honored. Not cursed."

"My dearest wish as a boy was to have fought alongside my hero, Huma Dragonbane," said Sturm. "And now Huma, this man I have long honored, this man who has become my friend, has placed his trust in me. And I must refuse. Not only that, but I will disappear without telling him why. He will think I am a coward, that I ran away out of fear."

"He will think I did worse—betrayed the memory of his friend," said Raistlin.

Raistlin spoke the word "*Dulak,*" and the light of the crystal went dark. By unspoken mutual consent, they both stopped and turned to look back at the altar of Paladine.

Huma and Gwyneth were praying, their hands clasped.

"They are under no illusions as to the outcome of this battle," said Raistlin quietly. "They are daring to fight a god. The time is fast approaching when they must say their goodbyes, when she will shed her mortal form and become what she truly is."

Huma and Gwyneth turned from the god to face each other.

"Steel and silver," Huma said.

Gwyneth smiled. "One last kiss."

Their lips met. Huma drew her close and held her fast, as though he would hold on to her forever. Then, with that one final kiss, he let her go.

The image of the elven woman disappeared, flesh transforming to silver scales: the neck growing long, gracefully arching. Silver hair became a silver mane. Silver wings seemed to lift her to her full height. Her silver body shone in the light of the candles.

Outside the temple, the storm raged with increasing fury. Inside, all was quiet. The gods held their breath, waiting.

Sturm and Raistlin turned away and continued walking.

"We have no choice," said Raistlin. "We must go back."

"As Tas would say, we have to save the song," said Sturm.

"All the songs," said Raistlin. "Even those that will never be sung."

CHAPTER
THIRTY-EIGHT

"All I did was flip a switch," Tas said miserably as he and Kairn and Destina started down the stairs, going to the temple to find their friends. "I didn't mean to change history! I was just trying to keep Knopple from getting skewered!"

"Maybe he only changed history a little," Destina said. "After all, Immolatus *was* wounded by the dragonlances, and he *did* flee the battle."

"That is true," said Kairn.

"So if that's true, did I save the song or not?" Tas asked anxiously.

"Hopefully, you saved it," said Kairn.

They came to the bottom of the stairs and halted before going farther to see what was happening.

The storm was closing in on the tower. The clouds had conquered the sun, and the constant lightning lit the darkness as if in mockery. The crashing thunder rumbled across the ground and rain pelted down with stinging force.

Most of the soldiers had left the repairs on the gate to return to their posts. Only a few remained, probably waiting for orders. Sir Reginald was speaking with one of them in front of Noble's Gate.

Both were soaking wet, huddling beneath the remnants of the wall for shelter. Destina studied the soldier.

"That man could be Tully," she said tensely. "I can't see his face, but he is about the same height and weight. What do we do? Sturm and Raistlin are meeting us inside the temple and that man is blocking the entrance."

"I'll go see if it's him," Tas offered. "I know Tully. He called me a thief—"

"No, Tas, don't!" Kairn cautioned. "If that is Tully and he sees you, he will know Destina is here with you. We need to find another way to enter."

"We could get in the way I got out when I went to save the song," said Tas. "There's a room that is like a really big closet where the clerics keep their old clothes. They named the room 'Christy.' I saw a sign over the door."

Kairn looked puzzled at first, then his expression cleared. "You mean the sacristy. It's a room where the High Clerist and his knights changed into their ceremonial robes before holding services. And you're right. It leads into the temple. But it's over by Merchant's Gate. We'll have to risk venturing out into the open, but I doubt anyone will be able to see us in the storm. Still, we should take precautions. Put on my cloak, Destina, and we must get rid of this torch. In this instance, darkness is our ally."

He draped his cloak around Destina's shoulders and she pulled the hood over her head.

"I'll lead!" said Tas. "I remember the way."

Kairn left the torch in a sconce and they ran out into the rain, following Tas. They circled around Noble's Gate, giving it a wide berth, and followed the outer wall of the tower until they were in sight of the next gate, known as Merchant's Gate. Halfway between the two gates was a door.

He pointed. "That's Christy. The door was unlocked when I was here. Someone might have locked it again, but don't worry. I still have my tools."

The door was still unlocked, much to Tas's disappointment, and they hurried inside the sacristy, grateful to be under shelter, out of the storm. The wind slammed the door shut behind them. The rain beat against the window, rattling the frame. Jagged bolts of lightning flared through the glass, illuminating the room one moment and plunging it into shadow the next. Kairn leaned his quarterstaff against the wall and dropped his rucksack beside it. He lit one of the oil lamps, and Destina found its steady white glow reassuring.

The sacristy was in disarray with books and objects scattered around the room.

"I didn't do this," said Tas immediately. "Well, I did pull that table over under the window, but that's because I couldn't reach it to crawl out. But I didn't make this mess."

"According to history, when the knights received word that Palanthas had fallen, the High Clerist and his fellows laid down their pens to pick up their swords," said Kairn. "They rode to the rescue of the city but fell victim to Immolatus."

Destina could see where they had flung their robes aside to put on their armor. Books lay open on the desks. Pens stood in the ink-wells. She looked down at someone's work. The page ended in mid-sentence, never to be finished. All those who had ridden out that fateful day had died in the dragon's attack at Westgate Pass.

Destina wearily sat down. She had wrapped Kairn's cloak closely around her neck, but she could still feel the Graygem burning through the thick cloth. The heat radiating from the jewel was growing stronger, almost painful. Tas leaned his hoopak against the wall beside Kairn's staff and came over to give Destina a soothing pat on the shoulder.

"I will still be your bodyguard. I have my hoopak, even though I am missing Goblinslayer."

"You said the knife was magical and would return to you," said Destina, smiling.

"It will. I just never know when." Tas looked at her oddly. "I can see light shining from beneath your cloak. I think it's the—" he sneezed. "Drat!" He wiped his nose. "It's giving me a squirmy feeling and I didn't even try to touch it."

Destina wrapped the cloak more closely around her throat. "We should leave, Kairn!"

Kairn cast the Graygem a troubled glance. "I will go fetch Sturm and Raistlin. You and Tas wait here for us."

"I'll keep an eye on your rucksack," Tas offered.

"Tas and I both will," said Destina.

Kairn looked reassured and opened the door that led to the temple. He was about to enter when he suddenly stopped and turned back in alarm.

Tas cocked his head, listening. "Do you hear that? A kind of terrible hooting sound. There it is again!"

"It's just the wind, Tas—" Destina began.

"That's not the wind!" Kairn said grimly. "Those are the ogre war horns! Takhisis has launched her assault!"

The tower's defenders answered with horns of their own, trumpeting defiance. Looking out the window, they could see soldiers running to their posts through the storm that struck with increasing fury. Kairn grabbed his quarterstaff and started to enter the temple. Destina joined him at the door.

"I will come with you. We dare not wait any longer."

Tas had hold of his hoopak, crowding in beside them. "I'm coming, too."

Kairn opened the door. The four candles burned on the altar, but their flames burned low and she could see little else. If their friends were in the temple, they were lost in the shadows.

"Lord Huma!" a man shouted. "I seek Lord Huma!"

A soldier had entered the temple and was standing amid the ruins of Noble's Gate, peering uncertainly into the darkness.

"I am here," Huma called.

The soldier walked swiftly down the aisle. "My lord! Sir Reginald sent me to tell you that Sargonnas and his minotaurs have taken Westgate Pass and are sweeping down on us from the north."

"I know that man's voice," Tas said, wrinkling his brow. "I remember not liking it."

Kairn frowned, perplexed. "Either history has changed drastically or he is lying. The minotaurs did not fight at the battle of the High Clerist's Tower. The people of Palanthas rose up in rebellion and drove them from the city."

The soldier in the temple was continuing to talk excitedly. "The armies of Takhisis are striking from the east, Lord Huma! Sir Reginald fears they will breech the outer walls!"

"Then we are too late!" Destina said, stricken. She saw Tas staring at her, his eyes wide. "What is it? What is wrong?"

"Your neck is glowing like it's on fire!"

"He is right, Destina," said Kairn. "The Graygem is blazing!"

Gray light shone through the folds of the cloak, as though the jewel had burned through the thick folds of the cloth. She tried to cover it with her hand to hide the glow, but it was too hot to touch. The Graygem was no longer content to hide. It was deliberately making itself known.

"Destina! It's him!" Tas pointed toward the soldier in the temple. "I knew I knew him! He's the bad man who called me a thief!"

The soldier had come to stand before the altar. He removed his helm to speak to Huma and tucked it beneath his arm. The light of the candles illuminated his face.

"Tas is right," Destina said. "That is Tully!"

CHAPTER
THIRTY-NINE

Raistlin and Sturm left the front of the temple to walk back toward Noble's Gate, planning to wait there for their friends. They could hear the storm raging outside and see the lightning flaring through the gaping holes in the walls left by the dragon. They did not expect to wait long and began to grow worried as time passed without any sign of their companions. Then they heard a sneeze and a shrill voice saying, "Drat!"

Raistlin shifted his head. "Tasslehoff!"

"It came from that room over there, the sacristy," said Sturm.

Raistlin was starting to head that direction when Sturm stopped him.

"Listen!" he said in urgent tones.

"For what?" Raistlin asked, annoyed at being detained.

"The sounds of war," said Sturm grimly.

Raistlin listened intently and now he could hear, above the tumult of the storm, bellowing ram's horns, the raucous blare of trumpets, and the pounding beat of massive drums carried into battle by ogres.

"The war horns of Takhisis," said Raistlin. "She will not wait for

Dragons of Fate 347

history. She has come for the Graygem. Let us hope Tas found Brother Kairn and Destina!"

They were starting toward the sacristy when a soldier came running into the temple. He came to a halt, almost directly in front of the sacristy, blocking their way.

"Lord Huma!" the soldier shouted, peering into the darkness. "I seek Lord Huma!"

"I am here," said Huma, turning from the altar.

Raistlin could see him silhouetted against the candlelight. Gwyneth stood near him, her wings folded at her side. The soldier ran past Raistlin and Sturm, never noticing them in his haste. His attention was fixed on Huma.

"We should leave now," Sturm urged.

"Wait!" said Raistlin. "Look at his sword!"

The soldier was wearing a helm, but something about him seemed familiar. Rainwater streamed from his armor, which consisted of a breastplate over chain and leather, and he carried an unusually long sword at his side. The sword was so long that he was forced to keep his hand on it as he ran to avoid tripping over it.

"That is a greatsword," said Sturm, frowning. "The Solamnic knights never used greatswords in this battle or any other. Such swords are impractical, far too unwieldy."

"My lord! Sir Reginald sent me to tell you that Sargonnas and his minotaurs have taken Westgate Pass and are sweeping down on us from the north."

"Did that happen?" Raistlin asked.

Sturm shook his head. "I have no idea. You'd have to ask Brother Kairn. Speaking of him, we should go—"

"The armies of Takhisis are striking from the east, Lord Huma!" The soldier stumbled over the sword, but he managed to keep his footing and continued down the aisle. "Sir Reginald sent me to tell you that he fears they will breech the outer walls!"

The soldier came to halt in front of Huma and respectfully removed his helm, tucking it under his arm. The light of the candles shone full on his face.

Sturm gave a soft gasp. "Isn't that—"

"Mullen Tully," said Raistlin grimly. "Go find Brother Kairn! Tell him he must take Destina and you and Tas back to our own time!"

"What about you?" Sturm demanded.

"I am needed here," said Raistlin. "As you say, there is something wrong about that sword."

Sturm frowned and did not move. "We cannot leave you! The future—"

"Is doomed if Takhisis captures the Graygem!" Raistlin said vehemently. "Listen to me for once in your life, Sturm Brightblade! Go to Destina and take her centuries away from here!"

Sturm hesitated a moment longer, then gave a brief nod and ran down the aisle toward the sacristy.

Raistlin walked down the aisle, keeping to the shadows, continuing to study the sword Tully was wearing. As Sturm had said, it was not the type of sword an ordinary yeoman would carry. It was far too heavy and clumsy. Caramon himself would have had difficulty wielding it.

Huma was asking Tully questions as Gwyneth stood nearby, her silver scales shimmering in the light of the candles. Tully was quite calm around her and did not appear awed or overwhelmed or frightened to find himself in the presence of a silver dragon. He behaved as if being around dragons was an everyday occurrence.

"Which it would be, since he worked for Immolatus," Raistlin muttered.

Huma dismissed Tully with a grateful nod and ordered him to return to his post.

"Sir Reginald suggested that I remain here with you, sir, in case you needed me to carry a message," said Tully in respectful tones.

"A good idea," said Huma, and then he spoke to Gwyneth. "You and I will take to the air."

They continued speaking but Raistlin didn't hear what they said. He was watching Tully, who had slipped into the shadows between two rows of pews and stood there, ill at ease, fidgeting with the sword. He nervously clasped and unclasped his fingers around the hilt, and he kept looking at it, as though uncertain about it.

"Because it is magic," said Raistlin. "And he does not trust it."

Those not skilled in magic needed training to use magical artifacts. Raistlin had no doubt that Immolatus or whoever had given Tully this sword had simply handed it to him and bid him carry out his orders. Tully was nervous, undoubtedly wondering if the magic would work, afraid it might not. Or perhaps even more afraid it might.

Raistlin drew closer, making no sound and careful not to let Tully see him. He need not have worried. Tully could not take his eyes from Huma and Gwyneth.

"Tsaran korilath ith hakon!" Raistlin whispered the words of the spell beneath his breath and pointed his finger at the sword. A faint aura, visible only to him, shimmered around the blade.

He was right. The sword had been imbued with magic, and although he had no idea what evil spells had been cast on this particular blade, he had to assume they would be lethal.

Raistlin sucked in a breath to shout a warning to Huma, only to feel the familiar pain in his chest. His breath caught in his throat. He struggled to speak and then realized in sickening fear that he was going to have to struggle to stay alive. The attack was a bad one—the worst he had ever suffered.

His lungs burned. He tasted blood in his mouth. He fumbled for his handkerchief and pressed it to his lips. It was almost immediately soaked in blood. He could not breathe, and he grew weak and light-headed from lack of air. He clung to the staff as desperately as he was clinging to his life, but he grew too weak and he dropped it. The staff fell to the floor and rolled out of reach. Raistlin sank onto his hands and knees.

He cursed himself. He cursed the gods, for he would not die with the magic burning in his blood.

He would die choking on it.

CHAPTER
FORTY

Destina watched Tully slide into an aisle between two pews close to the altar, hiding in the shadows.

She clasped the Graygem tightly, trying to conceal its blazing light, afraid Tully would see it. But a single ray escaped from her fingers, glided over the pews, and crawled up the side of the marble altar of Paladine, as though taunting the gods.

Huma had picked up one of the large mounted dragonlances and was talking to Gwyneth.

"You and I will fly to battle. First I have to speak to Brightblade. He is probably outside with Sir Reginald. Wait for me in the courtyard at Knight's Gate."

Raistlin and Sturm must have recognized Tully the same moment as Destina, for Sturm broke into a run, coming toward them.

Raistlin continued on down the aisle toward the altar. Destina hoped he was going to warn Huma about Tully, but before he could, he began to cough. She could see he was having trouble breathing. He tried to stay upright, clinging to the staff of Magius. Clutching his chest, he collapsed, dropping the staff.

Tully's hand closed over the hilt of the greatsword. He began walking slowly toward Gwyneth. The dragon was speaking with Huma and did not hear Tully's stealthy footfalls. Destina could not count on Raistlin to help. For all she knew, he might be dying. Sturm had heard Raistlin coughing and he had paused, half turning.

Destina pushed past Kairn and ran into the temple and down the aisle toward Tully. She had the vague impression that Sturm tried to stop her, but she dodged out of his grasp. Kairn was calling after her but Destina ignored him.

"Tully, I am the one you seek!" she cried desperately. "I have the Graygem!"

Destina tugged on the chain. The clasp gave way, the chain slithered to the floor, and she was holding the Graygem in her hand. It burned with a fiery light and Tully halted, watching her warily. She could see fear in his eyes, for he knew the Graygem's terrible power, but she could also see longing and cunning. He took a step toward her.

The Graygem suddenly blazed up like dry tinder catching fire. The heat was intense, searing her flesh, and she dropped it with a cry. Freed of the chain forged by Reorx to hold it, the Graygem soared to the top of the dome of the rotunda and hung there, its gray light blazing fiercely in gleeful mockery of the sun.

Gwyneth and Huma had heard the shouting and noticed the strange glow, and both turned to see what was going on. The Graygem illuminated the temple with eerie gray light. It washed out the silver of Gwyneth's scales, dulled the gleam of Huma's armor, and glistened on the greatsword Tully drew from the leather loop on his belt.

Destina gave a wild cry and started toward him. Sturm dashed past her, his sword drawn. Raistlin was choking yet struggling to reach his staff. But it seemed to Destina that all of them were caught in a strong rip current that was sucking them under and dragging them back.

"Dragon!" Tully shouted. "Immolatus sent me!"

He grasped the hilt of the heavy sword in both hands and plunged it into Gwyneth's breast.

The magical sword, crafted in homage to the Dark Queen, flared red, sliding through scales and flesh, shattering bones, boring deep into the dragon's body. Gwyneth screamed and thrashed her wings, trying to escape, but she was impaled on the blade like a butterfly on a pin. Her frantic struggles almost caused Tully to lose his grip on the sword. He yanked it free, unleashing a torrent of the dragon's blood.

Gwyneth shuddered. She felt the bitter pain of coming death, and her loving gaze went to Huma. Her wings sagged. Her strength gave way and she sank down at the foot of the altar of Paladine, her breath coming in labored, rasping gasps.

Gray light gleamed on the greatsword that had pierced her heart. Gray light glistened on the blood that was flowing like an awful river.

Huma stood staring at her, paralyzed with shock and horror. He had not even had time to draw his sword. Tully turned toward him, the bloodstained sword in his hand.

Huma was aware of him but he paid no heed. Tully was no longer important. Huma sank to his knees beside Gwyneth and gently cradled her silver head in his arms. He bent over her and whispered, his words only for her.

"Huma! Look out!" Sturm shouted in anguish, running toward him as fast as he could.

Huma must have heard his warning. He must have heard Tully's footsteps behind him. He must have known he was going to die, but he did not take his eyes from Gwyneth's. He held her close, his touch seeming to ease her terrible pain.

Tully plunged the greatsword, still wet with Gwyneth's blood, into Huma's back. The sword sliced through his armor, and the knight pitched forward and died without a cry. Gwyneth gave an anguished moan. Her tears fell, sparkling silver, and mingled with his blood. She closed her eyes, shuddered, and lay lifeless beside him.

Tully saw Sturm coming toward him. Raising the bloody sword, Tully whipped around to face his next foe. Sturm swung his sword in a slashing arc. Tully ducked the stroke that would have taken off his head and lunged at Sturm, aiming for his heart. Sturm's legacy, the old-fashioned armor, decorated with the Solamnic rose, deflected the killing stroke. The blade pierced his chest and Sturm staggered from the blow. He tried to recover, to continue fighting, but he fell to the floor. Raistlin crawled over to him and attempted to staunch the bleeding with the handkerchief that was stained with his own blood.

The Graygem flared and then flew down from the ceiling and landed at Tully's feet, gray light pulsing.

The Measure says: *When there is no hope, there is duty.*

Rushing waters of the River of Time caught Destina and swept her toward Tully. She heard Kairn shouting. She heard Tasslehoff's heartbroken wail.

Tully picked up the jewel. He seemed to bask in the light. He gazed, fascinated, into the ever-shifting, ever-changing Graygem, and he did not see Destina until she was almost on him. Startled, he flung the Graygem at her and scrambled backward. He struck at her clumsily with the sword, but his hands were slick with blood, the greatsword was heavy and unwieldy, and he lost his grip on it.

Destina dove for it, caught hold of it, and flung it away, sending it spinning into the ruins of the altar. The sword shattered on the marble, its splintered shards sparkling with gray light.

Destina swept up the Graygem in her hand and turned to run, but Tully seized her by her long hair. He twisted it in his hand and dragged her back, then wrapped his arm around her and put his knife to her throat. He swung around to face Kairn.

"Put down the staff and back off, monk!" Tully warned him. "As you see, I know how to kill."

Kairn laid down his staff but he didn't back away. He was watching for his chance to save her.

"Hand me the Graygem, Lady Destina," said Tully, jabbing her neck with his knife.

He stank of blood. The gray light glittered on the blade. Destina clung to the Graygem and, strangely, it seemed to cling to her.

"If you don't, I'll take it from your corpse—" Tully began, but never finished.

A whirlwind of brightly colored clothing wielding a hoopak erupted from the darkness.

"You ruined the song!" Tas cried in a choked voice as he clouted Tully on the back of his head.

Tully groaned and staggered and dropped the knife. Destina escaped from his grasp and sprang away from him. Kairn caught hold of her, then kicked away the knife. It slid across the floor and vanished under one of the pews.

Tully was still reeling from the unexpected blow. He swayed a little but managed to stay on his feet. Rounding on Tas, Tully tried to backhand him. Tas deftly rapped him on the knuckles with the hoopak and then hit him again on the forehead, knocking Tully to the floor.

Tully landed on his back. Glacing around for a weapon, he saw the mage's staff lying on the floor, temptingly near. The crystal on the top gave off a soft, enticing glow.

Tully grabbed the staff and jumped to his feet.

Raistlin smiled. "He is yours, Magius. Avenge your friend."

The crystal flared red as the light of Lunitari's bright eyes, the red of a mage's robes, the red of a true friend's blood. Flame blazed from the crystal and swirled around Tully.

The magical fire consumed his leather armor, burned his clothes, and set his hair ablaze. Crazed with terror, Tully screamed horribly and broke into a panicked run that only fanned the flames. He flailed about in agony until he collapsed in a writhing heap. His flesh bubbled and blackened. His face seemed to melt. The fire raged until there was nothing left of him but a pile of greasy ash and a blackened smudge on the stone.

The staff sank to the floor, near Raistlin.

A crack of thunder shook the walls of the High Clerist's Tower. The five heads of Takhisis, Queen of Darkness, cried out victory in hideous, triumphant howls. The altar of Paladine crumbled into dust. The candles toppled, their flames drowned in blood. The dragonlances clattered to the floor. One came to rest against Huma's lifeless hand as the shadow of a five-headed dragon obliterated the altar of Paladine.

Destina heard the clash of arms and the screams of the dying. The Graygem was dark and cold in her hand.

"The High Clerist's Tower has fallen," said Raistlin, who was still kneeling at Sturm's side. "We have only moments before Takhisis finds us. Brother Kairn, this would be a good time for us to leave!"

The clamor outside was growing louder. The lights of a hundred torches flared, and they could see goblins silhouetted against the glare, surging inside the temple, shrieking in glee as they caught sight of those standing by the altar.

Kairn looked over his shoulder, stricken. "I left my rucksack with the Device in the sacristy! I'll have go back—"

"You can't!" Destina cried. "You'll never reach it!"

"You mean this rucksack?" Tas asked, holding it up. "I guess you must have dropped it. I didn't look inside. Well, I might have looked inside, but I didn't touch the Device, only maybe just a little poke—"

Kairn sighed in relief and took the rucksack from him. He took out the silver globe with trembling hands.

"Each of us must place our hands on it," he explained hurriedly. "I will name the date and recite the rhyme, and it will take us back to the Inn of the Last Home."

"The Graygem has changed history. The gods only know what we will find on our return," Raistlin said grimly. He added with a glance at the broken altar, "If there *are* gods . . ."

Destina looked at the bodies of Huma and Gwyneth, lying together, and her tears blurred her sight. She grasped the Graygem in one hand and rested her other hand on the globe.

Sturm was still breathing, though he was unconscious. Raistlin placed the knight's limp hand on the globe and laid his hand over Sturm's. Tasslehoff put his small hand on the Device and gripped his hoopak in the other.

"I hope Goblinslayer can find me," he said with a sigh.

"Autumn 351 AC, Inn of the Last Home, the night of the reunion and the blue crystal staff," said Kairn. "With this poem that almost rhymes, now we travel back in time."

They could hear the roar of dragons outside the High Clerist's Tower and the enemy shouting in glee.

"All hail, Queen Takhisis, ruler of Solamnia!"

"I promise I will find a way to undo what I have done," Destina vowed. "I swear on my father's life!"

The River of Time swept them up, carried them away, and flung them on a far distant shore.

CHAPTER

FORTY-ONE

The River of Time tossed and tumbled Kairn and at last deposited him, shaken and disoriented, on solid ground in the deep shadows cast by the leaves and branches of an enormous vallenwood tree. Kairn needed a moment to recover from the tumultuous journey, but he dared not take long, for someone might have seen him and been alarmed by his sudden arrival, materializing out of nowhere. The hour must have been past sunset, for the sky was lit by flame-red afterglow in the west, darkening to the east with a few stars already visible. He was standing.

Kairn tucked the Device of Time Journeying into the rucksack, then glanced swiftly about, trying to figure out where he was. And, if possible, when. Above him, he could see the lights shining through stained glass windows and he recognized the Inn of the Last Home. The leaves of the vallenwood seemed to catch the dying sun's fire, for they gleamed red and gold.

Kairn sighed deeply in relief. The first part of the journey was complete. The Device had brought them to the inn in the autumn. He would leave Sturm and Raistlin here in their own time to be reunited with their friends. He would take Destina and Tas back with him to the Great Library, to their own time. Given the terrible news Kairn had to report to Astinus, he dreaded returning. Although, he reflected, Astinus undoubtedly already knew.

Kairn was surprised to realize with concern that he had heard nothing from those who had traveled through time with him. Tasslehoff, at least, should be talking, exclaiming over the journey. Kairn turned to locate those he had brought with him, and his relief evaporated. He was alone.

Kairn searched frantically about, but his companions were nowhere in sight. He reminded himself sternly that he was a scholar, an aesthetic. He forced himself to calm down and think like one.

He reasoned that since they had returned to their own time, Raistlin and Sturm might already be inside the inn, meeting with their old friends as they had done in the past. Time might have corrected itself. The river might have swept away the terrible events in the past and might now be flowing as it should.

But where were Destina and Tasslehoff? Tas could be inside the inn with Sturm and Raistlin and his friends Tanis and Flint. But if so, which Tasslehoff? The one that belonged in the future with him and Destina? Or the one that belonged in the Inn of the Last Home with his friends? Kairn had the sinking feeling that the Tas the Device had transported was the one that belonged in the future, and Gilean only knew what trouble he might cause.

The only way to find out was to enter the Inn of the Last Home.

The night was strangely quiet. Almost no one was about. Kairn remembered that on the night of the reunion, the inn had been bustling. People had traipsed up and down the stairs that wrapped around the trunk of the vallenwood, calling greetings to their friends. He should be hearing the sounds of cheer and good fellowship drifting down from above.

Kairn shivered. The autumn night was chill, but the shiver was more from dread than cold. The inn blazed with light, but he heard no laughter, no singing.

He located the the wooden stairs that spiraled around the enormous tree trunk and he began to climb. He was the only person on the stairs, and as he rounded a curve in the trunk and came within sight of the entrance, he saw a possible reason why.

Two draconian soldiers stood guard at the door.

"Gilean save us," Kairn murmured. "This is wrong. All wrong!"

No draconians had been anywhere near the Inn of the Last Home on the night of the reunion, much less guarding the door.

Kairn hastily tried to remember what he knew about them.

Draconians had been created by servants of Takhisis using evil magicks to corrupt and pervert the stolen eggs of good dragons. Different types of draconians came from different types of dragon eggs, each type with its own special skills and appearance. Draconians resembled dragons, for they were covered in scales, with reptilian heads and razor-sharp teeth, tails, and claws. But unlike dragons, they were the size of humanoids and they walked upright on two legs. Their hands resembled human hands, and they were capable of wielding a variety of weapons.

Most draconians had vanished after the War of the Lance and Kairn had never seen one himself. He remembered from his reading that the different types could be distinguished by the color of their scales.

The draconians stood directly beneath two torches that had been placed on either side of the door. Kairn judged by the bronze color of their scales that these soldiers were Bozaks, known to be skilled warriors, cunning and cruel. Bozaks were ideally suited to the military, for they were intelligent, independent-minded, and extremely loyal. These two were part of a military force, for they both wore blue leather armor and carried curved-bladed swords in their belts.

Bozaks had wings but were unable to fly, although Kairn remembered reading that they could jump from great heights and use their wings to sail down to the ground. He also remembered that they were capable of casting magical spells.

Kairn stopped climbing, his hand clutching the railing. He was tempted to turn around and run back down the stairs, but the Bozaks had already seen him. Their reptilian eyes were on him, and if he fled at the sight of them, they would be suspicious and likely give chase.

He continued up the stairs, carrying his rucksack over his shoulder and his quarterstaff in his hand. The Bozaks observed his progress but said nothing until he came level with them at the top of the stairs.

"What is your business?" one asked, speaking Common.

"I have traveled far this day," said Kairn, managing a strained smile. "I am in need of food and drink and a warm fire."

"Name?" the other draconian asked.

"Kairn," said Kairn, thinking this an odd question.

"He's not on the list," said one.

"You may enter," said the other, "but first we have to examine the staff and search the rucksack."

Kairn handed over the staff but held on to the rucksack. The Bozak who took the staff held it in both hands and then, to Kairn's astonishment, struck the staff hard against the porch rail. He did this twice, then handed it back to Kairn.

"It's made of wood," he stated.

"Of course," said Kairn, puzzled. "What were you expecting?"

The Bozak didn't answer. "Open the rucksack."

"Is that necessary?" Kairn ventured to protest. "I am carrying only clothes and supplies."

"I have my orders." The Bozak held out a clawed hand.

Kairn said a silent prayer asking for Gilean's blessing, then delivered the rucksack. The Bozak opened it, rummaged around among his stockings and shirts, and then pulled out the Device of Time Journeying. He eyed it curiously.

"What is this?"

"A toy for my child," Kairn replied.

The Bozak held the globe to the window to view it in the light. The silver globe was dull and lusterless, and the jewels that studded it looked cheap, as though made of paste. The Bozak tossed it back into the rucksack and handed the rucksack to Kairn.

"You may enter."

Kairn said a silent prayer of thanks to Gilean and closed and cinched the rucksack. He pushed open the door and edged his way past the Bozaks, keeping a wary eye on them. The two had lost interest in him, however, and continued whatever discussion they had been having before his arrival.

Inside the inn, the light of the fire was bright and Kairn had to pause a moment for his eyes to adjust. When they did, he searched for Destina and the others. His search didn't take long, for the inn was almost empty. A few customers sat at tables, talking in low voices. A rotund man wearing fine clothes lorded over a table. He appeared to consider himself to be someone of importance. An old man in shabby, hooded gray robes sat at a table in a corner. He wore his hood over his head but he appeared to be closely observing a man and a woman who were sitting near the fireplace.

They were both dressed in furs and leather. The man was unusually tall with dark hair and a stern expression. Kairn could not see the woman's face, but as she drew back the hood of her cloak, he saw that her hair was the color of gold spun with moonlight. She was carrying a staff, a very plain wooden staff.

Kairn recognized them from history, and he recognized, with a feeling of dread, one other person.

She had black, curly hair that she wore cut short, brown eyes, and a crooked smile. She was wearing a chain mail vest over a long blue leather tunic trimmed in silver that was cinched by a leather belt, blue leggings, and tall riding boots. She carried a sword at her waist. A blue helm made to look like a dragon's head lay in front of her on the table, along with her gloves.

Kitiara Uth Matar. Dragon Highlord of the Blue Dragonarmy and one of the most infamous persons in the history of Krynn.

She occupied a large round table by herself. Hearing the door open, she turned to see who had entered. She studied Kairn, but apparently he wasn't the person she had been expecting, for she scowled and kicked over a chair in disappointment.

Kitiara was the only one of the friends who had not attended the reunion. This night, she was the only one who had. Kairn's feeling of dread increased.

"Tika!" Kitiara shouted. "Come over here. I need to talk to you."

"I'll be with you in a moment, Kit," Tika told her.

A woman with red curls and a smattering of freckles hurried past, carrying a plate in one hand and a mug of ale in the other. She set the plate of food down in front of the rotund man, then stood glaring at him, her hands on her hips.

"There are your potatoes, Hederick. Otik says he fried them crispy, the way you like them."

"I hope so," said the man in lofty tones. "Otherwise I will send them back again."

"I'm sure you will," Tika muttered, but only after she had turned her back on him and walked over to Kitiara's table. Tika bent down to pick up the chair.

"What do you need, Kit? Can I bring you more ale? Or something to eat?"

"Have you seen Tanis?" Kit asked. "I thought he might have come in through the kitchen."

"I haven't seen him, Kit," said Tika patiently. "Like I told you when you came in tonight, I haven't seen Tanis in a long time. I don't even know where he is these days."

"He was supposed to be here tonight," said Kitiara, frustrated. "They all were supposed to be here. Caramon and Raistlin are going to join me and they were counting on seeing their old friends."

"I'll be glad to see Caramon again," said Tika with a fond smile. "But as for that brother of his, I hope he trips on his black robes, falls down the stairs, and breaks his scrawny neck."

Kit said nothing. She stared, brooding, down at the table.

"I expect Tanis and the others simply forgot," Tika said. "Five years is a long time."

"They wouldn't forget," said Kitiara. "Especially Tanis. Bring me a jug of dwarf spirits."

"I'll add some potatoes along with it," said Tika. "You shouldn't drink that rotgut on an empty stomach."

As she was hurrying back to the kitchen, she caught sight of Kairn.

"Sit anywhere you like, sir," she told him, and waved her hand at the numerous empty tables.

Two people in the inn looked up when they heard Tika use the appellation "Brother." One was the rotund man, who shifted his vast bulk around to glower at Kairn. The other was the old man in the hooded gray robes. He looked intently at Kairn, his eyes glittering from the shadows of his hood, and made a swift, negating motion with his hand, as though warning him away.

Kairn decided that was sound advice. He still had no idea where Destina and the others were, but he knew now where they were not. They were not in the Inn of the Last Home on the night of the reunion.

He hurried back toward the door, feeling physically sick.

"Stop him!" a voice boomed. "Stop the foul monk!"

Kairn paused, his hand on the door, uncertain what to do. He heard a chair scrape behind him and, glancing nervously over his shoulder, he saw the large man, Hederick, approaching him from behind, his expression dark and forbidding.

Kairn considered making a run for it, dashing through the door and down the stairs. Unfortunately the Bozaks standing guard outside had also heard Hederick's shout and were moving to block his escape.

Kairn slowly turned. "I am not a monk, sir. You are mistaken."

Hederick cast a sly glance at Kitiara, as if to make certain she was taking notice, then proclaimed dramatically, "You wear the gray robes of the servants of the false god Gilean. I rejoiced to hear your so-called Great Library was razed to the ground, but it seems a few vermin survived."

Hederick stole another glance at Kitiara, but she wasn't paying attention to him. She had propped her feet on a chair and was frowning at her boots. Tika placed a jug of dwarf spirits in front of Kit, then came to intervene.

"Small wonder we don't have any customers anymore, Hederick!" Tika scolded, her green eyes flashing. "You High Seekers scare them all away. The lad's wearing gray robes. So what? That doesn't make him a monk. Go back to your dinner. I've just taken an apple pie out of the oven and I'll bring you a slice."

Hederick was not to be deterred, however. "I want this monk taken into custody."

Kitiara had poured herself a mug of spirits and was now regarding Kairn with interest. He had no choice. He'd have to make a run for it. He couldn't let them discover the Device of Time Journeying. Gripping his quarterstaff, he prepared to slam through the door and fight his way past the draconians.

Kairn yanked open the door and came to face-to-face with Raistlin.

The mage was wearing black robes trimmed in silver. He had golden skin and hourglass eyes, and he carried the staff of Magius. Kairn stared at him in petrified astonishment.

"I was wondering where you were," said Raistlin, sounding annoyed. He took hold of Kairn's arm, then looked past him at Hederick.

"I suggest you try the apple pie, Seeker," Raistlin told him. "My brother tells me it is very good. Isn't the pie good, Caramon?"

"I can attest to it. Tika's a wonderful cook," said a big man with a jovial face. He wore blue armor that matched Kitiara's and a blue helm like hers. He rested his hand on the hilt of his sword and rattled it in the scabbard. "I suggest you go back to your eating and stop causing trouble."

"Yes, Hederick," said Kitiara, grinning at him in derision. "Some of us are here to enjoy ourselves."

Hederick seemed to deflate. He swallowed, mumbled something, and slunk back to his table. He sullenly demanded more ale.

"Come outside, where we can talk in peace," said Raistlin. "Caramon, report to Kit. I'll join you in a moment. And keep an eye on that buffoon Hederick."

"I'll have some of that pie, too," said Caramon. He paused and looked back worriedly at Raistlin. "Are you sure you are all right? Is your headache better?"

"I am fine," said Raistlin irritably. "Fully recovered."

Caramon nodded, then thrust his way past Kairn and entered the inn. He plopped himself down in a chair alongside Kitiara.

Raistlin escorted Kairn out onto the porch.

"This man is with me," he told the Bozaks. "I need to speak to him in private."

The two Bozaks acknowledged Raistlin with a respectful nod and walked to the far end of the porch, out of earshot.

"Where are Destina and the others—Tasslehoff and Sturm?" Raistlin demanded in a low voice.

Kairn was still trying to recover from his shock.

"I have no idea," he said unhappily. "I thought they might be in the inn, but they're not."

"Then we must hope that wherever they are, they are together," said Raistlin. "At least since I am here and you are here, we have to assume they are here as well."

"Do you know what has happened?" Kairn asked.

"History has changed, Brother, as we feared," said Raistlin. "Queen Takhisis rules the world and has done so since the end of the Third Dragon War. Your Device of Time Journeying dropped me down into these robes on this night. I was looking for you when

I came across Caramon. Since I needed to find out what was going on, I feigned a concussion and told him I had amnesia. I asked him who I was and what we were doing here. Fortunately, Caramon is not particularly astute, and he readily told me. He and I are in the Blue Dragonarmy, commanded by Kitiara, Dragon Highlord of the Blue Dragon. She is based in Solamnia but she has traveled here to Solace to attend the reunion. Is Tanis here? Flint?"

Kairn shook his head. "Kitiara has been asking about Tanis. Tika said she hadn't seen him. But two people are here who were in the inn that night and I fear for their safety. Goldmoon and Riverwind."

"So they are here," said Raistlin in thoughtful tones. "Does Goldmoon have her staff with her?"

"Yes, and I think the draconians are searching for it," said Kairn in sudden understanding. "They took my staff and slammed it against the railing, undoubtedly to see if it was made of blue crystal. I wondered at the time what they were doing."

The door to the inn opened and Caramon poked his head out. "Kit is asking about you, Raist."

"I will be there in a moment," Raistlin snapped.

Caramon nodded and shut the door.

"I have to go and so must you," said Raistlin. "Return to your own time. Tell Astinus what has happened. I will stay here and try to find Destina and the others. Fortunately, I expect to be here for some time. Kit came here to see Tanis and she won't leave until she finds him."

"Can we fix time?" Kairn asked desperately. "Could Destina and I go back to undo what we have done?"

"First we must find Destina," said Raistlin dryly. "Ask your question of Astinus. I do not know the answer. I'll keep the Bozaks occupied so that they do not interfere with you."

Raistlin walked over to speak to the Bozaks, who treated him with respectful deference.

Once certain they were no longer paying any attention to him, Kairn hurried down the stairs. His mind reeled. He was not watching where he was going and an unfortunate stumble almost sent him plunging to his death. He slowed down and concentrated on looking where he put his feet.

Reaching the ground, he sought refuge in the deep shadows beneath the vallenwood. Raistlin had gone inside the inn, presumably going to join his half-sister. The two Bozaks had returned to their posts.

Kairn tried to grasp the enormity of the terrible situation but his mind fumbled. He could only hope Astinus could advise him.

Kairn took the Device of Time Journeying from the rucksack. He held the globe in shaking hands and brought the poem to mind, sincerely thankful that Alice Ranniker had kept it simple, for he was so shaken, he doubted if he could have remembered anything more complex.

Kairn spoke the words, his voice trembling. "'And with a poem that almost rhymes, now I travel back in time.'"

The waters of the River of Time closed over him.

ACKNOWLEDGMENTS

I would like to acknowledge the assistance of my Astinus, Shivam Bhatt, who has always been there to answer all sorts of questions from the mundane to the strange.

I would like the acknowledge the help of Paul Morrisey at Wizards of the Coast, who has been very helpful and supportive.

I would like to acknowledge our editor at Random House Worlds, Anne Groell, who has done an excellent job of helping us tell our story.

I would like to acknowledge our friend and bard, Michael Williams, whose poetry has always been such an important part of Dragonlance.

MARGARET WEIS

My profound thanks to everyone who has made this book possible. To Anne Groell and all of the people at PRH across the spectrum who have applied their craft of turning dreams into the books we hold and share. To R. A. Salvatore, who led the way for this series to be. To my family, who puts up with this creative, eccentric grandfather who still plays games, builds models, and paints miniatures.

To my wife, who matches me step for step in the adventure of art and creation, and who introduced me to D&D in the first place. And finally, to all of you who down the years have read our words and created these worlds afresh . . . I am forever grateful.

TRACY HICKMAN

REFERENCES

DRAGONLANCE CHRONICLES
By Margaret Weis and Tracy Hickman
TSR, INC., 1984–1985

Dragons of Autumn Twilight
Dragons of Winter Night
Dragons of Spring Dawning

DRAGONLANCE LEGENDS
By Margaret Weis and Tracy Hickman
TSR, INC., 1986

Time of the Twins
War of the Twins
Test of the Twins

DRAGONLANCE LOST CHRONICLES
By Margaret Weis and Tracy Hickman
WIZARDS OF THE COAST, 2006–2009

Dragons of Dwarven Depths
Dragons of the Highlord Skies
Dragons of the Hourglass Mage

The Second Generation
By Margaret Weis and Tracy Hickman
TSR, INC., 1994

Dragons of Summer Flame
By Margaret Weis and Tracy Hickman
TSR, INC., 1995

The Soulforge
By Margaret Weis
WIZARDS OF THE COAST, 1998

Brothers in Arms
By Margaret Weis and Don Perrin
WIZARDS OF THE COAST, 1999

Dragonlance Adventures
By Tracy Hickman and Margaret Weis
TSR, INC., 1987

Atlas of the Dragonlance World
By Karen Wynn Fonstad
TSR, INC., 1987

Dragons of War
By Tracy and Laura Hickman
WIZARDS OF THE COAST, 1985

PHOTOS: COURTESY OF THE AUTHORS

MARGARET WEIS and TRACY HICKMAN published their first novel in the Dragonlance Chronicles series, *Dragons of Autumn Twilight*, in 1984. More than thirty-five years later they have collaborated on over thirty novels together in many different fantasy worlds. Hickman is currently working with his son, Curtis Hickman, for The VOID, creating stories and designs for whole-body, fully immersive VR experience. Weis teaches the competitive dog-racing sport flyball. She and Hickman are working on future novels in this series.

MARGARET WEIS
margaretweis.com
Facebook.com/Margaret.weis
X: @WeisMargaret

TRACY HICKMAN
trhickman.com
Facebook.com/trhickman
X: @trhickman

ABOUT THE TYPE

This book was set in Caslon, a typeface first designed in 1722 by William Caslon (1692–1766). Its widespread use by most English printers in the early eighteenth century soon supplanted the Dutch typefaces that had formerly prevailed. The roman is considered a "workhorse" typeface due to its pleasant, open appearance, while the italic is exceedingly decorative.

DISCOVER MORE FROM
DEL REY &
RANDOM HOUSE
WORLDS!

READ EXCERPTS
from hot new titles.

STAY UP-TO-DATE
on your favorite authors.

FIND OUT about exclusive
giveaways and sweepstakes.

CONNECT WITH US ONLINE!
@DelReyBooks

DelReyBooks.com
RandomHouseWorlds.com